VOODOO!

VOODOO!

A CHRESTOMATHY OF NECROMANCY

EDITED BY

BILL PRONZINI

ARBOR HOUSE
NEW YORK

ACKNOWLEDGMENTS

PAPA BENJAMIN, by Cornell Woolrich. Copyright © 1935 by Popular Publications, Inc.; copyright renewed © 1962 by Cornell Woolrich. Originally published in *Dime Mystery* as "Dark Melody of Madness." Reprinted by permission of The Chase Manhattan Bank, N.A., Executor of the Estate of Cornell Woolrich.

". . . DEAD MEN WORKING IN THE CANE FIELDS," by W.B. Seabrook. From *The Magic Island,* copyright © 1929 by Harcourt, Brace & Company, Inc. Reprinted by permission of A. Watkins, Inc., Agents for the Estate of W.B. Seabrook.

MOTHER OF SERPENTS, by Robert Bloch. Copyright © 1936 by Weird Tales, Inc. First published in *Weird Tales.* Reprinted by permission of the author and the author's agents, Scott Meredith Literary Agency, Inc., 845 Third Avenue, New York, New York 10022.

THE DIGGING AT PISTOL KEY, by Carl Jacobi. Copyright © 1947 by Weird Tales, Inc. First published in *Weird Tales.* Reprinted by permission of Arkham House Publishers, Inc., Sauk City, Wisconsin 53583.

SEVEN TURNS IN A HANGMAN'S ROPE, by Henry S. Whitehead. Copyright © 1932 by The Butterick Publishing Company. First published in *Adventure.* Reprinted by permission of Arkham House Publishers, Inc., Sauk City, Wisconsin 53583.

POWERS OF DARKNESS, by John Russell. Copyright © 1927 by John Russell. From *The Lost God and Other Adventure Stories.* Reprinted by permission of Lorraine Gordon, Conservator for Lily Russell, widow of John Russell.

EXÚ, by Edward D. Hoch. Copyright © 1980 by Edward D. Hoch. An original story published by permission of the author.

SEVENTH SISTER, by Mary Elizabeth Counselman. Copyright © 1942 by Weird Tales, Inc. First published in *Weird Tales.* Reprinted by permission of Arkham House Publishers, Inc., Sauk City, Wisconsin 53583.

THE DEVIL DOLL, by Bryce Walton. Copyright © 1947 by Popular Publications, Inc. First published in *Dime Mystery.* Reprinted by permission of the author.

KUNDU, by Morris West. From the novel *Kundu,* copyright © 1956 by Morris L. West. Reprinted by permission of the author and his agents, Paul R. Reynolds, Inc.

THE CANDIDATE, by Henry Slesar. Copyright © 1961 by Greenleaf Publishing Company. First published in *Rogue.* Reprinted by permission of the author.

CONTENTS

INTRODUCTION

It begins with the drums.

In a hidden clearing, by firelight under a moonless sky, the small band of worshipers stands waiting and listening to the steady throbbing beat of hands on the *rada* skins. The young goat tied near the *vodun* altar, already washed and anointed with perfume and wearing brightly colored bits of cloth, makes frightened bleats; no one notices. The two priests, the *papaloi* and the *mamaloi*, take their places on the altar next to an ornamented box containing the holy serpent known as Damballah.

Soon the *papaloi* starts chanting the words *"Papa Legba, ouvri barrie pou nous passer"*—asking Legba, master of the barrier which divides men from the world of spirits, to open the gate so that he and his followers may pass through and become one with the *loa*, the gods of voodoo. Then, one by one, the other believers approach to swear their devotion and ask their private favors.

The rhythm of the drums quickens. The *papaloi* touches the serpent box with one hand, clutches the *mamaloi*'s hand with the other; their bodies begin to tremble, to undulate in time to the thudding beat. It is not long before he lifts his queen atop the box, where her writhings become more intense, spasmodic, arms and legs thrusting out at acute angles, head lolling as if broken on the stem of her neck. She screams, then cries out a sacred invocation to Baron Samedi, the ruler of the cemetery, the symbol of death —and the worshipers know that she is possessed and the words she speaks are no longer her own but those of the serpent within the box.

A sharp knife flashes; the goat makes its final bleating cry. Earthenware bowls are quickly placed to catch the blood from its slit throat.

Now the *papaloi* commences the ancient *afro-americaine* chant, and the others can feel the power of the *loa* seizing control of their bodies too. They enter into a series of convulsions, moaning and shrieking with the ecstasy of their possession. Hands are clasped to increase the flow of power, like electrical current, from one twitching body to another; the chant rises and falls to the staccato pulse of the drums.

Eh! Eh! Bomba hen hen!
Canga bafie te
Danga moune de te
Canga do ki li!
Canga li!

The *papaloi* takes up a bowl of the kid's blood, hands it to the *mamaloi*. She drinks, passes the bowl on. Other bowls are lifted; dark fluid stains the lips and chins of the believers.

Both the chant and the rhythm of the drums increase to a feverish tempo. The movements of those in the clearing grow frenzied: they spin, leap, bend and twist, spread-eagle themselves on the earth, slither along it on their bellies in emulation of the serpent Damballah; they tear off their clothing, and the women clutch their breasts and lift them high, present them as offerings to the *loa*. Hands and bodies touch, blood-wet mouths fuse and slide apart; they bite, claw, scratch, fondle one another. For some, the intensity of the experience is too great, and they fall unconscious and are carried away into the shadows behind the fires. But the others go on, driven to ever greater paroxysms, naked flesh gleaming eerily in the firelight.

And the drums and the chant go on, too—*Eh! Eh! Bomba hen hen!*—far into the night.

It is only when dawn approaches, and but a few worshipers are left who have not succumbed to exhaustion, that the *loa* have been satisfied and the ceremony reaches its completion. Only then that the *rada* skins are still. For it ends as it begins—with the drums. This is always so.

And it is always so, too, that somewhere between the beginning and the ending there is a flashing knife, and a final bleating cry, and bowls placed quickly to catch blood from a slit throat.

But it is not always so that the cry and the blood come from a goat or other animal. Sometimes, in other clearings on other dark nights, the voodoo gods receive a different and more powerful form of sacrifice.

Sometimes the victim is human. . . .

There is some disagreement as to the origin of voodoo, both as a word and as a religion in the Americas. The most widely accepted version is that it originated in the West African province of Dahomey, from which most slaves were imported to the New World more than two hundred years ago. Among the Fon and other tribes of this region, there was a widespread belief in *vodu* or *vodun*—a word which translates as "something apart and holy" or, simply, as "god." And the god they worshiped was the serpent (traditionally, a python) because they believed that the first man and woman who came into the world were blind and it was the snake who bestowed sight upon the human race.

The second theory is that voodoo is of French origin and can be traced to the followers of Peter Valdo, also known as Father Valdesius, a member of the Catholic clergy in the twelfth century who founded a sect known as Vaudois. This sect was said to have practiced both witchcraft and human sacrifice, and thus the word *vaudois* eventually became a generic term for sorcerers and servants of black magic. Early French colonists, according to this theory, brought the practice of vaudois to Haiti, where the word was corrupted to *voudou.*

In either case, voodoo came to the "brave new world" in the early 1700s and spread rapidly among the oppressed slaves. Life for them under the yoke of French and Spanish settlers was appalling: they were "tamed" in slave camps upon arrival, then worked in chains from dawn to dusk, frequently whipped and branded with the fleur-de-lis, locked in guarded quarters at night, and forbidden by law to assemble for any purpose. On some plantations, atrocities against blacks almost exceed belief: slaves turned loose and hunted down for sport; slaves buried alive in vertical positions so that only their heads remained above ground, after which heavy balls were bowled at them for sport by the colonists—the object being to split open or knock off as many as possible. Less sadistic masters made superficial attempts to convert their slaves to Catholicism, but in the main blacks were allowed no religion at all. The consensus was that they had no souls.

The fact that voodoo nonetheless managed to flourish frightened the plantation owners, who considered it to be a "terrible weapon" which might one day rally the slaves to revolt. (Part of their fear, too, lay in their own deep-rooted European beliefs in the powers of black magic and the supernatural, and in such voodoo-related beings as werewolves, witches and demons.) Those blacks who were discovered to practice this "unholy" religion were beaten, imprisoned or executed. A number of restrictions on slave traffic were put into effect as well. Louisiana governor Gálvez, for example, forbade the importation of blacks from Martinique in 1782 because their voodooism "would make the lives of the citizens unsafe"; a similar ban on slaves from Santo Domingo occurred ten years later.

One of the reasons voodoo thrived in spite of all efforts to suppress it was that the slaves came from many classes of African society, including that of priests and magicians. Once arrived in the Americas, all classes were forced to live, work, and even die together, and voodoo was the only common bond; its teachings, therefore, were carefully handed down from one generation to the next. By the time most of the cruel laws and restrictions were abolished by American authorities in Louisiana after the Purchase of 1803, voodoo was a powerful and organized force both in this country and throughout the Caribbean.

Its greatest strength, of course, was in Haiti, the "Magic Island," where it still flourishes today. On such West Indian islands as Jamaica and Trinidad, it took shallower roots and evolved somewhat differently into the form known as Obeah. Other variations, called Macumba and Santería, were and still are practiced in Latin America. And there are examples of primitive magic, of spiritism (sometimes combined with Christianity), in such divers places as Hawaii, the islands of the South Seas and New Guinea.

In the West Indies the early voodoo ceremonies were those primitive ones which were born in Dahomey, Senegal, and other African provinces. But as time passed, certain Roman Catholic features were incorporated into them to create the curious mixture which exists today. God is considered the ruler of the universe and the creator and sustainer of all life; but it is the *loa*, or lesser gods, who serve to give men and women direct contact with God and His supernatural forces, and who are concerned with the existence of humans and with their fate after death. Sacrifice and the drinking of blood are justified as offerings to the *loa*, rather than to God Himself, for favors, good fortune and good health.

But some voodoo was and is of a darker and more pagan variety. For one, there is the Sect Rouge (or *cochons gris*—gray pigs or hairless pigs) of Haiti. Although the Red Sect has a long tradition on the Magic Island, few people will discuss it and little has been written about it. Some believe it is only a myth, another of Haiti's many voodoo legends; but there are others who will swear otherwise, and infrequent but documented evidence to corroborate their belief.

Members of the Sect Rouge are said to dress in red robes and headwear in the shape of horns or straw hats with sharp tall witches' crowns; to carry candles and whips. They meet late at night in the countryside and then move in a column to the nearest cemetery. There they make offerings of food, drink and money to Papa Legba, Baron Samedi and other *loa*—imploring help in obtaining a "goat without horns," a human being who can be sacrificed.

The *houngan* or priest dances chanting around the cemetery graves; candles and bowls of animal blood are placed on top of them. Then the sect leaves, again in a column, and goes to the nearest crossroads, which is considered the best place to find a victim. Once an unwary traveler has been taken—once rags have been stuffed into his mouth and a cord of intestines wound around his neck—he is transported to a secluded clearing and immediately killed with a ceremonial knife. After the killing, the corpse is carved into several pieces and his flesh eaten and his blood drunk. (The belief in Haiti is widespread that these victims are first turned into beasts ready for slaughter. Some of the animals brought to slaughterhouses are thought to be human beings who escaped from the Sect Rouge after being magically transformed; according to the superstition, these creatures are recognizable by the sad expression in their eyes.)

There are other voodoo sects reputed to believe in human sacrifice, both in the Caribbean and in the United States. Some of these also believe, as do many other voodoo followers, in the use of the voodoo fetish called the devil doll to destroy an enemy. These dolls are small, usually six inches or so in height, and made of earth or clay or wax and bits of rags; resemblance to the victim is unnecessary, but in order for the dolls to work they must contain nail parings, strands of hair or something else from the victim's body. Magical incantations are then said over the fetish, after which sharp things are jabbed into it, or string is tied around its neck, or its limbs are squeezed into odd shapes or pulled off entirely—a simulation of whatever it is the believer wishes to happen, fatally or otherwise, to his enemy. In some instances, depending on the type of magic used, the victim is to feel pain the instant the doll is savaged; in other cases, where an even more torturous vengeance is desired, the victim may not feel pain for weeks or months, but is given the doll immediately so he will know well in advance of what lies in store for him.

Universal among all voodoo sects is belief in the living dead. In Haiti and other places, the fear of zombies is severe; people are not only afraid that they themselves will become zombies after death, but that a member of their family will become one, or that a zombie might harm them while they are alive. Some families go to great lengths to protect their dead: a thirty-six hour watch after burial in a cemetery, so that there can be no possibility of revival; burial at a well-traveled crossroads; bodies cut open and the hearts damaged to assure absolute death; a knife placed in the right hand of the corpse, in the hope that it will stab anyone who tries to disturb it. When someone dies suddenly, young people in particular, and if a body stays warm after death, chances are the person expired from unnatural causes and a plot is afoot to turn him or her into a zombie. Special care is always taken in these cases.

A Haitian legend about zombies, recounted by Kyle Kristos in his book *Voodoo,* concerns a rich farmer who needs cheap labor for his farm and who makes an arrangement with a voodoo magician or *bocor.* The *bocor,* after performing a certain ritual once the sun has set, mounts a horse facing the tail and rides to the victim's house. Once there, he puts his lips to the crack of the door and sucks out the soul of his prey. Before long the victim dies; and following the funeral the *bocor* watches the cemetery interment without facing anyone in the mourning party. Later, after midnight, he returns to claim the body by unearthing it or opening its crypt, calling out the victim's name to awaken it, then chaining the corpse and beating it about the head to make it respond.

On the way to his voodoo temple, the *bocor* takes the zombie past the house where it lived in order to gain complete control of it; otherwise the zombie might one day pass the house and remember it. At the temple the corpse is given a drop of special liquid—and from then on it will do the *bocor's* (and the farmer's) bidding, without question and without being conscious of who it once was. Nor will it ever speak, unless by accident it is given salt to eat.

But this is, of course, a legend. There is really no such thing as a corpse resurrected from the grave, mindless and soulless, capable of carrying out the orders of a voodoo priest; those purportedly documented zombie cases in Haiti may almost always be explained as living men and women who fell under a *bocor*'s spell, cast through hypnosis and the use of drugs. (Similarly, it is not supernatural forces which cause the victim of a devil-doll curse to succumb according to what was done to the doll; it is the power of suggestion, the victim's own mind, which leads him into self-destruction.) Necromancy may be at the core of voodoo, but there is nothing magical in the effects of its ceremonies.

And yet . . .

There are, after all, some cases which seem to defy logical explanation. Is that illusion or is it truth? *Is* it possible that sometimes, in certain instances, the power of voodoo really does work?

Perhaps.

Yes, perhaps. For there *are* more things in heaven and earth, you know, than are dreamt of in our philosophy.

The first significant writing on the subject of voodoo was published in 1884 and authored by Spencer St. John, a former British consul in Haiti (or Hayti, as it was then spelled). The book, entitled *Hayti; or the Black Republic,* included a number of lavish descriptions of voodoo ceremonies, as well as accounts of such atrocities as cannibalism and the sacrificing of children, and was thus the basis for much of the early horror fiction on the voodoo theme. Unfortunately, there is as much romanticized fact and outright fiction in the book as there is valid material (and not a little racism to boot).

The same is true, although to a far less exaggerated and less offensive degree, of perhaps the most well-known "nonfiction" work on voodoo, W.B. Seabrook's *The Magic Island*. Published in 1929 and widely read, it relates Seabrook's own adventures in Haiti with voodoo and offers native accounts of such legendary figures as werewolves and fire-hags. One of the book's most provocative chapters, dealing with zombies, appears later in these pages—and it is left to the reader to determine how much of the information recounted therein is nonfiction and how much pure storytelling.

Of the dozens of works about West Indian voodoo, perhaps the most authoritative and objective are Hugh B. Cave's *Haiti: Highroad to Adventure* (1952), Alfred Metraux's *Voodoo in Haiti* (1959), and Kyle Kristos' *Voodoo* (1976). Robert Tallant's *Voodoo in New Orleans* (1946) is a superior history of *vodun* practices in that city and its outlying areas. And on the subjects of primitive magic and spiritism elsewhere, both Migene Gonzalez-Wippler's *Santería: African Magic in Latin America* (1973) and A.J. Langguth's *Macumba: White and Black Magic in Brazil* (1975) are fascinating and informative.

There are no works of fiction which may be termed "voodoo classics"; however, a number of novels and collections of short stories are quite good and deserve to reach a wider audience than they have thus far.

Charles G. Chesnutt (1858–1932), a black lawyer from North Carolina, was the first American to publish fiction dealing with the "conjuring practices" of slaves. His short stories, some humorous and some weird, appeared in *The Atlantic* in the 1880s and 1890s—the first, "The Goophered Grapevine," in 1887—and were collected in 1899 under the title *The Conjure Woman;* all are post–Civil War plantation tales narrated by a white Northerner but for the most part told in a North Carolina black dialect. Although they were popular at first, it is a sad comment on the times to note that their popularity underwent a rapid decline when it was revealed Chesnutt was a black, not a white, author. As a result of this prejudicial rejection, he wrote no more fiction during the last thirty-three years of his life.

A pair of Haitian writers, Philippe Thoby-Marcelin and Pierre Marcelin, authored three novels between 1944 and 1951—*Canapé Vert, The Beast of the Haitian Hills,* and *The Pencil of God* —which were lavishly praised by such critics as Edmund Wilson and Waldo Frank, the latter commenting that they "capture the profound rhythms of Haitian life." *Canapé Vert,* which deals with the voodoo religion in depth, was judged by John Dos Passos to be the best Latin American novel of 1944.

Hugh B. Cave's 1959 novel, *The Cross on the Drum,* is a first-rate study of the conflicts between Christianity and voodoo on the mythical Caribbean island of St. Joseph; the book contains a considerable amount of voodoo lore (as does Cave's recent macabre tale of voodoo and zombieism, *Legion of the Dead,* published in 1979). Other noteworthy novels include bestselling author Morris West's second book, *Kundu* (1956)—a searing account of primitive magic on New Guinea, excerpts from which are included here; Robert Tallant's meticulously researched *Voodoo Queen* (1956), a fictionalized biography of New Orleans's famous nineteenth-century voodoo priestess, Marie Laveau; Sax Rohmer's Fu Manchu adventure, *The Island of Fu Manchu* (1941); and a 1930 mystery entitled *Voodoo* by John Esteven— a pseudonym of historical novelist Samuel Shellabarger—which has several well-portrayed and chilling voodoo scenes (although the book is marred by certain fantastic and foolish notions about blacks).

Two excellent volumes of West Indian voodoo stories by Henry S. Whitehead, *Jumbee and Other Uncanny Tales* and *West India*

Lights, were published in the 1940s by Arkham House. Several of the stories are considered by aficionados to be superior examples of the literature of the weird and macabre; one of these, "Seven Turns in a Hangman's Rope," appears in these pages.

As for voodoo films, there are only a few, and but two of those are of any quality. The best is Val Lewton's masterful *I Walked with a Zombie* (1943), starring Frances Dee and Tom Conway and set in Haiti. Although it was released as a "B" horror movie, it had fine production values, atmospheric direction by Jacques Tourneur, and a superior script by Curt Siodmak (his plot was freely adapted from *Jane Eyre* and made liberal use of authentic voodoo practices as described in a series of newspaper articles of the time; it also vividly expressed one of Lewton's obsessive themes—the conflict between the powers of reason and the powers of the unknown).

Another unusual film was the 1932 *White Zombie,* with Bela Lugosi and Madge Bellamy as stars and Haiti again as the setting. Despite almost uniform bad acting, which makes for giggles instead of shudders at certain moments when viewed today, there are some well-done scenes of ritualized death and brooding horror. One, the best in the film, takes place in a sugar mill owned by Lugosi and depicts a horde of black zombies operating a cane-crushing machine; one of the zombies accidentally falls into the crusher and is ground up with the sugar cane, while the others continue about their methodical and mindless duties.

With the exceptions of *The Ghost Breakers,* a 1940 comedy vehicle for Bob Hope in which zombies play a minor role, and *The Devil's Own* (1966), a mildly interesting British screech-and-shudder vehicle for Joan Fontaine, the remaining voodoo films are what Hollywood itself calls "drek"—godawful melodramas which mostly seem to star Bela Lugosi and John Carradine and which mostly seem to deal with a bastardized form of the zombie legend. Even their titles are more or less interchangeable: *Revenge of the Zombies, Revolt of the Zombies, Zombies on Broadway; The Voodoo Man, Voodoo Woman, Voodoo Tiger.*

There are as few short stories on the voodoo theme as films, but among them are several outstanding works; all of the best are presented in the pages which follow. Joining Henry S. Whitehead's "Seven Turns in a Hangman's Rope" are such tales of traditional voodoo (that is, the West Indian variety) as Cornell Woolrich's "Papa Benjamin," Robert Bloch's "Mother of Serpents" and Carl Jacobi's "The Digging at Pistol Key." Locales include Haiti, New Orleans, Trinidad and the Virgin Islands.

Unusual examples of voodoo elsewhere and otherwise, in addition to the excerpt from Morris West's *Kundu,* are Robert Louis Stevenson's "The Isle of Voices," John Russell's "Powers of Darkness," Edward D. Hoch's "Exú," Mary Elizabeth Counselman's "Seventh Sister" and Bryce Walton's "The Devil Doll." The settings here are as diverse as the thematic approaches: Hawaii, Papua, Brazil, Alabama, New York City, New Guinea.

And for a proper finale, there is Henry Slesar's "The Candidate"—a story of the "ultimate" voodoo adapted to contemporary society.

Twelve stories in all, and all written by past and present masters of the bizarre and the special.

With pens dipped in blood. . . .

The time has come; only a matter of seconds remain before the first ceremony begins.

So prepare yourself. Turn up the lights; lay another log on the fire. For some of the rituals you're about to witness are truly strange and truly terrifying, and they are best viewed from within a shadowless room.

Listen, now.

Listen.

There. Can you hear it?

There—the first throbbing beat of the voodoo drums. . . .

—BILL PRONZINI
San Francisco, California
October 1979

PART I

TRADITIONAL VOODOO

PAPA BENJAMIN

BY CORNELL WOOLRICH

Think of New Orleans and any number of things come immediately to mind: gutbucket jazz, the Mardi Gras, the French Quarter, Storyville, riverboat gamblers and Creole beauties and gentlemen fighting duels over a lady's honor. Yes, and of course voodoo. For close to two centuries New Orleans has been the center of voodoo practice in this country; for close to two centuries thousands have worshiped and hundreds have died at shrines hidden among its cemetery gravestones, inside its decaying buildings, along its backwater canals. The beat of voodoo drums is as much a part of the city's rhythms as the throbbing notes from a jazzman's horn.

Only a few works of fiction, however, capture both the mystery of voodoo and the unique flavor of New Orleans. The two novels which best accomplish that difficult feat are Robert Tallant's Voodoo Queen and Kenneth Perkins's Voodoo'd. The best short story by far is Cornell Woolrich's "Papa Benjamin."

First published in 1936 in Dime Mystery, a "shudder pulp" magazine, "Papa Benjamin" is the tale of what happens to a successful band leader named Eddie Bloch when he makes a commercial musical number of the voodoo rhythm and thus "mocks the spirits with the chant that summons them." Its brooding atmosphere, its feelings of cosmic malevolence and palpably mounting terror, make it not only a classic of voodoo fiction but one of Woolrich's most powerful stories.

The ability to create that sense of palpable dread was the primary reason Cornell Woolrich achieved his considerable reputation as a master of the suspense story. No writer past or present rivals him in the art of expressing the kind of pure terror found in such stories as "Papa Benjamin" and "Rear Window" and such novels as The Bride Wore Black, Phantom Lady *(as by William Irish), and* The Night Has a Thousand Eyes *(written under the pseudonym George Hopley). The cinematic quality of his work is another reason for its success, and accounts for the remarkable total of twenty-eight feature films and twenty-five teleplays based on his novels and stories. ("Papa Benjamin," in fact, was adapted for the screen in 1961 as a segment of the TV series* Thriller.) *A tragic figure who lived most of his life in New York City hotel rooms, both alone and with his domineering mother, Woolrich died in 1968 at the age of sixty-five.*

AT four in the morning, a scarecrow of a man staggers dazedly into the New Orleans police headquarters building. Behind him at the curb a lacquered Bugatti purrs like a drowsy cat, the finest car that ever stood out there. He weaves his way through the anteroom, deserted at that early hour, and goes in through the open doorway beyond. The sleepy desk sergeant looks up; an idle detective scanning yesterday's *Times-Picayune* on the two hind legs of a chair tipped back against the wall raises his head; and as the funnel of light from the cone-shaped reflector overhead plays up their visitor like flashlight powder, their mouths drop open and their eyes bat a couple of times. The two front legs of the detective's chair come down with a thump. The sergeant braces himself, eager, friendly, with the heels of both hands on his desk top and his elbows up in the air. A patrolman comes in from the back room, wiping a drink of water from his mouth. His jaw also hangs when he sees who's there. He sidles nearer the detective and says behind the back of his hand, "That's Eddie Bloch, ain't it?"

The detective doesn't take the trouble to answer. It's like telling him what his own name is. The three stare at the figure under the light, interested, respectful, almost admiring. There is nothing professional in their scrutiny, they are not the police studying a suspect; they are nobodies looking at a celebrity. They take in the rumpled tuxedo, the twig of gardenia that has shed its petals, the tie hanging open in two loose ends. His topcoat was slung across his arm originally; now it trails along the dusty station-house floor behind him. He gives his hat the final, tortured push that dislodges it. It drops and rolls away behind him. The policeman picks it up and brushes it off—he never was a bootlicker in his life, but this man is Eddie Bloch.

Still it's his face, more than who he is or how he's dressed, that would draw stares anywhere. It's the face of a dead man—the face of a dead man on a living body. The shadowy shape of the skull seems to peer through the transparent skin; you can make out its bone structure as though an X-ray were outlining it. The eyes are stunned, shocked, haunted gleams, set in a vast purple hollow that bisects the face like a mask. No amount of drink or dissipation could do this to anyone, only long illness and the foreknowledge of death. You see faces like that looking up at you from hospital cots when all hope has been abandoned—when the grave is already waiting.

Yet, strangely enough, they knew who he was just now. Instant recognition of who he was came first—realization of the shape he's in comes after that, more slowly. Possibly it's because all three of them have been called on to identify corpses in the morgue in their day. Their minds are trained along those lines. And this man's face is known to hundreds of people. Not that he has ever broken or even fractured the most trivial law, but he has spread happiness around him, set a million feet to dancing in his time.

The desk sergeant's expression changes. The patrolman mutters under his breath to the detective, "Looks like he just came out of a bad smashup with his car." "More like a drinking bout, to me," answers the detective. They are simple men, capable within their limitations, but those are the only explanations they can find for what they now see before them.

The desk sergeant speaks. "Mr. Eddie Bloch, am I right?" He extends his hand across the desk in greeting.

The man can hardly stand up. He nods, he doesn't take the hand.

"Is there anything wrong, Mr. Bloch? Is there anything we can do for you?" The detective and the patrolman come over closer. "Run in and get him a drink of water, Latour," the sergeant says anxiously. "Have an accident, Mr. Bloch? Been held up?"

The man steadies himself with one arm against the edge of the sergeant's desk. The detective extends an arm behind him, in case he should fall backward. He keeps fumbling, continually fumbling in his clothes. The tuxedo jacket swims on him as his movements shift it around. He is down to about a hundred pounds in weight, they notice. Out comes a gun, and he doesn't even have the strength to lift it up. He pushes it and it skids across the desk top, then spins around and points back at him.

He speaks, and if the unburied dead ever spoke, this is the voice they'd use. "I've killed a man. Just now. A little while ago. At half-past three."

They're completely floored. They almost don't know how to handle the situation for a minute. They deal with killers every day, but killers have to be gone out after and dragged in. And when fame and wealth enter into it, as they do once in a great while, fancy lawyers and protective barriers spring up to hedge the killers in on all sides. This man is one of the ten idols of America, or was until just lately. People like him don't kill people. They don't come in out of nowhere at four in the morning and stand before a simple desk sergeant and a simple detective, stripped to their naked souls, shorn of all resemblance to humanity, almost.

There's silence in the room for a minute, a silence you could cut with a knife. Then he speaks again, in agony. "I tell you I've killed a man! Don't stand there looking at me like that! I've killed a man!"

The sergeant speaks, gently, sympathetically. "What's the matter, Mr. Bloch, been working too hard?" He comes out from behind the desk. "Come on inside with us. You stay here, Latour, and look after the telephone."

And when they've accompanied him into the back room: "Get him a chair, Humphries. Here, drink some of this water, Mr. Bloch. Now what's it all about?" The sergeant has brought the gun along with him. He passes it before his nose, then breaks it open. He looks at the detective. "He's used it all right."

"Was it an accident, Mr. Bloch?" the detective suggests respectfully. The man in the chair shakes his head. He's started to shiver all over, although the New Orleans night is warm and mellow. "Who'd you do it to? Who was it?" the sergeant puts in.

"I don't know his name," Bloch mumbles. "I never have. They call him Papa Benjamin."

His two interrogators exchange a puzzled look. "Sounds like—" The detective doesn't finish it. Instead he turns to the seated figure and asks almost perfunctorily: "He was a white man, of course?"

"He was colored," is the unexpected answer.

The thing gets more crazy, more inexplicable, at every step. How should a man like Eddie Bloch, one of the country's best-known band leaders, who used to earn a thousand dollars every week for playing at Maxim's, come to kill a nameless colored man —and then be put into this condition by it? These two men have never seen anything like it in their time; they have subjected suspects to forty-eight-hour grillings and yet compared to him now those suspects were fresh as daisies when they got through with them.

He has said it was no accident and he has said it was no hold-up. They shower questions at him, not to confuse him but rather to try to help him pull himself together. "What did he do, forget his place? Talk back to you? Become insolent?" This is the South, remember.

The man's head goes from side to side like a pendulum.

"Did you go out of your mind for a minute? Is that how it was?" Again a nodded no.

The man's condition has suggested one explanation to the detective's mind. He looks around to make sure the patrolman outside isn't listening. Then very discreetly: "Are you a needle-user, Mr. Bloch? Was he your source?"

The man looks up at them. "I've never touched a thing I shouldn't. A doctor will tell you that in a minute."

"Did he have something on you? Was it blackmail?"

Bloch fumbles some more in his clothes; again they dance around on his skeletonized frame. Suddenly he takes out a cube of money, as thick as it is wide, more money than these two men have ever seen before in their lives. "There's three thousand dollars there," he says simply and tosses it down like he did the gun. "I took it with me tonight, tried to give it to him. He could have had twice as much, three times as much, if he'd said the word, if he'd only let up on me. He wouldn't take it. That was when I had to kill him. That was all there was left for me to do."

"What was he doing to you?" They both say it together.

"He was killing me." He holds out his arm and shoots his cuff. The wristbone is about the size of the sergeant's own thumb joint. The expensive platinum wristwatch that encircles it has been pulled in to the last possible notch and yet it still hangs almost like a bracelet. "See? I'm down to one hundred and two. When my shirt's off, my heart's so close to the surface you can see the skin right over it move like a pulse with each beat."

They draw back a little, almost they wish he hadn't come in here. That he had headed for some other precinct instead. From the very beginning they have sensed something here that is over their heads, that isn't to be found in any of the instruction books. Now they come out with it. "How?" Humphries asks. "How was he killing you?"

There's a flare of torment from the man. "Don't you suppose I would have told you long ago, if I could? Don't you suppose I would have come in here weeks ago, months ago, and demanded protection, asked to be saved—if I could have told you what it was? If you would have believed me?"

"We'll believe you, Mr. Bloch," the sergeant says soothingly. "We'll believe anything. Just tell us—"

But Bloch in turn shoots a question at them, for the first time since he has come in. "Answer me! Do you believe in anything you can't see, can't hear, can't touch—?"

"Radio," the sergeant suggests not very brightly, but Humphries answers more frankly, "No."

The man slumps down again in his chair, shrugs apathetically. "If you don't, how can I expect you to believe me? I've been to the biggest doctors, biggest scientists in the world—they wouldn't believe me. How can I expect you to? You'll simply say I'm cracked, and let it go at that. I don't want to spend the rest of my life in an asylum—" He breaks off and sobs. "And yet it's true, it's true!"

They've gotten into such a maze that Humphries decides it's about time to snap out of it. He asks the one simple question that should have been asked long ago, and the hell with all this mumbo-jumbo. "Are you sure you killed him?" The man is broken physically and he's about ready to crack mentally too. The whole thing may be a hallucination.

"I know I did. I'm sure of it," the man answers calmly. "I'm already beginning to feel a little better. I felt it the minute he was gone."

If he is, he doesn't show it. The sergeant catches Humphries' eye and meaningfully taps his forehead in a sly gesture.

"Suppose you take us there and show us," Humphries suggests. "Can you do that? Where'd it happen, at Maxim's?"

"I told you he was colored," Bloch answers reproachfully. Maxim's is tony. "It was in the Vieux Carré. I can show you where, but I can't drive anymore. It was all I could do to get down here with my car."

"I'll put Desjardins on it with you," the sergeant says and calls through the door to the patrolman, "Ring Dij and tell him to meet Humphries at the corner of Canal and Royal right away!" He turns and looks at the huddle on the chair. "Buy him a bracer on the way. It doesn't look like he'll last till he gets there."

The man flushes a little—it would be a blush if he had any blood left in him. "I can't touch alcohol any more. I'm on my last legs. It goes right through me like—" He hangs his head, then raises it again. "But I'll get better now, little by little, now that he's—"

The sergeant takes Humphries out of earshot. "Pushover for a padded cell. If it's on the up-and-up, and not just a pipe dream, call me right back. I'll get the commissioner on the wire."

"At this hour of the night?"

The sergeant motions toward the chair with his head. "He's Eddie Bloch, isn't he?"

Humphries takes him under the elbow, pries him up from the chair. Not roughly, but just briskly, energetically. Now that things are at last getting under way, he knows where he's at; he can handle them. He'll still be considerate, but he's businesslike now; he's into his routine. "All right, come on Mr. Bloch, let's get up there."

"Not a scratch goes down on the blotter until I'm sure what I'm doing," the sergeant calls after Humphries. "I don't want this whole town down on my neck tomorrow morning."

Humphries almost has to hold him up on the way out and into the car. "This it?" he says. "Wow!" He just touches it with his nail and they're off like velvet. "How'd you ever get this into the Vieux Carré without knocking over the houses?"

Two gleams deep in the skull jogging against the upholstery, dimmer than the dashboard lights, are the only sign that there's life beside him. "Used to park it blocks away—go on foot."

"Oh, you went there more than once?"

"Wouldn't you—to beg for your life?"

More of that screwy stuff, Humphries thinks disgustedly. Why should a man like Eddie Bloch, star of the mike and the dance floor, go to some colored man in the slums and beg for his life?

Royal Street comes whistling along. He swerves in toward the curb, shoves the door out, sees Desjardins land on the running board with one foot. Then he veers out into the middle again without even having stopped. Desjardins moves in on the other side of Bloch, finishes dressing by knotting his necktie and buttoning his vest. "Where'd you get the Aquitania?" he wants to know, and then, with a look beside him, "Holy Kreisler, Eddie Bloch! We used to hear you every night on my Emerson—"

"Matter?" Humphries squelches. "Got a talking jag?"

"Turn," says a hollow sound between them and three wheels take the Bugatti around into North Rampart Street. "Have to leave it here," he says a little later, and they get out. "Congo Square," the old stamping ground of the slaves.

"Help him," Humphries tells his mate tersely, and they each brace him by an elbow.

Staggering between them with the uneven gait of a punch-drunk pug, quick and then slow by turns, he leads them down a ways, and then suddenly cuts left into an alley that isn't there at all until you're smack in front of it. It's just a crack between two houses, noisome as a sewer. They have to break into Indian file to get through at all. But Bloch can't fall down; the walls almost scrape both his shoulders at once. One's in front, one behind him.

"You packed?" Humphries calls over his head to Desjardins, up front.

"Catch cold without it," the other's voice comes back out of the gloom.

A slit of orange shows up suddenly from under a window sill and a shapely coffee-colored elbow scrapes the ribs of the three as they squirm by. "This far 'nough, honey," a liquid voice murmurs.

"Bad girl, wash y'mouth out with soap," the unromantic Humphries warns over his shoulder without even looking around. The sliver of light vanishes as quickly as it came.

The passage widens out in places into moldering courtyards dating back to French or Spanish colonial days, and once it goes under an archway and becomes a tunnel for a short distance. Desjardins cracks his head and swears with talent and abandon.

"Y'left out—" the rearguard remarks dryly.

"Here," pants Bloch weakly, and stops suddenly at a patch of blackness in the wall. Humphries washes it with his torch and crumbling mildewed stone steps show up inside it. Then he motions Bloch in, but the man hangs back, slips a notch or two lower down against the opposite wall that supports him. "Let me stay down here! Don't make me go up there again," he pleads. "I don't think I can make it anymore. I'm afraid to go back in there."

"Oh, no!" Humphries says with quiet determination. "You're showing us," and scoops him away from the wall with his arm. Again, as before, he isn't rough about it, just businesslike. Dij keeps the lead, watering the place with his own torch. Humphries trains his on the band leader's forty-dollar custom-made patent-leather shoes jerking frightenedly upward before him. The stone steps turn to wood ones splintered with usage. They have to step over a huddled black drunk, empty bottle cradled in his arms. "Don't light a match," Dij warns, pinching his nose, "or there'll be an explosion."

"Grow up," snaps Humphries. The Cajun's a good dick, but can't he realize the man in the middle is roasting in hell-fire? This is no time—

"In here is where I did it. I closed the door again after me."
Bloch's skull face is all silver with his life sweat as one of their
torches flicks past it.

Humphries shoves open the sagging mahogany panel that was
first hung up when a Louis was still king of France and owned this
town. The light of a lamp far across a still, dim room flares up and
dances crazily in the draft. They come in and look.

There's an old broken-down bed, filthy with rags. Across it
there's a motionless figure, head hanging down toward the floor.
Dij cups his hand under it and lifts it. It comes up limply toward
him, like a small basketball. It bounces down again when he lets
it go—even seems to bob slightly for a second or two after. It's
an old, old colored man, up in his eighties, even beyond. There's
a dark spot, darker than the weazened skin, just under one bleared
eye and another in the thin fringe of white wool that circles the
back of the skull.

Humphries doesn't wait to see any more. He turns, flips out and
down, and all the way back to wherever the nearest telephone can
be found, to let headquarters know that it's true after all and they
can rouse the police commissioner. "Keep him there with you,
Dij," his voice trails back from the inky stairwell, "and no quiz-
zing. Pull in your horns till we get our orders!" The scarecrow
with them tries to stumble after him and get out of the place,
groaning, "Don't leave me here! Don't make me stay here—!"

"I wouldn't quiz you on my own, Mr. Bloch," Dij tries to
reassure him, nonchalantly sitting down on the edge of the
bed next to the corpse and retying his shoelace. "I'll never
forget it was your playing 'Love in Bloom' on the air one
night in Baton Rouge two years ago gave me the courage to
propose to my wife—"

But the commissioner would, and does, in his office a couple hours later. He's anything but eager about it, too. They've tried to shunt him, Bloch, off their hands in every possible legal way open to them. No go. He sticks to them like flypaper. The old colored man *didn't* try to attack him, or rob him, or blackmail him, or kidnap him, or anything else. The gun didn't go off accidentally, and he didn't fire it on the spur of the moment either, without thinking twice, or in a flare of anger. The commissioner almost beats his own head against the desk in his exasperation as he reiterates over and over: "But why? Why? Why?" And for the steenth time, he gets the same indigestible answer, "Because he was killing me."

"Then you admit he did lay hands on you?" The first time the poor commissioner asked this, he said it with a spark of hope. But this is the tenth or twelfth and the spark died out long ago.

"He never once came near me. I was the one looked him up each time to plead with him. Commissioner Oliver, tonight I went down on my knees to that old man and dragged myself around the floor of that dirty room after him, on my *bended knees,* like a sick cat—begging, crawling to him, offering him three thousand, ten, any amount, finally offering him my own gun, asking him to shoot me with it, to get it over with quickly, to be kind to me, not to drag it out by inches any longer! No, not even that little bit of mercy! Then I shot—and now I'm going to get better, now I'm going to live—"

He's too weak to cry; crying takes strength. The commissioner's hair is about ready to stand on end. "Stop it, Mr. Bloch, stop it!" he shouts, and he steps over and grabs him by the shoulder in defense of his own nerves, and can almost feel the shoulder bone cutting his hand. He takes his hand away again in a hurry. "I'm going to have you examined by an alienist!"

The bundle of bones rears from the chair. "You can't do that!

You can't take my mind from me! Send to my hotel—I've got a trunkful of reports on my condition! I've been to the biggest minds in Europe! Can you produce anyone that would dare go against the findings of Buckholtz in Vienna, Reynolds in London? They had me under observation for months at a time! I'm not even on the borderline of insanity, not even a genius or musically talented. I don't even write my own numbers, I'm mediocre, uninspired—in other words completely normal. I'm saner than you are at this minute, Mr. Oliver. My body's gone, my soul's gone, and all I've got left is my mind, but you can't take that from me!"

The commissioner's face is beet red. He's about ready for a stroke, but he speaks softly, persuasively. "An eighty-odd-year-old colored man who is so feeble he can't even go upstairs half the time, who has to have his food pulleyed up to him through the window in a basket, is killing—whom? A white stumblebum his own age? No-o-o, Mr. Eddie Bloch, the premier bandsman of America, who can name his own price in any town, who's heard every night in all our homes, who has about everything a man can want—that's who!"

He peers close, until their eyes are on a level. His voice is just a silky whisper. "Tell me just one thing, Mr. Bloch." Then like the explosion of a giant firecracker, "How?" He roars it out, booms it out.

There's a long-drawn intake of breath from Eddie Bloch. "By thinking thought-waves of death that reach me through the air."

The poor commissioner practically goes all to pieces on his own rug. "And you don't need a medical exam!" he wheezes weakly.

There's a flutter, the popping of buttons, and Eddie Bloch's coat, his vest, his shirt, undershirt, land one after another on the floor around his chair. He turns. "Look at my back! You can count every vertebra through the skin!" He turns back again. "Look at my ribs. Look at the pulsing where there's not enough skin left to cover my heart!"

Oliver shuts his eyes and turns toward the window. He's in a particularly unpleasant spot. New Orleans, out there, is stirring, and when it hears about this, he's going to be the most unpopular man in town. On the other hand, if he doesn't see the thing through now that it's gone this far he's guilty of a dereliction of duty, malfeasance in office.

Bloch, slowly dressing, knows what he's thinking. "You want to get rid of me, don't you? You're trying to think of a way of covering this thing up. You're afraid to bring me up before the grand jury on account of your own reputation, aren't you?" His voice rises to a scream of panic. "Well, I want protection! I don't want to go out there again—to my death! I won't accept bail! If you turn me loose now, even on my own recognizance, you may be as guilty of my death as he is. How do I know my bullet stopped the thing? How does any of us know what becomes of the mind after death? Maybe his thoughts will still reach me, still try to get me. I tell you I want to be locked up, I want people around me day and night, I want to be where I'm safe—!"

"Shh, for God's sake, Mr. Bloch! They'll think I'm beating you up—" The commissioner drops his arms to his sides and heaves a gigantic sigh. "That settles it! I'll book you all right. You want that and you're going to get it! I'll book you for the murder of one Papa Benjamin, even if they laugh me out of office for it!"

For the first time since the whole thing has started, he casts a look of real anger, ill-will, at Eddie Bloch. He seizes a chair, swirls it around, and bangs it down in front of the man. He puts his foot on it and pokes his finger almost in Bloch's eye. "I'm not two-faced. I'm not going to lock you up nice and cozy and then soft-pedal the whole thing. If it's coming out at all, then all of it's coming out. Now start in! Tell me everything I want to know, and what I want to know is—everything!"

The strains of "Good Night Ladies" die away; the dancers leave the floor, the lights start going out, and Eddie Bloch throws down his baton and mops the back of his neck with a handkerchief. He weighs about two hundred pounds, is in the pink, and is a good-looking brute. But his face is sour right now, dissatisfied. His outfit starts to case its instruments right and left, and Judy Jarvis steps up on the platform, in her street clothes, ready to go home. She's Eddie's torch singer, and also his wife. "Coming, Eddie? Let's get out of here." She looks a little disgusted herself. "I didn't get a hand tonight, not even after my rumba number. Must be staling. If I wasn't your wife, I'd be out of a job I guess."

Eddie pats her shoulder. "It isn't you, honey. It's us, we're beginning to stink. Notice how the attendance has been dropping the past few weeks? There were more waiters than customers tonight. I'll be hearing from the owner any minute now. He has the right to cancel my contract if the intake drops below five grand."

A waiter comes up to the edge of the platform. "Mr. Graham'd like to see you in his office before you go home, Mr. Bloch."

Eddie and Judy look at each other. "This is it now, Judy. You go back to the hotel. Don't wait for me. G'night, boys." Eddie Bloch calls for his hat and knocks at the manager's office.

Graham rustles a lot of accounts together. "We took in forty-five hundred this week, Eddie. They can get the same ginger ale and sandwiches any place, but they'll go where the band has something to give 'em. I notice the few that do come in don't even get up from the table any more when you tap your baton. Now, what's wrong?"

Eddie punches his hat a couple of times. "Don't ask me. I'm getting the latest orchestrations from Broadway sent to me hot off the griddle. We sweat our bald heads off rehearsing—"

Graham swivels his cigar. "Don't forget that jazz originated here in the South, you can't show this town anything. They want something new."

"When do I scram?" Eddie asks, smiling with the southwest corner of his mouth.

"Finish the week out. See if you can do something about it by Monday. If not, I'll have to wire St. Louis to get Kruger's crew. I'm sorry, Eddie."

"That's all right," broad-minded Eddie says. "You're not running a charity bazaar."

Eddie goes out into the dark dance room. His crew has gone. The tables are stacked. A couple of old colored crones are down on hands and knees slopping water around on the parquet. Eddie steps up on the platform a minute to get some orchestrations he left on the piano. He feels something crunch under his shoe, reaches down, picks up a severed chicken's claw lying there with a strip of red-tag tied around it. How the hell did it get up there? If it had been under one of the tables, he'd have thought some diner had dropped it. He flushes a little. D'ye mean to say he and the boys were so rotten tonight that somebody deliberately threw it at them while they were playing?

One of the scrubwomen looks up. The next moment, she and her mate are on their feet, edging nearer, eyes big as saucers, until they get close enough to see what it is he's holding. Then there's a double yowl of animal fright, a tin pail goes rolling across the floor, and no two stout people, white or colored, ever got out of a place in such a hurry before. The door nearly comes off its hinges, and Eddie can hear their cackling all the way down the quiet street outside until it fades away into the night. "For gosh sake!" thinks the bewildered Eddie, "they must be using the wrong brand of gin." He tosses the object out onto the floor and goes back to the piano for his music scores. A sheet or two has slipped down behind it and he squats to collect them. That way the piano hides him.

The door opens again and he sees Johnny Staats (traps and percussion) come in in quite a hurry. He thought Staats was home in bed by now. Staats is feeling himself all over like he was rehearsing the shim-sham and he's scanning the ground as he goes along. Then suddenly he pounces—and it's on the very scrap of garbage Eddie just now threw away! And as he straightens up with it, his breath comes out in such a sign of relief that Eddie can hear it all the way across the still room. All this keeps him from hailing Staats as he was going to a minute ago and suggesting a cup of java. But, "Superstitious," thinks broad-minded Eddie. "It's his good-luck charm, that's all, like some people carry a rabbit's foot. I'm a little that way myself, never walk under a ladder—"

Then again, why should those two mammies go into hysterics when they lamp the same object? And Eddie recalls now that some of the boys have always suspected Staats has colored blood, and tried to tell him so years ago when Staats first came in with them, but he wouldn't listen to them.

Staats slinks out again as noiselessly as he came in, and Eddie decides he'll catch up with him and kid him about his chicken claw on their way home together. (They all roost in the same hotel.) So he takes his music sheets, some of which are blank, and he leaves. Staats is way down the street—in the *wrong direction,* away from the hotel! Eddie hesitates for just a minute, and then he starts after Staats on a vague impulse, just to see where he's going, just to see what he's up to. Maybe the fright of the scrub-women and the way Staats pounced on that chicken claw just now have built up to this, without Eddie's really knowing it.

And how many times afterward he's going to pray to his God that he'd never turned down that other way this night—away from his hotel, his Judy, his boys—away from the sunlight and the white man's world. Such a little thing to decide to do, and afterward no turning back—ever.

He keeps Staats in sight, and they hit the Vieux Carré. That's all right. There are a lot of quaint places here a guy might like to drop in. Or maybe he has some Creole sweetie tucked away, and Eddie thinks, I'm lower than a ditch to spy like this. But then suddenly right before his eyes, half way up the narrow lane he's turned into—there isn't any Staats any more! And no door opened and closed again either. Then when Eddie gets up to where it was, he sees the crevice between the old houses, hidden by an angle in the walls. So that's where he went! Eddie almost has a peeve on by now at all this hocus-pocus. He slips in himself and feels his way along. He stops every once in a while and can hear Staats' quiet footfall somewhere way up in front. Then he goes on again. Once or twice the passage spreads out a little and lets a little green-blue moonlight partway down the walls. Then later, there's a little flare of orange light from under a window and an elbow jogs him in the appendix. "You'd be happier here. Doan go the rest of the way," a soft voice breathes. A prophecy if he only knew it!

But hardboiled Eddie just says, "G'wan to bed, y' dirty stay-up!" out of the corner of his mouth, and the light vanishes. Next a tunnel and he bangs the top of his head and his eyes water. But at the other end of it, Staats has finally come to a halt in a patch of clear light and seems to be looking up at a window or something, so Eddie stays where he is, inside the tunnel, and folds the lapels of his black jacket up over his white shirt front so it won't show.

Staats just stands there for a spell, with Eddie holding his breath inside the tunnel, and then finally he gives a peculiar, dismal whistle. There's nothing carefree or casual about it. It's a hollow swampland sound, not easy to get without practice. Then he just stands there waiting, until without warning another figure joins him in the gloom. Eddie strains his eyes. A gorillalike, Negro roustabout. Something passes from Staats' hand to his—the chicken claw possibly—then they go in, into the house Staats has been facing. Eddie can hear the soft shuffle of feet going upstairs on the inside, and the groaning, squeaking of an old decayed door —and then silence.

He edges forward to the mouth of the tunnel and peers up. No light shows from any window, the house appears to be untenanted, deserted.

Eddie hangs onto his coat collar with one hand and strokes his chin with the other. He doesn't know just what to do. The vague impulse that has brought him this far after Staats begins to peter out now. Staats has some funny associates—something funny is going on in this out-of-the-way place at this unearthly hour of the morning—but after all, a man's private life is his own. He wonders what made him do this; he wouldn't want anyone to know he did it. He'll turn around and go back to his hotel now and get some shut-eye; he's got to think up some novelty for his routine at Maxim's between now and Monday or he'll be out on his ear.

Then just as one heel is off the ground to take the turn that will start him back, a vague, muffled wailing starts from somewhere inside that house. It's toned down to a mere echo. It has to go through thick doors and wide, empty rooms and down a deep, hollow stairwell before it gets to him. Oh, some sort of a revival meeting, is it? So Staats has got religion, has he? But what a place to come and get it in!

A throbbing like a faraway engine in a machine shop underscores the wailing, and every once in a while a *boom* like distant thunder across the bayou tops the whole works. It goes *boom-putta-putta-boom-putta-putta-boom!* And the wailing, way up high at the moon: *Eeyah-eeyah-eeyah—!*

Eddie's professional instincts suddenly come alive. He tries it out, beats time to it with his arm as if he were holding a baton. His fingers snap like a whip. "My God, that's grand! That's gorgeous! Just what I need! I gotta get up there!" So a chicken foot does it, eh?

He turns and runs back, through the tunnel, through the courtyards, all the way back where he came from, stooping here, stooping there, lighting matches recklessly and throwing them away as he goes. Out in the Vieux Carré again, the refuse hasn't been collected. He spots a can at the corner of two lanes, topples it over. The smell rises to heaven, but he wades into it ankle-deep like any levee-rat, digs into the stuff with both forearms, scattering it right and left. He's lucky, finds a verminous carcass, tears off a claw, wipes it on some newspaper. Then he starts back. Wait a minute! The red rag, red strip around it! He feels himself all over, digs into all his pockets. Nothing that color. Have to do without it, but maybe it won't work without it. He turns and hurries back through the slit between the old houses, doesn't care how much noise he makes. The flash of light from Old Faithful, the jogging elbow. Eddie stoops, he suddenly snatches in at the red kimono sleeve, his hand comes away with a strip of it. Bad language, words that even Eddie doesn't know. A five-spot stops it on the syllable, and Eddie's already way down the passage. If only they haven't quit until he can get back there!

They haven't. It was vague, smothered when he went away; it's louder, more persistent, more frenzied now. He doesn't bother about giving the whistle, probably couldn't imitate it exactly anyhow. He dives into the black smudge that is the entrance to the house, feels greasy stone steps under him, takes one or two and then suddenly his collar is four sizes too small for him, gripped by a big ham of a hand at the back. A sharp something that might be anything from a pocket-knife blade to the business edge of a razor is creasing his throat just below the apple and drawing a preliminary drop or two of blood.

"Here it is, I've got it here!" gasps Eddie. What kind of religion is this, anyway? The sharp thing stays, but the hand lets go his collar and feels for the chicken claw. Then the sharp thing goes away too, but probably not very far away.

"Whyfor you didn't give the signal?"

Eddie's windpipe gives him the answer. "Sick here, couldn't."

"Light up, lemme see yo' face." Eddie strikes a match and holds it. "Yo' face has never been here before."

Eddie gestures upward. "My friend—up there—he'll tell you!"

"Mr. Johnny yo' friend? He ax you to come?"

Eddie thinks quickly. The chicken claw might carry more weight than Staats. "That told me to come."

"Papa Benjamin sen' you that?"

"Certainly," says Eddie stoutly. Probably their deacon, but it's a hell of a way to—The match stings his fingers and he whips it out. Blackness and a moment's uncertainty that might end either way. But a lot of savoir faire, a thousand years of civilization, are backing Eddie up. "You'll make me late, Papa Benjamin wouldn't like that!"

He gropes his way on up in the pitch blackness, thinking any minute he'll feel his back slashed to ribbons. But it's better than standing still and having it happen, and to back out now would bring it on twice as quickly. However, it works, nothing happens.

"Fust thing y'know, all N'yorleans be comin' by," growls the African watchdog sulkily, and flounders down on the staircase with a sound like a tired seal. There is some other crack about "darkies lookin' lak pinks," and then a long period of scratching.

But Eddie's already up on the landing above and so close to the *boom-putta-boom* now it drowns out every other sound. The whole framework of the decrepit house seems to shake with it. The door's closed but the thread of orange that outlines it shows it up to him. Behind there. He leans against it, shoves a little. It gives. The squealings and the grindings it emits are lost in the torrent of noise that comes rushing out. He sees plenty, and what he sees only makes him want to see all the more. Something tells him the best thing to do is slip in quietly and close it behind him before he's noticed, rather than stay there peeping in from the outside. Little Snowdrop might always come upstairs in back of him and catch him there. So he widens it just a little more, oozes in, and kicks it shut behind him with his heel—and immediately gets as far away from it as he can. Evidently no one has seen him.

Now, it's a big shadowy room and it's choked with people. It's lit by a single oil lamp and a hell of a whole lot of candles, which may have shone out brightly against the darkness outside but are pretty dim once you get inside with them. The long flickering shadows thrown on all the walls by those cavorting in the center are almost as much of a protection to Eddie, as he crouches back amidst them, as the darkness outside would be. He's been around, and a single look is enough to tell him that whatever else it is, it's no revival meeting. At first, he takes it for just a gin or rent party with the lid off, but it isn't that either. There's no gin there, and there's no pairing off of couples in the dancing—rather it's a roomful of devils lifted bodily up out of hell. Plenty of them have passed out cold on the floor all around him and the others keep stepping over them as they prance back and forth, only they don't always step over but sometimes *on*—on prostrate faces and chests and outstretched arms and hands. Then there are others who have gone off into a sort of still trance, seated on the floor with their backs to the wall, some of them rocking back and forth, some just staring glassy-eyed, foam drooling from their mouths. Eddie quickly slips down among them on his haunches and gets busy. He too starts rocking back and forth and pounding the floor beside him with his knuckles, but he's not in any trance, he's getting a swell new number for his repertoire at Maxim's. A sheet of blank score paper is partly hidden under his body, and he keeps dropping one hand down to it every minute jotting down musical notes with the stub of pencil in his fingers. "Key of A," he guesses. "I can decide that when I instrument it. Mi-re-do, mi-re-do. Then over again. Hope I didn't miss any of it."

Boom-putta-putta-boom! Young and old, black and tawny, fat and thin, naked and clothed, they pass from right to left, from left to right, in two concentric circles, while the candle flames dance crazily and the shadows leap up and down on the walls. The hub of it all, within the innermost circle of dancers, is an old, old man, black skin and bones, only glimpsed now and then in a space between the packed bodies that surround him. An animal pelt is banded about his middle; he wears a horrible juju mask over his face—a death's head. On one side of him, a squatting woman clacks two gourds together endlessly, that's the "putta" of Eddie's rhythm; on the other, another beats a drum, that's the "boom." In one upraised hand he holds a squalling fowl, wings beating the air; in the other a sharp-bladed knife. Something flashes in the air, but the dancers mercifully get between Eddie and the sight of it. Next glimpse he has, the fowl isn't flapping any more. It's hanging limply down and veins of blood are trickling down the old man's shriveled forearm.

"That part don't go into my show," Eddie thinks facetiously. The horrible old man has dropped the knife; he squeezes the lifeblood from the dead bird with both hands now, still holding it in midair. He sprinkles the drops on those that cavort around him, flexing and unflexing his bony fingers in a nauseating travesty of the ceremony of baptism.

Drops spatter here and there about the room, on the walls. One lands near Eddie and he edges back. Revolting things go on all around him. He sees some of the crazed dancers drop to their hands and knees and bend low over these red polka dots, licking them up from the floor with their tongues. Then they go about the room on all fours like animals, looking for others.

"Think I'll go," Eddie says to himself, tasting last night's supper all over again. "They ought to have the cops on them."

He maneuvers the score sheet, filled now, out from under him and into his side pocket; then he starts drawing his feet in toward him preparatory to standing up and slipping out of this hell hole. Meanwhile a second fowl, black this time (the first was white), a squeaking suckling pig, and a puppy dog have gone the way of the first fowl. Nor do the carcasses go to waste when the old man has dropped them. Eddie sees things happening on the floor, in between the stomping feet of the dancers, and he guesses enough not to look twice.

Then suddenly, already reared a half-inch above the floor on his way up, he wonders where the wailing went. And the clacking of the gourds and the boom of the drum and the shuffling of the feet.

He blinks, and everything has frozen still in the room around him. Not a move, not a sound. Straight out from the old man's gnarled shoulder stretches a bony arm, the end dipped in red, pointing like an arrow at Eddie. Eddie sinks down again that half-inch. He couldn't hold that position very long, and something tells him he's not leaving right away after all.

"White man," says a bated breath, and they all start moving in on him. A gesture of the old man sweeps them into motionlessness again.

A cracked voice comes through the grinning mouth of the juju mask, rimmed with canine teeth. "Whut you do here?"

Eddie taps his pockets mentally. He has about fifty on him. Will that be enough to buy his way out? He has an uneasy feeling, however, that none of this lot is as interested in money as they should be—at least not right now. Before he has a chance to try it out, another voice speaks up. "I know this man, *papaloi*. Let me find out."

Johnny Staats came in here tuxedoed, hair slicked back, a cog in New Orleans' nightlife. Now he's barefooted, coatless, shirtless —a tousled scarecrow. A drop of blood has caught him squarely on the forehead and been traced, by his own finger or someone else's, into a red line from temple to temple. A chicken feather or two clings to his upper lip. Eddie saw him dancing with the rest, groveling on the floor. His scalp crawls with repugnance as the man comes over and squats down before him. The rest of them hold back, tense, poised, ready to pounce.

The two men talk in low, hoarse voices. "It's your only way, Eddie. I can't save you—"

"Why, I'm in the very heart of New Orleans! They wouldn't dare!" But sweat oozes out on Eddie's face just the same. He's no fool. Sure the police will come and sure they'll mop this place up. But what will they find? His own remains along with that of the fowls, the pig and the dog.

"You'd better hurry up, Eddie. I can't hold them back much longer. Unless you do, you'll never get out of this place alive and you may as well know it! If I tried to stop them, I'd go too. You know what this is, don't you? This is voodoo!"

"I knew that five minutes after I was in the room." And Eddie thinks to himself, "You son-of-a-so-and-so! You better ask Mombo-jombo to get you a new job starting in tomorrow night!" Then he grins internally and, clown to the very end, says with a straight face, "Sure I'll join. What d'ye suppose I came here for anyway?"

Knowing what he knows now, Staats is the last one he'd tell about the glorious new number he's going to get out of this, the notes for which are nestled in his inside pocket right now. And he might even get more dope out of the initiation ceremonies if he pretends to go through with them. A song or dance for Judy to do with maybe a green spot focused on her. Lastly, there's no use denying there *are* too many razors, knives and the like, in the room to hope to get out and all the way back where he started from without a scratch.

Staats' face is grave, though. "Now don't kid about this thing. If you knew what I know about it, there's a lot more to it than there seems to be. If you're sincere, honest about it, all right. If not, it might be better to get cut to pieces right now than to tamper with it."

"Never more serious in my life," says Eddie. And deep down inside he's braying like a jackass.

Staats turns to the old man. "His spirit wishes to join our spirits."

The *papaloi* burns some feathers and entrails at one of the candle flames. Not a sound in the room. The majority of them squat down all at once. "It came out all right," Staats breathes. "He reads them. The spirits are willing."

"So far so good," Eddie thinks. "I've fooled the guts and feathers."

The *papaloi* is pointing at him now. "Let him go now and be silent," the voice behind the mask cackles. Then a second time he says it, and a third, with a long pause between.

Eddie looks hopefully at Staats. "Then I can go after all, as long as I don't tell anyone what I've seen?"

Staats shakes his head grimly. "Just part of the ritual. If you went now, you'd eat something that disagreed with you tomorrow and be dead before the day was over."

More sacrificial slaughtering, and the drum and gourds and wailing start over again, but very low and subdued now as at the beginning. A bowl of blood is prepared and Eddie is raised to his feet and led forward, Staats on one side of him, an anonymous colored man on the other. The *papaloi* dips his already caked hand into the bowl and traces a mark on Eddie's forehead. The chanting and wailing grow louder behind him. The dancing begins again. He's in the middle of all of them. He's an island of sanity in a sea of jungle frenzy. The bowl is being held up before his face. He tries to draw back, his sponsors grip him firmly by the arms. "Drink!" whispers Staats. "Drink—or they'll kill you where you stand!"

Even at this stage of the game, there's still a wisecrack left in Eddie, though he keeps it to himself. He takes a deep breath. "Here's where I get my vitamin A for today!"

Staats shows up at orchestra rehearsal next A.M. to find somebody else at drums and percussion. He doesn't say much when Eddie shoves a two-week check at him, spits on the floor at his feet and growls: "Beat it, you filthy—"

Staats only murmurs, "So you're crossing them? I wouldn't want to be in your shoes for all the fame and money in this world, guy!"

"If you mean that bad dream the other night," says Eddie, "I haven't told anybody and I don't intend to. Why, I'd be laughed at. I'm only remembering what I can use of it. I'm a white man, see? The jungle is just trees to me; the Congo just a river; the nighttime just a time for electric lights." He whips out a couple of C's. "Hand 'em these for me, will ya, and tell 'em I've paid up my dues from now until doomsday and I don't want any receipt. And if they try putting rough-on-rats in my orange juice, they'll find themselves stomping in a chain gang!"

The C's fall where Eddie spat. "You're one of us. You think you're pink? Blood tells. You wouldn't have gone there—you couldn't have stood that induction—if you were. Look at your fingernails sometime, look in a mirror at the whites of your eyes. Good-bye, dead man."

Eddie says good-bye to him, too. He knocks out three of his teeth, breaks the bridge of his nose, and rolls all over the floor on top of him. But he can't wipe out that wise, knowing smile that shows even through the gush of blood.

They pull Eddie off, pull him up, pull him together. Staats staggers away, smiling at what he knows. Eddie, heaving like a bellows, turns to his crew. "All right, boys. All together now!" *Boom-putta-putta-boom-putta-putta-boom!*

Graham shoots five C's on promotion and all New Orleans jams its way into Maxim's that Saturday night. They're standing on each other's shoulders and hanging from the chandeliers to get a look. "First time in America, the original VOODOO CHANT," yowl the three-sheets on every billboard in town. And when Eddie taps his baton, the lights go down and a nasty green flood lights the platform from below and you can hear a pin drop. "Good evening, folks. This is Eddie Bloch and his Five Chips, playing to you from Maxim's. You're about to hear for the first time on the air the Voodoo Chant, the age-old ceremonial rhythm no white man has ever been permitted to listen to before. I can assure you this is an accurate transcription, not a note has been changed." Then very softly and faraway it begins: *Boom-putta-putta-boom!*

Judy's going to dance and wail to it, she's standing there on the steps leading up to the platform, waiting to go on. She's powdered orange, dressed in feathers, and has a small artificial bird fastened to one wrist and a thin knife in her other hand. She catches his eye, he looks over at her, and he sees she wants to tell him something. Still waving his baton he edges sideways until he's within earshot.

"Eddie, don't! Stop them! Call it off, will you? I'm worried about you!"

"Too late now," he answers under cover of the music. "We've started already. What're you scared of?"

She passes him a crumpled piece of paper. "I found this under your dressing-room door when I came out just now. It sounds like a warning. There's somebody doesn't want you to play that number!"

Still swinging with his right hand, Eddie unrolls the thing under his left thumb and reads it:

You can summon the spirits but can you dismiss them again? Think well.

He crumples it up and tosses it away. "Staats trying to scare me because I canned him."

"It was tied to a little bunch of black feathers," she tries to tell him. "I wouldn't have paid any attention, but my maid pleaded with me not to dance this when she saw it. Then she ran out on me—"

"We're on the air," he reminds her between his teeth. "Are you with me or aren't you?" And he eases back center again. Louder and louder the beat grows, just like it did two nights ago. Judy swirls on in a green spot and begins the unearthly wail Eddie's coached her to do.

A waiter drops a tray of drinks in the silence of the room out there, and when the headwaiter goes to bawl him out he's nowhere to be found. He has quit cold and a whole row of tables has been left without their orders. "Well, I'll be—!" says the captain and scratches his head.

Eddie's facing the crew, his back to Judy, and as he vibrates to the rhythm, some pin or other that he's forgotten to take out of his shirt suddenly catches him and strikes into him. It's a little below the collar, just between the shoulder blades. He jumps a little, but doesn't feel it any more after that.

Judy squalls, tears her tonsils out, screeches words that neither he nor she know the meaning of but that he managed to set down on paper phonetically the other night. Her little body goes through all the contortions, tamed down of course, that that brownskin she-devil greased with lard and wearing only earrings performed that night. She stabs the bird with her fake knife and sprinkles imaginary blood in the air. Nothing like this has ever been seen before. And in the silence that suddenly lands when it's through, you can count twenty. That's how it's gotten under everyone's skin.

Then the noise begins. It goes over like an avalanche. But just the same, more people are ordering strong drinks all at once than has ever happened before in the place, and the matron in the women's restroom has her hands full of hysterical sob-sisters.

"Try to get away from me, just try!" Graham tells Eddie at curfew time. "I'll have a new contract, gilt-edged, ready for you in the morning. We've already got six-grand worth of reservations on our hands for the coming week—one of 'em by telegram all the way from Shreveport!"

Success! Eddie and Judy taxi back to their rooms at the hotel, tired but happy. "It'll be good for years. We can use it for our signature on the air, like Whiteman does the Rhapsody."

She goes into the bedroom first, snaps on the lights, calls to him a minute later: "Come here and look at this—the cutest little souvenir!" He finds her holding a wax doll, finger high, in her hands. "Why, it's you, Eddie, look! Small as it is it has your features! Well isn't that the clev—!"

He takes it away from her and squints at it. It's himself all right. It's rigged out in two tiny patches of black cloth for a tuxedo, and the eyes and hair and features are inked onto the wax.

"Where'd you find it?"

"It was in your bed, up against the pillow."

He's fixing to grin about it, until he happens to turn it over. In the back, just a little below the collar, between the shoulder blades, a short but venomous-looking black pin is sticking.

He goes a little white for a minute. He knows who it's from now and what it's trying to tell him. But that isn't what makes him change color. He's just remembered something. He throws off his coat, yanks at his collar, turns his back to her. "Judy, look down there, will you? I felt a pin stick me while we were doing that number. Put your hand down. Feel anything?"

"No, there's nothing there," she tells him.

"Musta dropped out."

"It couldn't have," she says. "Your belt line's so tight it almost cuts into you. There couldn't have been anything there or it'd still be there now. You must have imagined it."

"Listen, I know a pin when I feel one. Any mark on my back, any scratch between the shoulders?"

"Not a thing."

"Tired, I guess. Nervous." He goes over to the open window and pitches the little doll out into the night with all his strength. Damn coincidence, that's all it was. To think otherwise would be to give them their inning. But he wonders what makes him feel so tired just the same—Judy did all the exercising, not he—yet he's felt all in ever since that number tonight.

Out go the lights and she drops off to sleep right with them. He lies very quiet for a while. A little later he gets up, goes into the bathroom where the lights are whitest of all, and stands there looking at himself close to the glass. "Look at your fingernails sometime; look at the whites of your eyes," Staats had said. Eddie does. There's a bluish, purplish tinge to his nails that he never noticed before. The whites of his eyes are faintly yellow.

It's warm in New Orleans that night but he shivers a little as he stands there. He doesn't sleep any more that night. . . .

In the morning, his back aches as if he were sixty. But he knows that's from not closing his eyes all night, and not from any magic pins.

"Oh, my God!" Judy says, from the other side of the bed; "look what you've done to him!" She shows him the second page of the *Picayune*. "John Staats, until recently a member of Eddie Bloch's orchestra, committed suicide late yesterday afternoon in full view of dozens of people by rowing himself out into Lake Pontchartrain and jumping overboard. He was alone in the boat at the time. The body was recovered half an hour later."

"I didn't do that," says Eddie grimly. "I've got a rough idea what did, though." Late yesterday afternoon. The night was coming on, and he couldn't face what was coming to him for sponsoring Eddie, for giving them all away. Late yesterday afternoon—that meant *he* hadn't left that warning at the dressing room or left that death sentence on the bed. He'd been dead himself by then—not white, not black, just yellow.

Eddie waits until Judy's in her shower, then he phones the morgue. "About Johnny Staats. He worked for me until yesterday, so if nobody's claimed the body send it to a funeral parlor at my exp—"

"Somebody's already claimed the remains, Mr. Bloch. First thing this morning. Just waited until the examiner had established suicide beyond a doubt. Some colored organization, old friends of his it seems—"

Judy comes in and remarks: "You look all green in the face."

Eddie thinks: "I wouldn't care if he was my worst enemy, I can't let that happen to him! What horrors are going to take place tonight somewhere under the moon?" He wouldn't even put cannibalism beyond them. The phone's right at his fingertips, and yet he can't denounce them to the police without involving himself, admitting that he was there, took part at least once. Once that comes out, bang! goes his reputation. He'll never be able to live it down—especially now that he's played the Voodoo Chant and identified himself with it in the minds of the public.

So instead, alone in the room again, he calls the best-known private agency in New Orleans. "I want a bodyguard. Just for tonight. Have him meet me at closing time at Maxim's. Armed, of course."

It's Sunday and the banks are closed, but his credit's good anywhere. He raises a G in cash. He arranges with a reliable crematorium for a body to be taken charge of late tonight or early in the morning. He'll notify them just where to call for it. Yes, of course! He'll produce the proper authorization from the police. Poor Johnny Staats couldn't get away from "them" in life, but he's going to get away from them in death, all right. That's the least anyone could do for him.

Graham slaps a sawbuck-cover on that night, more to give the waiters room to move around in than anything else, and still the place is choked to the roof. This voodoo number is a natural, a wow.

But Eddie's back is ready to cave in, while he stands there jogging with his stick. It's all he can do to hold himself straight.

When the racket and the shuffling are over for the night, the private dick is there waiting for him. "Lee is the name."

"Okay, Lee, come with me." They go outside and get in Eddie's Bugatti. They whizz down to the Vieux, scrounge to a stop in the middle of Congo Square, which will still be Congo Square when its official name of Beauregard is forgotten.

"This way," says Eddie, and his bodyguard squirms through the alley after him.

" 'Lo, suga' pie," says the elbow-pusher, and for once, to her own surprise as much as anyone else's, gets a tumble.

" 'Lo, Eglantine," Eddie's bodyguard remarks in passing. "So you moved?"

They stop in front of the house on the other side of the tunnel. "Now here's what," says Eddie. "We're going to be stopped halfway up these stairs in here by a big orangutan. Your job is to clean him, tap him if you want, I don't care. I'm going into a room up there, you're going to wait for me at the door. You're here to see that I get out of that room again. We may have to carry the body of a friend of mine down to the street between us. I don't know. It depends on whether it's in the house or not. Got it?"

"Got it."

"Light up. Keep your torch trained over my shoulder."

A big, lowering figure looms over them, blocking the narrow stairs, apelike arms and legs spread-eagled in a gesture of malignant embrace, receding skull, teeth showing, flashing steel in hand. Lee jams Eddie roughly to one side and shoves up past him. "Drop that, boy!" Lee says with slurring indifference, but then he doesn't wait to see if the order's carried out or not. After all, a weapon was raised to two white men. He fires three times, from two feet away and considerably below the obstacle, hits where he aimed to. The bullets shatter both kneecaps and the elbow joint of the arm holding the knife.

"Be a cripple for life now," he remarks with quiet satisfaction. "I'll put him out of his pain." So he crashes the butt of gun down on the skull of the writhing colossus, in a long arc like the overhand pitch of a baseball. The noise of the shots goes booming up the narrow stairwell to the roof, to mushroom out there in a vast rolling echo.

"Come on, hurry up," says Eddie, "before they have a chance to do away with—"

He lopes on up past the prostrate form, Lee at his heels. "Stand there. Better reload while you're waiting. If I call your name, for Pete's sake don't count ten before you come in to me!"

There's a scurrying back and forth and an excited but subdued jabbering going on on the other side of the door. Eddie swings it wide and crashes it closed behind him, leaving Lee on the outside. They all stand rooted to the spot when they see him. The *papaloi* is there and about six others, not so many as on the night of Eddie's initiation. Probably the rest are waiting outside the city somewhere, in some secret spot, wherever the actual burial, or burning, or—feasting—is to take place.

Papa Benjamin has no juju mask on this time, no animal pelt. There are no gourds in the room, no drum, no transfixed figures ranged against the wall. They were about to move on elsewhere, he just got here in time. Maybe they were waiting for the dark of the moon. The ordinary kitchen chairs on which the *papaloi* was to be carried on their shoulders stands prepared, padded with rags. A row of baskets covered with sacking are ranged along the back wall.

"Where is the body of John Staats?" raps out Eddie. "You claimed it, took it away from the morgue this morning." His eyes are on those baskets, on the bleared razor he catches sight of lying on the floor near them.

"Better far," cackles the old man, "that you had followed him. The mark of doom is on yo' even now—" A growl goes up all around.

"Lee," grates Eddie, "in here!" Lee stands next to him, gun in hand. "Cover me while I take a look around."

"All of you over in that corner there," growls Lee, and kicks viciously at one who is too slow in moving. They huddle there, cower there, glaring, spitting like a band of apes. Eddie makes straight for those baskets, whips the covering off the first one. Charcoal. The next. Coffee beans. The next. Rice. And so on.

Just small baskets that Negro women balance on their heads to sell at the marketplace. He looks at Papa Benjamin, takes out the wad of money he's brought with him. "Where've you got him? Where's he buried? Take us there, show us where it is."

Not a sound, just burning, shriveling hate in waves that you can almost feel. He looks at that razor blade lying there, bleared, not bloody, just matted, dulled, with shreds and threads of something clinging to it. Kicks it away with his foot. "Not here, I guess," he mutters to Lee and moves toward the door.

"What do we do now, boss?" his henchman wants to know.

"Get the hell out of here I guess, where we can breathe some air," Eddie says, and moves on out to the stairs.

Lee is the sort of man who will get what he can out of any situation, no matter what it is. Before he follows Eddie out, he goes over to one of the baskets, stuffs an orange in each coat pocket, and then prods and pries among them to select a particularly nice one for eating on the spot. There's a thud and the orange goes rolling across the floor like a volleyball. "Mr. Bloch!" he shouts hoarsely, "I've found—him!" And he looks pretty sick.

A deep breath goes up from the corner where the Negroes are. Eddie just stands and stares, and leans back weakly for a minute against the doorpost. From out of the layers of oranges in the basket, the five fingers of a hand thrust upward, a hand that ends abruptly, cleanly at the wrist.

"His signet," says Eddie weakly, "there on the little finger— I know it."

"Say the word! Should I shoot?" Lee wants to know.

Eddie shakes his head. "They didn't—he committed suicide. Let's do what we have to—and get out of here!"

Lee turns over one basket after the other. The stuff in them spills and sifts and rolls out upon the floor. But in each there's something else. Bloodless, pallid as fish flesh. That razor, those shreds clinging to it, Eddie knows now what it was used for. They take one basket, they line it with a verminous blanket from the bed. Then with their bare hands they fill it with what they have found, and close the ends of the blanket over the top of it, and carry it between them out of the room and down the pitch-black stairs, Lee going down backward with his gun in one hand to cover them from the rear. Lee's swearing like a fiend. Eddie's trying not to think what the purpose, the destination of all those baskets was.

The watchdog is still out on the stairs, with a concussion.

Back through the lane they struggle and finally put their burden down in the before-dawn stillness of Congo Square. Eddie goes up against a wall and is heartily sick. Then he comes back again and says: "The head—did you notice—?"

"No, we didn't," Lee answers. "Stay here, I'll go back for it. I'm armed. I could stand anything now, after what I just been through."

Lee's gone about five minutes. When he comes back, he's in his shirt, coatless. His coat's rolled up under one arm in a bulky bulge. He bends over the basket, lifts the blanket, replaces it again, and when he straightens up, the bulge in his folded coat is gone. Then he throws the coat away, kicks it away on the ground. "Hidden away in a cupboard," he mutters. "Had to shoot one of 'em through the palm of the hand before they'd come clean. What were they up to?"

"Practice cannibalism maybe, I don't know. I'd rather not think."

"I brought your money back. It didn't seem to square you with them."

Eddie shoves it back at him. "Pay for your suit and your time."

"Aren't you going to tip off the squareheads?"

"I told you he jumped in the lake. I have a copy of the examiner's report in my pocket."

"I know, but isn't there some ordinance against dissecting a body without permission?"

"I can't afford to get mixed up with them, Lee. It would kill my career. We've got what we went there for. Now just forget everything you saw."

The hearse from the crematorium contacts them there in Congo Square. The covered basket's taken on, and what's left of

Johnny Staats heads away for a better finish than was coming to him.

"G'night, boss," says Lee. "Any time you need any other little thing—"

"No," says Eddie, "I'm getting out of New Orleans." His hand is like ice when they shake.

He does. He hands Graham back his contract, and a split week later he's playing New York's newest, in the frantic Fifties. With a white valet. The chant, of course, is still featured. He has to; it's his chief asset, his biggest draw. It introduces him and signs him off, and in between Judy always dances it for a high spot. But he can't get rid of that backache that started the night he first played it. First he goes and tries having his back baked for a couple of hours a day under a violet-ray lamp. No improvement.

Then he has himself examined by the biggest specialist in New York. "Nothing there," says the big shot. "Absolutely nothing the matter with you: liver, kidneys, blood—everything perfect. It must be all in your own mind."

"You're losing weight, Eddie," Judy says, "you look bad, darling." His bathroom scales tell him the same thing. Down five pounds a week, sometimes seven, never up an ounce. More experts. X-rays this time, blood analysis, gland treatments, everything from soup to nuts. Nothing doing. And the dull ache, the lassitude, spreads slowly, first to one arm, then to the other.

He takes specimens of everything he eats, not just one day, but every day for weeks, and has them chemically analyzed. Nothing. And he doesn't have to be told that anyway. He knows that even in New Orleans, way back in the beginning, nothing was ever put into his food. Judy ate from the same tray, drank from the same coffeepot he did. Nightly she dances herself into a lather, and yet she's the picture of health.

So that leaves nothing but his mind, just as they all say. "But

I don't believe it!" he tells himself. "I don't believe that just sticking pins into a wax doll can hurt me—me or anyone!"

So it isn't his mind at all, but some other mind back there in New Orleans, some other mind *thinking,* wishing, ordering him dead, night and day.

"But it can't be done!" says Eddie. "There's no such thing!" And yet it's being done; it's happening right under his own eyes. Which leaves only one answer. If going three thousand miles away on dry land didn't help, then going three thousand miles away across the ocean will do the trick. So London next, and the Kit-Kat Club. Down, down, down go the bathroom scales, a little bit each week. The pains spread downward into his thighs. His ribs start showing up here and there. He's dying on his feet. He finds it more comfortable now to walk with a stick—not to be swanky, not to be English—to rest as he goes along. His shoulders ache each night just from waving that lightweight baton at his crew. He has a music stand built for himself to lean on, keeps it in front of his body, out of sight of the audience while he's conducting, and droops over it. Sometimes he finishes up a number with his head lower than his shoulders, as though he had a rubber spine.

Finally he goes to Reynolds, famous the world over, the biggest alienist in England. "I want to know whether I'm sane or insane." He's under observation for weeks, months; they put him through every known test, and plenty of unknown ones, mental, physical, metabolic. They flash lights in front of his face and watch the pupils of his eyes; they contract to pinheads. They touch the back of his throat with sandpaper; he nearly chokes. They strap him to a chair that goes around and around and does somersaults at so many revolutions per minute, then ask him to walk across the room; he staggers.

Reynolds takes plenty of pounds, hands him a report thick as a telephone book, sums it up for him. "You are as normal, Mr. Bloch, as anyone I have ever handled. You're so well-balanced you haven't even got the extra little touch of imagination most actors and musicians have." So it's not his own mind, it's coming from the outside, is it?

The whole thing from beginning to end has taken eighteen months. Trying to outdistance death, with death gaining on him slowly but surely all the time. He's emaciated. There's only one thing left to do now, while he's still able to crawl aboard a ship —that's to get back to where the whole thing started. New York, London, Paris, haven't been able to save him. His only salvation, now, lies in the hands of a decrepit colored man skulking in the Vieux Carré of New Orleans.

He drags himself there, to that same half-ruined house, without a bodyguard, not caring now whether they kill him or not, almost wishing they would and get it over with. But that would be too easy an out, it seems. The gorilla that Lee crippled that night shuffles out to him between two sticks, recognizes him, breathes undying hate into his face, but doesn't lift a finger to harm him. The spirits are doing the job better than he could ever hope to. Their mark is on this man, woe betide anyone who comes between them and their hellish satisfaction. Eddie Bloch totters up the stairs unopposed, his back as safe from a knife as if he wore steel armor. Behind him the Negro sprawls upon the stairs to lubricate his long-awaited hour of satisfaction with rum—and oblivion.

He finds the old man alone there in the room. The Stone Age and the twentieth century face each other, and the Stone Age has won out.

"Take it off me," says Eddie brokenly. "Give me my life back —I'll do anything, anything you say!"

"What has been done cannot be undone. Do you think the spirits of the earth and of the air, of fire and water, know the meaning of forgiveness?"

"Intercede for me, then. You brought it about. Here's money, I'll give you twice as much, all I earn, all I ever hope to earn—"

"You have desecrated the *obiah*. Death has been on you from that night. All over the world and in the air above the earth you have mocked the spirits with the chant that summons them. Nightly your wife dances it. The only reason she has not shared your doom is because she does not know the meaning of what she does. You do. You were here among us."

Eddie goes down on his knees, scrapes along the floor after the old man, tries to tug at the garments he wears. "Kill me right now, then, and be done with it. I can't stand any more—" He bought the gun only that day, was going to do it himself at first, but found he couldn't. A minute ago he pleaded for his life, now he's pleading for death. "It's loaded, all you have to do is shoot. Look! I'll close my eyes—I'll write a note and sign it, that I did it myself—"

He tries to thrust it into the witch doctor's hand, tries to close the bony, shriveled fingers around it, tries to point it at himself. The old man throws it down, away from him. Cackles gleefully, "Death will come, but differently—slowly, oh, so slowly!"

Eddie just lies there flat on his face, sobbing dryly. The old man spits, kicks at him weakly. He pulls himself up somehow, stumbles toward the door. He isn't even strong enough to get it open at the first try. It's that little thing that brings it on. Something touches his foot, he looks, stoops for the gun, turns. Thought is quick but the old man's mind is even quicker. Almost before the thought is there, the old man knows what's coming. In a flash, scuttling like a crab, he has shifted around to the other side of the bed, to put something between them. Instantly the situation's reversed, the fear has left Eddie and is on the old man now. He's lost the aggression. For a minute only, but that minute is all Eddie needs. His mind beams out like a diamond, like a lighthouse through a fog. The gun roars, jolting his weakened body down to his shoes. The old man falls flat across the bed, his head too far over, dangling down over the side of it like an overripe pear. The bed frame sways gently with his weight for a minute, and then it's over.

Eddie stands there, still off-balance from the kickback. So it was as easy as all that! Where's all his magic now? Strength, willpower flood back through him as if a faucet was suddenly turned on. The little smoke there was can't get out of the sealed-up room, it hangs there in thin layers. Suddenly he's shaking his fist at the dead thing on the bed. "I'm gonna live now! I'm gonna live, see?" He gets the door open, sways with it for a minute. Then he's feeling his way down the stairs, past the unconscious watchdog, mumbling it over and over but low, "Gonna live now, gonna live!"

The commissioner mops his face as if he were in the steam room of a Turkish bath. He exhales like an oxygen tank. "Judas, Joseph and Mary, Mr. Bloch, what a story! Wish I hadn't asked you; I won't sleep tonight." Even after the accused has been led from the room, it takes him some time to get over it. The upper right-hand drawer of his desk helps some—just two fingers. So does opening the windows and letting in a lot of sunshine.

Finally he picks up the phone and gets down to business. "Who've you got out there that's absolutely without a nerve in his body? I mean a guy with so little feeling he could sit on a hatpin and turn it into a paper clip. Oh, yeah, that Cajun, Desjar-

dins, I know him. He's the one goes around striking parlor matches off the soles of stiffs. Well, send him in here."

"No, stay outside," wheezes Papa Benjamin through the partly
open door to his envoy. "I'se communin' with the *obiah* and yo'
unclean, been drunk all last night and today. Deliver the summons. Reach yo' hand in to me, once fo' every token, yo' knows
how many to take."

The crippled Negro thrusts his huge paw through the aperture,
and from behind the door the *papaloi* places a severed chicken
claw in his upturned palm. A claw bound with a red rag. The
messenger disposes of it about his tattered clothing, thrusts his
hand in for another. Twenty times the act is repeated, then he
lets his arm hang stiffly at his side. The door starts closing slowly.

"Papaloi," whines the figure on the outside of it, "why you
hide yo' face from me, is the spirits angry?"

There's a flicker of suspicion in his yellow eyeballs in the dimness, however. Instantly the opening of the door widens. Papa
Benjamin's familiar wrinkled face thrusts out at him, malignant
eyes crackling like fuses. "Go!" shrills the old man, " 'liver my
summons. Is you want me to bring a spirit down on you?" The
messenger totters back. The door slams.

The sun goes down and it's nighttime in New Orleans. The
moon rises, midnight chimes from St. Louis Cathedral, and
hardly has the last note died away when a gruesome swampland
whistle sounds outside the deathly still house. A fat Negress,
basket on arm, comes trudging up the stairs a moment later, opens
the door, goes in to the *papaloi,* closes it again, traces an invisible
mark on it with her forefinger and kisses it. Then she turns and
her eyes widen with surprise. Papa Benjamin is in bed, covered
up to the neck with filthy rags. The familiar candles are all lit, the

bowl for the blood, the sacrificial knife, the magic powders, all the paraphernalia of the ritual are laid out in readiness, but they are ranged about the bed instead of at the opposite end of the room as usual.

The old man's head, however, is held high above the encumbering rags, his beady eyes gaze back at her unflinchingly, the familiar semicircle of white wool rings his crown, his ceremonial mask is at his side. "I am a little tired, my daughter," he tells her. His eyes stray to the tiny wax image of Eddie Bloch under the candles, hairy with pins, and hers follow them. "A doomed one, nearing his end, came here last night thinking I could be killed like other men. He shot a bullet from a gun at me. I blew my breath at it, it stopped in the air, turned around, and went back in the gun again. But it tired me to blow so hard, strained my voice a little."

A revengeful gleam lights up the woman's broad face. "And he'll die soon, *papaloi?*"

"Soon," cackles the weazened figure in the bed. The woman gnashes her teeth and hugs herself delightedly. She opens the top of her basket and allows a black hen to escape and flutter about the room.

When all twenty have assembled, men and women, old and young, the drum and the gourds begin to beat, the low wailing starts, the orgy gets under way. Slowly they dance around the three sides of the bed at first, then faster, faster, lashing themselves to a frenzy, tearing at their own and each other's clothes, drawing blood with knives and fingernails, eyes rolling in an ecstasy that colder races cannot know. The sacrifices, feathered and furred, that have been fastened to the two lower posts of the bed, squawk and flutter and fly vertically up and down in a barnyard panic. There is a small monkey among them tonight, clawing, biting, hiding his face in his hands like a frightened child. A bearded Negro, nude torso glistening like patent leather, seizes one of the frantic fowls, yanks it loose from its moorings, and holds it out toward the witch doctor with both hands. "We'se thirsty, *papaloi*, we'se thirsty fo' the blood of ou' enemies."

The others take up the cry. "We'se hung'y, *papaloi*, fo' the bones of ou' enemies!"

Papa Benjamin nods his head in time to the rhythm.

"Sac'fice, *papaloi*, sac'fice!"

Papa Benjamin doesn't seem to hear them.

Then back go the rags in a gray wave and out comes the arm at last. Not the gnarled brown toothpick arm of Papa Benjamin, but a bulging arm thick as a piano leg, cuffed in serge, white at the wrist, ending in a regulation police revolver with the clip off. The erstwhile witch doctor's on his feet at a bound, standing erect atop the bed, back to the wall, slowly fanning his score of human devils with the mouth of his gun, left to right, then right to left again, evenly, unhurriedly. The resonant bellow of a bull comes from his weazened slit of a mouth instead of *papaloi*'s cracked falsetto. "Back against that wall there, all of you! Throw down them knives and jiggers!"

But they're slow to react; the swift drop from ecstasy to stupefaction can't register right away. None of them are over bright anyway or they wouldn't be here. Mouths hang open, the wailing stops, the drums and gourds fall still, but they're still packed close about this sudden changeling in their midst, with the familiar shriveled face of Papa Benjamin and the thickset body, business suit, of a white man—too close for comfort. Blood lust and religious mania don't know fear of a gun. It takes a cool head for that, and the only cool head in the room is the withered cocoanut atop the broad shoulders behind that gun. So he shoots twice, and a woman at one end of the semicircle, the drum beater, and a man at the other end, the one still holding the sacrificial fowl, drop in their tracks with a double moan. Those in the middle slowly draw back step by step across the room, all eyes on the figure reared up on the bed. An instant's carelessness, the wavering of an eye, and they'll be in on him in a body. He reaches up with his free hand and rips the dead witch-doctor's features from his face, to breathe better, see better. They dissolve into a crumpled rag before the blacks' terrified eyes, like a stocking cap coming off someone's head—a mixture of paraffin and fiber, called moulage —a death mask taken from the corpse's own face, reproducing even the fine lines of the skin and its natural color. Moulage. So the twentieth century has won out after all. And behind them is the grinning, slightly perspiring, lantern-jawed face of Detective Jacques Desjardins, who doesn't believe in spirits unless they're under a neat little label. And outside the house sounds the twenty-first whistle of the evening, but not a swampland sound this time; a long, cold, keen blast to bring figures out of the shadows and doorways that have waited there patiently all night.

Then the door bursts inward and the police are in the room. The prisoners, two of them dangerously wounded, are pushed and carried downstairs to join the crippled doorguard, who has been in custody for the past hour, and single file, tied together with ropes, they make their way through the long tortuous alley out into Congo Square.

In the early hours of that same morning, just a little more than twenty-four hours after Eddie Bloch first staggered into police headquarters with his strange story, the whole thing is cooked, washed and bottled. The commissioner sits in his office listening attentively to Desjardins. And spread out on his desk as strange an array of amulets, wax images, bunches of feathers, balsam leaves, *ouangas* (charms of nail parings, hair clippings, dried blood, powdered roots), green mildewed coins dug up from coffins in graveyards, as that room has ever seen before. All this is state's evidence now, to be carefully labeled and docketed for the use of the prosecuting attorney when the proper time comes. "And this," explains Desjardins, indicating a small dusty bottle, "is methylene blue, the chemist tells me. It's the only modern thing we got out of the place, found it lying forgotten with a lot of rubbish in a corner that looked like it hadn't been disturbed for years. What it was doing there or what they wanted with it I don't—"

"Wait a minute," interrupts the commissioner eagerly. "That fits in with something poor Bloch told me last night. He noticed a bluish color under his fingernails and a yellowness to his eyeballs, but *only* after he'd been initiated that first night. This stuff probably had something to do with it, an injection of it must have been given him that night in some way without his knowing it. Don't you get the idea? It floored him just the way they wanted it to. He mistook the signs of it for a giveaway that he had colored blood. It was the opening wedge. It broke down his disbelief, started his mental resistance to crumbling. That was all they needed, just to get a foothold in his mind. Mental suggestion did the rest, has been doing it ever since. If you ask me, they pulled the same stunt on Staats originally. I don't believe he had colored blood any more than Bloch has. And as a matter of fact the theory that it shows up in that way generations later is all the bunk anyway, they tell me."

"Well," says Dij, looking at his own grimy nails, "if you're just going to judge by appearances that way, I'm full-blooded Zulu."

His overlord just looks at him, and if he didn't have such a poker face, one might be tempted to read admiration or at least approval into the look. "Must have been a pretty tight spot for a minute with all of them around while you put on your act!"

"Nah, I didn't mind," answered Dij. "The only thing that bothered me was the smell."

Eddie Bloch, the murder charge against him quashed two months ago, and the population of the state penitentiary increased only this past week by the admission of twenty-three ex-voodoo-worshipers for terms varying from two to ten years, steps up on the platform at Maxim's for a return engagement. Eddie's pale and washed-out looking, but climbing slowly back up through the hundred-and-twenties again to his former weight. The ovation he gets ought to do anyone's heart good, the way they clap and stamp and stand up and cheer. And at that, his name was kept out of the recently concluded trial. Desjardins and his mates did all the states-witnessing necessary.

The theme he comes in on now is something sweet and harmless. Then a waiter comes up and hands him a request. Eddie shakes his head. "No, not in our repertoire any more." He goes on leading. Another request comes, and another. Suddenly someone shouts it out at him, and in a second the whole place has taken up the cry. "The Voodoo Chant! Give us the Voodoo Chant!"

His face gets whiter than it is already, but he turns and tries to smile at them and shake his head. They won't quit, the music can't be heard, and he has to tap a lay-off. From all over the place, like a cheering section at a football game, "We want the Voodoo Chant! We want—!"

Judy's at his side. "What's the matter with 'em anyway?" he asks. "Don't they know what that thing's done to me?"

"Play it, Eddie, don't be foolish," she urges. "Now's the time, break the spell once and for all, prove to yourself that it can't hurt you. If you don't do it now, you'll never get over the idea. It'll stay with you all your life. Go ahead. I'll dance it just like I am."

"Okay," he says.

He taps. It's been quite some time, but he can rely on his outfit. Slow and low like thunder far away, coming nearer. *Boom-putta-putta-boom!* Judy whirls out behind him, lets out the first preliminary screech, *Eeyaeeya!*

She hears a commotion in back of her, and stops as suddenly as she began. Eddie Bloch's fallen flat on his face and doesn't move again after that.

They all know, somehow. There's an inertness, a finality about it that tells them. The dancers wait a minute, mill about, then melt away in a hush. Judy Jarvis doesn't scream, doesn't cry, just stands there staring, wondering. That last thought—did it come from inside his own mind just now—or outside? Was it two months on its way, from the other side of the grave, looking for him, looking for him, until it found him tonight when he played the chant once more and laid his mind open to Africa? No policeman, no detective, no doctor, no scientist, will ever be able to tell her. Did it come from inside or from outside? All she says is, "Stand close to me, boys—real close to me, I'm afraid of the dark."

"...DEAD MEN WORKING IN THE CANE FIELDS"

BY W.B. SEABROOK

As noted in the Introduction, " '. . . Dead Men Working in the Cane Fields' " is a chapter from W.B. Seabrook's The Magic Island, *a flamboyant and exaggerated firsthand account of voodoo in Haiti in the 1920s. (Other chapters in the book have even more lurid titles: "Goat-Cry, Girl-Cry," "The Altar of Skulls," "The God Incarnate," "A Nymph in Bronze." And the several illustrations by one Alexander King, most of which are stereotypical black caricatures, also add to the book's sensationalism.)*

Nevertheless, no matter what percentage is factual and what percentage fictional, Seabrook's account of zombies and zombieism offers more than a few shudders. Take, for example, this passage:

But the zombies shuffled through the marketplace, recognizing neither father nor wife nor mother, and as they turned leftward up the path leading to the graveyard, a woman whose daughter was in the procession of the dead threw herself screaming before the girl's . . . feet and begged her to stay; but the grave-cold feet of the daughter and the feet of the other dead shuffled over her and onward; and as they approached the graveyard, they began to shuffle faster and rushed among the graves, and each before his own empty grave began clawing at the stones and earth to enter it again; and as their cold hands touched the earth of their own graves, they fell and lay there, rotting carrion.

A well-known explorer and author during the early years of this century, William B. Seabrook produced a number of (supposedly) authentic records of black magic, spiritualism, and witchcraft throughout the world. Another of his books, Witchcraft, *received as much attention in its day as did* The Magic Island *and is a prized item among students and collectors of the occult. Although he wrote relatively little fiction per se, two excellent short stories, "The Salamander" and "The Witch's Vengeance," often appear in anthologies of the supernatural and the macabre. He died during World War II, not long after the publication of his autobiography,* No Hiding Place, *in 1942.*

PRETTY mulatto Julie had taken baby Marianne to bed. Constant Polynice and I sat late before the doorway of his *caille,* talking of fire-hags, demons, werewolves and vampires, while a full moon, rising slowly, flooded his sloping cotton fields and the dark rolling hills beyond.

Polynice was a Haitian farmer, but he was no common jungle peasant. He lived on the island of La Gonave. He seldom went over to the Haitian mainland, but he knew what was going on in Port-au-Prince, and spoke sometimes of installing a radio.

A countryman, half peasant born and bred, he was familiar with every superstition of the mountains and the plain, yet too intelligent to believe them literally true—or at least so I gathered from his talk.

He was interested in helping me toward an understanding of the tangled Haitian folklore. It was only by chance that we came presently to a subject which—though I refused for a long time to admit it—lies in a baffling category on the ragged edge of things which are beyond either superstition or reason. He had been telling me of fire-hags who left their skins at home and set the cane fields blazing; of the vampire, a woman sometimes living, sometimes dead, who sucked the blood of children and who could be distinguished because her hair always turned an ugly red; of the werewolf—*chauché*, in Creole—a man or woman who took the form of some animal, usually a dog, and went killing lambs, young goats, sometimes babies.

All this, I gathered, he considered to be pure superstition, as he told me with tolerant scorn how his friend and neighbor Osmann had one night seen a gray dog slinking with bloody jaws from his sheep-pen, and who, after having shot and exorcised and buried it, was so convinced he had killed a certain girl named Liane who was generally reputed to be a *chauché* that when he met her two days later on the path to Grande Source, he believed she was a ghost come back for vengeance, and fled howling.

As Polynice talked on, I reflected that these tales ran closely parallel not only with those of the Negroes in Georgia and the Carolinas, but with the medieval folklore of white Europe. Werewolves, vampires and demons were certainly no novelty. But I recalled one creature I had been hearing about in Haiti, which sounded exclusively local—the zombie.

It seemed (or so I had been assured by Negroes more credulous than Polynice) that while the zombie came from the grave, it was neither a ghost, nor yet a person who had been raised like Lazarus from the dead. The zombie, they say, is a soulless human corpse, still dead, but taken from the grave and endowed by sorcery with a mechanical semblance of life—it is a dead body which is made to walk and act and move as if it were alive. People who have the power to do this go to a fresh grave, dig up the body before it has had time to rot, galvanize it into movement, and then make of it a servant or slave, occasionally for the commission of some crime, more often simply as a drudge around the habitation or the farm, setting it dull heavy tasks, and beating it like a dumb beast if it slackens.

As this was revolving in my mind, I said to Polynice: "It seems to me that these werewolves and vampires are first cousins to those we have at home, but I have never, except in Haiti, heard of anything like zombies. Let us talk of them for a little while. I wonder if you can tell me something of this zombie superstition. I should like to get at some idea of how it originated."

My rational friend Polynice was deeply astonished. He leaned over and put his hand in protest on my knee.

"Superstition? But I assure you that this of which you now speak is not a matter of superstition. Alas, these things—and other evil practices connected with the dead—exist. They exist to an extent that you whites do not dream of, though evidences are everywhere under your eyes.

"Why do you suppose that even the poorest peasants, when they can, bury their dead beneath solid tombs of masonry?

"Why do they bury them so often in their own yards, close to the doorway?

"Why, so often, do you see a tomb or grave set close beside a busy road or footpath where people are always passing?

"It is to assure the poor unhappy dead such protection as we can.

"I will take you in the morning to see the grave of my brother, who was killed in the way you know. It is over there on the little ridge which you can see clearly now in the moonlight, open space all around it, close beside the trail which everybody passes going to and from Grande Source. Through four nights we watched yonder, in the peristyle, Osmann and I, with shotguns—for at that time both my dead brother and I had bitter enemies—until we were sure the body had begun to rot.

"No, my friend, no, no. There are only too many true cases. At this very moment, in the moonlight, there are zombies working on this island, less than two hours' ride from my own habitation. We know about them, but we do not dare to interfere so long as our own dead are left unmolested. If you will ride with me tomorrow night, yes, I will show you dead men working in the cane fields. Close even to the cities, there are sometimes zombies. Perhaps you have already heard of those that were at Hasco. . . ."

"What about Hasco?" I interrupted him, for in the whole of Haiti, Hasco is perhaps the last name anybody would think of connecting with either sorcery or superstition.

The word is American-commercial-synthetic, like Nabisco, Delco, Socony. It stands for the Haitian-American Sugar Company—an immense factory plant, dominated by a huge chimney, with clanging machinery, steam whistles, freight cars. It is like a chunk of Hoboken. It lies in the eastern suburbs of Port-au-Prince, and beyond it stretch the cane fields of the Cul-de-Sac.

Hasco makes rum when the sugar market is off, pays low wages, twenty or thirty cents a day, and gives steady work. It is modern big business, and it sounds it, looks it, smells it.

Such, then, was the incongruous background for the weird tale Constant Polynice now told me.

The spring of 1918 was a big cane season, and the factory, which had its own plantations, offered a bonus on the wages of new workers. Soon heads of families and villages from the mountain and the plain came trailing their ragtag little armies, men, women, children, trooping to the registration bureau and thence into the fields.

One morning an old black headman, Ti Joseph of Colombier, appeared leading a band of ragged creatures who shuffled along behind him, staring dumbly, like people walking in a daze. As Joseph lined them up for registration, they still stared, vacant-eyed like cattle, and made no reply when asked to give their names.

Joseph said they were ignorant people from the slopes of Morne-au-Diable, a roadless mountain district near the Dominican border, and that they did not understand the Creole of the plains. They were frightened, he said, by the din and smoke of the great factory, but under his direction they would work hard in the fields. The farther they were sent away from the factory, from the noise and bustle of the railroad yards, the better it would be.

Better indeed, for these were not living men and women but poor unhappy zombies whom Joseph and his wife Croyance had dragged from their peaceful graves to slave for him in the sun—and if by chance a brother or father of the dead should see and recognize them, Joseph knew that it would be a very bad affair for him.

So they were assigned to distant fields beyond the crossroads, and camped there, keeping to themselves like any proper family or village group; but in the evening when other little companies, encamped apart as they were, gathered each around its one big common pot of savory millet or plantains, generously seasoned with dried fish and garlic, Croyance would tend *two* pots upon the fire, for as everyone knows, the zombies must never be permitted to taste salt or meat. So the food prepared for them was tasteless and unseasoned.

As the zombies toiled day after day dumbly in the sun, Joseph sometimes beat them to make them move faster, but Croyance began to pity the poor dead creatures who should be at rest—and pitied them in the evenings when she dished out their flat, tasteless *bouillie*.

Each Saturday afternoon, Joseph went to collect the wages for them all, and what division he made was no concern of Hasco, so long as the work went forward. Sometimes Joseph alone, and sometimes Croyance alone, went to Croix de Bouquet for the Saturday night *bamboche* or the Sunday cockfight, but always one of them remained with the zombies to prepare their food and see that they did not stray away.

Through February this continued, until Fête Dieu approached, with a Saturday-Sunday-Monday holiday for all the workers. Joseph, with his pockets full of money, went to Port-au-Prince and left Croyance behind, cautioning her as usual; and she agreed to remain and tend the zombies, for he promised her that at the Mardi Gras she should visit the city.

But when Sunday morning dawned, it was lonely in the fields, and her kind old woman's heart was filled with pity for the zombies, and she thought, "Perhaps it will cheer them a little to see the gay crowds and the processions at Croix de Bouquet, and since all the Morne-au-Diable people will have gone back to the mountain to celebrate Fête Dieu at home, no one will recognize them, and no harm can come of it." And it is the truth that Croyance also wished to see the gay procession.

So she tied a new bright-colored handkerchief around her head, aroused the zombies from the sleep that was scarcely different from their waking, gave them their morning bowl of cold, unsalted plantains boiled in water, which they ate dumbly uncomplaining, and set out with them for the town, single file, as the country people always walk. Croyance, in her bright kerchief, leading the nine dead men and women behind her, past the railroad crossing, where she murmured a prayer to Legba, past the great white-painted wooden Christ, who hung life-sized in the glaring sun, where she stopped to kneel and cross herself—but the poor zombies prayed neither to Papa Legba nor to Brother Jesus, for they were dead bodies walking, without souls or minds.

They followed her to the market square, before the church where hundreds of little thatched, open shelters, used on weekdays for buying and selling, were empty of trade, but crowded here and there by gossiping groups in the grateful shade.

To the shade of one of these market booths, which was still unoccupied, she led the zombies, and they sat like people asleep with their eyes open, staring, but seeing nothing, as the bells in the church began to ring, and the procession came from the priest's house—red-purple robes, golden crucifix held aloft, tinkling bells and swinging incense pots, followed by little black boys in white lace robes, little black girls in starched white dresses, with shoes and stockings, from the parish school, with colored ribbons in their kinky hair, a nun beneath a big umbrella leading them.

Croyance knelt with the throng as the procession passed, and wished she might follow it across the square to the church steps, but the zombies just sat and stared, seeing nothing.

When noontime came, women with baskets passed to and fro in the crowd, or sat selling bonbons (which were not candy but little sweet cakes), figs (which were not figs but sweet bananas), oranges, dried herring, biscuit, casava bread, and *clairin* poured from a bottle at a penny a glass.

As Croyance sat with her savory dried herring and biscuit baked with salt and soda, and provision of *clairin* in the tin cup by her side, she pitied the zombies who had worked so faithfully for Joseph in the cane fields, and who now had nothing, while all the other groups around were feasting, and as she pitied them, a woman passed, crying,

"*Tablettes! Tablettes pistaches! T'ois pour dix cobs!*"

Tablettes are a sort of candy, in shape and size like cookies, made of brown cane sugar (*rapadou*); sometimes with *pistaches,* which in Haiti are peanuts, or with coriander seed.

And Croyance thought, "These *tablettes* are not salted or seasoned, they are sweet, and can do no harm to the zombies just this once."

So she untied the corner of her kerchief, took out a coin, a gourdon, the quarter of a gourde, and bought some of the *tablettes,* which she broke in halves and divided among the zombies, who began sucking and mumbling them in their mouths.

But the baker of the *tablettes* had salted the *pistache* nuts before stirring them into the *rapadou,* and as the zombies tasted the salt, they knew that they were dead and made a dreadful outcry and arose and turned their faces toward the mountain.

No one dared stop them, for they were corpses walking in the sunlight, and they themselves and all the people knew that they were corpses. And they disappeared toward the mountain.

When later they drew near their own village on the slopes of Morne-au-Diable, these dead men and women walking single file in the twilight, with no soul leading them or daring to follow, the people of their village, who were also holding *bamboche* in the marketplace, saw them drawing closer, recognized among them fathers, brothers, wives and daughters whom they had buried months before.

Most of them knew at once the truth, that these were zombies who had been dragged dead from their graves, but others hoped that a blessed miracle had taken place on this Fête Dieu, and rushed forward to take them in their arms and welcome them.

But the zombies shuffled through the marketplace, recognizing neither father nor wife nor mother, and as they turned leftward up the path leading to the graveyard, a woman whose daughter was in the procession of the dead threw herself screaming before the girl's shuffling feet and begged her to stay; but the grave-cold feet of the daughter and the feet of the other dead shuffled over her and onward; and as they approached the graveyard, they began to shuffle faster and rushed among the graves, and each before his own empty grave began clawing at the stones and earth to enter it again; and as their cold hands touched the earth of their own graves, they fell and lay there, rotting carrion.

That night the fathers, sons and brothers of the zombies, after restoring the bodies to their graves, sent a messenger on muleback down the mountain, who returned next day with the name of Ti Joseph and with a stolen shirt of Ti Joseph's which had been worn next his skin and was steeped in the grease-sweat of his body.

They collected silver in the village and went with the name of Ti Joseph and the shirt of Ti Joseph to a *bocor* beyond Trou Caiman, who made a deadly needle *ouanga*, a black bag *ouanga*, pierced all through with pins and needles, filled with dry goat dung, circled with cock's feathers dipped in blood.

And lest the needle *ouanga* be slow in working or be rendered weak by Joseph's counter-magic, they sent men down to the plain, who lay in wait patiently for Joseph, and one night hacked off his head with a machete. . . .

When Polynice had finished this recital, I said to him, after a moment of silence, "You are not a peasant like those of the Cul-de-Sac; you are a reasonable man, or at least it seems to me you are. Now how much of that story, honestly, do you believe?"

He replied earnestly: "I did not see these special things, but there were many witnesses, and why should I not believe them when I myself have also seen zombies? When you also have seen them, with their faces and their eyes in which there is no life, you will not only believe in these zombies who should be resting in their graves, you will pity them from the bottom of your heart."

Before finally taking leave of La Gonave, I did see these "walking dead men," and I did, in a sense, believe in them and pitied them, indeed, from the bottom of my heart. It was not the next night, though Polynice, true to his promise, rode with me across the Plaine Mapou to the deserted, silent cane fields where he had hoped to show me zombies laboring. It was not on any night. It was in broad daylight one afternoon, when we passed that way again, on the lower trail to Picmy. Polynice reined in his horse and pointed to a rough, stony, terraced slope—on which four laborers, three men and a woman, were chopping the earth with machetes, among straggling cotton stalks, a hundred yards distant from the trail.

"Wait while I go up there," he said, excited because a chance had come to fulfill his promise. "I think it is Lamercie with the zombies. If I wave to you, leave your horse and come." Starting up the slope, he shouted to the woman, "It is I, Polynice," and when he waved later, I followed.

As I clambered up, Polynice was talking to the woman. She had stopped work—a big-boned, hard-faced black girl, who regarded us with surly unfriendliness. My first impression of the three supposed zombies, who continued dumbly at work, was that there was something about them unnatural and strange. They were plodding like brutes, like automatons. Without stooping down, I could not fully see their faces, which were bent expressionless over their work. Polynice touched one of them on the shoulder, motioned him to get up. Obediently, like an animal, he slowly stood erect—and what I saw then, coupled with what I had heard previously, or despite it, came as a rather sickening shock. The eyes were the worst. It was not my imagination. They were in truth like the eyes of a dead man, not blind, but staring, unfocused, unseeing. The whole face, for that matter, was bad enough. It was vacant, as if there was nothing behind it. It seemed not only expressionless, but incapable of expression. I had seen so much previously in Haiti that was outside ordinary normal experience that for the flash of a second I had a sickening, almost panicky lapse in which I thought, or rather felt, "Great God, maybe this stuff is really true, and if it is true, it is rather awful, for it upsets everything." By "everything" I meant the natural fixed laws and processes on which all modern human thought and actions are based. Then suddenly I remembered—and my mind seized the memory as a man sinking in water clutches a solid plank —the face of a dog I had once seen in the histological laboratory at Columbia. Its entire front brain had been removed in an experimental operation weeks before; it moved about, it was alive, but its eyes were like the eyes I now saw staring.

I recovered from my mental panic. I reached out and grasped one of the dangling hands. It was calloused, solid, human. Holding it, I said, *"Bonjour, compère."* The zombie stared without responding. The black wench, Lamercie, who was their keeper, now more sullen than ever, pushed me away—*"Z'affai' nèg' pas z'affai' blanc"* (Negroes' affairs are not for whites). But I had seen enough. "Keeper" was the key to it. "Keeper" was the word that had leapt naturally into my mind as she protested, and just as naturally the zombies were nothing but poor, ordinary demented human beings, idiots, forced to toil in the fields.

It was a good rational explanation, but it is far from being the end of this story. It satisfied me then, and I said as much to Polynice as we went down the slope. At first he did not contradict me, even said doubtfully, "Perhaps"; but as we reached the horses, before mounting, he stopped and said, "Look here, I respect your distrust of what you call superstition and your desire to find out the truth, but if what you were saying now were the whole truth, how could it be that over and over again, people who have stood by and seen their own relatives buried have, sometimes soon, sometimes months or years afterward, found those relatives working as zombies, and have sometimes killed the man who held them in servitude?"

"Polynice," I said, "that's just the part of it that I can't believe. The zombies in such cases may have resembled the dead persons, or even been 'doubles'—you know what doubles are, how two people resemble each other to a startling degree. But it is a fixed rule of reasoning in America that we will never accept the possibility of a thing's being 'supernatural' so long as any natural explanation, even farfetched, seems adequate."

"Well," said he, "if you spent many years in Haiti, you would have a very hard time to fit this American reasoning into some of the things you encountered here."

As I have said, there is more to this story—and I think it is best to tell it very simply.

In all Haiti, there is no clearer scientifically trained mind, no sounder pragmatic rationalist, than Dr. Antoine Villiers. When I sat later with him in his study, surrounded by hundreds of scientific books in French, German and English, and told him of what I had seen and of my conversations with Polynice, he said:

"My dear sir, I do not believe in miracles nor in supernatural events, and I do not want to shock your Anglo-Saxon intelligence, but this Polynice of yours, with all his superstition, may have been closer to the partial truth than you were. Understand me clearly. I do not believe that anyone has ever been raised literally from the dead—neither Lazarus, nor the daughter of Jairus, nor Jesus Christ himself—yet I am not sure, paradoxical as it may sound, that there is not something frightful, something in the nature of criminal sorcery if you like, in some cases at least, in this matter of zombies. I am by no means sure that some of them who now toil in the fields were not dragged from the actual graves in which they lay in their coffins, buried by their mourning families!"

"It is then something like suspended animation?" I asked.

"I will show you," he replied, "a thing which may supply the key to what you are seeking," and standing on a chair, he pulled down a paper-bound book from a top shelf. It was nothing mysterious or esoteric. It was the current official *Code Pénal* (Criminal Code) of the Republic of Haiti. He thumbed through it and pointed to a paragraph which read:

"*Article 249.* Also shall be qualified as attempted murder the employment which may be made against any person of substances which, without causing actual death, produce a lethargic coma more or less prolonged. If, after the administering of such substances, the person has been buried, the act shall be considered murder no matter what result follows."

MOTHER OF SERPENTS

BY ROBERT BLOCH

Like the Seabrook piece, "Mother of Serpents" tells of dark voodoo rites on the island of Haiti; but there all similarity ends. Robert Bloch's story is pure fiction (although it is based on factual material), and recounts the saga of a certain "educated man" who rose to become president of the republic after Toussaint l'Ouverture, Dessalines, and King Christophe freed it from its French oppressors in the 1800s. It is also one of the most chilling horror stories ever to use the voodoo theme.

The quality and the gooseflesh are not surprising, of course, considering that Robert Bloch has long been recognized as the premier contemporary writer of horror fiction. But what is remarkable is that "Mother of Serpents" was published in the great fantasy pulp Weird Tales *in 1936—when Bloch was just nineteen years old. (His first professional sale, also to* Weird Tales, *was*

68

*made two years previous, at the even more precocious age of seven-
teen.) That a teenager—even one of Bloch's talent—should produce a story of this craftsmanship is as unusual as its subject
matter.*

*In his forty-six year career Robert Bloch ("I have the heart of a
little boy; I keep it in a jar on my desk") has published hundreds
of fantasy/horror, science fiction, and mystery stories, a dozen or
so collections, some twenty novels (among them the classic* Psycho
and the near-classic The Scarf), *scores of television and movie
scripts, and countless articles and essays. His most recent books are
a pair of novels—*Strange Eons, *a horror tale built around H.P.
Lovecraft's Cthulhu mythos;* There is a Serpent in Eden, *a suspense story—and a collection entitled* Out of the Mouths of
Graves.

 VOODOOISM is a queer thing. Forty years ago
it was an unknown subject, save in certain
esoteric circles. Today there is a surprising
amount of information about it, due to research—and an even more surprising amount
of misinformation.

Recent popular books on the subject are, for the most part,
sheer romantic fancy; elaborated with the incomplete theorizings
of ignoramuses.

Perhaps, though, this is for the best. For the truth about voodoo is such that no writer would care, or dare, to print it. Some
of it is worse than their wildest fancies. I myself have seen certain
things I do not dare to discuss. It would be useless to tell people

anyway, for they would not believe me. And once again, this may
be for the best. Knowledge can be a thousand times more terrifying than ignorance.

I know, though, for I have lived in Haiti, the dark island. I have
learned much from legend, stumbled on many things through
accident, and the bulk of my knowledge comes from the one really
authentic source—the statements of the blacks. They're not talk-
ative people, as a rule, those old natives of the back hill country.
It took patience and long familiarity with them before they un-
bent and told me their secrets.

That's why so many of the travel books are so palpably false—
no writer who visits Haiti for six months or a year could possibly
ingratiate himself into the confidence of those who know the
facts. There are so few who really do know; so few who are not
afraid to tell.

But I have learned. Let me tell you of the olden days; the old
times, when Haiti rose to an empire, borne on a wave of blood.

It was many years ago, soon after the slaves had revolted.
Toussaint l'Ouverture, Dessalines and King Christophe freed
them from their French masters, freed them after uprisings and
massacres and set up a kingdom founded on cruelty more fantastic
than the despotism that reigned before.

There were no happy blacks in Haiti then. They had known
too much of torture and death; the carefree life of their West
Indian neighbors was utterly alien to these slaves and descendants of slaves. A strange mixture of races flourished: fierce
tribesmen from Ashanti, Damballah and the Guinea Coast;
sullen Caribs; dusky offspring of renegade Frenchmen; bastard
admixtures of Spanish, Negro and Indian blood. Sly, treacher-
ous half-breeds and mulattos ruled the coast, but there were

even worse dwellers in the hills behind.

There were jungles in Haiti, impassable jungles, mountain-ringed and swamp-scourged forests filled with poisonous insects and pestilential fevers. White men dared not enter them, for they were worse than death. Blood-sucking plants, venomous reptiles, diseased orchids filled the forests, forests that hid horrors Africa had never known.

For that is where the real voodoo flourished, back there in the hills. Men lived there, it is said, descendants of escaped slaves, and outlaw factions that had been hunted from the coast. Furtive rumors told of isolated villages that practiced cannibalism, mixed in with dark religious rites more dreadful and perverted than anything spawned in the Congo itself. Necrophilism, phallic worship, anthropomancy and distorted versions of the Black Mass were commonplace. The shadow of Obeah was everywhere. Human sacrifice was common, the offering up of roosters and goats an accepted thing. There were orgies around the voodoo altars, and blood was drunk in honor of Baron Samedi and the old black gods brought from ancient lands.

Everybody knew about it. Each night the *rada-* drums boomed out from the hills, and fires flared over the forests. Many known *papalois* and conjure-doctors resided on the edge of the coast itself, but they were never disturbed. Nearly all the "civilized" blacks still believed in charms and philtres; even the churchgoers reverted to talismans and incantations in time of need. So-called "educated" Negroes in Port-au-Prince society were admittedly emissaries from the barbarian tribes of the interior, and despite the outward show of civilization the bloody priests still ruled behind the throne.

Of course there were scandals, mysterious disappearances, and occasional protests from emancipated citizens. But it was not wise to meddle with those who bowed to the Black Mother, or incur the anger of the terrible old men who dwelt in the shadow of the Snake.

Such was the status of sorcery when Haiti became a republic. People often wonder why there is still sorcery existent there today; more secretive, perhaps, but still surviving. They ask why the ghastly zombies are not destroyed, and why the government has not stepped in to stamp out the fiendish blood-cults that still lurk in the jungle gloom.

Perchance this tale will provide an answer; this old, secret tale of the new republic. Officials, remembering the story, are still afraid to interfere too strongly, and the laws that have been passed are very loosely enforced.

Because the Serpent Cult of Obeah will never die in Haiti— in Haiti, that fantastic island whose sinuous shoreline resembles the yawning jaws of a monstrous *snake*.

One of the earliest presidents of Haiti was an educated man. Although born on the island, he was schooled in France, and studied extensively while abroad. His accession to the highest office of the land found him an enlightened, sophisticated cosmopolite of the modern type. Of course he still liked to remove his shoes in the privacy of his office, but he never displayed his naked toes in an official capacity. Don't misunderstand—the man was no Emperor Jones; he was merely a polished ebony gentleman whose natural barbarity occasionally broke through its veneer of civilization.

He was, in fact, a very shrewd man. He had to be in order to become president in those early days; only extremely shrewd men ever attained that dignity. Perhaps it would enlighten you a bit to say that in those times the term "shrewd" was a polite Haitian synonym for "crooked." It is therefore easy to realize the president's character when you know that he was regarded as one of the most successful politicians the republic ever produced.

In his short reign he was opposed by very few enemies; and those that did work against him usually disappeared. The tall, coal-black man with the physical skull-conformation of a gorilla harbored a remarkably crafty brain beneath his beetling brow.

His ability was phenomenal. He had an insight into finance which profited him greatly; profited him, that is, in both his official and unofficial capacity. Whenever he saw fit to increase the taxes he increased the army as well, and sent it out to escort the state tax-collectors. His treaties with foreign countries were masterpieces of legal lawlessness. This black Machiavelli knew that he must work fast, since presidents had a peculiar way of dying in Haiti. They seemed peculiarly susceptible to disease— "lead poisoning," as our modern gangster friends might say. So the president worked very fast indeed, and he did a masterful job.

This was truly remarkable, in view of his humble background. For his was a success saga in the good old Horatio Alger manner. His father was unknown. His mother was a conjure woman in the hills, and though quite well-known, she had been very poor. The president had been born in a log cabin; quite the classic setting for a future distinguished career. His early years had been most uneventful, until his adoption, at thirteen, by a benevolent Protestant minister. For a year he lived with this kind man, serving as houseboy in his home. Suddenly the poor minister died of an obscure ailment; this was most unfortunate, for he had been quite wealthy and his money was alleviating much of the suffering in this particular section. At any rate, this rich minister died, and the poor conjure woman's son sailed to France for a university education.

As for the conjure woman, she bought herself a new mule and said nothing. Her skill at herbs had given her son a chance in the world, and she was satisfied.

It was eight years before the boy returned. He had changed a great deal since his departure; he preferred the society of whites and the octoroon society people of Port-au-Prince. It is recorded that he rather ignored his old mother, too. His newly acquired fastidiousness made him painfully aware of the woman's ignorant simplicity. Besides, he was ambitious, and he did not care to publicize his relationship with such a notorious witch.

For she was quite famous in her way. Where she had come from and what her original history was, nobody knew. But for many years her hut in the mountains had been the rendezvous of strange worshipers and even stranger emissaries. The dark powers of Obeah were evoked in her shadowy altar-place amidst the hills, and a furtive group of acolytes resided there with her. Her ritual fires always flared on moonless nights, and bullocks were given in bloody baptism to the Crawler of Midnight. For she was a Priestess of the Serpent.

The Snake-God, you know, is the real deity of the Obeah cults. The blacks worshiped the Serpent in Dahomey and Senegal from time immemorial. They venerate the reptiles in a curious way, and there is some obscure linkage between the snake and the crescent moon. Curious, isn't it—this serpent superstition? The Garden of Eden had its tempter, you know, and the Bible tells of Moses and his staff of snakes. The Egyptians revered Set, and the ancient Hindus had a cobra god. It seems to be general throughout the world—the kindred hatred and reverence of serpents. Always they seem to be worshiped as creatures of evil. American Indians believed in Yig, and Aztec myths follow the pattern. And of course the Hopi ceremonial dances are of the same order.

But the African Serpent legends are particularly dreadful, and the Haitian adaptations of the sacrificial rites are worse.

At the time of which I speak some of the voodoo groups were believed to actually breed snakes; they smuggled the reptiles over from the Ivory Coast to use in their secret practices. There were tall tales current about twenty-foot pythons which swallowed infants offered up to them on the Black Altar, and about *sendings* of poisonous serpents which killed enemies of the voodoo-masters. It is a known fact that several anthropoid apes had been smuggled into the country by a peculiar cult that worshiped gorillas; so the serpent legends may have been equally true.

At any rate, the president's mother was a priestess, and equally as famous, in a way, as her distinguished son. He, just after his return, had slowly climbed to power. First he had been a tax-gatherer, then treasurer, and finally president. Several of his rivals died, and those who opposed him soon found it expedient to dissemble their hatred; for he was still a savage at heart, and savages like to torment their enemies. It was rumored that he had constructed a secret torture chamber beneath the palace, and that its instruments were rusty, though not from disuse.

The breach between the young statesman and his mother began to widen just prior to his presidential incumbency. The immediate cause was his marriage to the daughter of a rich octoroon planter from the coast. Not only was the old woman humiliated because her son contaminated the family stock (she was pure Negro, and descendant of a Niger slave-king), but she was further indignant because she had not been invited to the wedding.

It was held in Port-au-Prince. The foreign consuls were there, and the cream of Haitian society was present. The lovely bride had been convent-bred, and her antecedents were held in the highest esteem. The groom wisely did not deign to desecrate the nuptial celebration by including his rather unsavory parent.

She came, though, and watched the affair through the kitchen doorway. It was just as well that she did not make her presence known, as it would have embarrassed not only her son, but several others as well—official dignitaries who sometimes consulted her in their unofficial capacity.

What she saw of her son and his bride was not pleasing. The man was an affected dandy now, and his wife was a silly flirt. The atmosphere of the pomp and ostentation did not impress her; behind their debonair masks of polite sophistication she knew that most of those present were superstitious Negroes who would have run to her for charms or oracular advice the moment they were in trouble. Nevertheless, she took no action; she merely smiled rather bitterly and hobbled home. After all, she still loved her son.

The next affront, however, she could not overlook. This was the inauguration of the new president. She was not invited to this affair either, yet she came. And this time she did not skulk in the shadows. After the oath of office was administered she marched boldly up to the new ruler of Haiti and accosted him before the very eyes of the German consul himself. She was a grotesque figure; an ungainly little harridan barely five feet tall, black, barefooted, and clad in rags.

Her son quite naturally ignored her presence. The withered crone licked her toothless gums in terrible silence. Then, quite calmly, she began to curse him—not in French, but in native patois of the hills. She called down the wrath of her bloody gods upon his ungrateful head, and threatened both him and his wife with vengeance for their smug ingratitude. The assembled guests were shocked.

So was the new president. However, he did not forget himself. Calmly he motioned to his guards, who led the now hysterical witch-woman away. He would deal with her later.

The next night when he saw fit to go into the dungeon and reason with his mother, she was gone. Disappeared, the guards told him, rolling their eyes mysteriously. He had the jailer shot, and went back to his official chambers.

He was a little worried about that curse business. You see, he knew what the woman was capable of. He did not like those threats against his wife, either. The next day he had some silver bullets moulded, like King Henry in the old days. He also bought an *ouanga* charm from a devil-doctor of his own acquaintance. Magic would fight magic.

That night a serpent came to him in dreams; a serpent with green eyes that whispered in the way of men and hissed at him with shrill and mocking laughter as he struck at it in his sleep. There was a reptilian odor in his bedroom the next morning, and a nauseous slime upon his pillow that gave forth a similar stench. And the president knew that only his charm had saved him.

That afternoon his wife missed one of her Paris frocks, and the president questioned his servants in his private torture chamber below. He learned some facts he dared not tell his bride, and thereafter he seemed very sad. He had seen his mother work with wax images before—little mannikins resembling men and women, dressed in parts of their stolen garments. Sometimes she stuck pins into them or roasted them over a slow fire. Always the real people sickened and died. This knowledge made the president quite unhappy, and he was still more overwrought when messengers returned and said that his mother was gone from her old hut in the hills.

Three days later his wife died, of a painful wound in her side which no doctors could explain. She was in agony until the end, and just before her passing it was rumored that her body turned blue and bloated up to twice its normal size. Her features were eaten away as if with leprosy, and her swollen limbs looked like those of an elephantiasis victim. Loathsome tropical diseases abound in Haiti, but none of them kill in three days. . . .

After this the president went mad.

Like Cotton Mather of old, he started on a witch-hunting crusade. Soldiers and police were sent out to comb the country-side. Spies rode up to hovels on the mountain peaks, and armed patrols crouched in far-off fields where the living dead-men work, their glazed and glassy eyes staring ceaselessly at the moon. *Mamalois* were put to the question over slow fires, and possessors of forbidden books were roasted over flames fed by the very tomes they harbored. Bloodhounds yammered in the hills, and priests died on altars where they were wont to sacrifice. Only one order had been specially given: the president's mother was to be captured alive and unharmed.

Meanwhile he sat in the palace with the embers of slow insanity in his eyes—embers that flared into fiendish flame when the guards brought in the withered crone, who had been captured near that awful grove of idols in the swamp.

They took her downstairs, although she fought and clawed like a wildcat, and then the guards went away and left her son with her alone. Alone, in a torture chamber, with a mother who cursed him from the rack. Alone, with frantic fires in his eyes, and a great silver knife in his hand. . . .

The president spent many hours in his secret torture chamber during the next few days. He seldom was seen around the palace, and his servants were given orders that he must not be disturbed. On the fourth day he came up the hidden stairway for the last time, and the flickering madness in his eyes was gone.

Just what occurred in the dungeon below will never be rightly known. No doubt that is for the best. The president was a savage at heart, and to the brute, prolongation of pain always brings ecstasy. . . .

It is recorded, though, that the old witch-woman cursed her son with the Serpent's Curse in her dying breath, and that is the most terrible curse of all.

Some idea of what happened may be gained by the knowledge of the president's revenge; for he had a grim sense of humor, and a barbarian's idea of retribution. His wife had been killed by his mother, who fashioned a waxen image. He decided to do what would be exquisitely appropriate.

When he came up the stairs that last time, his servants saw that he bore with him a great candle, fashioned of corpse-fat. And since nobody ever saw his mother's body again, there were curious surmises as to where the corpse-fat was obtained. But then, the president's mind leaned toward grisly jests. . . .

The rest of the story is very simple. The president went directly to his chambers in the palace, where he placed the candle in a holder on his desk. He had neglected his work in the last few days, and there was much official business for him to transact. For a while he sat in silence, staring at the candle with a curious satisfied smile. Then he called for his papers and announced that he would attend to them immediately.

He worked all that night, with two guards stationed outside his door. Sitting at his desk, he pored over his task in the candlelight —the candlelight from the corpse-fat taper.

Evidently his mother's dying curse did not bother him at all. Once satisfied, his blood-lust abated, he discounted all possibility of revenge. Even he was not superstitious enough to believe that the sorceress could return from her grave. He was quite calm as he sat there, quite the civilized gentleman. The candle cast ominous shadows over the darkened room, but he did not notice—until it was too late. Then he looked up to see the corpse-fat candle wriggle into monstrous life.

His mother's curse. . . .

The candle—the corpse-fat candle—was *alive!* It was a sinuous, twisting thing, weaving in its holder with sinister purpose.

The flame-tipped end seemed to glow strongly into a sudden terrible semblance. The president, amazed, saw the fiery face—his mother's; a tiny wrinkled face of flame, with a corpse-fat body that darted out toward the man with hideous ease. The candle was lengthening as if the tallow were melting; lengthening, and reaching out towards him in a terrible way.

The president of Haiti screamed, but it was too late. The glowing flame on the end snuffed out, breaking the hypnotic spell that had held the man betranced. And at that moment the candle leapt, while the room faded into dreadful darkness. It was a ghastly darkness, filled with moans, and the sound of a thrashing body that grew fainter, and fainter. . . .

It was quite still by the time the guards had entered and turned up the lights once more. They knew about the corpse-fat candle and the witch-mother's curse. That is why they were the first to announce the president's death; the first to fire a bullet into his temple and claim he committed suicide.

They told the president's successor the story, and he gave orders that the crusade against voodoo be abandoned. It was better so, for the new man did not wish to die. The guards had explained why they shot the president and called it suicide, and his successor did not wish to risk the Serpent Curse.

For the president of Haiti had been strangled to death by his mother's corpse-fat candle—*a corpse-fat candle that was wound around his neck like a giant snake.*

THE DIGGING AT PISTOL KEY

BY CARL JACOBI

The form of voodoo known as Obeah is practiced on such West Indian islands as Jamaica and Trinidad, chiefly by peasants who have been observed "speaking incantations over broken eggshells, bones, tufts of hair and other disagreeable objects." It is said that some Obeahs—those in whom the Power is strongest—are even able to reach from beyond the grave to destroy a hated enemy. This may only be superstition, of course. Then again, it may be something more.

"The Digging at Pistol Key," which first appeared in Weird Tales *in 1947, makes a strong case for the mystical (and deadly) qualities of Obeah. At the same time it tells a suspenseful tale of murder, greed, vengeance and the search for buried treasure on the narrow promontory near Port-of-Spain, Trinidad, known as Pistol Key. The chills it offers may be of the rippling rather than hair-raising variety, but those ripples do tend to linger a while . . .*

A native of Minneapolis, where he was born in 1908, Carl Jacobi published his first stories while a student at the University of

*Minnesota. After graduation in 1931 he became a news reporter
and book and play reviewer for the Minneapolis* Star *and remained
with that paper for several years, leaving finally to edit an advertising and radio trade journal and to devote more time to his fiction
writing. His stories have appeared in such diverse magazines as*
MacLean's, Weird Tales, Galaxy Science Fiction, The Toronto
Star, Thrilling Mystery *and* Railroad Stories. *The best of his
fantasy/horror tales appear in three Arkham House collections:*
Revelations in Black *(recently reprinted in paperback),* Portraits in
Moonlight, *and* Disclosures in Scarlet.

 ALTHOUGH he had lived in Trinidad for more
than fifteen years, Jason Cunard might as
well have remained in Devonshire, his original home, for all the local background he had
absorbed. He read only British newspapers,
the *Times* and the *Daily Mail,* which he
received by weekly post, and he even had his tea sent him from
a shop in Southampton, unmindful of the fact that he could have
obtained the same brand, minus the heavy tax, at the local im-
porter in Port-of-Spain.

Of course, Cunard got into town only once a month, and then
his time was pretty well occupied with business matters concerning his sugar plantation. He had a house on a narrow promontory
midway between Port-of-Spain and San Fernando which was
known as Pistol Key. But his plantation sprawled over a large tract
in the center of the island.

Cunard frankly admitted there was nothing about Trinidad he

liked. He thought the climate insufferable, the people—the Brit-
ishers, that is—provincial, and the rest of the population, a poly-
glot of races that could be grouped collectively as "natives and
foreigners." He dreamed constantly of Devonshire, though he
knew of course he would never go back.

Whether it was due to this brooding or his savage temper, the
fact remained that he had the greatest difficulty in keeping house
servants. Since his wife had died two years ago, he had had no less
than seven: Caribs, quadroons, and Creoles of one sort or another.
His latest, a lean, gangly black boy, went by the name of Christopher, and was undoubtedly the worst of the lot.

As Cunard entered the house now, he was in a distinctly bad
frame of mind. Coming down the coast highway, he had had the
misfortune to have a flat tire and had damaged his clothes considerably in changing it. He rang the antiquated bell-pull savagely.

Presently Christopher shambled through the connecting doorway.

"Put the car in the garage," Cunard said tersely. "And after
dinner repair the spare tire. Some fool left a broken bottle on the
road."

The Negro remained standing where he was, and Cunard saw
then that he was trembling with fear.

"Well, what the devil's the matter?"

Christopher ran his tongue over his upper lip. "Can't go out
dere, sar," he said.

"Can't . . . Why not?"

"De holes in de yard. Der Dere again."

For the first time in more than an hour Cunard permitted
himself to smile. While he was totally without sympathy for the
superstitions of these blacks, he found the intermittent recur-
rence of these holes in his property amusing. For he knew quite

well that superstition had nothing to do with them.

It all went back to that most diabolical of buccaneers, Francis L'Ollonais and his voyage to the Gulf of Venezuela in the middle of the seventeenth century. After sacking Maracaibo, L'Ollonais sailed with his murderous crew for Tortuga. He ran into heavy storms and was forced to put back in here at Trinidad.

Three or four years ago some idiot by the idiotic name of Arlanpeel had written and published a pamphlet entitled *Fifty Thousand Pieces of Eight* in which he sought to prove by various references that L'Ollonais had buried a portion of his pirate booty on Pistol Key. The pamphlet had sold out its small edition, and Cunard was aware that copies had now become a collector's item. As a result, Pistol Key had come into considerable fame. Tourists stopping off at Port-of-Spain frequently telephoned Cunard, asking permission to visit his property, a request which of course he always refused.

And the holes! From time to time during the night Cunard would be awakened by the sound of a spade grating against gravel, and looking out his bedroom window, he would see a carefully shielded lantern down among the cabbage palms. In the morning there would be a shallow excavation several feet across with the dirt heaped hastily on all four sides.

The thought of persons less fortunate than himself making clandestine efforts to capture a mythical fortune dating to the seventeenth century touched Cunard's sense of humor.

"You heard me, Christopher," he snapped to the houseboy, "put the car in the garage."

But the black remained cowering by the door until Cunard, his patience exhausted, dealt him a sharp slap across the face with the flat of his hand. The boy's eyes kindled, and he went out silently.

Cunard went up to his bathroom and washed the road grime

from his hands. Then he proceeded to dress for his solitary dinner, a custom which he never neglected. Downstairs, he got to thinking again about those holes in his yard and decided to have a look at them. He took a flashlight and went out the rear entrance and under the cabbage palms. Fireflies in the darkness and a belated *Qu'-est-ce-qu'il-dit* bird asked its eternal question.

Forty yards from the house he came upon the diggings Christopher had reported. That they were the work of some ambitious fortune hunter was made doubly apparent by the discarded tape-measure and the cheap compass which lay beside the newly turned earth.

Again Cunard smiled. It would be "forty paces from this point to the north end of a shadow cast by a man fifteen hands high," or some such fiddle faddle. Even if L'Ollonais had ever buried money here—and there was no direct evidence that he had—it had probably been carted away long years ago.

He saw Christopher returning from the garage then. The houseboy was walking swiftly, mumbling a low litany to himself. In his right hand he held a small cross fashioned of two bent twigs.

Back in the house, Cunard told himself irritably that Christopher was a fool. After all, he had seen his mother come into plenty of trouble because of her insistence on practicing Obeah. She had professed to be an Obeah-woman and was forever speaking incantations over broken eggshells, bones, tufts of hair and other disagreeable objects. Employed as a laundress by Cunard, he had discovered her one day dropping a white powder into his teacup, and unmindful of her plea that it was merely a good-health charm designed to cure his recurrent spells of malaria, he had turned her over to the Constabulary. He had pressed charges too, testifying that the woman had attempted to poison him. Largely because of his influence, she had been convicted and sent to the Convict

Depot at Tobago. Christopher had stayed on because he had no other place to go.

The meal over, Cunard went into the library with the intention of reading for several hours. Although the *Times* and the *Daily Mail* reached him in bundles of six copies a fortnight or so after they were published, he made it a practice to read only Monday's copy on Monday and so on through the week, thus preserving the impression that he was still in England.

But this night as he strode across to his favorite chair, he drew up short with a gasp. The complete week's bundle of newspapers had been torn open and their contents scattered about in a wild and disorganized pile. To add to this sacrilege, one of the sheets had a ragged hole in it where an entire column had been torn out. For an instant Cunard was speechless. Then he wheeled on Christopher.

"Come here," he roared. "Did you do this?"

The houseboy looked puzzled.

"No, sar," he said.

"Don't lie to me. How dare you open my papers?"

But Christopher insisted he knew nothing of the matter. He had placed the papers on their arrival in the library and had not touched them since.

Cunard's rage was mounting steadily. A mistake he might have excused, but an out-and-out lie. . . .

"Come with me," he said in a cold voice.

Deliberately he led the way into the kitchen, looked about him carefully. Nothing there. He went back across the little corridor to the houseboy's small room under the stairway. While Christopher stood protesting in the doorway, Cunard marched across to the table and silently picked up a torn section of a newspaper.

"So you did lie!" he snarled.

The sight of the houseboy with his perpetual grin there in the doorway was too much for the planter. His rage beyond control, he seized the first object within reach—a heavy length of wood resting on a little bracket mounted on the wall—and threw it with all his strength.

The missile struck Christopher squarely on the temple. He uttered no cry, but remained motionless a moment, the grin frozen on his face. Then his legs buckled and he slumped slowly to the floor.

Cunard's fists clenched. "That'll teach you to respect other people's property," he said. His anger, swift to come, was receding as quickly, and noting that the houseboy lay utterly still, he stepped forward and stirred him with his foot.

Christopher's head rolled horribly.

Quickly Cunard stooped and felt for a pulse. None was discernible. With trembling fingers he drew out a pocket mirror and placed it by the boy's lips. For a long moment he held it there, but there was no resultant cloud of moisture. Christopher was dead!

Cunard staggered across to the chair and sat down. Christopher's death was one thing and one thing only—murder! The fact that he was a man of color and Cunard an influential planter would mean nothing in Crown court of law. He could see the bewigged magistrate now; he could hear the evidence of island witnesses, testifying as to his uncontrollable temper, his savage treatment of servants.

Even if there were not actual danger of incarceration—and he knew there was—it would mean the loss of his social position and prestige.

And then Cunard happened to think of the holes in his yard. A new one—a grave for the dead houseboy—would never be noticed, and he could always improvise some sort of story that the boy had run off. As far as Cunard knew, other than the old crone who was his mother, Christopher had no other kin, having come originally from Jamaica.

The planter was quite calm now. He went to his room, changed to a suit of old clothes and a pair of rubber-soled shoes. Then, returning to the little room under the stairs, he rolled the body of the houseboy into a piece of sailcloth and carried it out into the yard.

He chose a spot near the far corner of his property where a clump of bamboo grew wild and would effectually shield him from any prying eyes. But there were no prying eyes, and half an hour later Cunard returned to the house. Then he carefully cleaned the clinging loam from the garden spade, washed his shoes and brushed his trousers.

It was when he went again to the room under the stairs to gather together Christopher's few possessions that he saw the piece of wood that had served as the death missile. Cunard picked it up and frowned. The thing was an Obeah fetish apparently, an ugly little carving with a crude likeness of an animal head and a squat human body. The lower half of the image ended in a flat panel, the surface of which was covered with wavy lines, so that the prostrate figure looked as if it were partially immersed in water. Out of that carved water two arms extended upward, as in supplication, and they were arms that were strangely reminiscent for Cunard. Christopher's mother had had arms like that, smooth and strangely youthful for a person of her age. There was even a chip of white coral on one of the fingers like the coral ring the old woman always wore.

Cunard threw the thing into the pile of other objects he had gathered: spare clothes, several bright-colored scarves, a sack of cheap tobacco, made a bundle of them and burned them in the old-fashioned cook stove with which the kitchen was equipped.

The last object to go into the fire was the newspaper clipping, and the planter saw then with a kind of grim horror that Christopher had not lied at all, that the top of the paper in fact bore a dateline several months old and was one of a lot he had given to the houseboy "to look at de pictures."

For several days after that Cunard did not leave his house. He felt nervous and ill-at-ease, and he caught himself looking out the window toward the bamboo thicket on more than one occasion. Curiously too, there was an odd murmuring in his ears like the sound of distant water flowing.

On the third day, however, he was sufficiently himself to make a trip to town. He drove the car at a fast clip to Port-of-Spain, parked on Marine Square and went about his business. He was walking down Frederick Street half an hour later when he suddenly became aware that an aged Negro woman with head tied in a red kerchief was following him.

Cunard didn't have a direct view of her until just as he turned a corner, and then only a glance, but his heart stopped dead still for an instant. Surely that black woman was Christopher's mother whom he had sent to prison. True, her face was almost hidden by the folds of the loosely draped kerchief, but he had seen her hand, and there was the coral ring on it. Wild thoughts rushed to Cunard's head. Had the woman been released then? Had she missed her son, and did she suspect what had happened?

Cunard drew up in a doorway, but the old crone did not pass him, and when he looked back down the street, she was nowhere in sight.

Nevertheless the incident unnerved him. When, later in the day, he met Inspector Bainley of the Constabulary, he seized the opportunity to ask several questions that would ease his mind.

"Where have you been keeping yourself?" Bainley asked. "I haven't seen much of you lately."

Cunard lit a cigar with what he hoped was a certain amount of casualness.

"I've been pretty busy," he replied. "My houseboy skipped, you know. The blighter simply packed off without warning."

"So?" said Bainley. "I thought Christopher was a pretty steady chap."

"In a way," said Cunard. "And in a way he wasn't." And then: "By the way, do you remember his mother? I was wondering whether she had been released. I thought I saw her a moment ago on the street."

The inspector smiled a thin smile. "Then you were seeing things," he said. "She committed suicide over at the Convict Depot at Tobago two months ago."

Cunard stared.

"At least we called it suicide," Inspector Bainley went on. "She took some sort of an Obeah potion when she found we weren't going to let her go, and simply lay back and died. It was rather odd that the medico couldn't find any trace of poison though."

Cunard was rather vague about the rest of the day's events. He recalled making some trifling purchases, but his mind was wandering, and twice he had to be reminded to pick up his change. At four o'clock he abruptly found himself thinking of his old friend, Hugh Donay, and the fact that Donay had employed Christopher's mother a year or so before she had entered Cunard's services. Donay had a villa just outside of town, and it would take only a few moments to see him. Of course there was no reason to see him. If Bainley said the old woman had committed suicide, that settled it. Yet Cunard told himself the inspector might have been mistaken or perhaps joking. He himself was a strong believer in his powers of observation, and it bothered him to have doubts cast upon them.

The planter drove through the St. Clair district and turned into a driveway before a sprawling house with roof of red tile. Donay, a thin waspish man, was lounging in a hammock and greeted Cunard effusively.

"Tried to get you by phone the other day," he said, "but you weren't at home. Had something I wanted to tell you. About that L'Ollonais treasure that's supposed to be buried on your property."

Cunard frowned. "Have you started believing that too?"

"This was an article in the *Daily Mail,* and it had some new angles that were rather interesting. I get my paper here in town before you do out there on Pistol Key, you know."

Cunard attempted to swing the conversation into other channels, but Donay was persistent.

"Funny thing about that article," he said. "I read it the same day the burglar was here."

"Burglar?" Cunard lifted his eyes.

"Well," Donay said, "Jim Barrett was over here, and I showed him the paper. Barrett said it was the first description he had read that sounded logical and that the directions given for locating the treasure were very clear and concise. Just at that moment there was a sound in the corridor, and Barrett leaped up and made a dash for the kitchen.

"I might tell you that for several days I thought prowlers were about. The lock on the cellar door was found broken, and several times I'd heard footsteps in the laundry room. Several things were out of place in the laundry room too, though what anyone would want there is more than I can see.

"Anyway, Barrett shouted that someone was in the house. We followed the sounds down into the cellar, and just as we entered the door into the laundry room, there was a crash and the sound of glass breaking."

Donay smiled sheepishly as if to excuse all these details.

"It was only a bottle of bluing," he went on, "but what I can't figure out is how the prowler got in and out of that room without our seeing anyone pass. There's only one door, you know, and the windows are all high up."

"Was anything stolen?" Cunard asked.

"Nothing that I'm aware of. That bluing though was running across the floor toward a hamper of clean linen, and without thinking I used the first thing handy to wipe it up. It happened to be the newspaper with that treasure article in it. So I'm afraid . . ."

"It doesn't matter. I can read it in my copy," Cunard said. But even as he spoke, a vision of his own torn paper flashed to him.

"That isn't quite all," Donay said. "The next day I found every blessed wastebasket in the house turned upside down and their contents scattered about. Queer, isn't it?"

The conversation changed after that, and they talked of idle things. But just before he left Cunard said casually:

"By the way, my houseboy, Christopher's run off. Didn't his mother work for you as a laundress or something?"

"That's right," Donay said, "I turned her over to you when I took a trip up to the States. Don't you remember?"

Cunard drove through town again, heading for the highway to Pistol Key. He had just turned off Marine Square when he suddenly slammed down hard on the brakes. The woman darted from the curb directly into his path, and with the lowering sun in his eyes, he did not see her until it was too late. Cunard got out of the car, shaking like a leaf, fully expecting to find a crumpled body on the bumper.

But there was no one there, and a group of Portuguese street laborers eyed him curiously as he peered around and under the car. He was almost overcome with relief, but at the same time he was disturbed. For in that flash he had seen of the woman against the sun, he was almost sure he had seen the youthful dark-skinned arms of Christopher's mother.

Back at Pistol Key Cunard spent the night. The sensation of distant running water was stronger in his ears now. "Too much quinine," he told himself. "I'll have to cut down on the stuff."

He lay awake for some time, thinking of the day's events. But as his brain went over the major details in retrospection, he found himself supplying the missing minor details and so fell into a haze of peaceful drowsiness.

At two o'clock by the radium clock on the chiffonier, he awoke abruptly. The house was utterly still, but through the open window came an intermittent metallic sound. It died away, returned after an interval of several minutes. Cunard got out of bed, put on his brocaded dressing robe and strode to the window. A full moon illumined the grounds save where the palmistes cast their darker shadow, and there was no living person in evidence.

Below him and slightly to the left there was a freshly dug hole. But it was not that that caused Cunard to pass his hands before his eyes as if he had been dreaming. It was the sight of a spade alternately disappearing in the hole and reappearing to pile the loosened soil on the growing mound. A spade that moved slowly, controlled by aged yet youthful-appearing arms and hands, but arms unattached to any human body.

In the morning Cunard called the Port-of-Spain *Journal,* instructing them to run an advertisement for a houseboy, a task which he had neglected the day before. Then he went out to his post box to get the mail.

The morning mist had not yet cleared. It hung over the hibiscus hedges like an endless line of white shrouds. As he reached the end of the lane, Cunard thought he saw a figure turn from the post box and move quickly toward a grove of ceiba trees. He thought nothing of it at first, for those trees flanked the main road which was traveled by residents of the little native settlement at the far end of Pistol Key. But then he realized that the figure had moved away from the road, in a direction leading obliquely toward his own house.

Still the matter did not concern him particularly until he opened the post box. There was a single letter there, and it had not come by regular mail; the dirty brown envelope bore neither stamp nor cancellation mark. Inside was a torn piece of newspaper.

Cunard realized at once that it was the missing piece from his *Daily Mail.* But who besides Christopher could have had access to the house and who would steal a newspaper column and return it in the post box?

It was like him that he made no attempt to read the paper until he had returned to the library. Then he matched it with the torn sheet still on his desk. The two pieces fitted exactly. He sat back and began to read.

The first part was a commonplace enough account of the opening of new auction parlors in Southwick Street, London, and a description of some of the more unusual articles that had been placed for sale there. Cunard, reading swiftly, found his eye attracted to the following:

Among the afternoon offerings was the library of the late Sir Adrian Fell of Queen Anne's Court, which included an authentic first edition of McNair's *Bottle of Heliotrope* and a rare quarto volume of *Lucri Causa*. There was also a curious volume which purported to be the diary of the Caribbean buccaneer, Francis L'Ollonais, written while under the protection of the French West India Company at Tortuga.

This correspondent had opportunity to examine the latter book and found some interesting passages. According to the executors of the estate, it had been obtained by Sir Adrian on his trip to Kingston in 1904, and so far as is known, is the only copy in existence.

Under the heading, "The Maracaibo Voyage," L'Ollonais describes his destruction of that town, of his escape with an enormous booty, and of the storms which beset him on his return trip to Tortuga. It is here that the diary ceases to be a chronological date-book and becomes instead a romantic narrative.

L'Ollonais, driven southward, managed to land on Trinidad, on a promontory known as Pistol Key. There "By a greate pile of stones whiche looked fair like two horses running," he buried the equivalent of fifty thousand pieces of eight. His directions for locating the treasure are worth quoting:

"Sixty paces from the south forward angle of the horse rock to the crossing of a line west by south west by the compass from a black pointed stone shaped like a broken needle near the shore. At this point if a man will stand in the light of a full moon at the eleventh hour, the shadow of his head will fall upon the place."

Cunard lowered the paper and thoughtfully got a cigar out of the silver humidor on the table. So there was truth in that story of hidden treasure after all. Perhaps the money was still there, and he had been a fool to ridicule the motive behind those holes in his yard. He smoked in silence.

How many persons, he wondered, had seen that newspaper story. There was Hugh Donay and Jim Barrett, of course, but they didn't count. Few others here subscribed to the *Daily Mail.* Of those that did, the odds were against any of them wading through such a dull account. The fact remained, however, that someone had read it in his own copy and had been sufficiently interested to tear it from the sheet. Who was that person? And why had they seen fit to return it by way of his post box?

The landmarks he knew only too well. He had often remarked that that stone near the end of his property resembled two galloping horses. And the black stone "like a broken needle" was still there, a rod or two from shore.

Suddenly fear struck Cunard—fear that he might already be too late. He leaped from his chair and ran out into the grounds.

There were four holes and the beginning of a fifth in evidence. But, moving quickly from one to another, the planter saw with relief that all were shallow and showed no traces of any object having been taken from them.

Cunard hastened back to the house where he procured a small but accurate compass and a ball of twine. Then he went into the toolhouse and brought out a pair of oars for the dory that was moored at the water's edge on a little spit of sand.

An hour later his work was finished. He had rowed the dory out to the needle point of rock and fastened one end of the twine to it. The other end he stretched across to the horse rock in the corner of his property. Then he counted off the required sixty paces and planted a stick in the ground to mark the spot. After that there was nothing he could do until night. He hoped there would be no clouds to obstruct the moon.

Still there was the possibility someone might blunder here while he was in the house, and after a moment's thought Cunard returned to the toolhouse and rummaged through the mass of odds and ends that had collected there through the years. He found an old doorbell that had been discarded when the more musical chimes had been installed in the house, also several batteries and a coil of wire.

During the war Cunard had made a superficial study of electricity and wireless as part of what he considered his patriotic duties, and he now proceeded to wire a crude but efficient alarm system around the general area where he conceived the treasure to be.

Back in the house, he settled himself to wait the long hours until moonrise. In the quiet of inactivity he was conscious again of that sound of distant water flowing. He made a round of all taps in the house, but none was leaking.

During his solitary dinner he caught himself glancing out the window into the grounds, and once he thought he saw a shadow move across the lawn and into the trees. But it must have been a passing cloud, for he didn't see it again.

At two P.M. a knock sounded on the door. Cunard was surprised and somewhat disconcerted to see Inspector Bainley standing on the veranda.

"Just passing by," Bainley said, smiling genially. "Had a sudden call from the native village out on the Key. Seems a black boy got into some trouble out there. Thought it might be your Christopher."

"But that's impos—" Cunard checked himself. "I hardly think it likely," he amended. "Christopher would probably go as far as he could, once he started."

They drank rum. The inspector seemed in no hurry to leave, and Cunard was torn between two desires, not to be alone and to be free from Bainley's gimlet eyes which always seemed to be moving about restlessly.

Finally he did go, however. The throb of his car was just dying off down the road when Cunard heard a new sound which electrified him to attention. The alarm bell!

Yet there was no one in the grounds. The wires were undisturbed, and the makeshift switch he had fashioned was still open. The bell was silent when he reached it.

With the moon high over his shoulder Cunard wielded his spade rapidly. The spot where the shadow of his head fell was disagreeably close to the bamboo thicket where he had buried Christopher, but as a matter of fact, he wasn't quite sure where that grave was, so cleverly had he hidden all traces of his work.

The hole had now been dug to a depth of four feet, but there was no indication anything had been buried there. Cunard toiled strenuously another half hour. And then quite suddenly his spade struck something hard and metallic. A wave of excitement swept over him. He switched on his flashlight and turned it in the hole. Yes, there it was, the rusted top of a large iron chest—the treasure of L'Ollonais.

He resumed digging, but as he dug, he became aware that the sand, at first dry and hard, had grown moist and soggy. The spade became increasingly heavy with each scoop, and presently water was running off it, glistening in the moonlight. Water began to fill the bottom of the hole, too, making it difficult for Cunard to work.

But it was not until ten minutes later that he saw something protruding from the water. In the moonlight two slender dark objects were reaching outward, a pair of Negro feminine arms gently weaving to and fro.

Cunard stiffened while a wave of horror swept over him. They were dark-skinned arms of an aged Negress, yet somehow they were smooth and youthful. The middle finger of the left hand bore a ring of white coral.

Cunard screamed and lunged backward. Too late, one of those grasping hands encircled his ankle and jerked him forward. And as he fell across the hole, those hands wrapped themselves about his throat and drew his head slowly but deliberately downward. . . .

"Yes, it's a queer case," Inspector Bainley said, tamping tobacco into his pipe. "But then of course no more queer than a lot of things that happen here in the islands."

"You say this fellow, Cunard, murdered his houseboy, Christopher?" the warrant-officer said.

Bainley nodded. "I knew his savage temper would get the better of him some day. He buried the body in the yard and apparently rigged up that alarm arrangement to warn him of any trespassers. Then he contrived that story which he told me, that Christopher had run off.

"Of course we know now that Cunard was trying to find that buried treasure by following the directions given in that newspaper clipping. But that doesn't explain why he disregarded those directions and attempted to dig open the houseboy's grave again. Or why, before he had finished, he thrust his head into the shallow hole and lay in the little pool of seepage water until he drowned."

SEVEN TURNS
IN A HANGMAN'S ROPE

BY HENRY S. WHITEHEAD

The Spanish Main in the 1820s, a cutthroat pirate named Captain Fawcett and a dashing rogue known as Saul Macartney, a woman called Camilla who has mastered the art of voodoo as well as any slave, and a century-old painting of a gallows execution, in which one of the condemned men bleeds fresh blood . . . these are just some of the ingredients to be found in "Seven Turns in a Hangman's Rope." Blended together by the artful hand of Henry S. Whitehead, they form a savory and unusual brew of swashbuckling adventure, historical romance, and shivery horror.

Although the story's initial publication was in the pulp Adventure *in 1932, it reached its most appreciative audience—aficionados of the macabre—only when it was included in Whitehead's first posthumous collection,* Jumbee and Other Uncanny Tales, *in 1944. This book, and a second collection which appeared two years later,* West India Lights, *contain a total of thirty-one of his best stories of voodoo and the supernatural; among them are the oft-reprinted and highly acclaimed "Cassius," "Jumbee," "The Lips," "The Ravel Pavane," and "Sea Change."*

Born in New Jersey in 1882, Henry St. Clair Whitehead wrote and sold his first story the year after graduating from Harvard in the same class with Franklin Delano Roosevelt. In 1909 he entered divinity school, was ordained minister in the Episcopal Church three years later, and subsequently did missionary work in the West Indies. In addition to macabre, adventure, and juvenile fiction for such magazines as Weird Tales, Strange Tales, Adventure, *and* Outdoors, *he wrote extensively for church papers and published* The Invitations of Our Lord, Neighbors of the Early Church, *and other religious books until his death in Florida in 1932.*

 I first became acutely aware of the dreadful tragedy of Saul Macartney one sunny morning early in the month of November of the year 1927. On that occasion, instead of walking across the hall from my bathroom after shaving and the early morning shower, I turned to the left upon emerging and, in my bathrobe and slippers, went along the upstairs hallway to my workroom on the northwest corner of the house into which I had just moved, in the west coast town of Frederiksted on the island of Santa Cruz.

This pleasant room gave a view through its several windows directly down from the hill on which the house was located, across the pretty town with its red roofs and varicolored houses, directly upon the indigo Caribbean. This workroom of mine had a north light from its two windows on that side and, as I used it only during the mornings, I thus escaped the terrific sun drenching to which, in the absence of any shade without, the room was subjected during the long West Indian afternoon.

The occasion for going in there was my desire to see, in the clear morning light, what that ancient oil painting looked like; the canvas which, without its frame, I had tacked up on the south wall the evening before.

This trophy, along with various other items of household flotsam and jetsam, had been taken the previous afternoon, which was a day after my arrival on the island, out of a kind of lumber room wherein the owners of the house had plainly been storing for the best part of a century the kinds of things which accumulate in a family. Of the considerable amount of material which my houseman, Stephen Penn, had taken out and stacked and piled in the upper hallway, there happened to be nothing of interest except this good-sized painting—which was about three feet by five in size. Stephen had paused to examine it curiously and it was this which drew my attention to it.

Under my first cursory examination, which was little more than a glance, I had supposed the thing to be one of those ubiquitous Victorian horrors of reproduction which fifty years ago might have been observed on the walls of most middle-class front parlors, and which were known as chromos. But later that evening, on picking it up and looking at it under the electric light, I found that it was honest paint, and I examined it more closely and with a constantly increasing interest.

The painting was obviously the work of a fairly clever amateur. The frame of very old and dry wood had been riddled through and through by woodworms; it literally fell apart in my hands. I left it there on the floor for Stephen to brush up the next morning and took the canvas into my bedroom where there was a better light. The accumulations of many years' dust and grime had served to obscure its once crudely bright coloration. I carried it into my bathroom, made a lather of soap and warm water, and gave it a careful and much needed cleansing, after which the scene delineated before me assumed a surprising freshness and clarity.

After I had dried it off with a hand towel, using great care lest I crack the ancient pigment, I went over it with an oiled cloth. This process really brought it out, and although the canvas was something more than a century old, the long obscured and numerous figures with which it had been almost completely covered seemed once more as bright and clear—and quite as crude—as upon the long distant day when that rather clever amateur artist had laid down his (or perhaps her) brush after putting on the very last dab of vermilion paint.

The subject of the old painting, as I recognized quite soon, was an almost forgotten incident in the history of the old Danish West Indies. It had, quite obviously, been done from the viewpoint of a person on board a ship. Before me, as the setting of the scene, was the well-known harbor of St. Thomas with its dull red fort at my right—looking exactly as it does today. At the left-hand margin were the edges of various public buildings which have long since been replaced. In the midst, and occupying nearly the entire spread of the canvas, with Government Hill and its fine houses sketched in for background, was shown the execution of Fawcett, the pirate, with his two lieutenants; an occasion which had constituted a general holiday for the citizens of St. Thomas, and which had taken place, as I happened to be aware, on the eleventh of September, 1825. If the picture had been painted at that time, and it seemed apparent that such was the case, the canvas would be just one hundred and two years old.

My interest now thoroughly aroused, I bent over it and examined it with close attention. Then I went into my workroom and brought back my large magnifying glass.

My somewhat clever amateur artist had left nothing to the imagination. The picture contained no less than two hundred and three human figures. Of these only those in the remoter backgrounds were sketched in roughly in the modern manner. The actual majority were very carefully depicted with a laborious infinitude of detail; and I suspected then, and since have found every reason to believe, that many, if not most of them, were portraits! There before my eyes were portly Danish worthies of a century ago, with their ladyfolk, all of whom had come out to see Captain Fawcett die. There were the officers of the garrison. There were the *gendarmes* of the period, in their stiff-looking uniforms after the manner of Frederick the Great.

There were Negroes, some with large gold rings hanging from one ear; Negresses in their bebustled gingham dresses and bare feet, their foulards or varicolored head handkerchiefs topped by the broad-brimmed plaited straw hats which are still to be seen along modern St. Thomas's concrete drives and sidewalks. There was the executioner, a huge, burly, fierce-looking black man; with the policemaster standing beside and a little behind him, gorgeous in his glistening white drill uniform with its gilt decorations. The two stood on the central and largest of the three scaffolds.

The executioner was naked to the waist and had his woolly head bound up in a tight-fitting scarlet kerchief. He had only that moment sprung the drop, and there at the end of the manila rope (upon which the artist had carefully painted in the seven turns of the traditional hangman's knot placed precisely under the left ear of the miscreant now receiving the just reward of his innumerable villainies) hung Captain Fawcett himself, the gruesome central figure of this holiday pageant—wearing top boots and a fine plum-colored laced coat.

On either side, and from the ropes of the two smaller gibbets, dangled those two lesser miscreants, Fawcett's mates. Obviously their several executions, like the preliminary bouts of a modern boxing program, had preceded the main event of the day.

The three gibbets had been erected well to the left of the central space which I have described. The main bulk of the spectators was consequently to the right as one looked at the picture, on the fort side.

After more than a fascinating hour with my magnifying glass, it being then eleven o'clock and time to turn in, I carried the brittle old canvas into my workroom and by the rather dim light of a shaded reading lamp fastened it carefully at a convenient height against the south wall with thumbtacks. The last tack went through the arm of the hanging man nearest the picture's extreme left-hand margin. After accomplishing this I went to bed.

The next morning, as I have mentioned, being curious to see how the thing looked in a suitable light, I walked into the work-room and looked at it.

I received a devastating shock.

My eye settled after a moment or two upon that dangling mate whose body hung from its rope near the extreme left-hand margin of the picture. I found it difficult to believe my eyes. In this clear morning light the expression of the fellow's face had changed startlingly from what I remembered after looking at it closely through my magnifying glass. Last night it had been merely the face of a man just hanged; I had noted it particularly because, of all the more prominent figures, that face had been most obviously an attempt at exact portraiture.

Now it wore a new and unmistakable expression of acute agony.

And down the dangling arm, from the point which that last thumbtack had incontinently transfixed, there ran, and dripped off the fellow's fingers, a stream of bright, fresh red blood. . . .

II

Between the time when the clipper schooner, which had easily overhauled the Macartney trading vessel *Hope*—coming north across the Caribbean and heavily laden with sacked coffee from Barranquilla—had sent a challenging shot from its swivel-gun across the *Hope*'s bows, and his accomplishing the maneuver of coming about in obedience to that unmistakable summons, Captain Saul Macartney had definitely decided what policy he should follow.

He had made numerous voyages in the *Hope* among the bustling trade ports of the Caribbean and to and from his own home port of St. Thomas, and never before, by the Grace of God and the Macartney luck, had any freetrader called up on him to stand and deliver on the high seas. But, like all seafaring men of Captain Macartney's generation, plying their trade in those latitudes in the early 1820s, he was well aware of what was now in store for him, his father's ship and the members of his crew. The *Hope* would be looted; then probably scuttled, in accordance with the freetraders' well nigh universal policy of destroying every scrap of evidence against them. As for himself and his men, they would be confronted with the formula—

"Join, or go over the side!"

A pirate's recruit was a pirate, at once involved in a status which was without the law. His evidence, even if he were attempting the dangerous double game of merely pretending to join his captor, was worthless.

There was no possible ray of hope, direct resistance being plainly out of the question. This might be one of the better established freebooters, a piratical captain and following whose notoriety was already so widespread, who was already so well known, that he would not take the trouble to destroy the *Hope;* or, beyond the usual offer made to all volunteers for a piratical crew—constantly in need of such replacements—to put the captured vessel, officers and crew through the mill; once they were satisfied that there was nothing aboard this latest prize to repay them for the trouble and risk of capture and destruction.

The *Hope,* laden almost to her gunwales with sacked coffee, would provide lean pickings for a freetrader, despite the value of her bulk cargo in a legitimate port of trade like Savannah or Norfolk. There were cases, known to Captain Macartney, where a piratical outfit under the command of some notable such as Edward Thatch—often called Teach, or Blackbeard—or England, or Fawcett, or Jacob Brenner, had merely sheered off and sailed away in search of more desirable game as soon as it was plain that the loot was neither easily portable nor of the type of value represented by bullion, silks, or the strong box of some interisland trading supercargo.

It was plain enough to Captain Saul Macartney, whose vessel had been stopped here about a day's sail south-southwest of his home port of St. Thomas, capital of the Danish West Indies, and whose cargo was intended for delivery to several ship's brokerage houses in that clearinghouse port for the vast West Indian shipping trade, that this marauder of the high seas could do nothing with his coffee. These ideas were prominent in his mind in the interval between his shouted orders and the subsequent period during which the *Hope*, her way slacking rapidly, hung in the wind, her jibs, booms, and loose rigging slapping angrily while the many boats from the freetrading vessel were slung outboard in a very brisk and workmanlike manner and dropped one after the other into the water alongside until every one—seven in all—had been launched.

These boats were so heavily manned as to leave them very low in the water. Now the oars moved with an almost delicate precision as though the rowers feared some mischance even in that placid sea. The *Hope*'s officers and crew—all of the latter Negroes —crowded along their vessel's starboard rail, the mates quiet and collected as men taking their cue from their superior officer; the crew goggle-eyed, chattering in low tones among themselves in groups and knots, motivated by the sudden looming terror which showed in a gray tinge upon their black skins.

Then, in a strident whisper from the first mate, a shrewd and experienced bucko, hailing originally from Portsmouth, New Hampshire, wise in the ways of these tropical latitudes from twenty years' continuous seafaring:

"God! It's Fawcett himself!"

Slowly, deliberately, as though entirely disdainful of any possible resistance, the seven boats drew toward the doomed *Hope*. The two foremost edged in close alongside her starboard quarter and threw small grapples handily from bow and stern and so hung in under the *Hope*'s lee.

Captain Saul Macartney, cupping his hands, addressed over the heads of the intervening six boatloads the man seated in the sternsheets of the outermost boat:

"Cargo of sacked Brazil coffee, captain, and nothing else to make it worth your while to come aboard me—if you'll take my word for it. That's the facts, sir, so help me God!"

In silence from all hands in the boats and without any immediate reply from Fawcett, this piece of information was received. Captain Fawcett sat there at the sternsheets of his longboat, erect, silent, presumably pondering what Captain Saul Macartney had told him. He sat there calm and unruffled, a fine gold-laced tricorn hat on his head, which, together with the elegance of his wine-colored English broadcloth coat, threw into sharp relief his brutal, unshaven face with its sinister, shining white scar—the result of an old cutlass wound—which ran diagonally from the upper corner of his left ear forward down the cheek, across both lips, clear to the edge of his prominent chin.

Fawcett, the pirate, ended his reflective interval. He raised his head, rubbed a soiled hand through his beard's stubble, and spat outboard.

"Any ship's biscuit left aboard ye?" he inquired, turning his eye along the *Hope's* freeboard and thence contemplatively about her masts and rigging. "We're short."

"I have plenty, captain. Will it answer if I have it passed over the side to ye?"

The two vessels and the seven heavily laden boats lay tossing silently in the gentle swell. Not a sound broke the tension while Captain Fawcett appeared to deliberate.

Then a second time he spat over the side of his longboat and rubbed his black stubbly chin with his hand, reflectively. Then he looked across his boats directly at Captain Saul Macartney. The ghost of a sour grin broke momentarily the grim straight line of his maimed and cruel mouth.

"I'll be comin' aboard ye, captain," he said very slowly, "if ye have no objection to make."

A bellow of laughter at this sally of their captain's rose from the huddled pirate crew in the boats and broke the mounting tension. A Negro at the *Hope*'s rail cackled hysterically, and a chorus of gibes at this arose from the motley crews of the boats grappled alongside.

In the silence which followed Captain Fawcett muttered a curt, monosyllabic order. The other five boats closed in with haste, two of them passing around the *Hope*'s stern and another around her bow. It was only a matter of a few seconds before the entire seven hung along the *Hope*'s sides like feasting wolves upon the flanks of a stricken deer. Then at a second brief order their crews came over the rails quietly and in good order, Fawcett himself arriving last upon the *Hope*'s deck. No resistance of any kind was offered. Captain Macartney had had the word passed quietly on that score while the pirates' boats were being slung into the water.

After the bustling scramble involved in nearly a hundred men climbing over the *Hope*'s rail from the seven boats and which was, despite the excellent order maintained, a maneuver involving considerable noisy activity, another and even a more ominous silence settled down upon the beleaguered *Hope*.

Supported by his two mates, one of whom was a small, neat, carefully dressed fellow, and the other an enormous German who sported a cavalryman's moustache and walked truculently, Captain Fawcett proceeded directly aft, where he turned and faced forward, a mate on either side of him, and leaned against the superstructure of Captain Macartney's cabin.

Macartney's mates, taking pattern from this procedure, walked over from the rail and flanked him where he stood just aft of the *Hope*'s foremast. The rest of the freebooters, having apparently been left free by their officers to do as they pleased for the time being, strolled about the deck looking over the vessel's superficial equipment, and then gathered in little knots and groups about the eleven Negro members of the *Hope*'s crew.

Through this intermingling the comparative silence which had followed their coming aboard began to be dissipated with raillery, various low-voiced sallies of crude wit at the Negroes' expense, and an occasional burst of nervous or raucous laughter. All this, however, was carried on, as Captain Macartney took it in, in what was to him an unexpectedly restrained and quiet manner, utterly at variance with the reputed conduct of such a group of abandoned villains at sea, and to him, at least, convincing evidence that something sinister was in the wind.

This expectation had its fulfillment at a harsh blast from the whistle which, at Fawcett's nod, the huge German mate had taken from his pocket and blown.

Instantly the pirates closed in and seized those members of the *Hope*'s Negro crew who stood nearest them; several, sometimes five or six, men crowding in to overpower each individual. Five or six of the pirates who had been as though without purpose near the forward hatchway which led below decks began forthwith to knock out the wedges. The *Hope*'s Negroes, with a unanimity which bespoke the excellent discipline and strategy which Fawcett was generally understood to maintain, were hustled forward and thrust into the forecastle; the hatch of which, as soon as they were all inside, was forthwith closed tight and at once nailed fast by the undersized little Englishman who was Fawcett's ship's carpenter.

None of the *Hope*'s crew had been armed. None seemed to Captain Macartney to have been even slightly injured in the course of this rough and effective handling. Captain Macartney surmised, and rightly, that the pirates' intention was to preserve them alive either for ultimate sale into slavery, which was of

course then extant throughout the West India Islands, or, perhaps, to convey them as shore servants to Fawcett's settlement
which, it was generally believed, was well in the interior of the
island of Andros in the Bahama group, where a network of inter-
lacing creeks, rendering anything like pursuit and capture well
nigh out of the question, had made this private fastness a strong-
hold.

But Captain Macartney had little time to waste thinking over
the fate of his crew. With perhaps a shade less of the roughness
with which the Negroes had been seized he and his mates were
almost simultaneously surrounded and marched aft to face their
captors. It seemed plain that the usual choice was to be given only
to the three of them.

Fawcett did not hesitate this time. He looked at the three men
standing before him, lowered his head, relaxed his burly figure and
barked out—

"Ye'll join me or go over the side."

He pointed a dirty finger almost directly into the face of the
older mate, who stood at his captain's right hand.

"You first," he barked again. "Name yer ch'ice, and name it
now."

The hardbitten New Hampshire Yankee stood true to the
traditions of an honest sailorman.

"To hell with ye, ye damned scalawag," he drawled, and spat
on the deck between Captain Fawcett's feet.

There could be but one reply on the part of a man of Fawcett's
heady character to such an insult as this. With a speed that baffled
the eye the great pistol which hung from the right side of his belt
beneath the flap of his fine broadcloth coat was snatched free, and
to the accompaniment of its tearing roar, its huge ounce ball
smote through the luckless Yankee's forehead. As the acrid cloud

of smoke from this detonation blew away Captain Macartney observed the huge German mate lifting the limp body which, as though it had been that of a child, he carried in great strides to the nearer rail and heaved overboard.

Fawcett pointed with his smoking weapon at Macartney's other mate, a small-built fellow, originally a British subject from the Island of Antigua. The mate merely nodded comprehendingly. Then—

"The same as Elias Perkins told ye, ye blasted swab, and may ye rot deep in hell."

But Fawcett's surly humor appeared to have evaporated, to have discharged itself in the pistoling of the other man whose scattered brains had left an ugly smear on the *Hope*'s clean deck. He merely laughed and, with a comprehensive motion of his left hand, addressed the larger of his mates, who had resumed his position at his left.

"Take him, Franz," he ordered.

The huge mate launched himself upon the Antiguan like a ravening beast. With lightninglike rapidity his enormous left arm coiled crushingly about the doomed man's neck. Simultaneously, his open right hand against his victim's forehead, he pushed mightily. The little Antiguan's spine yielded with an audible crack and his limp body slithered loosely to the deck. Then with a sweeping, contemptuous motion the huge mate grasped the limp form in one hand, lifting it by the front of the waistcoat and, whirling about, hurled it with a mighty pitch far outboard.

The German mate had not yet resumed his place beside Fawcett when Captain Saul Macartney addressed the pirate leader.

"I'm joining you, captain," he said quietly.

And while the surprised Fawcett stared at him the newly enlisted freebooter, who had been Captain Saul Macartney of the

schooner *Hope,* with a motion which did not suffer by compari-
son with Fawcett's for its swiftness, had produced a long dirk,
taken the two lightning strides necessary for an effective stroke,
and had plunged his weapon with a mighty upward thrust from
under the ribs through the German mate's heart.

Withdrawing it instantly, he stooped over the sprawled body
and wiped the dirk's blade in a nonchalant and leisurely manner
on the dead ruffian's fine cambric shirt frill. As he proceeded to
this task he turned his head upward and slightly to the left and
looked squarely in the eye the stultified pirate captain who stood
motionless and staring in his surprise at this totally unexpected
feat of his newest recruit. From his crouching position Saul Macartney spoke, quietly and without emphasis—

"Ye see, sir, I disliked this larrikin from the minute I clapped
eyes on him and I'll call your attention to the fact that I'm a sound
navigator, and—" Saul Macartney smiled and showed his handsome teeth—"I'll ask your notice preliminary to my acting with
you aft that it might equally well have been yourself that I
scragged, and perhaps that'll serve to teach ye the manner of man
that you're now taking on as an active lieutenant!"

Then Saul Macartney, his bantering smile gone now, his Macartney mouth set in a grim line, his cleansed dirk held ready in
his sound right hand, stood menacingly before Captain Fawcett,
their breasts almost touching, and in a quarterdeck voice inquired:

"And will ye be taking it or leaving it, Captain Fawcett?"

III

It was more than two months later when the *Hope,* her hull now
painted a shining black, her topmasts lengthened all round by six

feet, her spread of canvas vastly increased, eight carronade ports newly cut along her sides, and renamed the *Swallow,* entered the harbor of St. Thomas, dropped her anchor and sent over her side a narrow longboat.

Into this boat, immediately after its crew of six oarsmen had settled down upon their thwarts and laid their six long sweeps out upon the harbor water, interested onlookers observed two officers descend over the *Swallow*'s side, where they occupied the stern-sheets together. As the boat, rowed man-o'-war style, rapidly approached the wharves it was observed by those on shore that the two men seated astern were rather more than handsomely dressed.

The shorter and heavier man wore a fine sprigged long coat of English broadcloth with lapels, and a laced tricorn hat. His companion, whose appearance had about it something vaguely familiar, was arrayed in an equally rich and very well tailored, though somewhat plainer, coat of a medium blue which set off his handsome figure admirably. This person wore no hat at all, nor any shade for his head against the glare of the eleven o'clock sun save a heavy crop of carefully arranged and naturally curly hair as black as a crow's wing.

So interesting, indeed, to the loungers along the wharves had been the entrance of this previously unknown vessel into the harbor and the subsequent coming ashore of these two fine gentlemen, that a considerable knot of sightseers was already assembled on the particular jetty toward which the longboat, smartly rowed, came steadily closer and closer. The hatless gentleman, who was by far the taller and handsomer of the two, appeared to be steering, the taut tiller ropes held firmly in his large and very shapely hands.

It was the Herr Rudolph Bernn, who had observed the crowd

collecting on the jetty through the open windows of his airy shipping office close at hand, and who had clapped on his pith sun helmet and hastened to join the group, who was the first to recognize this taller officer.

"Gude Gott! If id iss nod der Herr Captain Saul Macartney. Gude Gott, how dey will be rejoiced—Oldt Macartney andt de Miss Camilla!"

Within five minutes the rapidly approaching longboat had been laid aside the pier head in navy style. Without any delay the two gentlemen, whose advent had so greatly interested the St. Thomas harbor watchers, stepped ashore with an air and mounted the jetty steps side by side. At once Saul Macartney, whose fine clothes so well became him, forged ahead of his well-dressed, shaved and curled companion. He wore the dazzling smile which revealed his magnificent teeth and which had served to disarm every woman upon whom it had been consciously turned since his eighth year or thereabouts.

Like a conquering hero this handsome young man—who had taken clearance from the South American port of Barranquilla nearly three months before and subsequently disappeared into thin air along with his vessel and all hands off the face of the water—now stepped jauntily across the jetty toward the welcoming group whose numbers were, now that the news of his homecoming was beginning to trickle through the town, constantly increasing. He was instantaneously surrounded by these welcoming acquaintances who sought each to outdo his neighbor in the enthusiastic fervency of his congratulatory greetings.

During this demonstration the redoubtable and notorious Captain Fawcett stood quietly looking on through its milling course, a sardonic smile faintly relieving the crass repulsiveness of his maimed countenance. The pirate had been "shaved to the blood" that morning; dressed for the occasion with the greatest care. His carefully arranged locks were redolent of the oil of Bergamot, filched a week before out of the accessories of a lady passenger taken from the luckless vessel on which she had been coming out to the West Indies to join her planter husband. This lady had, after certain passing attentions from Saul Macartney, gone over the *Swallow*'s side in plain sight of the volcanic cone of Nevis, the island of her destination.

That Macartney had brought Captain Fawcett ashore with him here in St. Thomas was a piece of judgment so lamentably bad as to need no comment of any kind. His doing so initiated that swift course of events which brought down upon his handsome head that ruinous doom which stands, probably, as unique among the annals of retribution; that devasting doom which, for its horror and its strangeness, transcends and surpasses, in all human probability, even the direst fate, which, in this old world's long history, may have overtaken any other of the sons of men.

But the sheer effrontery of that act was utterly characteristic of Saul Macartney.

In the course of the long, painstaking, and probably exhaustive research which I, Gerald Canevin, set in motion in order to secure the whole range of facts forming the basis of this narrative—an investigation which has extended through more than three years and has taken me down some very curious bypaths of antique West Indian history as well as into contact with various strange characters and around a few very alluring corners of research— one aspect of the whole affair stands out in my mind most prominently. This is the fact that—as those many who nowadays increasingly rely for guidance upon the once discredited but now reviving science of astrology would phrase it—Saul Macartney was in all ways "a typical Sagittarian!"

One of the more readily accessible facts which I looked up out of ancient, musty records in the course of this strange affair was the date of his birth. He had been born in the city of St. Thomas on the twenty-eighth of November, in the year 1795. He was thus twenty-nine—in his thirtieth year and the full vigor of his manhood—at the time when Captain Fawcett had captured the *Hope* and, having lightened that vessel by emptying her hold of her cargo which he consigned to the sea, and having scuttled his own disabled vessel, had sailed for his home base among the Andros creeks.

From there a month later the transformed *Swallow* had emerged to maraud upon the Spanish Main. He was not yet out of his twenties when he had chosen to tempt fate by coming ashore with Fawcett in St. Thomas. He was still short of thirty when a certain fateful day dawned in the month of September, 1825.

True to this hypothetical horoscope of his and to every sidereal circumstance accompanying it, Saul Macartney was an entirely self-centered person. With him the "main chance" had always been paramount. It was this addiction to the main chance which had caused him to join Fawcett. A similar motive had actuated him in the notable coup which had at once, because of its sheer directness and the courage involved in it, established him in the high esteem of the pirate captain. There had been no sentiment in his killing of the gigantic mate, Franz. He was not thinking of avenging his own faithful lieutenant whom that hulking beast had slain with his bare hands before his eyes a moment before he had knifed the murderer.

His calculating sense of self-interest had been the sole motive behind that act. He could quite as easily have destroyed Fawcett himself, as he characteristically pointed out to that ruffian. He would have done so with equal ruthlessness save for his knowledge of the fact that he would have been overwhelmed immediately thereafter by Fawcett's underlings.

There is very little question but what he would have before very long succeeded to the command of the *Swallow* and the control of the considerable commerce in the slave trade and other similar illegitimate sources of revenue which went with the command of this piratical enterprise. He had already inaugurated the replacement of Captain Fawcett by himself in the esteem of that freebooter's numerous following well before the refurbished *Swallow* had sailed proudly out upon her current voyage. His unquestionable courage and enormous gift of personality had already been for some time combining actively to impress the pirate crew. Among them he was already a dominating figure.

Since well before he had attained manly maturity he had been irresistible to women. He was a natural fighter who loved conflict for its own sake. His skill with weapons was well nigh phenomenal. In the prosecution of every affair which concerned his own benefit, he had always habituated himself to going straight to the mark. He was, in short, as it might be expressed, both with respect to women and the securing of his own advantage in general affairs, thoroughly spoiled by an unbroken course of getting precisely what he wanted.

This steady impact of continuous success and the sustained parallel effect of unceasing feminine adulation had entrenched in his character the fatal conviction that he could do as he pleased in every imaginable set of conditions.

The first reversal suffered in this unbroken course of selfish domination inaugurated itself not very long after he had stepped ashore with Captain Fawcett beside him. After ten minutes or so, Macartney gradually got himself free from the crowd of friends congratulating him there on the jetty.

Stimulated as he always was by such adulation, highly animated, his Irish blue eyes flashing, his smile unabated, his selfish heart full to repletion of his accustomed self-confidence, he disentangled himself from the still-increasing crowd and, with several bows and various wavings of his left hand as he backed away from them, he rejoined Fawcett, linked his right arm through the crook of the pirate captain's left elbow and proceeded to conduct him into the town. Those fellows on the wharf were small fry! He would, as he smilingly mentioned in Fawcett's ear, prefer to introduce the captain at once into a gathering place where he would meet a group of gentlemen of greater importance.

They walked up into the town and turned to the left through the bustling traffic of its chief thoroughfare and, proceeding to the westward for a couple of hundred feet or so, turned in through a wide arched doorway above which, on its bracket, perched guardianlike a small gilded rooster. This was Le Coq d'Or, rendezvous of the more prosperous merchants of the flourishing city of St. Thomas.

A considerable number of these prosperous worthies were already assembled at the time of their arrival in Le Coq d'Or. Several Negroes under the direction of the steward of this clublike clearinghouse were already bringing in and placing on the huge polished mahogany table the planter's punch, swizzles of brandy or rum, and sangaree such as always accompanied this late-morning assembly. It lacked only a minute or two of eleven, and the stroke of that hour was sacred at Le Coq d'Or and similar foregathering places as the swizzle hour. No less a personage than M. Daniell, some years before a refugee from the Haitian revolution and now a merchant prince here in the Danish colonial capital, was already twirling a carved swizzle stick in the fragrant iced interior of an enormous silver jug.

But this hospitable activity, as well as the innumerable conversations current about that board, ceased abruptly when these city burghers had recognized the tall, handsome gentleman in blue broadcloth who had just stepped in among them. It was, indeed, practically a repetition of what had occurred on the jetty, save that here the corporate and individual greetings were, if anything, more intimate and more vociferous.

Here were the natural associates, the intimates, the social equals of the Macartneys themselves—a well-to-do clan of proud, self-respecting personages deriving from the class of Irish Protestant high gentry which had come into these islands three generations before upon the invitation of the Danish Colonial Government.

Among those who rose out of their chairs to surround Saul Macartney with hilarious greetings was Denis Macartney, his father. He had suspected that the Old Man would be there. The two clasped each other in a long and affectionate embrace, Denis Macartney agitated and tearful, his son smiling with an unforced whimsicality throughout the intensive contact of this reunion. At last the Old Man, his tears of happiness still flowing, held off and gazed fondly at his handsome, strapping son, a pair of still trembling hands upon the shoulders of the beautiful new broadcloth coat.

"An ' where, in God's own name, have ye been hidin' yourself away, me boy?" he asked solicitously.

The others grouped about, and now fallen silent, hovered about the edge of this demonstration, the universal West Indian courtesy only restraining their common enthusiasm to clasp the Macartney prodigal by his bronzed and shapely hands, to thump his back, to place kindly arms about his broad shoulders, later to thrust brimming goblets of cut crystal upon him that they might drink his health and generously toast his safe and unexpected return.

"I'll tell ye all about that later, sir," said Saul Macartney, his dazzling smile lighting up his bronzed face. "Ye'll understand, sir, my anxiety to see Camilla; though, of course, I looked in upon ye first off."

And thereupon, in his sustained bravado, in the buoyancy of his fatal conviction that he, Saul Macartney, could get away with anything whatever he might choose to do, and taking full advantage of the disconcerting effect of his announcement that he must run off, he turned to Captain Fawcett, who had been standing close behind him and, an arm about the captain's shoulders, presented him formally to his father, to M. Daniell and, with a comprehensive wave of his disengaged arm, to the company at large; and, forthwith, well before the inevitable effect of this act could record itself upon the corporate mind of such a group, Saul Macartney had whirled about, reached the arched doorway almost at a run, and disappeared in the blinding glare, on his way to call upon his cousin Camilla.

The group of gentlemen assembled in Le Coq d'Or that morning, intensely preoccupied as they had been with the unexpected restoration to their midst of the missing mariner, Macartney, had barely observed the person who had accompanied him. They were now rather abruptly left facing their new guest, and their immediate reaction after Macartney's hasty departure was to stage a greeting for this very evil-looking but highly dandified fellow whom they found in their midst. To this they proceeded forthwith, actuated primarily by the unfailing and highly developed courtesy which has always been the outstanding characteristic of the Lesser Antilles.

There was not a man present who had not winced at the name which Saul Macartney had so clearly pronounced in the course of his threefold introduction of Captain Fawcett. For this name, as that of one of the principal maritime scourges of the day, was indeed very familiar to these men, attuned as they were to seafaring matters. Several of them, in fact, vessel owners, had actually been sufferers at the hands of this man who now sat among them.

Courtesy, however—and to a guest in this central sanctum—came first. Despite their initial suspicion, by no single overt act, nor by so much as a single glance, did any member of that polished company allow it to be suspected that he had at least given harborage to the idea that Saul Macartney had brought Fawcett the pirate here to Le Coq d'Or and left him among them as a guest.

Besides, doubtless, it occurred to each and every one of these excellent gentlemen, apart from the impossibility of such a situation being precipitated by anyone named Macartney—which was an additional loophole for them—the name of Fawcett was by no means an uncommon one; there might well be half a dozen Fawcetts on Lloyd's List who were or had been commanders of ships. It was, of course, possible that this overdressed, tough-looking seahawk had fooled the usually astute Saul.

As for Fawcett himself, the wolf among these domestic cattle, he was enjoying the situation vastly. The man was intelligent and shrewd, still capable of drawing about him the remnants of a genteel deportment; and, as the details of his projected coming ashore here had been quite fully discussed with Saul Macartney, he had anticipated and was quite well prepared to meet the reaction released at the first mention of that hated and dreaded name of his, and which he now plainly sensed all about him. There was probably even a touch of pride over what his nefarious reputation could evoke in a group like this to nerve him for the curiuos ordeal which had now begun for him.

It was, of course, his policy to play quietly a conservative—an almost negative—role. He busied now his always alert mind with this, returning courtesy for courtesy as his hosts toasted him formally, assured him of their welcome, exchanged with him those general remarks which precede any real breaking of the ice between an established group and some unknown and untried newcomer.

It was Old Macartney who gave him his chief stimulation by inquiring:

"An' what of me dear son, captain? Ye will have been in his company for some time, it may be. It would be more than gracious of ye to relate to us—if so be ye're aware of it, perchance—what occurred to him on that last voyage of his from Sout' America."

At this really unexpected query the entire room fell silent. Every gentleman present restrained his own speech as though a signal had been given. Only the Negro servants, intent upon their duties, continued to speak to each other under their breaths and to move soft-footedly about the room.

Captain Fawcett recognized at once that Mr. Denis Macartney's question contained no challenge. He had even anticipated it, with a thin yarn of shipwreck, which he and Saul had concocted together. In a sudden access of whimsical bravado he abandoned this cooked-up tale. He would give them a story. . . .

He turned with an elaborate show of courtesy to Old Macartney. He set down his half-emptied goblet, paused, wiped his maimed mouth with a fine cambric handkerchief and set himself, in the breathless silence all about him, to reply.

"The freetraders took him, sir," said Captain Fawcett. Then

he nodded twice, deprecatingly; next he waved a hand, took up his goblet again, drank off its remaining contents in the sustained, pregnant silence, and again turned to Saul's father.

Settling himself somewhat more comfortably in his chair, he then proceeded to relate, with precise circumstantial detail, exactly what had actually taken place, only substituting for himself as the captor the name of the dreaded Jacob Brenner, who, like himself, had a place of refuge among the Andros creeks, and whom Captain Fawcett regarded with profound and bitter detestation as his principal rival.

He told his story through in the atmosphere of intense interest all about him. He made Captain Saul Macartney pretend to join the cutthroat Brenner and, the wish greatly father to the thought, brought his long yarn to a successful conclusion with the doughty Saul staging a desperate hand-to-hand encounter with his captor after going ashore with him on Andros Island, together with a really artistic sketching-in of his escape from the pirate settlement in a dinghy through the intricacies of the mosquito-infested creeks; and his ultimate harborage—"well nigh by chance, or a trace of what he names 'the Macartney luck,' sir"—with himself.

"I've a very pleasant little spot there on Andros," added Captain Fawcett.

Then, satisfying another accession of his whimsicality:

"I'm certain any of you would be pleased with it, gentlemen. It's been good—very good and pleasurable, I do assure you—to have had Captain Macartney with me."

And Fawcett, the pirate, whose own longboat had fetched him ashore here from that very vessel whose capture by freetraders on the high seas he had just been so graphically recounting, with a concluding short bow and a flourish of the left hand, took up his recently replenished crystal goblet and, again facing the senior

Macartney, toasted him roundly on this, the glad occasion of his seafaring son's prosperous return.

Saul Macartney walked rapidly across the crowded main thoroughfare so as to avoid being recognized and stopped. He turned up a precipitous, winding and abruptly cornered street of varying width, and, following it between the many closely walled residences among which it wound, mounted at a rapid stride to a point two-thirds of the way up the hill. Here he paused to readjust his clothes and finally to wipe the sweat induced by his pace from his bronzed face with another fine cambric handkerchief like that being used by his colleague about this time down there at Le Coq d'Or. The two of them had divided evenly four dozen of these handkerchiefs not long before from the effects of a dandified French supercargo now feeding the fishes.

It was a very sultry day in the middle of the month of May, in that spring period when the *rada* drums of the Negroes may be heard booming nightly from the wooded hills in the interior of the islands; when the annual shift in the direction of the trade wind between the points east and west of north seems to hang a curtain of sultriness over St. Thomas on its three hillsides. It was one of those days when the burros' tongues hang out of dry mouths as they proceed along dusty roads; when centipedes leave their native dust and boldly cross the floors of houses; when ownerless dogs slink along the inner edges of the baking, narrow sidewalks in the slits of house shade away from the sun.

Saul Macartney had paused near the entrance to the spacious mansion of his uncle, Thomas Lanigan Macartney, which stood behind a stately grille of wrought iron eleven feet high, in its own grounds, and was approached through a wide gateway above which the cut stone arch supported a plaque on which had been carved the Macartney arms. Through this imposing entrance, his face now comfortably dry and his fine broadcloth coat readjusted to his entire satisfaction, Saul Macartney now entered and proceeded along the broad, shell-strewn path with its two borders of cemented pink conch shells toward the mansion.

Through the accident of being his father's first-born son and the rigid application of the principle of primogeniture which had always prevailed among the Macartney clan in the matter of inheritances, old T. L. Macartney possessed the bulk of the solid Macartney family fortune. He had married the only daughter of a retired Danish general who had been governor of the colony. Dying in office, the general had left behind him the memory of a sound administration and another substantial fortune which found its way through that connection into the Macartney coffers.

The only reason why Saul Macartney had not led his heavenly endowed cousin, Camilla, to the altar long before, was merely because he knew he could marry her any time. Camilla's lips had parted and her blue eyes become mysterious, soft and melting, at every sight of him since about the time she was eight and he ten. As for Saul Macartney, he could not remember the time when it had not been his settled intention to marry his cousin Camilla when he got ready. He was as sure of her as of the rising and setting of the sun; as that failure was a word without meaning to him; as that the Santa Cruz rum was and always would be the natural drink of gentlemen and sailors.

Jens Sorensen, the black butler, who had witnessed his arrival, had the door open with a flourish when Saul was halfway between the gate and the gallery. His bow as this favored guest entered the house was profound enough to strain the seams of his green broadcloth livery coat.

But black Jens received no reward for his assiduousness from the returned prodigal, beyond a nod. This was not like Saul in the least, but black Jens understood perfectly why Captain Macartney had not quizzed him, paused to slap mightily his broad back under his green coat, or to tweak the lobe of his right ear ornamented with its heavy ring of virgin gold, all of which attentions black Jens could ordinarily expect from this fine gentleman of his family's close kinfolk. There had been no time for such persiflage.

For, hardly had black Jens's huge, soft right hand begun the motion of closing the great door, when Camilla Macartney, apprised by some subtlety of "the grapevine route" of her cousin's arrival, appeared on the threshold of the mansion's great drawing room, her lips parted, her eyes suffused with an inescapable emotion. Only momentarily she paused there. Then she was running toward him across the polished mahogany flooring of the wide hallway, and had melted into the firm clasp of Saul Macartney's brawny arms. Raising her head, she looked up into his face adoringly and Saul, responding, bent and kissed her long and tenderly. No sound save that occasioned by the soft-footed retirement of black Jens to his pantry broke the cool silence of the dignified hall. Then at last in a voice from Camilla Macartney that was little above a whisper:

"Saul—Saul, my darling! I am so glad, so glad! You will tell me all that transpired—later, Saul, my dear. Oh, it has been a dreadful time for me."

Withdrawing herself very gently from his embrace, she turned and, before the great Copenhagen mirror against the hallway's south wall, made a small readjustment in her coiffure—her hair was of the purest, clearest Scandinavian gold, of a spun-silk fineness. Beckoning her lover to follow, she then led the way into the mansion's drawing room.

As they entered, Camilla a step in advance of Macartney, there arose from a mahogany and rose-satin davenport the thickset figure of a handsome young man of about twenty-four, arrayed in the scarlet coat of His Britannic Majesty's line regiments of infantry. This was Captain the Honorable William McMillin, who, as a freshly commissioned coronet-of-horse, had actually fought under Wellington at Waterloo ten years before. Recently he had attained his captaincy, and sold out to undertake here in the Danish West Indies the resident management of a group of Santa Cruzian sugar estates, the property of his Scottish kinsfolk, the Comyns.

These two personable captains, one so-called because of his courtesy title, and the other with that honorable seafaring title really forfeited, were duly presented to each other by Camilla Macartney; and thereby was consummated another long stride forward in the rapid march of Saul Macartney's hovering doom.

The Scottish officer, sensing Saul's claim upon that household, retired ere long with precisely the correct degree of formality.

As soon as he was safely out of earshot Camilla Macartney rose and, seizing a small hassock, placed it near her cousin's feet. Seating herself on this, she looked up adoringly into his face and, her whole soul in her eyes, begged him to tell her what had happened since the day when he had cleared the *Hope* from Barranquilla.

Again Saul Macartney rushed forward upon his fate.

He told her, with circumstantial detail, the cooked-up story of shipwreck, including a touching piece of invention about three days and nights in the *Hope*'s boats and his timely rescue by his new friend, Fawcett, master of the *Swallow*—a very charitable gentleman, proprietor of a kind of trading station on Andros in the Bahamas. Captain Fawcett, who had considerably brought

the prodigal back to St. Thomas, was at the moment being entertained in Le Coq d'Or.

Camilla Macartney's eyes grew wide at the name of Saul's
rescuer. The first intimation of her subsequent change of attitude
began with her exclamation:

"Saul! Not—not Captain Fawcett, the pirate! Not that dreadful man! I had always understood that *his* lying-up place was on
the Island of Andros, among the creeks!"

Saul Macartney lied easily, reassuringly. He turned upon his
cousin—anxious, now, as he could see, and troubled—the full
battery of his engaging personality. He showed those beautiful
teeth of his in a smile that would have melted the heart of a
Galatea.

Camilla dropped the subject, entered upon a long explication
of her happiness, her delight at having him back. He must remain
for breakfast. Was his friend and benefactor, Captain Fawcett,
suitably housed? He might, of course, stay here—her father would
be so delighted at having him . . .

It was as though she were attempting, subconsciously, to anni-
hilate her first faint doubt of her cousin Saul, in this enthusiasm
for his rescuer. She rose and ran across the room, and jerked
violently upon the ornamental bell rope. In almost immediate
response to her ring black Jens entered the room softly, bowed
before his mistress with a suggestion of prostrating himself.

"A place for Captain Macartney at the breakfast table. Cham-
pagne; two bottles—no, four—of the 1801 Chablis—Is Miranda
well along with the shell-crustadas?"

Again Camilla Macartney was reassured. All these commands
would be precisely carried out.

Thereafter for a space, indeed, until the noon breakfast was
announced, conversation languished between the cousins. For the

first time in his life, had Saul Macartney been to the slightest degree critically observant, he would have detected in Camilla's bearing a vague hint that her mind toward him was not wholly at rest; but of this he noticed nothing. As always, and especially now under the stimulation of this curious game of bravado he and Fawcett were playing here in St. Thomas, no warning, no sort of premonition, had penetrated the thick veneer of his selfishness, his fatuous conviction that any undertaking of his must necessarily proceed to a successful outcome.

He sat there thinking of how well he had managed things; of the chances of the *Swallow*'s next venture on the Main; of the ripe physical beauty of Camilla; of various women here in the town.

And Camilla Macartney, beautiful, strangely composed, exquisitely dressed, as always, sat straight upright across from him, and looked steadily at her cousin, Saul Macartney. It was as though she envisaged vaguely how he was to transform her love into black hatred. A thin shadow of pain lay across her own Irish-blue eyes.

Captain the Honorable William McMillin, like many other personable young gentlemen before him, had been very deeply impressed with the quality of Camilla Macartney. But it was not only that West Indian gentlewoman's social graces and cool blond beauty that were responsible for this favorable impression. The young captain, a thoroughly hard-headed Scot with very much more behind his handsome forehead than the necessary knowledge of military tactics possessed by the ordinary line regiment officer, had been even more deeply impressed by other qualities obviously possessed by his West Indian hostess. Among these was her intellect; unusual, he thought, in a colonial lady not yet quite twenty-eight. Nothing like Miss Macartney's control of the many servants of the household had ever seemed possible to the captain.

From black Jens, the butler, to the third scullery maid, all of them, as they came severally under the notice of this guest, appeared to accord her a reverence hardly distinguishable from acts of worship. In going about the town with her, either walking for early evening exercise or in her father's barouche to make or return formal calls, the trained and observant eye of the young Scotsman had not failed to notice her effect upon the swarming Negro population of the town.

Obeisances from these marked her passage among them. The gay stridency of their street conversations lulled itself and was still at her passing.

Doffed hats, bows, veritable obeisances in rows and by companies swayed these street loiterers as her moving about among them left them hushed and worshipful in her wake.

Captain McMillin noted the very general respectful attitude of these blacks toward their white overlords, but, his eyes told him plainly, they appeared to regard Camilla Macartney as a kind of divinity.

In the reasonable desire to satisfy his mounting curiosity Captain McMillin had broached the matter to his hostess. A canny Scot, he had approached this matter indirectly. His initial questions had had to do with native manners and customs, always a safe general topic in a colony.

Camilla's direct answers had at once surprised him with their clarity and the exactitude of their information. It was unusual and —as the subject broadened out between them and Camilla told him more and more about the Negroes, their beliefs, their manner of life, their customs and practices—it began to be plain to Captain McMillin that it was more than unusual; if someone entitled to do so had asked him his opinion on Camilla Macartney's grasp of this rather esoteric subject, and the captain had answered freely and frankly, he would have been obliged to admit that it seemed to him uncanny.

For behind those social graces of hers which made Camilla Macartney a notable figure in the polite society of this Danish colonial capital, apart from the distinction of her family connection, her commanding position as the richest heiress in the colony, her acknowledged intellectual attainments, and the distinguished beauty of face and form which lent a pervading graciousness to her every act, Camilla Macartney was almost wholly occupied by two consuming interests.

Of these, the first, generally known by every man, woman and child in St. Thomas, was her preoccupation with her cousin, Saul Macartney. The other, unsuspected by any white person in or out of Camilla Macartney's wide acquaintance, was her knowledge of the magic of the Negroes.

The subject had been virtually an obsession with her since childhood. Upon it she had centered her attention, concentrated her fine mind and, using every possible opportunity which her independent position and the enormous amount of material at hand afforded, had mastered it in theory and practice throughout its almost innumerable ramifications.

There was, first, the Obeah. This, deriving originally from the Ashanti slaves, had come into the West Indies through the gate of Jamaica. It was a combined system of magical formulas and the use of drugs. Through it a skillful practitioner could obtain extraordinary results. It involved a very complete *materia medica*, and a background setting for the usage and practice thereof, which reached back through uncounted centuries into rituals that were the very heart of primitive savagery.

The much more greatly extended affair called voodoo, an extraordinary complex fabric of "black," "white," and revelatory occultism, had made its way through the islands chiefly through the Haitian doorway from its proximate source, Dahomey, whence the early French colonists of Hispaniola had brought their original quotas of black slaves.

Voodoo, an infinitely broader and more stratified system than the medicinal Obeah, involved much that appeared to the average white person mere superficial Negro "stupidness." But in its deeper and more basic aspects it included many very terrible things, which Camilla Macartney had encountered, succeeded in understanding, and appropriated into this terrific fund of black learning which was hers as this fell subject took her through the dim backgrounds of its origin to the unspeakable snake worship of Africa's blackest and deadliest interior.

The considerable Negro population of the island, from the most fanatical *hougan* presiding in the high hills over the dire periodic rites of the "baptism" and the slaughter of goats and bullocks and willingly offered human victims whose blood, mingled with red rum, made that unholy communion out of which grew the unnameable orgies of the deep interior heights, down to the lowliest pickaninny gathering fruits or stealing yams for the sustenance of his emaciated body—every one of these blacks was aware of this singular preoccupation; acknowledged the supremacy of this extraordinarily gifted white lady; paid her reverence; feared her acknowledged powers; would as soon have lopped off a foot as to cross her lightest wish.

Captain the Honorable William McMillin made up his mind that her grasp of these matters was extraordinary. His questionings and Camilla's informative replies had barely touched upon the edge of what she knew.

And the former captain, her cousin, Saul Macartney, did not

know that his heiress cousin cherished any interest except that which she had always demonstrated so plainly in his own direction.

Going in to breakfast, Saul Macartney was nearly knocked off his feet by the physical impact of his uncle's greeting. Camilla's father had been spending the morning overlooking a property of his east of the town, in the direction of Smith's Bay. He had thus missed meeting Saul at Le Coq d'Or, but had learned of his nephew's arrival on his way home. The town, indeed, was agog with it.

So sustained was his enthusiasm, the more especially after imbibing his share of the unusually large provision of wine for a midday meal which his daughter's desire to honor the occasion had provided, that he monopolized most of his nephew's attention throughout breakfast and later in the drawing room after the conclusion of that meal. It was perhaps because of this joviality on his uncle's part that Saul Macartney failed to observe the totally new expression which had rested like a very small cloud on Camilla Macartney's face ever since a short time before going into the dining room.

His uncle even insisted upon sending the prodigal home in the English barouche, and in this elegant equipage—with its sleek, Danish coach horses and the liveried Negroes on its box with cockades at the sides of their glistening silk toppers—he made the brief journey down one hill, a short distance through the town, and up another one to his father's house.

Here, it being well after two o'clock in the afternoon, and siesta hour, he found Fawcett, whom the Old Man had taken under his hospitable wing. The two had no private conversation together. Both were in high spirits and these Old Macartney fostered with his cordials, his French brandy and a carafe of very ancient rum.

The three men sat together over their liquor during the siesta hour, and during the session Old Macartney did most of the talking. He did not once refer to his son's capture by Brenner, the freebooter.

He confined himself in his desire to be entertaining to his son's benefactor, Captain Fawcett, to a joyous succession of merry tales and ripe, antique quips. Saul Macartney had therefore no reason to suspect, nor did it happen to occur to Fawcett to inform him, that the latter's account of Macartney's adventures since the time he had last been heard from until the present was in any wise different from the tale of shipwreck upon which they had agreed and which Macartney had told out in full to his cousin, Camilla.

The three had not finished their jovial session before various strange matters affecting them very nearly, odd rumors, now being discussed avidly in various offices, residences and gathering places about St. Thomas, were gathering headway, taking on various characteristic exaggerations and, indeed, running like wildfire through the town.

In a place like St. Thomas, crossroads and clearinghouse of the vast West Indian trade which came and went through that port and whose prosperity was dependent almost wholly upon shipping, even the town's riffraff was accustomed to think and express itself in terms of ships.

It was an unimportant, loquacious Negro youth who started the ball a-rolling. This fellow, a professional diver, came up to one of the wharves in his slab-sided, homemade rowboat where he lounged aft, submitting to the propulsion of his coal-black younger brother, a scrawny lad of twelve. This wharf rat had had himself rowed out to the vessel from which the two notables he had observed had come ashore that morning. It was from the lips of this black ne'er-do-well that various other wharfside loiterers learned that the beautiful clipper vessel lying out there at anchor was provided with eight carronade ports.

Out of the idle curiosity thus initially aroused there proceeded various other harbor excursions in small boats. The black diver had somehow managed to miss the stanchion of the "long tom" which Fawcett, in an interval of prudence, had had dismounted the night before. The fact that the *Swallow* carried such an armament, however, very soon trickled ashore.

This nucleus of interesting information was soon followed up and almost eclipsed in interest by the various discussions and arguments which were soon running rife among the shipping interests of the town over the extraordinary numbers of the *Swallow*'s crew.

A round dozen, together with the usual pair of mates to supplement the captain, as all these experts on ships were well aware, would ordinarily suffice for a vessel of this tonnage. Accounts and the terms of the various arguments varied between estimates ranging from seventy-five to a hundred men on board the *Swallow*.

A side issue within this category was also warmly discussed. Crews of vessels with home ports in the islands were commonly Negro crews. This unprecedented gathering of men was a white group. Only two—certain of the debaters held out firmly that they had observed three—Negroes were to be perceived aboard the *Swallow*, and one of these, a gigantic brown man who wore nothing but earrings and a pair of faded dungaree trousers, was plainly the cook in charge of the *Swallow*'s galley, and the other, or others, were this fellow's assistants.

But the town got its real fillip from the quite definite statement of a small-fry worthy, one Jeems Pelman, who really gave them something to wrangle about when he came ashore after a visit of scrutiny and stated flatly that this rakish, shining, black-hulled clipper was none other vessel than the Macartney's *Hope,* upon both hull and rigging of which he had worked steadily for three months in his own shipyard when the *Hope* was built during the winter of 1819.

All these items of easily authenticated information bulked together and indicated to the comparatively unsophisticated, as well as to the wiseacres, only one possible conclusion. This was that the Macartney vessel, in command of which Captain Saul Macartney was known to have cleared from a South American port three months earlier, had in some as yet unexplained fashion been changed over into a freetrading ship and that the harsh-featured seadog in his fine clothes who had accompanied Captain Macartney ashore that morning could very well be none other than its commander.

A certain lapse of time is ordinarily requisite for the loquacious stage of drunkenness to overtake the average hard-headed seafaring man. The crew of Fawcett's longboat, after three weeks' continuous duty at sea, had bestowed the boat safely, engaged the services of an elderly Negro to watch it in their absence, and drifted into the low rum shop nearest their landing place; and there not long after their arrival Fawcett's boatswain, a Dutch island bruiser, had been recognized by several former acquaintances as a sailorman who had gone out of the harbor of St. Eustasia in a small trading schooner which had disappeared off the face of the wide Caribbean three years previously.

The rum-induced garrulity of this gentleman, as the report of it went forth and flared through the town, corroborated the as yet tentative conclusion that a fully manned pirate ship lay for the time being at anchor in the peaceful harbor of St. Thomas; and that its master, whose identity as a certain Captain Fawcett had spread downward through the social strata from Le Coq d'Or itself, was here ashore, hobnobbing with the town's high gentry, and actually a guest of the Macartneys.

By three o'clock in the afternoon the town was seething with the news. There had been no such choice morsel to roll on the tongue since Henry Morgan had sacked the city of Panama.

The first corroboration of that vague, distressing, but as yet unformed suspicion which had lodged itself in Camilla Macartney's mind came to her through Jens Sorensen, the butler. The "grapevine route," so-called—that curious door-to-door and mouth-to-ear method of communication among the Negroes of the community—is very rapid as well as very mysterious. Black Jens had heard this devastating story relayed up to him from the lowest black riffraff of the town's waterfront a matter of minutes after the name of their guest, seeping downward from Le Coq d'Or, had met, mingled with, and crowned the damnatory group of successive details from the wharves.

To anyone familiar with the effect of voodoo upon the Negro mentality there would be nothing surprising in the fact that black Jens proceeded straight to his mistress to whisper the story without any delay. For fear is the dominant note of the voodooist. The St. Thomas Negroes were actuated in their attitude toward Camilla Macartney by something infinitely deeper than that superficial respect which Captain McMillin had noted. They feared her and her proven powers as they feared the dread demigod Damballah, tutelary manifestation of the unnamed Guinea-Snake himself.

For it was not as one who only inquires and studies that Camilla Macartney commanded awe and reverence from the St. Thomas Negroes. She had *practiced* this extraordinary art and it was her results as something quite tangible, definite and unmistakable which formed the background of that vast respect, and which had brought black Jens cringing and trembling into her presence on this particular occasion.

And black Jens had not failed to include in his report the drunken sailorman's leering account of that captive lady's treatment by Saul Macartney—how an innocent young wife, off Nevis, had been outrageously forced into Saul's cabin, and when he had tired of her, how he had sent her back to the deck to go across the plank of death.

What desolation penetrated deep and lodged itself there in Camilla Macartney's soul can hardly be guessed at. From that moment she was convinced of the deep infamy of that entrancing lover-cousin of hers whom she had adored with her whole heart since the remoteness of her early childhood.

But, however poignantly indescribable, however extremely devastating, may have been her private feelings, it is certain that she did not retire as the typical gentlewoman of the period would have done to eat out her heart in solitary desolation.

Within ten minutes, on the contrary, in response to her immediately issued orders, the English barouche with its sleek Danish horses, its cockaded servants on the box, was carrying her down the hill, rapidly along through the town, and then the heavy coach horses were sweating up the other hill toward her uncle's house. If the seed of hatred, planted by Saul's duplicity, were already sprouting, nevertheless she would warn him. She dreaded meeting him.

Saul Macartney, summoned away from the somewhat drowsy end of that afternoon's convivial session with Fawcett and the Old Man, found his cousin awaiting him near the drawing room door. She was standing, and her appearance was calm and collected. She addressed him directly, without preamble:

"Saul, it is known in the town. I came to warn you. It is running about the streets that this Captain Fawcett of yours is the pirate. One of his men has been recognized. He talked in one of the rum shops. They say that this ship is the *Hope,* altered into a different appearance. I advise you to go, Saul—go at once, while it is safe!"

Saul Macartney turned his old disarming smile upon his cousin. He could feel the liquor he had drunk warming him, but his hard Irish head was reasonably clear. He was not befuddled. He stepped toward her as though impulsively, his bronzed face flushed from his recent potations, his arms extended and spread in a carefree gesture as though he were about to take her in his embrace.

"Camilla, *allana,* ye should not sadden your sweet face over the likes of me. I know well what I'm about, me darling. And as for Fawcett—well, as ye're aware of his identity, ye'll know that he can care for himself. Very suitably, very suitably indeed."

He had advanced very close upon her now, but she stood unmoving, the serious expression of her face not changed. She only held up a hand in a slight gesture against him, as though to warn him to pause and think. Again Saul Macartney stepped lightly toward his doom.

"And may I not be having a kiss, Camilla?" His smiling face was unperturbed, his self-confidence unimpaired even now. Then, fatally, he added. "And now that ye're here, *acushla,* why should ye not have me present my friend, the captain? 'Twas he, ye'll remember, that brought me back to ye. I could be fetching him within the moment."

But Camilla Macartney merely looked at him with a level gaze.

"I am going now," she said, ignoring his suggestion and the crass insult to her gentility involved in it, and which beneath her calm exterior had outraged her and seared her very soul. The seed was growing apace. "I have warned you, Saul."

She turned and walked out of the room and out of the house: then across the tiled gallery and down the black marble steps, and out to her carriage.

Saul Macartney hastened back to his father and Fawcett. Despite his incurable bravado, motivated as always by his deep-seated selfishness, he had simply accepted the warning just given him at its face value. He addressed his drowsing father after a swift, meaningful glance at Fawcett:

"We shall be needing the carriage, sir, if so be it's agreeable to ye. We must be getting back on board, it appears, and I'll be hoping to look in on ye again in the morning, sir."

And without waiting for any permission, and ignoring his father's liquor-muffled protests against this abrupt departure, Saul Macartney rang the bell, ordered the family carriage to be waiting in the shortest possible time, and pressed a rix-dollar into the Negro butler's hand as an incentive to hasten the process.

Within a quarter of an hour, after hasty farewells to the tearful and now well-befuddled Old Man, these two precious scoundrels were well on their way through the town toward the jetty where they had landed, and where, upon arrival, they collected their boat's crew out of the rum shop with vigorous revilings and not a few hearty clouts, and were shortly speeding across the turquoise and indigo waters of St. Thomas harbor toward the anchored *Swallow*.

Inside half an hour from their going up over her side and the hoisting of the longboat, the *Swallow*, without reference to the harbormaster, clearance, or any other formality, was picking her lordly way daintily out past Colwell's Battery at the harbor mouth, and was soon lost to the sight of all curious watchers in the welcoming swell of the Caribbean.

This extraordinary visit of the supposedly long-drowned Captain Macartney to his native town, and the circumstances accompanying it, was a nine-days' wonder in St. Thomas. The widespread discussion it provoked died down after awhile, it being supplanted in current interest by the many occurrences in so busy a port-of-call. It was not, of course, forgotten, although it dropped out of mind as a subject for acute debate.

Such opinion as remained after the arguments had been abandoned was divided opinion. Could the vessel possibly have been the Macartneys' *Hope?* Was this Captain Fawcett who had brought Saul Macartney ashore Captain Fawcett, the pirate? Had Captain Saul Macartney really thrown in his lot with freetraders, or was such a course unthinkable on his part?

The yarn which Captain Fawcett had spun in Le Coq d'Or seemed the reasonable explanation—if it were true. In the face of the fact that no other counter-explanation had been definitely put forward by anybody, this version was tacitly accepted by St. Thomas society; but with the proviso, very generally made and very widely held, that this fellow must have been *the* Captain Fawcett after all. Saul Macartney had either been fooled by him, or else Saul's natural gratitude had served to cover, in his estimation of the fellow, any observed shortcomings on the part of this rescuer and friend-in-need.

Camilla Macartney made no allusion whatever, even within the family circle, to the story Saul had told *her.* She was not, of course, called upon to express any opinion outside. She was quite well aware that both versions were falsehoods.

She faced bravely, though with a sorely empty and broken heart, all her manifold social obligations in the town. Indeed, somewhat to distract her tortured mind, wherein that seed of hate was by now growing into a lusty plant, the heiress of the Macartney fortune engaged herself rather more fully than usual that summer season in the various current activities. She forced herself to a greater preoccupation than ever in her attention to her occult pursuits. She even took up afresh the oil painting, long ago abandoned by her, which had been one of her early "accomplishments."

It was during this period—a very dreadful one for her, succeeding as it did, abruptly upon her momentary happiness at her cousin Saul's restoration to the land of the living which had dissipated her acute and sustained grief over his presumptive loss at sea in the *Hope*—that she undertook, with what obscure premonitory motive derived from curious skill in the strange and terrible arts of the black people can only be darkly surmised— another and very definite task.

This was the painting of a panoramic view of the town as seen from the harbor. At this she toiled day after day from the awninged afterdeck of one of the smaller Macartney packet vessels. This boat had been anchored to serve her purpose at the point of vantage she had selected. She worked at her panorama in the clear, pure light of many early summer mornings. Before her on the rather large canvas she had chosen for this purpose there gradually grew into objectivity the wharves, the public buildings, the fort, the three hills with their red-roofed mansions, set amid decorative trees. Her almost incredible industry was, really, a symptom of the strange obsession now beginning to invade her reason. Camilla Macartney had suffered a definite mental lesion.

The scrupulous courtesy of the St. Thomians, that graceful mantle of manners which has never been allowed to wear thin, was unobtrusively interposed between the respected Macartneys and the dreadful scandal which had reached out and touched their impeccable family garment of respectability. By no word spoken, by no overt act, by not so much as a breath were they reminded of Captain Macartney's recent visit ashore or his hasty and irregular departure. Captain McMillin, therefore, as a guest of Camilla's father, heard nothing of it. He sensed, however, a certain indefinite undercurrent of family trouble and, yielding to this sure instinct, ended his visit with all the niceties of high breeding and departed for Santa Cruz.

Just before he left, on the morning after the farewell dinner which had been given as a final gesture in his honor, the captain managed to convey to Camilla the measure of his appreciation. He placed, as it were, his sword at her disposal! It was very nicely made—that gesture of gallantry. It was not to be mistaken for the preliminary to a possible later offer of marriage. It was anything but braggadocio. And it was somehow entirely appropriate to the situation. The handsome, upstanding captain left with his hostess precisely the impression he intended; that is, he left her the feeling that he was an adequate person to depend upon in a pinch, and that she had been invited to depend upon him should the pinch come.

A third of the way up one of the low mountains northward and behind the three gentle hills on the southern slopes of which the ancient city of St. Thomas is built, there stood—and still stands —a small stone gentry residence originally built in the middle of the eighteenth century by an exiled French family which had taken refuge in this kindly Danish colony and played at raising vanilla up there on their airy little estate overlooking the town and the sea.

This place was still known by its original name of Ma Folie— a title early bestowed upon it by Mme. la Marquise, who had looked up at it through a window in her temporary apartment in the Hotel du Commerce, in the town, while the roofing was being placed upon her new house, there and then assuring herself that only perched upon the back of one of those diminutive burros which cluttered up the town streets could anyone like herself possibly manage the ascent to such a site.

Ma Folie was now one of the many Macartney properties. It belonged to Camilla, having come to her as a portion of her maternal inheritance, and upon it she had reestablished the vanilla planting, helped out by several freshly cleared acres in cocoa. No donkey was required nowadays to convey a lady up the tortuous, steep, little trail from the town to Ma Folie. A carriage road led past its unpretentious square entrance posts of whitewashed, cemented stone, and when Camilla Macartney visited her hillside estate the English barouche carried her there, the long climb causing the heavy coach horses to sweat mightily and helping, as the coal-black coachman said, to keep them in condition.

It was up here that she had long ago established what might be called her laboratory. It was at Ma Folie, whose village housed only Negroes selected by herself as her tenant-laborers, that she had, in the course of years, brought the practice of the "strange art" to its perfection. She had for some time now confined her practice to meeting what might be called charitable demands upon her.

Talismans to protect; amulets to attract or repel; potent *ouangas*—only such modest products of the fine art of voodoo as these went out from that occult workshop of hers at Ma Folie—went out into the eager, outstretched hands of the afflicted whose manifold plights had engaged Camilla Macartney's sympathy; to the relief of those abject ones who called upon her, in fear and trembling, as their last resort against who knows what obscure devilish attacks, what outrageous charmings, wrought by that inimical ruthlessness of one Negro to another which Caucasians hardly suspect.

No vanilla pod, no single cocoa bean, had been stolen from Ma Folie estate since Camilla Macartney had planted it afresh nine years before. . . .

It was at about ten o'clock in the morning of a day near the middle of August that a kind of tremor of emotion ran through the town of St. Thomas, a matter of minutes after a report of the official watcher and the many other persons in the town and along the wharves whose sustained interest in shipping matters caused their eyes to turn ever and anon toward the wide harbor mouth. The *Swallow*, which three months before had literally run away, ignoring all the niceties of a ship's departure from any port and even the official leavetaking, was coming in brazenly, lilting daintily along under the stiff trade, her decks visibly swarming with the many members of her efficient and numerous crew.

She came up into the wind like a little man-o'-war, jauntily, her sails coming down simultaneously with a precision to warm the hearts of those ship-wise watchers, her rigging slatting with reports like musket shots, the furling and stowing of canvas a truly marvelous demonstration of the efficiency which now reigned aft.

These details of rapid-fire seamanship, swiftly as they were being handled, were as yet incomplete when the longboat went straight down from its davits into the water and Saul Macartney followed his boat's crew over the side and picked up his tiller ropes.

The *Swallow*'s anchorage this time was closer in, and it seemed no time at all to the thronging, gaping watchers on the jetty before he sprang ashore and was up the steps. There was no rum shop for the boat's crew this time. Without their officer's even looking back at them over his shoulder the oarsmen pushed off, turned about and rowed back to the *Swallow*.

Saul Macartney was, if possible, even more debonair than ever. His self-confident smile adorned his even more heavily bronzed face. He was hatless, as usual, and his handsome figure was mightily set off by a gaily sprigged waistcoat and a ruffled shirt of fine cambric which showed between the silver braided lapels of the maroon-colored coat of French cloth with a deep velvet collar, the pantaloons of which, matching the coat's cloth, were strapped under a pair of low boots of very shining black leather.

The throng on the jetty was plainly in a different mood as compared to the vociferous, welcoming mob of three months before. They stayed close together in a little phalanx this time and from them came fewer welcoming smiles.

Plainly sensing this, Saul Macartney bestowed on this riffraff of the wharves no more than a passing glance of smiling raillery. He passed them and entered the town with rapid, purposeful strides as though intent on some very definite business and, utterly ignoring the hum of released though muted conversation which rose behind him as though from an aroused swarm of bees, entered the main thoroughfare, turned sharply to his left along it, proceeded in this direction some forty feet, and turned into the small office of one Axel Petersen, a purveyor of ships' stores.

Blond, stout, genial Axel Petersen stared from his broad, comfortable desk at this entrance and allowed his lower jaw to sag. Then he rose uncertainly to his feet and his four neatly garbed mulatto clerks rose from their four respective high stools with him and, in precise conformity with their employer's facial reaction, their four pairs of mottled-iris eyes rounded out altogether like saucers, and their four lower jaws sagged in unison.

Saul Macartney threw back his head and laughed aloud. Then, addressing Petersen:

"Axel, Axel! I couldn't've thought it of ye! 'Tis but stores I'm after, man—vast stores, the likes of which ye might be selling in the course of a week to five vessels, if so be ye had the fortune to get that many all in one week!" Then, a shade more seriously, " 'Tis pork I want; beans, coffee in sacks, limes by the gunny sack —a hundred and one things, all of them written down to save ye trouble, ye great, feckless porker! And here—beside the list which I'm handing ye now—is the reassurance—"

And Saul Macartney, thrusting his list of ship's supplies neatly printed on a long slip of paper under the nose of the stultified Petersen, slapped down upon the desktop beside it the bulging purse which he had hauled out of the tail pocket of his beautiful, maroon-colored French coat.

"There's two hundred and fifty English sovereigns there forninst ye, Axel. Ye can have it counted out or do it yourself, and if that does not suffice to cover the list, why, there's another shot in the locker behind it, ye *omadhoun*—ye fat robber of pettifogging ships' stewards!"

And before the protruding, bemused blue eyes of portly Axel Petersen Saul Macartney shook banteringly a thick sheaf of Bank of England ten-pound notes. By the time he had returned these to the same capacious pocket, he was at the door, had paused, turned and, leaning for an instant nonchalantly against its jamb, remarked—

"Ye're to have the stores piled on your wharf not an instant later than two o'clock this day." Then, the bantering smile again to the fore, and shaking a long, shapely forefinger toward the goggling dealer in ships' stores, he added, "Ye'll observe, Axel.

I'm not taking your stores by force and arms. I'm not sacking the town—this time!"

Then Saul Macartney was gone, and Axel Petersen, muttering unintelligibly as he assembled his scattered wits and those of his four clerks, the heavy purse clutched tightly by its middle in one pudgy hand, and the long list of the *Swallow*'s required stores held a little unsteadily before his nearsighted blue eyes, methodically began the process of getting this enormous order assembled.

It was with a perfectly calm exterior that Camilla Macartney received her cousin Saul a quarter of an hour later. The turmoil beneath this prideful reserve might, perhaps, be guessed at; but as the art of guessing had never formed any part of Saul Macartney's mental equipment, he made no effort in that direction.

He began at once with his usual self-confident directness upon what he had come to say.

"Camilla, *acushla,* I've come to ye in haste, 'tis true, and I'm asking your indulgence for that. 'Twas gracious of ye, as always, to be here at home when I chanced to arrive.

"I'll go straight to the point, if so be ye have no objections to make, and say in plain words what I well know to have been in the hearts of the two of us this many a year. I'm askin' ye now, Camilla—I'm begging ye with my whole soul to say that ye'll drive down with me now, Camilla, to the English Church, and the two of us be married, and then sail with me for the truly magnificent home I've been establishing for ye over on Andros."

Camilla Macartney continued to sit, outwardly unmoved, where she had received him when black Jens had shown him into the drawing room. She had not been looking at her cousin during this characteristically confident and even impulsive declaration of his. Her eyes were upon her hands which lay, lightly clasped, in her lap, and she did not raise them to reply. She did not, however, keep him waiting. She said in a perfectly level voice in which there was apparently no single trace or indication of the tearing, internal emotion which surged through her outraged heart at this last and unforgivable insult—

"I shall not become your wife, Saul—now or ever."

Then, as he stood before her, his buoyant self-confidence for once checked, his face suddenly configured into something like the momentary grotesqueness of Axel Petersen's, she added, in that same level tone, which had about it now, however, the smallest suggestion of a rising inflection:

"Do not come to me again. Go now—at once."

This final interview with her cousin Saul was unquestionably the element which served to crystallize into an active and sustained hatred the successive emotional crises and their consequent abnormal states of mind which the events here recorded had stirred up within this woman so terribly equipped for vengeance. The seed of hatred was now a full-grown plant.

Upon a woman of Camilla Macartney's depth and emotional capacity the felonious behavior of Saul Macartney had had a very terrible, and a very deep-reaching, mental effect. She had adored and worshiped him for as long as she could remember. He had torn down and riven apart and left lying about her in brutally shattered fragments the whole structure of her life. He had smashed the solid pride of her family into shreds. He had disgraced himself blatantly, deliberately, with a ruthless abandon. He had piled insult to her upon insult. He had taken her pure love for him, crushed and defiled it.

And now these irresistible blows had had the terrible effect of breaking down the serene composure of this gentlewoman. All her love for her cousin and all her pride in him were transformed into one definite, flaming and consuming purpose: She must wipe out those dreadful stains!

Arrived in the empty library, Camilla Macartney went straight to the great rosewood desk, and without any delay wrote a letter. The black footman who hurried with this missive down the hill actually passed Saul Macartney, likewise descending it. Within a very short time after its reception the captain of the little packet-vessel—upon which, anchored quite close to shore, Camilla Macartney had been painting her nearly finished panorama of the town—had gone ashore to round up his full crew. The packet itself, with Camilla Macartney on board, sailed out of St. Thomas harbor that afternoon in plain sight of the restocked *Swallow*, whose great spread of gleaming white canvas showed gloriously under the afternoon's sun as she laid her course due southwest. The packet, laying hers to the southward, rolled and tossed at a steady eight-knot clip under the spanking trade, straight for the Island of Santa Cruz.

Captain the Honorable William McMillin was summoned from his seven o'clock dinner in his estate house up in the gentle hills of the island's north side, and only his phlegmatic Scottish temperament, working together with his aristocratic self-control, prevented *his* shapely jaw from sagging and his blue eyes from becoming saucerlike when they had recorded for him the identity of this wholly unexpected visitor. Camilla Macartney wasted none of the captain's time, nor was her arrival cause for any cooling of the excellent repast from which he had arisen to receive her.

"I have not," said she downrightly in response to the astonished captain's initial inquiry as to whether she had dined. "And," she added, "I should be glad to sit down with you at once, if that meets your convenience, sir. It is, as you may very well have surmised, a very deep and pressing matter upon which I have ventured to come to you. That, I should imagine, would best be discussed while we sit at table, and so without delay."

Again the captain demonstrated his admirable manners. He merely bowed and led the way to the door of his dining room.

Once seated opposite Captain McMillin, Camilla Macartney again went straight to her point. The captain quite definitely forgot to eat in the amazing and immediate interest of what she proceeded to say.

"I am offering the reward of a thousand English sovereigns for the apprehension at sea and the bringing to St. Thomas for their trials of the freetrader, Fawcett, and his mates. It may very well be no secret to you, sir, that a member of our family is one of these men. I think that any comment between us upon that subject will be a superfluity. You will take note, if you please, that it is I, a member of our family, who offer the reward I have named for his apprehension. You will understand—everything that is involved.

"Earlier this day it was proposed to me that I should sail away upon a ship without very much notice. I have come here to you, sir, on one of my father's vessels—Captain Stewart, her commander, a trusted man in our employ, has accompanied me all the way to your door. He is here now, waiting in the hired *calèche* which I secured in Frederiksted for the drive here to your house. Perhaps you will be good enough to have some food taken to him.

"I have come, Captain McMillin, in all this haste, actually to request you to do the same thing that I mentioned—you made me see, when you were our guest, that I could wholly rely upon you, sir. I am here to ask you, as a military man, to command the expedition which I am sending out. I am asking you to sail back with Captain Stewart and me for St. Thomas—tonight."

Captain McMillin looked at Camilla Macartney across the length of his glistening mahogany dining table. He had been listening very carefully to her speech. He rang his table bell now that he was sure she was finished, and when his serving man answered this summons, ordered him to prepare a repast for the waiting ship's captain, and to send in to him his groom. Then, with a bow to his guest, and pushing back his chair and rising, he said:

"You will excuse me, Miss Macartney, I trust, for the little time I shall require to pack. It will not occupy me very long."

IV

The story of how the *Hyperion*, newest and swiftest of all the Macartney vessels, was outfitted and armed for the pursuit and capture of Captain Fawcett is a little epic in itself. It would include among many details extant the intensive search among the shipping resources of St. Thomas, for the swivelgun which, two days after Captain McMillin's arrival on the scene, was being securely bolted through the oak timbers of the *Hyperion's* afterdeck.

A surprisingly complete record of this extraordinary piece of activity survives among the ancient colonial archives. Perhaps the recording clerk of the period, in his Government House office, was, like everyone else in St. Thomas, fascinated by the ruthless swiftness with which that job, under the impact of Camilla Macartney's eye, was pushed through to a successful conclusion in precisely forty-eight hours. Nothing like this rate of speed had ever been heard of, even in St. Thomas. The many men engaged in this herculean task at Pelman's Shipyard worked day and night continuously in three eight-hour shifts.

It is significant that these shipwrights and other skilled artisans were all Negroes. They had assembled in their scores and dozens from every quarter of the widespread town, irrespective of age or the exactions of their current employment, from the instant that the grapevine route spread through the black population of the town the summons to this task which Camilla Macartney had quietly uttered in the ear of her butler, Jens Sorensen.

The *Hyperion*, under the command of her own officers but with the understanding that Captain McMillin was in sole charge of the expedition, came up with the *Swallow* a little under four days from the hour of her sailing out of St. Thomas harbor.

Captain McMillin caught Fawcett at a vast disadvantage. The *Swallow*, very lightly manned at the moment, hung in stays, her riding sails flapping with reports like pistol shots as her graceful head was held into the wind. She lay some ten shiplengths away to the leeward of an American merchant vessel about which the *Swallow*'s boats—now nine in number—were grouped, a single member of the crew in each. Fawcett and his two lieutenants, and nine-tenths of his crew of cutthroats, were ransacking their prize, whose officers, crew and passengers had been disposed of under nailed hatches. They appeared, indeed, to be so thoroughly occupied in this nefarious work as to have ignored entirely any preparations for meeting the *Hyperion*'s attack—a circumstance sufficiently strange to have impressed Captain McMillin profoundly.

The *Hyperion*'s officers, unable to account for this singular quiescence on the part of the pirates, attributed it to their probably failing to suspect that the *Hyperion* was anything but another trading vessel which had happened to blunder along on her course into this proximity. With a strange, quick gripping at the heart, quite new in his experience, Captain McMillin permitted himself to suspect, though for a brief instant only, that something of the strange power which he had glimpsed in his contacts with Camilla

Macartney, might in some extraordinary fashion be somehow responsible for this phenomenon.

But this thought, as too utterly ridiculous for harborage in a normal man's mind, he put away from him instanter.

The strategy of the situation appeared to be simple. And Captain McMillin formulated his plan of attack accordingly, after a brief consultation with his officers.

Realizing that there could be no effective gunnery from the handful of men in charge of the *Swallow*, Captain McMillin ordered a dozen men in charge of the *Hyperion*'s second mate over the side in the largest of the boats. The maneuver of dropping an already manned boat from the davits—a risky undertaking in any event—was handled successfully, an exceptionally quiet sea contributing to the management of this piece of seamanship.

This boat's crew, all Negroes and all armed with the pistols and cutlasses which had been hastily served out to them, had no difficulty whatever in getting over the *Swallow*'s side and making themselves masters of the pirate vessel. The dozen Negroes had butchered the seven members of the pirate crew left on board the *Swallow* within forty seconds of their landing upon her deck, and Mr. Matthews, the officer in charge of them, hauled down with his own hand the Jolly Roger which, true to the freetrading traditions of the Main, flaunted at the *Swallow*'s main peak.

The magnificent cooperation of the fifteen Negroes constituting the *Hyperion*'s deck crew made possible the next daring piece of seamanship which the *Hyperion*'s captain had agreed to attempt. This was Captain McMillin's plan.

The *Hyperion* should lay alongside the American vessel, grapple to her and board—with all hands—from deck to deck. This idea, almost unheard of in modern sea warfare, had suggested itself as practicable in this instance to Captain McMillin, from his reading. Such had been the tactics of the antique Mediterranean galleys.

For the purpose of retaining the outward appearance of a simple trader, Captain McMillin had concealed the thirty-three additional members of his heavily armed crew, and these had not been brought on deck until he was almost ready to have the grapples thrown. These reserves now swarmed upon the *Hyperion*'s deck in the midst of a bedlam of shouts, yells and curses, punctuated by pistol shots, from the pirate crew on board their prize.

These were taken at a vast disadvantage. Their prize vessel was immobile. They had, for what appeared to Captain McMillin some inexplicable reason, apparently failed until the very last moment to realize the *Hyperion*'s intentions. Most of them were busily engaged in looting their prize. Under this process five of the *Swallow*'s nine boats had already been laden gunwale deep with the miscellaneous plunder already taken out of the American ship. Two of these laden small boats and two others of the *Swallow*'s nine were crushed like eggshells as the *Hyperion* closed in and threw her grappling hooks.

Then, in a silence new and strange in Captain McMillin's previous experience in hand-to-hand fighting, his forty-eight black fighting men followed him over the rails and fell upon the pirates.

Within three minutes the American vessel's deck was a shambles. Camilla Macartney's black myrmidons, like militant fiends from some strange hell of their own, their eyeballs rolling, their white teeth flashing as they bared their lips in the ecstasy of this mission of wholesale slaughter, spread irresistibly with grunts and low mutterings and strange cries about that deck.

Not a member of the pirate crew escaped their ruthless on-slaught. Hard skulls were split asunder and lopped arms strewed the deck, and tough bodies were transfixed, and the gasping wounded were trampled lifeless in the terrible energy of these black fighting men.

Then abruptly, save for a harsh sobbing sound from laboring panting lungs after their terrific exertion, a strange silence fell, and toward Captain McMillin, who stood well nigh aghast over the utter strangeness of this unprecedented carnage which had just taken place under his eye and under his command, there came a huge, black, diffidently smiling Negro, his feet scarlet as he slouched along that moist and slippery deck, a crimson cutlass dangling loosely now from the red hand at the end of a red arm. This one, addressing the captain in a low, humble and deprecating voice, said—

"Come, now, please, me marster—come, please sar, see de t'ree gentlemahn you is tell us to sabe alive!"

And Captain McMillin, bemused, followed this guide along that deck slashed and scarlet with the lifeblood of those pulped heaps which had been Captain Fawcett's pirate crew, stepped aft to where, behind the main deckhouse, three trussed and helpless white men lay upon a cleaner section of that vessel's deck, under the baleful eye of another strapping black man with red feet and a naked red cutlass brandished in a red hand.

The *Swallow*, her own somewhat bloodsoiled deck now shining spotless under the mighty holystonings it had received at the hands of its prize crew of twelve under command of the *Hyperion*'s second mate, the Danish flag now flying gaily from her masthead, followed the *Hyperion* into St. Thomas harbor on the second day of September, 1825. The two vessels came up to their designated anchorages smartly, and shortly thereafter, and for the last time, Saul Macartney, accompanied by his crony, Captain Fawcett, and his colleague, the other pirate mate, was rowed ashore in the familiar longboat.

But during this short and rapid trip these three gentlemen did not, for once, occupy the sternsheets. They sat forward, their hands and feet in irons, the six oarsmen between them and Mr. Matthews, the *Hyperion's* mate, who held the tiller rope, and Captain the Honorable William McMillin, who sat erect beside him.

V

I have already recorded my first horrified reaction to the appearance of the handsome black-haired piratical mate whose painted arm my innocent thumbtack had penetrated. My next reaction, rather curiously, was the pressing, insistent, sudden impulse to withdraw that tack. I did so forthwith—with trembling fingers. I here openly confess.

My third and final reaction which came to me not long afterward and when I had somewhat succeeded in pulling myself together, was once more to get out my magnifying glass and take another good look through it. After all, I told myself, I was here confronted with nothing more in the way of material facts than a large-sized, somewhat crudely done and very old oil painting.

I got the glass and reassured myself. The "blood" was, of course —as now critically examined, magnified by sixteen diameters— merely a few spattered drops of the very same vermilion pigment which my somewhat clever amateur artist had used for the red roofs of the houses, the foulards of the Negresses and those many gloriously flaming flower blossoms.

Quite obviously these particular spatters of red paint had not been in the liquid state for more than a century. Having ascertained these facts beyond the shadow of any lingering doubt in the field of everyday material fact, my one remaining bit of surviving wonderment settled itself about the minor puzzle of just why I had failed to observe these spots of ancient, dry and brittle paint during the long and careful scrutiny to which I had subjected the picture the evening before. A curious coincidence, this—that the tiny red spots should happen to be precisely in the place where blood would be showing if it *had* flowed from my tack wound in that dangled painted arm.

I looked next, curiously, through my glass at the fellow's face. I could perceive now none of that acutely agonized expression which had accentuated my first startled horror at the sight of the blood.

And so, pretty well reassured, I went back to my bedroom and finished dressing. And thereafter, as the course of affairs proceeded, I could not get the thing out of my mind. I will pass over any attempt at describing the psychological processes involved and say here merely that by the end of a couple of weeks or so I was in that state of obsession which made it impossible for me to do my regular work, or, indeed, to think of anything else. And then, chiefly to relieve my mind of this vastly annoying preoccupation, I began upon that course of investigatory research to which I have already alluded.

When I had finished this, had gone down to the end of the last bypath which it involved, it was well on in the year 1930. It had taken three years, and—it was worth it.

I was in St. Thomas that season and St. Thomas was still operating under the régime which had prevailed since the spring of 1917, at which time the United States had purchased the old Danish West Indies from Denmark as a war measure, during the presidency of Woodrow Wilson.

In 1930 our naval forces had not yet withdrawn from our Virgin Island Colony. The administration was still actively under the direction of his Excellency Captain Waldo Evans, USN Retired, and the heads of the major departments were still the efficient and personable gentlemen assigned to those duties by the Secretary of the Navy.

My intimate friend, Dr. Pelletier, the pride of the USN Medical Corps, was still in active charge of the Naval Hospital, and I could rely upon Dr. Pelletier, whose interest in and knowledge of the strange and outré beliefs, customs and practices of numerous strange corners of this partly civilized world of ours were both deep and, as it seemed to me, virtually exhaustive.

To this good friend of mine, this walking encyclopedia of strange knowledge, I took, naturally, my findings in this very strange and utterly fascinating story of old St. Thomas. We spent several long evenings together over it, and when I had imparted all the facts while my surgeon friend listened, as is his custom, for hours on end without a single interruption, we proceeded to spend many more evenings discussing it, sometimes at the hospitable doctor's bachelor dinner table and afterward far into those tropic nights of spice and balm, and sometimes at my house which is quite near the old T.L. Macartney mansion on Denmark Hill.

In the course of these many evenings I added to the account of the affair which had emerged out of my long investigation two additional phases of this matter which I have not included in my account as written out here because, in the form which these took in my mind, they were almost wholly conjectural.

Of these, the first took its point of departure from the depiction of the rope, as shown in the painting, with which Saul Macartney had been hanged. I have mentioned the painstaking particularity with which the artist had put in the minor details of the composition. I have illustrated this by stating that the seven traditional turns of the hangman's knot were to be seen showing plainly under Captain Fawcett's left ear. The same type of knot, I may add here, was also painted in laboriously upon the noose which had done to death Fawcett's other mate.

But Saul Macartney's rope did not show such a knot. In fact, it showed virtually no knot at all. Even under the magnifying glass a knot expert would have been unable to name in any category of knots the inconspicuous slight enlargement at the place where Saul Macartney's noose was joined. Another point about this rope which might or might not have any significance, was the fact that it was of a color slightly but yet distinctly different from the hemp color of the other two. Saul Macartney's rope was of a faint greenish-blue color.

Upon this rather slight basis for conjecture I hazarded the following enlargement:

That Camilla Macartney, just after the verdict of the Danish Colonial High Court had become known to her—and I ventured to express the belief that she had known it before any other white person—had said in her quiet voice to her black butler, Jens Sorensen:

"I am going to Ma Folie. Tonight, at nine o'clock precisely, Ajax Mendoza is to come to me there."

And—this is merely my imaginative supplement, it will be remembered, based on my own knowledge of the dark ways of voodoo—burly black Ajax Mendoza, capital executioner in the honorable employ of the Danish Colonial Administration, whose father, Jupiter Mendoza, had held that office before him, and whose grandfather, Achilles Mendoza (whose most notable performance had been the racking of the insurrectionist leader, Black Tancrède, who had been brought back to the capital in chains after the perpetration of his many atrocities in the St. Jan Uprising of the slaves in 1733), had been the first of the line; that Ajax Mendoza, not fierce and truculent as he looked standing there beside the policemaster on Captain Fawcett's gallow platform, but trembling, and cringing, had kept that appointment to which he had been summoned.

Having received his orders, he had then hastened to bring to Camilla Macartney the particular length of thin manila rope which was later to be strung from the arm of Saul Macartney's gallows and had left it with her until she returned it to him before the hour of the execution; and that he had received it back and reeved it through its pulley with even more fear and trembling and cringings at being obliged to handle this transmuted thing whose very color was a terror and a distress to him, now that it had passed through that fearsome laboratory of "white missy who knew the Snake. . . ."

And my second conjectural hypothesis I based upon the fact which my research had revealed to me that all the members of the honorable clan of Macartney resident in St. Thomas had, with obvious propriety, kept to their closely shuttered several residences during the entire day of that public execution. That is, all of the Macartneys except the heiress of the great Macartney fortune, Camilla.

Half an hour before high noon on that public holiday the English barouche had deposited Camilla Macartney at one of the wharves a little away from the center of the town where that great throng had gathered to see the pirates hanged, and from there she had been rowed out to the small vessel which had that morning gone back to its old anchorage near the shore.

There, in her old place under the awning of the afterdeck, she had very calmly and deliberately set up her easel and placed before her the all-but-finished panorama upon which she had been working, and had thereupon begun to paint, and so had continued quietly painting until the three bodies of those pirates which had been left dangling "for the space of a whole hour," according to the sentence, "as a salutary example," and had then ended her work and gone back to the wharf carrying carefully the now finished panorama to where the English barouche awaited her.

By conjecture, on the basis of these facts, I managed somehow to convey to Dr. Pelletier, a man whose mind is attuned to such matters, the tentative, uncertain idea—I should not dare to name it a conviction—that Camilla Macartney, by some application of that uncanny skill of hers in the arts of darkness, had, as it were, caught the life principle of her cousin, Saul Macartney, as it escaped from his splendid body there at the end of that slightly discolored and curiously knotted rope, *and fastened it down upon her canvas within the simulacrum of that little painted figure through the arm of which I had thrust a thumbtack!*

These two queer ideas of mine, which had been knocking about inside my head, strangely enough did not provoke the retort, "Outrageous!" from Dr. Pelletier, a man of the highest scientific attainments. I had hesitated to put such thoughts into words, and I confess that I was surprised that his response in the form of a series of nods of the head did not seem to indicate the indulgence of a normal mind toward the drivelings of some imbecile.

Dr. Pelletier deferred any verbal reply to this imaginative climax of mine, placed as it was at the very end of our discussion. When he did shift his mighty bulk where it reclined in my Chinese rattan lounge chair on my airy west gallery—a sure preliminary to any remarks from him—his first words surprised me a little.

"Is there any doubt, Canevin, in your mind about the identity of this painted portrait figure of the mate with Saul Macartney himself?"

"No," said I. "I was able to secure two faded old ambrotypes of Saul Macartney—at least, I was given a good look at them. There can, I think, be no question on that score."

For the space of several minutes Pelletier remained silent. Then he slightly shifted his leonine head to look at me.

"Canevin," said he, "people like you and me who have *seen* this kind of thing working under our very eyes, all around us, among people like these West Indian blacks, well—we *know.*"

Then, more animatedly, and sitting up a little in his chair, the doctor said:

"On that basis, Canevin—on the pragmatic basis, if you will, and that, God knows, is scientific, based on observation—the only thing that we can do is to give this queer, devilish thing the benefit of the doubt. Our doubt, to say nothing of what the general public would think of such ideas!"

"Should you say that there is anything that can be done about it?" I inquired. "I have the picture, you know, and you have heard the—well, the *facts* as they have come under my observation. Is there any—what shall I say?—any *responsibility* involved on the basis of those facts and any conjectural additions that you and I may choose to make?"

"That," said Pelletier, "is what I meant by the benefit of the doubt. Thinking about this for the moment in terms of the limitations, the incompleteness, of human knowledge and the short distance we have managed to travel along the road to civilization, I should say that there is—a responsibility."

"What shall I do—if anything?" said I, a little taken aback at this downrightness.

Again Dr. Pelletier looked at me for a long moment, and nodded his head several times. Then:

"Burn the thing, Canevin. Fire—the solvent. Do you comprehend me? Have I said enough?"

I thought over this through the space of several silent minutes. Then, a trifle hesitantly because I was not at all sure that I had grasped the implications which lay below this very simple suggestion—

"You mean—?"

"That if there is anything in it, Canevin—that benefit of the doubt again, you see—if, to put such an outrageous hypothesis into a sane phrase, the life, the soul, the personality remains unreleased, and that because of Camilla Macartney's use of a pragmatic 'magical' skill such as is operative today over there in the hills of Haiti; to name only one focus of this particular *cultus* —well, then . . ."

This time it was I who nodded; slowly, several times. After that I sat quietly in my chair for long minutes in the little silence which lay between us. We had said, it seemed to me, everything that was to be said. I—we—had gone as far as human limitations permitted in the long investigation of this strange affair. Then I summoned my houseman, Stephen Penn.

"Stephen," said I, "go and find out if the charcoal pots in the kitchen have burned out since breakfast. I imagine that about this time there would be a little charcoal left to burn out in each of them. If so, put all the charcoal into one pot and bring it out here on the gallery. If not, fix me a new charcoal fire in the largest pot. Fill it about half full."

"Yes, sar," said Stephen, and departed on this errand.

Within three minutes the excellent Stephen was back. He set down on the tile floor beside my chair the largest of my four kitchen charcoal pots. It was half full of brightly glowing embers. I sent him away before I went into the house to fetch the painting. It is a curious fact that this faithful servitor of mine, a *zambo* or medium-brown Negro, and a native of St. Thomas, had manifested an increasing aversion to anything like contact with or even sight of the old picture, an aversion dating from that afternoon when he had discovered it, three years before, in the lumber room of my Santa Cruzian hired residence.

Then I brought it out and laid it flat, after clearing a place for it, on the large plain table which stands against the wall of the house on my gallery. Pelletier came over and stood beside me, and in silence we looked long and searchingly at Camilla Macartney's panorama for the last time.

Then, with the sharp, small blade of my pocketknife, I cut it cleanly through again and again until it was in seven or eight strips. A little of the brittle old paint cracked and flaked off in this process. Having piled the strips one on top of another, I picked up the topmost of the three or four spread newspapers which I had placed under the canvas to save the table top from my knife point, and these flakes and chips I poured first off the newspaper's edge upon the glowing embers. These bits of dry, ancient pigment hissed, flared up, and then quickly melted away. Then I burned the strips very carefully until all but one were consumed.

This, perhaps because of some latent dramatic instinct whose existence until that moment I had never really suspected, was the one containing the figure of Saul Macartney. I paused, the strip in my hand, and looked at Pelletier. His face was inscrutable. He nodded his head at me, however, as though to encourage me to proceed and finish my task.

With perhaps a trifle of extra care I inserted the end of this last strip into the charcoal pot.

It caught fire and began to burn through precisely as its predecessors had caught and burned, and finally disintegrated into a light grayish ash. Then a very strange thing happened—

There was no slightest breath of air moving in that sheltered corner of the gallery. The entire solid bulk of the house sheltered it from the steady northeast trade—now at three in the afternoon at its lowest daily ebb, a mere wavering, tenuous pulsing.

And yet, at the precise instant when the solid material of that last strip had been transmuted by the power of the fire into the whitish, wavering ghost of material objects which we name ash —from the very center of the still brightly glowing charcoal embers there arose a thin, delicate wisp of greenish-blue smoke which spiraled before our eyes under the impact of some obscure pulsation in the quiet air about us, then stiffened, as yet unbroken, into a taut vertical line, the upper end of which abruptly turned, curving down upon itself, completing the representation of the hangman's noose; and then, instantly, this contour wavered and broke and ceased to be, and all that remained there before our fascinated eyes was a kitchen charcoal pot containing a now rapidly dulling mass of rose-colored embers.

PART II

VOODOO ELSEWHERE AND OTHERWISE

THE ISLE OF VOICES

BY ROBERT LOUIS STEVENSON

Voodoo magic elsewhere and otherwise takes a variety of forms. One of the most fascinating is that of the early natives of the Hawaiian Islands, who believed that their sorcerers could read the stars, divine by the bodies of the dead and by the means of evil creatures, go alone into the highest parts of the volcanic mountains where the hobgoblins dwell and lay snares to entrap the spirits of the ancients. One such sorcerer is Kalamake, the wise man of the island of Molokai, who can make himself grow to such massive size that he is able to wade across the ocean and who can magically transport himself to the place called the Isle of Voices, where there is great wealth to be found—and the most fearful of all deaths as well.

Although it is not nearly as well known as The Strange Case of Dr. Jekyll and Mr. Hyde *and other macabre classics from the pen of Robert Louis Stevenson, "The Isle of Voices" ranks as one of his finest tales of this type. Not only is it beautifully and evocatively told, it also captures the voice and the spirit of Hawaii before the turn of the century with such deftness that it reads like native folklore. You'll not soon forget Kalamake, Keola, and the things that happen on the Isle of Voices. . . .*

Scottish novelist, essayist and poet Robert Louis Stevenson was born in Edinburgh in 1850 and studied both engineering and law before taking up writing in his middle twenties. Because he suffered from a respiratory illness, he traveled often in search of healthier climates; it was these travels, most notably those in America and in the South Seas, which led to such romantic adventure novels as Treasure Island, Kidnapped, The Master of the Ballantrae, *and* David Balfour, *and to such nonfiction travel and autobiographical works as* The Silverado Squatters, Across the Plains, *and* In the South Seas. *He also published collections of short stories* (The New Arabian Nights, Island Nights' Entertainments), *collections of essays and critical studies* (Virginibus Puerisque, Familiar Studies of Men and Books), *collections of poetry* (A Child's Garden of Verses, Underwoods, Ballads), *and novels in collaboration with his American stepson, Lloyd Osbourne* (The Wrong Box, The Wrecker). *He was only forty-four at the time of his death from tuberculosis in Samoa, where he had settled with his American wife five years before.*

KEOLA was married with Lehua, daughter of Kalamake, the wise man of Molokai, and he kept his dwelling with the father of his wife. There was no man more cunning than that prophet; he read the stars, he could divine by the bodies of the dead, and by the means of evil creatures: he could go alone into the highest parts of the mountain, into the region of the hobgoblins, and there he would lay snares to entrap the spirits of the ancients.

For this reason no man was more consulted in all the kingdom of Hawaii. Prudent people bought, and sold, and married, and laid out their lives by his counsels; and the king had him twice to Kona to seek the treasures of Kamehameha. Neither was any man more feared: of his enemies, some had dwindled in sickness by the virtue of his incantations, and some had been spirited away, the life and the clay both, so that folk looked in vain for so much as a bone of their bodies. It was rumored that he had the art or the gift of the old heroes. Men had seen him at night upon the mountains, stepping from one cliff to the next; they had seen him walking in the high forest, and his head and shoulders were above the trees.

This Kalamake was a strange man to see. He was come of the best blood in Molokai and Maui, of a pure descent; and yet he was more white to look upon than any foreigner; his hair the color of dry grass, and his eyes red and very blind, so that "Blind as Kalamake that can see across tomorrow," was a byword in the islands.

Of all these doings of his father-in-law, Keola knew a little by the common repute, a little more he suspected, and the rest he ignored. But there was one thing troubled him. Kalamake was a man that spared for nothing, whether to eat or to drink, or to wear; and for all he paid in bright new dollars. "Bright as Kalamake's dollars," was another saying in the Eight Isles. Yet he neither sold, nor planted, nor took hire—only now and then from his sorceries—and there was no source conceivable for so much silver.

It chanced one day Keola's wife was gone upon a visit to

Kaunakakai on the lee side of the island, and the men were forth at the sea-fishing. But Keola was an idle dog, and he lay in the verandah and watched the surf beat on the shore and the birds fly about the cliff. It was a chief thought with him always—the thought of the bright dollars. When he lay down to bed he would be wondering why they were so many, and when he woke at morn he would be wondering why they were all new; and the thing was never absent from his mind. But this day of all days he made sure in his heart of some discovery. For it seems he had observed the place where Kalamake kept his treasure, which was a lock-fast desk against the parlor wall, under the print of Kamehameha the fifth, and a photograph of Queen Victoria with her crown; and it seems again that, no later than the night before, he found occasion to look in, and behold! the bag lay there empty. And this was the day of the steamer; he could see her smoke off Kalaupapa; and she must soon arrive with a month's goods, tinned salmon and gin, and all manner of rare luxuries for Kalamake.

"Now if he can pay for his goods today," Keola thought, "I shall know for certain that the man is a warlock, and the dollars come out of the devil's pocket."

While he was so thinking, there was his father-in-law behind him, looking vexed.

"Is that the steamer?" he asked.

"Yes," said Keola. "She has but to call at Pelekunu, and then she will be here."

"There is no help for it then," returned Kalamake, "and I must take you in my confidence, Keola, for the lack of anyone better. Come here within the house."

So they stepped together into the parlor, which was a very fine room, papered and hung with prints, and furnished with a rocking-chair, and a table and a sofa in the European style. There was a shelf of books besides, and a family Bible in the midst of the table, and the lock-fast writing-desk against the wall; so that anyone could see it was the house of a man of substance.

Kalamake made Keola close the shutters of the windows, while he himself locked all the doors and set open the lid of the desk. From this he brought forth a pair of necklaces hung with charms and shells, a bundle of dried herbs, and the dried leaves of trees, and a green branch of palm.

"What I am about," said he, "is a thing beyond wonder. The men of old were wise; they wrought marvels, and this among the rest: but that was at night, in the dark, under the fit stars and in the desert. The same will I do here in my own house, and under the plain eye of day." So saying, he put the Bible under the cushion of the sofa so that it was all covered, brought out from the same place a mat of a wonderfully fine texture, and heaped the herbs and leaves on sand in a tin pan. And then he and Keola put on the necklaces and took their stand upon the opposite corners of the mat.

"The time comes," said the warlock, "be not afraid."

With that he set flame to the herbs, and began to mutter and wave the branch of palm. At first the light was dim because of the closed shutters; but the herbs caught strongly afire, and the flames beat upon Keola, and the room glowed with the burning; and next the smoke rose and made his head swim and his eyes darken, and the sound of Kalamake muttering ran in his ears. And suddenly, to the mat on which they were standing came a snatch or twitch, that seemed to be more swift than lightning. In the same wink the room was gone, and the house, the breath all beaten from Keola's body. Volumes of sun rolled upon his eyes and head, and he found himself transported to a beach of the sea, under a strong sun, with a great surf roaring: he and the warlock standing there on the same mat, speechless, gasping and grasping at one another, and passing their hands before their eyes.

"What was this?" cried Keola, who came to himself the first, because he was the younger. "The pang of it was like death."

"It matters not," panted Kalamake. "It is now done."

"And, in the name of God, where are we?" cried Keola.

"That is not the question," replied the sorcerer. "Being here, we have matter in our hands, and that we must attend to. Go, while I recover my breath, into the borders of the wood, and bring me the leaves of such and such an herb, and such and such a tree, which you will find to grow there plentifully—three handfuls of each. And be speedy. We must be home again before the steamer comes; it would seem strange if we had disappeared." And he sat on the sand and panted.

Keola went up the beach, which was of shining sand and coral, strewn with singular shells; and he thought in his heart:

"How do I not know this beach? I will come here again and gather shells."

In front of him was a line of palms against the sky; not like the palms of the Eight Islands, but tall and fresh and beautiful and hanging out withered fans like gold among the green, and he thought in his heart:

"It is strange I should not have found this grove. I will come here again, when it is warm, to sleep." And he thought, "How warm it has grown suddenly!" For it was winter in Hawaii, and the day had been chill. And he thought also, "Where are the gray mountains? And where is the high cliff with the hanging forests and the wheeling birds?" And the more he considered, the less he might conceive in what quarter of the islands he was fallen.

In the border of the grove, where it met the beach, the herb was growing, but the tree farther back. Now, as Keola went towards the tree, he was aware of a young woman who had nothing on her body but a belt of leaves.

"Well!" thought Keola, "they are not very particular about their dress in this part of the country." And he paused, supposing she would observe him and escape; and seeing that she still looked before her, he stood and hummed aloud. Up she leaped at the sound. Her face was ashen; she looked this way and that, and her mouth gaped with the terror of her soul. But it was a strange thing that her eyes did not rest upon Keola.

"Good day," said he. "You need not be so frightened, I will not eat you." And he had scarce opened his mouth before the young woman fled into the bush.

"These are strange manners," thought Keola, and, not thinking what he did, ran after her.

As she ran, the girl kept crying in some speech that was not practiced in Hawaii, yet some of the words were the same, and she knew she kept calling and warning others. And presently he saw more people running—men, women and children, one with another, all running and crying like people at a fire. And with that he began to grow afraid himself, and returned to Kalamake bringing the leaves. Him he told just what he had seen.

"You must pay no heed," said Kalamake. "All this is like a dream and shadows. All will disappear and be forgotten."

"It seemed none saw me," said Keola.

"And none did," replied the sorcerer. "We walk here in the broad sun invisible by reason of these charms. Yet they hear us; and therefore it is well to speak softly, as I do."

With that he made a circle round the mat with stones, and in the midst he set the leaves.

"It will be your part," he said, "to keep the leaves alight, and feed the fire slowly. While they blaze (which is but for a little moment) I must do my errand; and before the ashes blacken, the same power that brought us carries us away. Be ready now with the match; and do you call me in good time lest the flames burn out and I be left."

As soon as the leaves caught, the sorcerer leaped like a deer out of the circle, and began to race along the beach like a hound that has been bathing. As he ran, he kept stooping to snatch shells; and it seemed to Keola that they glittered as he took them. The leaves blazed with a clear flame that consumed them swiftly; and presently Keola had but a handful left, and the sorcerer was far off, running and stopping.

"Back!" cried Keola. "Back! The leaves are near done."

At that Kalamake turned, and if he had run before, now he flew. But fast as he ran, the leaves burned faster. The flame was ready to expire when, with a great leap, he bounded on the mat. The wind of his leaping blew it out; and with that the beach was gone, and the sun and the sea; and they stood once more in the dimness of the shuttered parlor, and were once more shaken and blinded; and on the mat betwixt them lay a pile of shining dollars. Keola ran to the shutters; and there was the steamer tossing in the swell close in.

The same night Kalamake took his son-in-law apart, and gave him five dollars in his hand.

"Keola," said he; "if you are a wise man (which I am doubtful of) you will think you slept this afternoon on the verandah, and dreamed as you were sleeping. I am a man of few words, and I have for my helpers people of short memories."

Never a word more said Kalamake, nor referred again to that affair. But it ran all the while in Keola's head—if he were lazy before, he would now do nothing.

"Why should I work," thought he, "when I have a father-in-law who makes dollars of seashells?"

Presently his share was spent. He spent it all upon fine clothes. And then he was sorry:

"For," thought he, "I had done better to have bought a concertina, with which I might have entertained myself all day long." And then he began to grow vexed with Kalamake.

"This man has the soul of a dog," thought he. "He can gather dollars when he pleases on the beach, and he leaves me to pine for a concertina! Let him beware: I am no child, I am as cunning as he, and hold his secret." With that he spoke to his wife Lehua, and complained of her father's manners.

"I would let my father be," said Lehua. "He is a dangerous man to cross."

"I care that for him!" cried Keola; and snapped his fingers. "I have him by the nose. I can make him do what I please." And he told Lehua the story. But she shook her head.

"You may do what you like," said she; "but as sure as you thwart my father, you will be no more heard of. Think of this person, and that person; think of Hua, who was a noble of the House of Representatives, and went to Honolulu every year: and not a bone or a hair of him was found. Remember Kamau, and how he wasted to a thread, so that his wife lifted him with one hand. Keola, you are a baby in my father's hands; he will take you with his thumb and finger and eat you like a shrimp."

Now Keola was truly afraid of Kalamake, but he was vain too; and these words of his wife's incensed him.

"Very well," said he, "if that is what you think of me, I will show how much you are deceived." And he went straight to his father-in-law.

"Kalamake," said he, "I want a concertina."

"Do you, indeed?" said Kalamake.

"Yes," said he, "and I may as well tell you plainly, I mean to have it. A man who picks up dollars on the beach can certainly afford a concertina."

"I had no idea you had so much spirit," replied the sorcerer. "I thought you were a timid, useless lad, and I cannot describe how much pleased I am to find I was mistaken. Now I begin to think I may have found an assistant and successor in my difficult business. A concertina? You shall have the best in Honolulu. And tonight, as soon as it is dark, you and I will go and find the money."

"Shall we return to the beach?" asked Keola.

"No, no!" replied Kalamake; "you must begin to learn more of my secrets. Last time I taught you to pick shells; this time I shall teach you to catch fish. Are you strong enough to launch Pili's boat?"

"I think I am," returned Keola. "But why should we not take your own?"

"I have a reason which you will understand thoroughly before tomorrow," said Kalamake. "Pili's boat is the better suited for my purpose. So, if you please, let us meet there as soon as it is dark; and in the meanwhile, let us keep our own counsel, for there is no cause to let the family into our business."

Honey is not more sweet than was the voice of Kalamake, and Keola could scarce contain his satisfaction.

"I might have had my concertina weeks ago," thought he, "and there is nothing needed in this world but a little courage." Presently after he spied Lehua weeping, and was half in a mind to tell her all was well.

"But no," thinks he; "I shall wait till I can show her the concertina; we shall see what the chit will do then. Perhaps she will understand in the future that her husband is a man of some intelligence."

As soon as it was dark father and son-in-law launched Pili's boat and set the sail. There was a great sea, and it blew strong from the leeward; but the boat was swift and light and dry, and skimmed the waves. The wizard had a lantern, which he lit and held with his finger through the ring, and the two sat in the stern and smoked cigars, of which Kalamake had always a provision, and spoke like friends of magic and the great sums of money which they could make by its exercise, and what they should buy first, and what second; and Kalamake talked like a father.

Presently he looked all about, and above him at the stars, and back at the island, which was already three parts sunk under the sea, and he seemed to consider ripely his position.

"Look!" says he, "there is Molokai already far behind us, and Maui like a cloud; and by the bearing of these three stars I know I am come to where I desire. This part of the sea is called the Sea of the Dead. It is in this place extraordinarily deep, and the floor is all covered with the bones of men, and in the holes of this part gods and goblins keep their habitation. The flow of the sea is to the north, stronger than a shark can swim, and any man who shall here be thrown out of a ship it bears away like a wild horse into the uttermost ocean. Presently he is spent and goes down, and his bones are scattered with the rest, and the gods devour his spirit."

Fear came on Keola at the words, and he looked, and by the light of the stars and the lantern, the warlock seemed to change.

"What ails you?" cried Keola, quick and sharp.

"It is not I who am ailing," said the wizard; "but there is one here sick."

With that he changed his grasp upon the lantern, and, behold —as he drew his finger from the ring, the finger stuck and the ring was burst, and his hand was grown to be the bigness of three.

At that sight Keola screamed and covered his face.

But Kalamake held up the lantern. "Look rather at my face!"

said he—and his head was huge as a barrel; and still he grew and grew as a cloud grows on a mountain, and Keola sat before him screaming, and the boat raced on the great seas.

"And now," said the wizard, "what do you think about that concertina? and are you sure you would not rather have a flute? No?" says he; "that is well, for I do not like my family to be changeable of purpose. But I begin to think I had better get out of this paltry boat, for my bulk swells to a very unusual degree, and if we are not the more careful, she will presently be swamped."

With that he threw his legs over the side. Even as he did so, the greatness of the man grew thirty-fold and forty-fold as swift as sight or thinking, so that he stood in the deep sea to the armpits, and his head and shoulders rose like the high isle, and the swell beat and burst upon his bosom, as it beats and breaks against a cliff. The boat ran still to the north, but he reached out his hand, and took the gunwale by the finger and thumb, and broke the side like a biscuit, and Keola was spilled into the sea. And the pieces of the boat the sorcerer crushed in the hollow of his hand and flung miles away into the night.

"Excuse me taking the lantern," said he; "for I have a long wade before me, and the land is far, and the bottom of the sea uneven, and I feel the bones under my toes."

And he turned and went off walking with great strides; and as soon as Keola sank in the trough he could see him no longer; but as often as he was heaved upon the crest, there he was striding and dwindling, and he held the lamp high over his head, and the waves broke white about him.

Since first the islands were fished out of the sea, there was never a man so terrified as this Keola. He swam indeed, but he swam as puppies swim when they are cast in to drown, and knew not wherefore. He could but think of the hugeness of the swelling of the warlock, of that face which was great as a mountain, of those shoulders that were broad as an isle, and of the seas that beat on them in vain. He thought, too, of the concertina, and shame took hold upon him; and of the dead men's bones, and fear shook him.

Of a sudden he was aware of something dark against the stars that tossed, and a light below, and a brightness of the cloven sea; and he heard speech of men. He cried out aloud and a voice answered; and in a twinkling the bows of a ship hung above him on a wave like a thing balanced, and swooped down. He caught with his two hands in the chains of her, and the next moment was buried in the rushing seas, and the next hauled on board by seamen.

They gave him gin and biscuit and dry clothes, and asked him how he came where they found him, and whether the light which they had seen was the lighthouse, Lae o Ka Laau. But Keola knew white men are like children and only believe their own stories; so about himself he told them what he pleased, and as for the light (which was Kalamake's lantern) he vowed he had seen none.

This ship was a schooner bound for Honolulu, and then to trade in the low islands; and by a very good chance for Keola she had lost a man off the bowsprit in a squall. It was no use talking. Keola durst not stay in the Eight Islands. Word goes so quickly, and all men are so fond to talk and carry news, that if he hid in the north end of Kauai or in the south end of Kaü, the wizard would have wind of it before a month, and he must perish. So he did what seemed the most prudent, and shipped sailor in the place of the man who had been drowned.

In some ways the ship was a good place. The food was extraordinarily rich and plenty, with biscuits and salt beef every day, and pea soup and puddings made of flour and suet twice a week, so that Keola grew fat. The captain also was a good man, and the crew no worse than other whites. The trouble was the mate, who was the most difficult man to please Keola had ever met with, and beat and cursed him daily, both for what he did and what he did not. The blows that he dealt were very sure, for he was strong; and the words he used were very unpalatable, for Keola was come of a good family and accustomed to respect. And what was the worst of all, whenever Keola found a chance to sleep, there was the mate awake and stirring him up with a rope's end. Keola saw it would never do; and he made up his mind to run away.

They were about a month out from Honolulu when they made the land. It was a fine starry night, the sea was smooth as well as the sky fair; it blew a steady trade; and there was the island on their weather bow, a ribbon of palm trees lying flat along the sea. The captain and the mate looked at it with the night glass, and named the name of it, and talked of it, beside the wheel where Keola was steering. It seemed it was an isle where no traders came. By the captain's way, it was an isle besides where no man dwelt; but the mate thought otherwise.

"I don't give a cent for the directory," said he. "I've been past here one night in the schooner *Eugenie:* it was just such a night as this; they were fishing with torches, and the beach was thick with lights like a town."

"Well, well," says the captain, "it's steep-to, that's the great point; and there ain't any outlying dangers by the chart, so we'll just hug the lee side of it. Keep her ramping full, don't I tell you!" he cried to Keola, who was listening so hard that he forgot to steer.

And the mate cursed him, and swore that Kanaka was for no use in the world, and if he got started after him with a belaying-pin, it would be a cold day for Keola. And so the captain and mate lay down on the house together, and Keola was left to himself.

"This island will do very well for me," he thought, "if no traders deal there, the mate will never come. And as for Kalamake, it is not possible he can ever get as far as this."

With that he kept edging the schooner nearer in. He had to do this quietly, for it was the trouble with these white men, and above all with the mate, that you could never be sure of them; they would all be sleeping sound, or else pretending, and if a sail shook, they would jump to their feet and fall on you with a rope's end. So Keola edged her up little by little, and kept all drawing. And presently the land was close on board.

With that, the mate sat up suddenly upon the house.

"What are you doing?" he roars. "You'll have the ship ashore!"

And he made one bound for Keola, and Keola made another clean over the rail and plump into the starry sea. When he came up again, the schooner had payed off on her true course and the mate stood by the wheel himself, and Keola heard him cursing. The sea was smooth under the lee of the island; it was warm besides, and Keola had his sailor's knife, so he had no fear of sharks. A little way before him the trees stopped; there was a break in the line of the land like the mouth of a harbor; and the tide, which was then flowing, took him up and carried him through. One minute he was without, and the next within, had floated there in a wide shallow water, bright with ten thousand stars, and all about him was the ring of the land with its string of palm trees.

The time of Keola in that place was in two periods—the period when he was alone, and the period when he was there with the tribe. At first he sought everywhere and found no man; only some houses standing in a hamlet, and the marks of fires. But the ashes of the fires were cold and the rains had washed them away; and the winds had blown, and some of the huts were overthrown. It was here he took his dwelling; and he made a fire drill, and a shell hook, and fished and cooked his fish, and climbed after green cocoanuts, the juice of which he drank, for in all the isle there was no water. The days were long for him, and the nights terrifying. He made a lamp of cocoa-shell, and drew the oil off the ripe nuts, and made a wick of fiber; and when evening came he closed up his hut, and lit his lamp, and lay and trembled till morning. Many a time he thought in his heart he would have been better in the bottom of the sea, his bones rolling there with the others.

All this while he kept by the inside of the island, for the huts were on the shore of the lagoon, and it was there the palms grew best, and the lagoon itself abounded with good fish. And to the outer side he went once only, and he looked but once at the beach of the ocean, and came away shaking. For the look of it, with its bright sand, and strewn shells, and strong sun and surf, went sore against his inclination.

"It cannot be," he thought, "and yet it is very like. And how do I know? These white men, although they pretend to know where they are sailing, must take their chances like other people. So that after all we have sailed in a circle, and I may be quite near to Molokai, and this may be the very beach where my father-in-law gathers his dollars."

It was perhaps a month later, when the people of the place arrived—the fill of six great boats. They were a fine race of men, and spoke a tongue that sounded very different from the tongue of Hawaii, but so many of the words were the same that it was not difficult to understand. The men besides were very courteous, and the women very towardly; and they made Keola welcome, and built him a house, and gave him a wife; and what surprised him the most, he was never sent to work with the young men.

And now Keola had three periods. First he had a period of being very sad, and then he had a period when he was pretty merry. Last of all, came the third, when he was the most terrified man in the four oceans.

The cause of the first period was the girl he had to wife. He was in doubt about the island, and he might have been in doubt about the speech, of which he had heard so little when he came there with the wizard on the mat. But about his wife there was no mistake conceivable, for she was the same girl that ran from him crying in the wood. So he had sailed all this way, and might as well have stayed in Molokai; and had left home and wife and all his friends for no other cause but to escape his enemy, and the place he had come to was that wizard's hunting ground, and the place where he walked invisible. It was at this period when he kept the most close to the lagoon side, and as far as he dared, abode in the cover of his hut.

The cause of the second period was talk he had heard from his wife and the chief islanders. Keola himself said little. He was never so sure of his new friends, for he judged they were too civil to be wholesome, and since he had grown better acquainted with his father-in-law the man had grown more cautious. So he told them nothing of himself, but only his name and descent, and that he came from the Eight Islands, and what fine islands they were; and about the king's palace in Honolulu, and how he was a chief friend of the king and the missionaries. But he put many questions and learned much. The island where he was was called the Isle of Voices; it belonged to the tribe, but they made their home upon another, three hours' sail to the southward. There they lived and had their permanent houses, and it was a rich island, where were eggs and chickens and pigs, and ships came trading with rum and tobacco. It was there the schooner had gone after Keola deserted; there, too, the mate had died, like the fool of a white man he was. It seems, when the ship came, it was the beginning of the sickly season in that isle, when the fish of the lagoon are poisonous, and all who eat of them swell up and die. The mate was told of it; he saw the boats preparing, because in that season the people leave that island and sail to the Isle of Voices; but he was a fool of a white man, who would believe no stories but his own, and he caught one of these fish, cooked it and ate it, and swelled up and died, which was good news to Keola. As for the Isle of Voices, it lay solitary the most of the year, only now and then a boat's crew came for copra, and in the bad season, when the fish at the main isle were poisonous, the tribe dwelt there in a body. It had its name from a marvel, for it seemed the seaside of it was all beset with invisible devils; day and night you heard them talking with one another in strange tongues; day and night little fires blazed up and were extinguished on the beach; and what was the cause of these doings no man might conceive. Keola asked them if it were the same in their own island where they stayed, and they told him no, not there; nor yet in any other of some hundred isles that lay all about them in that sea; but it was a thing peculiar to the Isle of Voices. They told him also that these fires and voices were ever on the seaside and in the seaward fringes of the wood, and a man might dwell by the lagoon two thousand years (if he could live so long) and never be any way troubled; and even on the seaside the devils did no harm if let alone. Only once a chief had cast a spear at one of the voices, and the same night he fell out of a cocoanut palm and was killed.

Keola thought a good bit with himself. He saw he would be all right when the tribe returned to the main island, and right enough where he was, if he kept by the lagoon, yet he had a mind to make things righter if he could. So he told the high chief he had once been in an isle that was pestered the same way, and the folk had found a means to cure that trouble.

"There was a tree growing in the bush there," says he, "and it seems these devils came to get the leaves of it. So the people of the isle cut down the tree wherever it was found, and the devils came no more."

They asked what kind of a tree this was, and he showed them the tree of which Kalamake burned the leaves. They found it hard to believe, yet the idea tickled them. Night after night the old men debated it in their councils, but the high chief (though he was a brave man) was afraid of the matter, and reminded them daily of the chief who cast a spear against the voices and was killed, and the thought of that brought all to a stand again.

Though he could not yet bring about the destruction of the trees, Keola was well enough pleased, and began to look about him and take pleasure in his days; and, among other things, he was the kinder to his wife, so that the girl began to love him greatly. One day he came to the hut, and she lay on the ground lamenting.

"Why," said Keola, "what is wrong with you now?"

She declared it was nothing.

The same night she woke him, and he saw by her face she was in sorrow.

"Keola," she said, "put your ear to my mouth that I may whisper, for no one must hear us. Two days before the boats begin to be got ready, go you to the seaside of the isle and lie in a thicket. We shall choose that place beforehand, you and I; and hide food; and every night I shall come near by there singing. So when a night comes and you do not hear me, you may know we are clean gone out of the island, and you may come forth again."

The soul of Keola died within him.

"What is this?" he cried. "I cannot live among devils. I will not be left behind upon this isle. I am dying to leave it."

"You will never leave it alive, my poor Keola," said the girl;

"for to tell you the truth, my people are eaters of men; but this they keep secret. And the reason they will kill you before we leave is because in our island ships come, and Donat-Kimaran comes and talks for the French, and there is a white trader there in a house with a verandah, and a catechist. Oh, that is a fine place indeed! The trader has barrels filled with flour; and a French warship once came in the lagoon and gave everybody wine and biscuit. Ah, my poor Keola, I wish I could take you there, for great is my love to you, and it is the finest place in the seas except Papeete."

So now Keola was the most terrified man in the four oceans. He had heard tell of eaters of men in the south islands, and the thing had always been a fear to him; and here it was knocking at his door. He had heard besides, by travelers, of their practices, and how when they are in a mind to eat a man, they cherish and fondle him like a mother with a favorite baby. And he saw this must be his own case; and that was why he had been housed, and fed, and wived, and liberated from all work; and why the old men and the chiefs discoursed with him like a person of weight. So he lay on his bed and railed upon his destiny; and the flesh curdled on his bones.

The next day the people of the tribe were very civil, as their way was. They were elegant speakers, and they made beautiful poetry, and jested at meals, so that a missionary must have died laughing. It was little enough Keola cared for their fine ways: all he saw was the white teeth shining in their mouths, and his gorge rose at the sight; and when they were done eating, he went and lay in the bush like a dead man.

The next day it was the same, and then his wife followed him.

"Keola," she said, "if you do not eat, I tell you plainly you will be killed and cooked tomorrow. Some of the old chiefs are murmuring already. They think you are fallen sick and must lose flesh."

With that Keola got to his feet, and anger burned in him.

"It is little I care one way or the other," said he. "I am between the devil and the deep sea. Since die I must, let me die the quickest way; and since I must be eaten at the best of it, let me rather be eaten by hobgoblins than by men. Farewell," said he, and walked to the seaside of that island.

It was all bare in the strong sun; there was no sign of man, only the beach was trodden, and all about him as he went, the voices talked and whispered, and the little fires sprang up and burned down. All tongues of the earth were spoken there: the French, the Dutch, the Russian, the Tamil, the Chinese. Whatever land knew sorcery, there were some of its people whispering in Keola's ear. That beach was thick as a cried fair, yet no man seen; and as he walked he saw the shells vanish before him, and no man to pick them up. I think the devil would have been afraid to be alone in such a company; but Keola was past fear and courted death. When the fires sprang up, he charged for them like a bull. Bodiless voices called to and fro; unseen hands poured sand upon the flames; and they were gone from the beach before he reached them.

"It is plain Kalamake is not here," he thought, "as I must have been killed long since."

With that he sat him down in the margin of the wood, for he was tired, and put his chin upon his hands. The business before his eyes continued; the beach babbled with voices, and the fires sprang up and sank, and the shells vanished and were renewed again even while he looked.

"It was a by-day when I was here before," he thought, "for it was nothing to this."

And his head was dizzy with the thought of these millions and millions of dollars, and all these hundreds and hundreds of persons culling them upon the beach, and flying in the air higher and swifter than eagles.

"And to think how they have fooled me with their talk of mints," says he, "and that money was made there, when it is clear that all the new coin in all the world is gathered on these sands! But I will know better the next time!" said he. And at last, he knew not very well how or when, sleep fell on Keola, and he forgot the island and all his sorrows.

Early the next day, before the sun was yet up, a bustle woke him. He awoke in fear, for he thought the tribe had caught him napping; but it was no such matter. Only, on the beach in front of him, the bodiless voices called and shouted one upon another, and it seemed they all passed and swept beside him up the coast of the island.

"What is afoot now?" thinks Keola. And it was plain to him it was something beyond ordinary, for the fires were not lighted nor the shells taken, but the bodiless voices kept posting up the beach, and hailing and dying away; and by the sound of them these wizards should be angry.

"It is not me they are angry at," thought Keola, "for they pass me close."

As when hounds go by, or horses in a race, or city folk coursing to a fire, and all men join and follow after, so it was now with Keola; and he knew not what he did, nor why he did it, but there, lo and behold! he was running with the voices.

So he turned one point of the island, and this brought him in view of a second; and there he remembered the wizard trees to have been growing by the score together in a wood. From this point there went up a hubbub of men crying not to be described;

and by the sound of them, those that he ran with shaped their course for the same quarter. A little nearer, and there began to mingle with the outcry the crash of many axes. And at this a thought came at last into his mind that the high chief had consented; that the men of the tribe had set to cutting down these trees; that word had gone about the isle from sorcerer to sorcerer, and these were all now assembling to defend their trees. Desire of strange things swept him on. He posted with the voices, crossed the beach, and came into the borders of the wood, and stood astonished. One tree had fallen, others were part hewed away. There was the tribe clustered. They were back to back, and bodies lay, and blood flowed among their feet. The hue of fear was on all their faces; their voices went up to heaven shrill as a weasel's cry.

Have you seen a child when he is all alone and has a wooden sword, and fights, leaping and hewing with the empty air? Even so the man-eaters huddled back to back and heaved up their axes and laid on, and screamed as they laid on, and behold! no man to contend with them! only here and there Keola saw an axe swinging over against them without hands; and time and again a man of the tribe would fall before it, clove in twain or burst asunder, and his soul sped howling.

For a while Keola looked upon this prodigy like one that dreams, and then fear took him by the midst as sharp as death, that he should behold such doings. Even in that same flash the high chief of the clan espied him standing, and pointed and called out his name. Thereat the whole tribe saw him also, and their eyes flashed, and their teeth clashed.

"I am too long here," thought Keola, and ran farther out of the wood and down the beach, not caring whither.

"Keola!" said a voice close by upon the empty sand.

"Lehua! is that you!" he cried, and gasped, and looked in vain for her; but by the eyesight he was stark alone.

"I saw you pass before," the voice answered; "but you would not hear me. Quick! get the leaves and the herbs, and let us flee."

"You are there with the mat?" he asked.

"Here, at your side," said she. And felt her arms about him. "Quick! the leaves and the herbs, before my father can get back!"

So Keola ran for his life, and fetched the wizard fuel; and Lehua guided him back, and set his feet upon the mat, and made the fire. All the time of its burning, the sound of the battle towered out of the wood; the wizards and the man-eaters hard at fight; the wizards, the viewless ones, roaring out aloud like bulls upon a mountain, and the men of the tribe replying shrill and savage out of the terror of their souls. And all the time of the burning, Keola stood there and listened, and shook, and watched how the unseen hands of Lehua poured the leaves. She poured them fast, and the flame burned high, and scorched Keola's hands, and she speeded and blew the burning with her breath. The last leaf was eaten, the flame fell, and the shock followed, and there were Keola and Lehua in the room at home.

Now, when Keola could see his wife at last he was mighty pleased, and he was mighty pleased to be home again in Molokai and sit down beside a bowl of poi—for they made no poi on board ships, and there was none in the Isle of Voices—and he was out of the body with pleasure to be clean escaped out of the hands of the eaters of men. But there was another matter not so clear, and Lehua and Keola talked of it all night and were troubled. There was Kalamake left upon the isle. If, by the blessing of God, he could but stick there, all were well: but should he escape and return to Molokai, it would be an ill day for his daughter and her husband. They spoke of his gift of swelling and whether he could wade that distance in the seas. But Keola knew by this time where that island was—and that is to say, in the Low or Dangerous Archipelago. So they fetched the atlas and looked upon the distance in the map, and by what they could make of it, it seemed a far way for an old gentleman to walk. Still, it would not do to make too sure of a warlock like Kalamake, and they determined at last to take counsel of a white missionary.

So the first one that came by Keola told him everything. And the missionary was very sharp on him for taking the second wife in the low island; but for all the rest, he vowed he could make neither head nor tail of it.

"However," says he, "if you think this money of your father's ill-gotten, my advice to you would be to give some of it to the lepers and some to the missionary fund. And as for this extraordinary rigmarole, you cannot do better than keep it to yourselves." But he warned the police at Honolulu that, by all he could make out, Kalamake and Keola had been coining false money, and it would not be amiss to watch them.

Keola and Lehua took his advice, and gave many dollars to the lepers and the fund. And no doubt the advice must have been good, for from that day to this, Kalamake has never more been heard of. But whether he was slain in the battle by the trees, or whether he is still kicking his heels upon the Isle of Voices, who shall say?

POWERS OF DARKNESS

BY JOHN RUSSELL

Some men never learn, it seems. This seems especially true of those who travel far from their "civilized" homelands to take up residence among primitive cultures, usually for the purpose of exploitation; men who strip away their own veneer of civilization and revert to attitudes and actions far more atavistic than those of the natives. The antagonist in "Powers of Darkness," Dobel, is such a man, and Papua, New Guinea, in the early 1900s is such a place.

But Dobel makes the mistake of underestimating a certain native sorcerer at Warange Station. The sorcerer's magic is great: he can turn pandanus seeds into yellow and crimson moths and then make them melt away into the shadows; he can bring a dead crocodile back to life merely by stroking it from head to tail. And even greater are the powers of darkness, particularly when a brutish nonbeliever like Dobel makes it necessary to call on them. The result is as satisfying as it is strange.

John Russell was a master of the wry, suspenseful and unusual adventure tale, of which "Powers of Darkness" is a fine example. (He also wrote excellent popular and crime fiction.) Born in Iowa in 1885, he wandered the world during the first few decades of this century and spent a considerable amount of time in the South Seas, where many of his staggering total of sixteen hundred short stories are set. The best of his work has been favorably compared to that of Kipling and O. Henry and can be found in such collections as The Red Mark *(a.k.a.* Where the Pavement Ends*),* Cops 'n Robbers, In Dark Places, *and* Far Wandering Men. *During and after World War II he wrote and adapted scripts for several Hollywood film companies, and continued writing until his death in 1956.*

NICKERSON, R.M., failed in judgment concerning his guest Dobel. This was the reason of his ordeal that night at Warange Station: a black night and a bitter ordeal. If Dobel had been a cannibal or a headhunter—wandering thief or fugitive murderer—Nickerson would have made no mistake. But himself he was a gentle soul, trained merely in all forms of conceivable wickedness, and although he disliked the gross stranger with the sly and slitted red eyes he had no intimation of the fellow's real nature. Not until Dobel showed such an utterly brutal manner of disbelief.

At the very first demonstration of the native Sorcerer—at the very first piece of native magic which Nickerson had been at diplomatic pains to stage and arrange for him—Dobel grabbed an empty beer bottle. "You black-faced swine. Dried shark liver!" he rumbled. "Try and fool me with your dam' faking tricks, will you?"

He made a motion as if to crown the Sorcerer, kneeling quietly there on the mat beside them, when Nickerson let out a cry, involuntary. "For God's sake, stop it, Dobel. Stop it—I say, you drunken idiot. . . . The man's my friend!"

Evidently Dobel had not really meant it just then: it was rather his line of humor, his revealing gesture. For he stopped and put down the bottle and leaned back in his chair again, with a grunt.

The two white men were sitting at dinner in Nickerson's palisaded station at the far end of the world. By way of information, the far end of the world is Papua. This is not only geographic, it is also entirely authentic, being well known to everybody who has survived it in person. Papua remains the last mystery on this big round globe. It remains largely impenetrable and unpenetrated beyond a coastal strip and a few gold mines. It remains an active hell of heat, fever, violence and sudden death. In fact, it remains . . . Whenever a hard-working explorer casts about for some place to get lost and to write his next book, he considers Papua on the map and then goes somewhere else.

However: Nickerson was used to it. For some years he had been what is called a "Resident Magistrate" in the nominal government thereabouts. This meant that he personated the whole British Empire over a theoretical "District" of monstrous mountains and reeking jungles. It also meant that he was supposed to control various unconquered tribes of large, muscular and extremely serious-minded black gentlemen who have been cannibals and headhunters from time immemorial and who see no particular reason why they should change their habits at the behest of strange armed intruders. As if messengers from Mars should sud-

denly descend upon us and make us all eat grass. But Nickerson
had done very well. With his handful of native police he had won
his wilder charges to a moderate righteousness. He liked his work:
yes, and he liked his black folk, because he respected them as lost
ancestors of ours left over from the Stone Age, with many singular
gifts and virtues of their own. So they in turn respected him, and
even obeyed him sometimes.

Dobel. . . . Well, Dobel was quite a different person. Nickerson
had received him as he did all dispensations, with the same kindly
simplicity, and with no more than a vague suspicion that there
occurs from time to time such sort of commercial adventurer for
the chastening of every colonial administrator—inevitable as the
worm in a walnut. Arriving from nowhere, equipped with creden-
tials, a brazen assurance and an unholy familiarity with the waterfront dives and lingos of a dozen tropical ports, Dobel had announced himself a coffee planter proposing to develop the
country. In which capacity, of course, he could claim aid, hospital-
ity and protection at Nickerson's station of Warange. This he
managed off-hand, and meanwhile conveyed without too much
subtlety an opinion of his host, his host's ideas, methods and
general worth that might have provoked the mildest man. But
Nickerson—poor chap!—he was the mildest man. And thus one
word leading to another, and because after all they were the only
two whites (outside the Brothers at Warange Mission) in a howling wilderness together, the little R.M. had finally invited his
uninvited guest to the private proof and demonstration as hereinbefore stated.

He was already sorry for it. He was due to be a great deal
sorrier. . . .

"Make him do it again."

"That's not quite fair, is it?" protested Nickerson.

"Didn't you say you'd show me some native stuff I couldn't explain?"

"I did. And you couldn't. And many others have tried—and couldn't."

"Well, you called him a friend," sneered Dobel. "Is he afraid to try it over?"

All this while the Sorcerer had stayed resting on his mat beside the table. Certainly there never was a sorcerer less under implication that he should roll up his sleeves. Naked except for a bark strip about his middle, he resembled some image in polished basalt from before the days of Egypt. Anywhere else he would have been amazing: here he was magnificent, with the features of an ancient Assyrian king—the hooked nose of power and the mouth of imperious pride. He stayed motionless and inscrutable, as becomes a high chief and a master of magic in Papua, until at Nickerson's quiet word again he proceeded to oblige.

Now, his magic was this:

Taking in his hands a few loose seeds of pandanus, with appropriate incantation he tossed them sharply into the lamplight. There they hung suspended an instant, when they took miraculous life of their own, spreading the wings of yellow and crimson moths that fluttered and circled as a brilliant flake-storm—melting away at last with the shadows.

At least, so it seemed, and the seeming was a gracious and a harmless fancy.

Perhaps such qualities were especially irritating to Dobel. Perhaps one of those synthetic insects flipped past and made him jump. Or perhaps the true animus of the man lay bedded in something deeper, of which his skepticism was merely the fat layer. At any rate, he liked it no better than the first time: once more he flushed with evil anger.

"Dam' blasted faker! Pig-snout—" he began to growl. But once more he checked abruptly: and this time for a very special reason.

A new and surprising figure had just glided in between the bead curtains of the inner verandah, carrying a tray with their next relay of drink.

Through their meal together the two white men had been waited upon by Nickerson's houseboys: rough-handed and half-tamed products of the cannibal frontier. But this was a girl! A girl, and the like of a girl to draw the bloodshot gaze of any Dobel, East or West. "What—ho!" he gurgled.

A native girl in a white man's house?

What made it better (or worse), she was attractive by any standard: slim and lithe. She wore a single white garment of the sort supplied by missionary enterprise for the suppression, one supposes, of the female form divine. But this garment had been often laundered, and if its effect was not displeasing the young lady herself seemed not unaware. No. If old Mother Hubbard had garbed her, old Mother Eve had endowed this copper-bronze child of hers with something much more elemental. It showed in the provocative face with sweeping lashes. It showed in the willing grace with which she leaned over to pour Dobel's glass. Timidly. Yet not too timidly, either. . . .

Well, of course there are things that merely happen, and there are other things that merely are not done. All depends upon how you look at them and how much you know. And who should know better than Dobel, who seemed to know everything?

"Well, *well*—!" he murmured, very softly, for him. He looked with great favor. He looked with very particular favor. Nickerson

was paying the girl no attention whatsoever. Neither was the
Sorcerer. Which left Dobel her sole appreciator.

He was highly appreciative. He watched while she filled the
drinks. He watched and let his slow gaze run along the smoothly
perfect contour of cheek and arm. He continued to watch when
she moved noiselessly away to the bead curtains, and there paused
to flash back a look at the gross white man that made him wet
his thick lips and chuckle in his thick throat. . . . Nevertheless it
was his further humor to say nothing about her—to make no
comment. Not yet. When he did speak, he was grinning.

"Ah. Very pretty. But it's only tricks."

"You saw what he did?"

"I saw something. But I hate to be fooled by a nigger. No—
nor anybody else!" added Dobel, with a red glint. "Nobody fools
me much!"

"Dobel—" Nickerson was almost pathetic. "It's my job to steer
you through and make you successful, and all that. But if you're
going to stay in this country you'll have to change your way with
these people. One thing: you must never use that word. They're
not—what you said. They're not a subject race at all. And we hold
them none too safe, if you know what that means. . . . Heavens,
man—you can't hit a native!"

"No?" drawled the other. "You can't hit 'em. And you can't
love 'em either, maybe?"

"That's true."

"I've heard a lot of such talk. . . . It don't mean a blasted thing."

"It means we're dealing with one of the most powerful chiefs
—a gentleman in his own fashion. It means he has to be treated
properly."

Dobel gave a bark of amusement. "Listen: I've dealt with all
shades of natives, black to pea-green—for twenty years. D'you

think you can teach me anything? If you do—carry on with the show!"

Nickerson hesitated. He had lived too long in the unaccountable spaces of the earth: he had forgotten how to account for a type like Dobel. He served a friendless Service, devil-ridden by political amateurs (Papua is not a Crown Colony, worse luck!). But, poor pay and all, he needed his place for his family back home. What if this annoying, accredited guest should start up complaints at headquarters? The mere thought gave him a shiver familiar to every empire-builder. Did people really act so? As a matter of fact, he could not tell: any more than he could judge just how drunk Dobel might be: any more than he could gauge the precise peril behind those sly and slitted eyes. At the present moment the fellow seemed not too awfully drunken—he was keeping a grin quite amiable with his gaze fixed over yonder toward the curtains somewhere. . . .

All of which will indicate the perplexity of Nickerson, R.M., and the reason of his mistake, as aforesaid. For presently he consulted again with the Sorcerer. (It was curious how he gained ease and confidence with that language.)

"I'm sorry, Dobel," he announced at last. "The old boy doesn't much fancy you."

"No?"

"No. He says if men like you had been the only white men in Papua, he would own a lot of fine smoked heads. . . . I'm quoting his drift."

"Yes?"

"Yes. And for that reason, as nearly as I can make out, he is willing to show you just one more thing you *can't* explain."

"Carry on," repeated Dobel.

Now, the only visible possessions of the Sorcerer were these: on one side of him his keen little belt-axe, and on the other his grass-woven sack. The weapon he had discarded in courtesy. The sack he kept for his oddments and conjuring stuff—his bag o' tricks, so to speak.

From out of that bag he dragged forth next an object which he threw with a limp flop on the mat before them. Not a pleasing object. It was a baby crocodile about ten inches long, and quite evidently it had passed some time ago from this crocodile vale of tears. It was already blue, the scales loosening from it. "He wants you to be sure this creature is dead," explained Nickerson.

"Faugh! . . . Guess I know a dead croc!"

"You're sure?"

"Of course," growled Dobel.

"Then hold tight," said Nickerson.

The Sorcerer exhibited a fragment of ordinary greenstone, delicately shaped, about the size of an arrowhead. Taking it between finger and thumb like a pencil, he began carefully to stroke the point. Then very gently, very slowly, he stroked the crocodile from head to tail. Some way, but in the way of an artist, he brought to that fantastic employ a silent suspense that grew and grew almost tangibly. Kneeling there in the aura of light, the big black man stroked gently—gently. And slowly—slowly, the result appeared on the dead animal. A pulsation ran through its flanks. Its scales brightened to a pallid green, firmed and quivered. All at once its sunken lids lifted on two gleaming, pin-pricked nodules. It stood propped on its four legs. And at the final touch —impossibly, unbelievably—with a flirt and a whisk it rattled over the mattings and was gone! The thump of its escape outside made an end to that manifestation—also an end to Dobel's restraint.

He rose with a roar. He wanted no bottle this time. All he used

was his fist, and a fist cruel as a knotted club, and he swung it with
scientific impact squarely to the jaw.

Like a cloud across the moon, like the dark wind that slashes
some sunny beach, so quickly they turned from comedy to tragedy
—never far apart anywhere, it may be, but surely never as close
as in this strange, deep and untamed land: tragicomedy and tragedy not very comic in Papua. . . .

"Good God!" Nickerson whispered.

As if stricken by the same foul blow he dropped on one knee
by the victim who lay limp and helpless as any crocodile, an inert
heap. "You beast. . . . You unspeakable beast!"

Dobel stayed straddled. "That's a' right. 'S only a sleep punch."

"How—*how* could you!"

"Time enough, too. I told you nobody was making a fool of
me."

"Fool—? Have you any sense of what you've done? All his
fighting men are camped outside the gates. Enough to swamp us,
and the whole district! . . . Death is out there. *Death!*"

True, in the hush they might have been aware of Papua around
them, stirring in the night. From the savage camp came the soft
throb of a tom-tom, like the beating of a heart. A sigh passed in
the jungle, stealthy and sinister—a hot breath that is like nothing
except a tiger's throat.

But it meant nothing to Dobel—he only stayed grinning—and
the sight of his hateful, impervious sneer was more than Nickerson could stand: it drove him near to madness. "Besides—when
I—when I said he was my friend!" he half-sobbed, and simply
threw himself at the fellow. Another mistake and about the worst
possible, of course, though doubtless the sort Dobel had been
playing for. Gleefully he took the little R.M., twisted him easily
as a banana stalk, slammed him against the wall.

Appalled—almost stunned—still Nickerson made the proper official effort. "That stops it, Dobel. You're going out of here. I'll have you deported. On the coasting-steamer tomorrow. . . . Consider yourself under arrest, sir!" With a shaking hand he felt for the police whistle on a cord about his neck.

Before he could touch it, Dobel ripped it away and bulked over him, the whole brutal assurance of the man projected like a cliff.

"*Me* going out? Y' sop and weakling—why, that's exactly what I come to do for *you!* . . .

"You didn't guess it yet? Why, I knew all about you, Mister Resident Magistrate, before I ever started here. Sure. Your record at headquarters: y'r silly reports on native habits and customs and such. Ho!" He gave his bark of laughter. " 'Habits an' customs.' Soon as I saw that, I knew where I'd catch you. Says I, 'Leave him to me. I'll get that dam' nigger-loving R.M. out of there!' "

Dazed—bewildered—still Nickerson was able to ask the proper official question.

" 'Order'?" echoed Dobel. "Order be blowed. No—I ain't in your service. I represent a company that gives their orders to any service. We hold a concession for this distric'. But first we reckoned to be rid of you. And how easy you made it! What? Did you never hear of laws and regulations—Section 89—against 'witchcraft or sorcery, or pretense to same'? And don't I find you promoting sorcery your own silly self, Mister Magistrate Nickerson?"

"You—you wanted it."

"Sure, did I. I wanted to see how much I could pin onto you. And if I needed any more—" Dobel's voice rose to a virtuous bellow. "If that ain't enough—don't I find you here in your own house with a good-lookin' brown girl?"

"Girl? . . . That girl?" stammered the unfortunate R.M. "Why, she's a Mission girl. From Warange Mission. She came over tonight because her father was here. The chief—the Sorcerer—he's her father!"

"Eyewash. D' you think I can't tell that kind? With her free-for-all ways? . . . Another one of your 'native habits,' I suppose!"

Poor Nickerson. "You're wrong. . . . On my honor!" This was what he gasped, and it deserves to live as a tribute to the female persuasion at large: "They only act so. It's—it's nothing against them. Only they can't help themselves—some of 'em!"

Whereat Dobel did laugh.

"My colonial oath. Of all the soft sops! Wait till I tell that for headquarters!"

True enough, it was naïve comedy close to grim tragedy again. True enough, it was Dobel's entire triumph. He laughed. He straddled there, the hateful and conquering fellow, with his red grin directed over Nickerson's shoulder toward the bead curtains. He finished his last drink. He stretched his great arms. "Well, that'll do for entertainment. I'll just be mooching along to my bungalow. . . . I'm taking that steamer tomorrow, you know. . . . Oh. I'll be back. Yes, yes! Only I got to file my report, you see—the report that's going to scupper y'r job for you, Mister Nonresident! Meanwhile, many thanks for the show."

And he swaggered out.

Poor R.M. He was like a man overtaken in a nightmare. It was not so much the insult, the humiliation that had been put upon him. It was not even the inevitable loss of post and pay. What wrung him was his mistake—his failure to judge and to understand the given crisis: as every empire-builder should and must. Did such things really happen? They seemed incredible—far beyond any magic.

This was the ordeal of Nickerson. R.M., when he turned mechanically to attend again on his stricken performer—and found the place empty. The Sorcerer had vanished. . . .

Outside lay Papua, primitive and incalculable: Papua, where mystery and death wait on every move. What could he do? To be sure, he had two armed sentries at the station gate. To be sure, he might rouse the rest of his police from their barrack. What good would his handful be, against Papua? . . . A wind sighed in the swamps and the trees—heady as the essence of vitality— heavy as the scent of a slaughterhouse. From the cannibal camp just beyond his flimsy palisade the tom-tom kept throbbing: and his own pulse kept time with it. Nobody else could have listened with such agony for another sound—like the gather and snarl of a breaking wave. Nobody else could have visioned so vividly the horror that has overwhelmed and blotted in blood so many outposts. (In Papua.)

It was rather with some vague idea of finishing more or less on his own feet with his face in front that he reeled over toward the bead curtains of the verandah and peered through.

A dim glint of moonshine slanted across the parade ground and made visible its sandy strip. And more besides. Something curious, and curiously illuminated and illuminating. Over yonder, by the clump of croton bushes. Over yonder, near the guest bungalow: two figures, interlaced. One a great hulking white man who held clipped in his arms a native woman: the other the slim, thin-garmented native woman who clung quite willingly to the white man. . . .

Well, there are things which happen and there are things which are not done: the burden is in judging them aright even among strange and dark spaces. But in that flash that burden was lifted from Nickerson, R.M. For then he understood, at last. Then it dawned upon him—the real nature of his guest and enemy. Then it came clear, what he had failed to conceive: the wickedness rejecting all belief and all decency—the only actual power of darkness.

A gentle chap, kindly and mild and earnest to the verge of simplicity, so indeed he was, as hereinbefore stated. But then he remembered that he was the administrator responsible for Warange Station. Then he also remembered that he represented in his own person on the pay of a chimney-sweep the whole British Empire. And further, for the first time that night, he remembered the pistol strapped on his thigh! His hand fell to it. As if released with a steel spring in all his slight frame, he took a single jump over the verandah and out onto the parade-ground.

He was just too late. At the same instant Papua had chosen her own tragedy once more. An inky shape rose out of the croton bushes. A polished belt-axe gleamed in the moonlight. . . . A sweeping gesture—a choking cry—and a cloud closing swiftly as a wink.

When Nickerson reached them, the two figures were still interlaced more or less, though rather differently. The man could scarcely hold the woman, sinking from his paralyzed arms. It was Nickerson who received her as she fell, limp and voiceless. It was Nickerson unaided who carried her back the entire distance. Finally it was Nickerson who brought her into his house and laid her carefully on the mat beside his table.

She looked quite handsome, the good-looking native girl—under the lamp. But her fringed lashes were lowered with no provocation now, and her graceful copper-bronze body was now neither timid nor bold, only pitiful and elemental. . . . Nickerson knelt beside it. His hands never shook. His face never altered. He had the deft detachment of any trained surgeon as he made his examination, and straightened up.

"She's dead."

"Good God—!" stammered Dobel.

"I suggest you had better make sure of that fact yourself. . . ."

"How could—how could she be—?"

"Instantaneous, I think. A blow at the base of the skull. But I would ask you to verify."

Dobel? . . . Dobel could verify nothing. The big, gross and swaggering fellow had gone like a punctured bladder of lard. He was all of a sop of terror: his joints sagging under him, the sweat steaming from his flabby cheeks and the eyes starting in his head. He tried to speak and made no more than whimpering noises in his thick throat.

Nickerson considered him, gauged him with one contemptuous scalpel glance and dismissed him from immediate mind. Nickerson had never been calmer in all his years of work. Icy and aloof, he stayed thinking, with the images and the measures of all his knowledge running clear—everything he had ever learned about his people—everything that had given him his control of cannibal and headhunter, wandering thief and fugitive murderer. And his thoughts followed somewhat along this line:

How had the Sorcerer escaped? To the right, into the crotons. What lay behind him? The palisade, surmountable, but sharp with spikes. What lay in front? The open parade-ground. And to the left—? The gate, and the only exit from Warange. . . . Meanwhile there had been no alarm, and the tom-tom was still drumming quietly outside. . . .

He shifted his pistol to his left hand. He edged with infinite precaution toward the verandah entrance. He poised silently by the curtains. From there, on a venture desperate as the last gasp of a swimmer—necessary as the last leap from under an avalanche

—from there he launched himself into outer shadow. And . . . simply plucked forth the black crouching bulk he found in that exact concealment!

The Sorcerer had nothing much to remark: there is little even a Sorcerer can say with the muzzle of eternity pressing against his ear. He had nothing much to do except precisely as he was told: there is little else for anybody when he feels the oiled click of a large-sized automatic pistol jarring into his bones. Besides, as Nickerson explained to him (it was interesting how explicit and convincing the R.M. could be with that language)—besides, the plain choice was between one corpse and two corpses: life or death: just an ordinary matter for adjustment any hour and any minute in Papua.

So presently the Sorcerer was kneeling on the mat again, in the same spot under the lamplight, as before. And presently he had opened his bag of oddments and conjuring stuff, and had brought out a fragment of greenstone shaped like an arrowhead—as before. And presently, with the subject of his demonstration in proper position—very gently, very slowly—he began to stroke— precisely as before. . . . And thereafter the souls of two white men —watching—were drawn from their roots and whirled upward . . . were tossed and torn in a suspense almost intolerable . . . waiting . . . while they glimpsed the depths of lost and forgotten fantasies in the backward abysm of time. . . .

The garrison of Warange Station are a very smart drill. They have often proved it, and it does them credit, and they are rather swanky about it. They are only a handful of native police. But they have practiced the call to arms, even at midnight, until they can do it generally—starting on the unannounced toot of the whistle —in something close to two minutes. (Nickerson's weekly reports are always meticulous in stating such details.) On this particular occasion it could hardly have been more than a few seconds over the two minutes when the little command stood ready.

The gates had been closed and the sentries doubled. Corporals Arigita and Sione had arrived one pace to the front. Behind them clicked to attention a rank of six privates—kilts, rifles and bandoliers complete. While Sergeant Bio, a prince of noncoms, stepped forward on the verandah before the wide-opened curtains in the lamplight, and saluted.

"Company under arms, *Tabauda!*"

The R.M. inspected them for a moment. They noticed nothing unusual about him. Except perhaps a certain added ring in his tone and a certain stiffening of his parade-ground manner as he snapped his orders.

What he said to the corporals was:

"Sione and Arigita—you see this fella black girl? You walk along with her one time to Mission House. You escort her safe and leave her there!" Whereat the corporals saluted, received their charge and tramped away, stolidly.

What he said to the sergeant was:

"Bio—you see this fella white man here? You take him and lock him in the lock-up. With irons if necessary. Tomorrow he goes by the coast-steamer. And he does not come back!" Whereat Bio saluted, fell in the prisoner between two guards, and started, smartly.

What the prisoner said, as he was led off nearly weeping, was: "Oh God—get me out of here! Take me away from this dam' country. . . . Oh, take me away!"

What Nickerson said to the Sorcerer was little more than a formal apology, ceremoniously delivered, for events that had happened. But what the Sorcerer said to Nickerson in reply deserves to be recorded.

They were alone there in Nickerson's house. The Sorcerer stood proud and inscrutable as a carven Assyrian statue—dignified as becomes a high chief and a master of magic and a gentleman in his own fashion, in Papua. And his answer substantially was this:

"*Tabauda:* nothing has happened. It has been a pleasant evening between friends. I am much honored by my visit. I am gratified if I have entertained you with my poor art. It is my hope that your days may be long in this land—and I would ask your lordly permission to depart!"

From outside in Papua somewhere there sounded the peaceful throbbing of a tom-tom. . . .

EXÚ

BY EDWARD D. HOCH

In Rio de Janeiro and other parts of Brazil, application of the voodoo form called Macumba is widespread. Spirit cults such as Umbanda, Quimbanda and Candomblé have large followings and even hold black magic ceremonies on Copacabana beach in the heart of Rio, with thousands of candles aglow, cabalistic signs drawn in the sand, worshipers gyrating in circles to the beat of drums and praying to Saravá, Yemanjá, the Old Black Slave and the devil Exú.

This story, brief though it is, vividly portrays the spiritist movement in modern Brazil—and serves up more than its fair share of goosebumps in the bargain. But "Exú" is also a thinking person's horror story: what you are witness to and what you are told in the final few hundred words may or may not be taken literally, and is open to more than one interpretation. In voodoo, as in other aspects of life, the answers are not always easy and obvious.

Born a half-century ago in upstate New York, Edward D. Hoch toiled in an advertising agency before and after beginning his *literary career in the mid-1950s. In the past twenty-five years he has published more than five hundred and fifty short stories in the mystery, fantasy/horror, science fiction and Western categories; four novels, three of which are science fiction mysteries; and four collections of stories, including two—*City of Brass *and* The Judges of Hades—*about Simon Ark, a man who claims to be 2,000 years old. Hoch has also edited one anthology for the Mystery Writers of America (who awarded his "The Oblong Room" an Edgar as the best short story of 1968) and the last five volumes of the annual* Best Detective Stories of the Year. *He lives with his wife in Rochester, New York, where at present he supports himself solely by writing short fiction.*

 ALMOST from the moment he arrived in Rio de Janeiro, Jennings knew he had come to the right place. There was something garish about the sights and sounds of the great city —something exotic and just a bit dangerous. He saw it in the paintings displayed at news kiosks, where pictures of Christ and Saint Sebastian vied for space with the spiritist divinities such as Yemanjá and the Old Black Slave.

And he heard it in the voices of the people, and in their music. That December a decade-old song of Rio, *Garôta de Ipanema*— "Girl from Ipanema"—was popular again and he heard it sung in Portuguese in the bars and cafes of the city.

He listened, and felt the old excitement building within him. On his second night in Rio he approached a singer at the conclusion of her act and invited her to join him for a drink. She stared at him, apparently sizing him up, and then accepted.

"Are you new to the city?" she asked, sipping at the tall glass before her. "You speak the language very well."

"New, yes. I am only here on a visit." He laid a one-hundred-cruzeiros banknote on the table between them. "I need some excitement."

"I do not—" she began, looking frightened.

"Where can I find voodoo?" he asked quietly, and the sound of his voice was almost obscured by the beat of the music.

She pushed the banknote away. "There is no voodoo in Rio. Only the spirit cults. Rio is a Catholic city."

"Then tell me of the spirit cults. Tell me of Quimbanda."

She shook her head. "I know nothing of this," she insisted.

Jennings grew impatient. He added a second banknote to the first. "I listened while you sang. I heard it in the lyrics of your song —the mention of Saravá and Yemanjá and the other spirit gods. Tell me where I can worship them."

She cast her dark eyes down at the table, studying the money. Finally she said, "Quimbanda is a cult of black magic. They worship the devil Exú."

"Where?" he asked again.

Her reply was so soft he barely heard it. "The cemetery of Inhaúma. Go there any night. Close to midnight." She scooped up the banknotes and was gone from his table.

Outside the cemetery a young woman with coal-black hair sat against a wall selling candles. Jennings was struck by the beauty of her face as he dropped a few coins in her cup and accepted a candle in return. A number of expensive cars were drawn up at the cemetery gates, and he could see the light of a hundred candles flickering in the blackness among the tombstones.

"Are you here every night?" he asked the young woman.

"Every night. They come to make an offering to Exú."

"The devil."

She shrugged. "If you wish."

He gestured toward the flickering lights. "Do you believe?"

"I only sell candles."

He left her and walked among the gravestones then, passing a black man eating fire as a circus entertainer might. There were bowls of food on the tombstones, offerings to the devil. Cigars were scattered about, and bottles of some strong-smelling alcoholic drink. There were black chickens with their throats cut, and the head of a goat resting in a bowl of its own blood.

And always the people, just beyond the edge of shadow, watching him.

Suddenly his arm was gripped from the side, and he saw a man all in black pull him away. It took him an instant to realize the man was a priest.

"You do not belong here," the priest said to him. "Come with me!"

Jennings followed him into the darkness, more curious than anything else. "I hardly expected to meet a priest here," he said at last. "These people are worshiping the devil."

"Not worshiping," the priest corrected, his pale face reflecting the candlelight. "Only making their foolish sacrifices to a deity who does not listen. My name is Father Aaral, and I have a parish church near here. I saw at once that you were not one of them, from the way you boldly walked among the tombstones. The cemetery at midnight is not a safe place for outsiders."

"I have come here to study the spirit cults," Jennings said.

"To study or to worship? This is not a new religion, my friend.

It is, in fact, a very old religion. Come back to the rectory with me and I will give you some coffee while we talk."

The December night was warm and Jennings had to remind himself it was only two days until New Year's Eve. He had never gotten used to the Southern Hemisphere with its seasonal reverses. But he went with Father Aaral, because he had seen enough for the moment of dead chickens and beheaded goats.

"The spirit cults of Rio," the priest began when they were settled in his rectory study, "are very closely allied with the Catholic Church. That is not surprising in a country that is ninety-three percent Catholic. Like the more traditional voodoo cults of the West Indies, they are a combination of African cult worship and elements borrowed from the Catholic religion. The cult of Candomblé climaxes its month-long initiation ceremony by taking new members—their heads shaven and bodies painted—to hear a Catholic mass in a church or cathedral. I have had them in my church on occasion."

"But the people in the cemetery tonight were not merely natives. Some were well-dressed white families."

"Quimbanda is a black magic subsidiary of the Umbanda cult. It is very dangerous because in worshiping the devil one attracts all sorts. I go to the cemetery because I have heard rumors of human sacrifice, though I have never seen any."

"I have come a long way to study these things," Jennings said.

"Be careful you do not study them too well."

"Where would you suggest I go?"

Father Aaral sighed. "In two nights it will be New Year's Eve. Go to the Copacabana beach and see the Umbanda pay special homage to the ruling divinity of the sea, Yemanjá."

"Yemanjá," Jennings repeated. "Yes, I have seen the pictures. A beautiful dark-haired goddess coming from the water."

"That is Yemanjá, and the coming of the new year is her night. Go there, and perhaps you will find what you seek."

"Thank you, father," Jennings said.

But in two nights' time he went instead to the cemetery once more, because the place held a strange fascination for him. He saw again the lovely dark-haired girl who sold candles by the entrance and wondered if she might be the sea goddess Yemanjá. "We must go to the beach later," he told her, but she only smiled.

Inside the gates the candles flickered once more, and the silent worshipers waited with their offerings. One young woman scattered popcorn, because that was said to be the devil's favorite delicacy. Another broke a bottle of liquor, scattering blue flame over the flickering candles.

He walked among them as he had two nights ago, turning occasionally from side to side. He saw the blood of the chickens, and came at last to the large bowl that had held the goat's head.

Tonight it held something else.

Tonight it held the head of Father Aaral.

He was running then, terrified, wanting only to get away. He had gone some distance before he realized that the dark-haired young woman was running with him. He held her hand, and they might have been lovers off on a spree.

"Where are we going?" she asked him once.

"To the beach. It's almost midnight."

"I am not Yemanjá," she told him. "That is all a dream."

But he ran on, dragging her along. "Did you see that back there?" he asked after a time, when they'd paused for breath. "In the cemetery?"

"I have seen many things in the cemetery. Sometimes it is better not to see too much."

They crossed the serpentine mosaic of Copacabana's prome-

nade and hurried across the beach. There were more candles here
—thousands of candles—and magical signs drawn in the sand.
There were pictures of the blue-clad Yemanjá, and a virginal
statue of her. And always the worshipers, moving in their circles.
Occasionally some would venture into the surf, casting a bouquet
of flowers or an offering of jewelry to the goddess of the sea.

"She will come at midnight," Jennings said.

"She will never come," the woman at his side said.

They moved further along the beach where all was frenzy and
the worshipers beat their drums while others whirled and gyrated
to the music. Here a medium with a ritual cigar told a fortune,
while another lit a final row of candles in the form of a cross.

It was midnight at last, and Jennings fell to his knees before
the young woman. "Behold, Yemanjá has come!" he shouted.

But the worshipers paid him no heed, because they knew this
was only the poor girl who sold candles at the cemetery.

"She did not come," the young woman said, helping him to his
feet. "There is no Yemanjá."

"There must be!" he insisted. "She must be here! She must be
real!"

"Why?"

"Because I am Exú," he said at last. "I am Exú and I am real."

"The devil." She said it simply, neither believing nor disbeliev-
ing.

"I am the one they worship back there, with their candles and
popcorn and orgies at midnight. I walked among them and they
did not recognize me. Even the priest did not recognize me."

"I recognize you, Exú," she told him.

The chanting grew louder all around them, and he reached out
his arm to her. "How can I tell them? How can I tell them that
I have no use for their blood and chickens and heads of priests?

There is more evil in the mind of man than even I would have thought possible."

"I will tell them for you," she said. "I will tell them tomorrow."

"By tomorrow I will be elsewhere."

Presently they slept there on the beach together, and at the first light of dawn when the young woman awakened she saw that the man named Jennings was no longer beside her. As far as she could see down the beach there was no sign of him.

She waded into the surf to wash herself, and as she emerged a young girl brought her flowers, thinking she was Yemanjá.

SEVENTH SISTER

BY MARY ELIZABETH COUNSELMAN

There were many superstitions involved in the voodoo and conjuring practices of blacks in the Old South. But perhaps the most unusual is that of the Seventh Sister—the seventh girl baby in a family, born on a night when the squinch-owl hollers and a dog howls three times and a martin gets into the house and batters its brains out against the walls before anyone can set it free. For she has the Power: she can touch warts and make them disappear; she can make bullbats fly out of the dusk; she can cause birds to die with blood on their feathers by pointing a chicken bone at them and shouting, "Bang, bang! Boom!"

The "Seventh Sister" here, however, is even stranger than most: she was born an albino. Her translucent pink eyes and cotton-colored hair frighten her brothers and sisters as much as her Power, and make her even more of an outcast; yet she wants desperately to belong, so desperately that she'll do almost anything for a little affection. Her tragic and poignant story, told in the plantation-black dialect of the pre-Depression years, has been hailed as a superior work in the field of weird fantasy.

Mary Elizabeth Counselman is an Alabaman by birth (in 1911) and still makes her home in that state. Shortly after attending the University of Alabama and Montevallo University, she began writing and selling stories to Collier's, The Saturday Evening Post, Good Housekeeping, Ladies' Home Journal, Weird Tales *and other magazines. She is considered by many to be the foremost woman writer of macabre fiction at work today; her recent Arkham House collection,* Half in Shadow, *which contains fourteen of her finest stories, gives strong support to that claim.*

 THE night Seven Sisters was born, a squinch-owl hollered outside the cabin from sundown until the moment of her birth. Then it stopped its quavering cry. Everything stopped—the whippoorwills in the loblollies; the katydids in the fig tree beside the well; even the tree-frogs, burring their promise of rain as "sheet lightning" flickered across the black sky.

The row of slave cabins behind the Old Place looked ramshackle and deserted; had been deserted, for a fact, ever since Grant took Richmond. Daylight or a moon would have shown their shingle roofs fallen in and their sagging porches overgrown with jimson weed and honeysuckle. Only one cabin was livable now and inhabited. Dody, grandson of a Saunders slave, had wandered back to the Old Place, with a wife and a flock of emaciated little pickaninnies.

They had not thrived on odd-job fare in the city. So Dody had come home, the first year of the Depression, serenely certain of his welcome. He knew Cap'm Jim and Miss Addie would give them a cabin with a truck garden, in return for whatever sporadic labor was needed on the old rundown plantation smack on the Alabama-Georgia line.

That was in '29, six years ago. Miss Addie was dead now and buried in the family cemetery on the south hill. Most of the land had been sold to meet taxes. Miss Addie's grandson, Cap'm Jim, alone was left. Cap'm Jim was a baby doctor in Chattanooga. He kept the Old Place closed up except for weekend trips down with his wife and two young sons.

The red clay fields lay fallow and uncultivated. The rail fences had fallen, and even the white-columned Place itself was leaky and in need of paint. Whenever Dody or Mattie Sue thought of it, they had one of the young-uns sweep the leaves and chicken-sign from the bare sanded clay of the front yard. But aside from that weekly chore, they had the deserted plantation all to themselves, and lived accordingly. The children grew fat and sassy on yams and chitterlings. Dody drank more homebrew and slept all day in the barrel-slat hammock. And Mattie cooked, quarreled and bore another pickaninny every year. . . .

That is, until Seven Sisters was born.

That night a squinch-owl hollered. And somewhere beyond the state highway, a dog howled three times. More than that, one of the martins, nesting in the gourd-pole in front of the cabin, got into the house and beat its brains out against the walls before anyone could set it free.

Three Signs! Small wonder that at sundown Mattie Sue was writhing in agony of premature childbirth. Not even the two greased axes, which Ressie and Clarabelle—her oldest unmarried daughters; aged fifteen and seventeen—had placed under her bed to cut the pain, did any good.

"Oh, Lawsy—Mammy done took bad!" Ressie whimpered.

She hovered over the fat groaning black woman on the bed, eyewhites large and frightened in her pretty Negro face. Ressie had seen many of her brothers and sisters come into the world. But always before, Mattie Sue had borne as easily and naturally as a cat.

"Do, my Savior!" Clarabelle whispered. "We got to git somebody to midwife her! Aunt Fan. . . . Go 'long and fotch her, quick! Oh, Lawsy. . . ." she wailed, holding high the kerosene lamp and peering down at the woman in pain. "I . . . I'se sho skeered. . . . What you waitin' on, fool? Run! . . . Oh, Lawsy, mammy . . . mammy?"

Ressie plunged out into the night. The *slap-slap* of her bare feet trailed into silence.

The cabin's front room was very still. Save for the regular moaning of Dody's wife—and an occasional snore from Dody himself, drunk and asleep on the kitchen floor—there was no sound within. The other children were clustered in one corner, silent as young foxes. Only the whites of their eyes were visible against the dark. Clarabelle tiptoed about in her mail-order print dress, her chemically straightened hair rolled up on curlers for the church social tomorrow.

Light from the sooty lamp threw stunted shadows. The reek of its kerosene and the smell of Negro bodies blended with the pungent odor of peaches hung in a string to dry beside the window. Hot summer scents drifted in: sun-baked earth, guano from the garden, the cloying perfume of a clematis vine running along the porch rafters.

It was all so familiar—the smells, the night-sounds. The broken and mended furniture, discarded by four generations of Saunderses. The pictures tacked on the plank walls—of a snow-scene, of a Spanish dancer, of the president—torn from old magazines

Cap'm Jim and Miss Ruth had cast aside. The last year's feed-store calendar, dated January 1934. The gilded wreath, saved from Miss Addie's funeral, now decorating the mantel with its purple and gilt ribbon rain-marred to read: ABID WI H MF.

Even the childbirth scene was familiar to all of Mattie's children except the youngest. And yet. . . .

There was an eerie quality about the night, throwing the familiar out of focus. The young-uns felt it, huddled, supperless, in the corner while Clarabelle fluttered ineffectually about the bed and its burden. It was so hot and oppressive, with a curious air of waiting. Even a rumble of thunder along the horizon sounded hushed and furtive.

And the screech-owl's cry drifted nearer.

The woman on the bed writhed and moaned again. Clarabelle twisted her black hands together, bright with pink nail polish— relic of the winters spent in Chattanooga as nurse for Cap'm Jim's youngest. She went to the open door for a fourth time, listening for the sound of approaching footsteps.

Aunt Fan had a cabin down the road about half a mile, and had washed for the Andrews as far back as anyone remembered. She was a church woman; in fact, one of her three husbands had been a preacher before he knifed a man and got sent away to prison. If anyone could help Mattie Sue in her extremity, it would be Aunt Fan. . . .

The squinch-owl wailed again. Clarabelle drew a quick circle on the cabin floor and spat in it. But the moaning of her mother went on and on, incoherent, rising and falling as though in imitation of the owl's ill-omened call.

Clarabelle stiffened, listening. The hurried *crunch-crunch* of shod feet came to her ears at last. With a gasp of relief she ran out to meet the pair—Ressie, returning, and a tiny wizened old

Negress with a wen in the center of her forehead, jutting out like a blunt horn.

"Aunt Fan, what I tell you? Listen yonder!" Ressie whimpered. "Dat ole squinch-owl been holl'in' fit to be tied ever since sundown!"

The old midwife poised on the porch step, head cocked. She grunted, and with a slow, precise gesture took off her apron, to don it again wrong-side out.

"Dah. Dat oughta fix 'im. What-at Mattie Sue? My land o' Goshen, dat young-un don't b'long to get borned for two month yet! She been workin' in de garden?"

"Well'm. . . ." Clarabelle started to lie, then nodded, contrite. "Seem like she did do a little weedin' yestiddy. . . ."

"Uh-huh! So dat's hit! I done tole her! Dat low-down triflin' Dody. . . ." Aunt Fan, with a snort that included all men, switched into the cabin.

Outside, the screech-owl chuckled mockingly, as though it possessed a deeper knowledge of the mystery of birth and death.

Ressie and Clarabelle hunched together on the front stoop. Through the door they could hear Aunt Fan's sharp voice ordering the pickaninnies out of her way into the kitchen. Mattie Sue's regular moaning had risen in timbre to a shrill cry. Clarabelle, squatting on the log step of the porch, whispered under her breath.

"Huh!" Ressie muttered. "Ain't no use prayin' wid dat ole squinch-owl holl'in' his fool head off! Oh, Lawsy, Clary, you reckon Aunt Fan can . . . ?"

The older girl shivered but did not reply. Her eyes, wide and shining from the window's glow, swept across the flat terrain. Fireflies twinkled in the scrub pines beyond the cornfield. A muffled roar from above caught her ear once. She raised her head.

Wing lights on a transport plane, racing the storm from Birmingham to Atlanta, winked down at her, then vanished in the clouds.

" 'Leb'm-thirty," she murmured. "Less hit's late tonight. . . . Daggone! If'n dat ole fool don't shet up his screechin'. . . ." She hushed herself, sheepishly fearful of her own blasphemy.

Of course there was nothing to all that stuff her mammy and Aunt Fan had passed down to them, huddling before the fire on rainy nights. Signs! Omens! Juju . . . Cap'm Jim had laughed and told them, often enough, that. . . .

The girl started violently. From the cabin a scream shattered the night. High-pitched. Final.

Then everything was still. The tree-frogs. The quarreling katydids. The whippoorwills. The muttering thunder. A trick of wind even carried away the sound of the transport plane.

And the screech-owl stopped hollering, like an evil spirit swallowed up by the darkness.

A few minutes later Aunt Fan came to the door, a tiny bundle in her arms swaddled in an old dress of Mattie's. The girls leaped to their feet, wordless, eager.

But the old Negress in the doorway did not speak. She was murmuring something under her breath that sounded like a prayer—or an incantation. There was a sinister poise to her tiny form framed in the lighted doorway, silent, staring out into the night.

Suddenly she spoke.

"Clary honey . . . Ressie. You' mammy done daid. Wan't nothin' I could do. But . . . my soul to Glory! Hit's somep'm funny about dis gal-baby! She white as cotton! I reckon yo' mammy musta had a sin on she soul, how come de Lawd taken her. . . ."

Clarabelle gasped a warning. A broad hulk had blotted out the lamplight behind Aunt Fan—Dody, awake, still drunk, and mean.

A tall sepia Negro, wearing only his overalls, he swayed against the door for support, glowering down at the bundle in Aunt Fan's arms.

"Woods-colt!" Dody growled. "I ain't gwine feed no woods-colt. . . . Git hit on out'n my cabin! I got eight young-uns o' my own to feed, workin' myself down to a frazzle. . . . Git hit on out, I done tole you!" he snarled, aiming a side swipe at Aunt Fan that would have knocked her sprawling if it had landed.

But the old Negress ducked nimbly, hopped out onto the porch, and glared back at Dody. Her tiny black eyes glittered with anger and outrage, more for herself than for the squirming handful of life in her embrace.

"You Dody Saunders!" Aunt Fan shrilled. "You big low-down triflin' piece o' trash! I gwine tell Cap'm Jim on you! Jes' wait and see don't I tell 'im! Th'owin' Mattie's own baby out'n de house like she want nothin' but a mess o' corn shucks! And Mattie layin' daid in yonder. . . ."

Dody swayed, bleary eyes trying to separate the speaker from her alcoholic image.

"Daid? M-mattie Sue . . . my Mattie Sue done daid? Oh, Lawsy —why'n you tell me . . . ?"

His blunt, brutal features crumpled all at once, childlike in grief. He whirled back into the cabin toward the quilt-covered bed. "Mattie?" the three on the porch heard his voice. "Mattie honey? Hit's your Dody—say somep'm, honey. . . . Don't sull up like dat and be mad at Dody! What I done now? . . . Mattie . . . ?"

Clarabelle and Ressie clung together, weeping.

Only Aunt Fan was dry-eyed, practical. In the dark she looked down at the mewling newborn baby. And slowly her eyes widened.

With a gesture almost of repugnance the old woman held the

infant at arm's length, peering at it in the pale glow from the open cabin door.

"My Lawd a-mercy!" she whispered. "No wonder Mattie Sue died a-birthin' dis-heah one! Makes no diff'rence if'n hit's a woods-colt or not, dis heah chile. . . ."

She stopped, staring now at Clarabelle and Ressie. They paused in their grieving, caught by Aunt Fan's queer tone. The old woman was mumbling under her breath, counting on her black fingers; nodding.

"Dat ole squinch-owl!" Ressie sobbed. "I knowed it! If'n hit hadn't a-hollered, mammy wouldn't. . . ."

"Squinch-owl don't mean nothin' tonight," Aunt Fan cut in with an odd intensity. "Eh, Lawd, hit's jes' stomp-down nachel dat a squinch-owl'd come around to holler at dis-heah birthin'. Nor neither hit wouldn't do no good to put no axes under Mattie's bed, nor do no prayin'. You know why? Dis-heah young-un got six sisters, ain't she? Dat makes she a seb'm-sister! *She gwine have de Power!*"

Like a solemn period to her words, a clap of thunder boomed in the west, scattering ten-pin echoes all over the sky.

"Yessirree, a seb'm-sister," Aunt Fan repeated, rubbing the wen on her wrinkled forehead for good luck. "Y'all gwine have trouble wid dis chile! Hit's a pyore pity she didn't die alongside she mammy."

Ressie and Clarabelle, saucer-eyed, peered at their motherless newborn sister, at her tiny puckered face that resembled nothing so much as a small monkey. But she was *white*, abnormally white! Paler than any "high yaller" pickaninny they had ever seen; paler even than a white baby. Her little eyes were a translucent watery pink. Her faint fuzz of hair was like cotton.

"De Lawd he'p us to git right!" Clarabelle whispered in awe.

"What us gwine do wid her? Pappy won't leave her stay here—
not no woods-colt, and *sho* not no seb'm-sister! Will you keep
care of her, Aunt Fan? Anyways, till after de funeral?"

The old Negress shook her head. With flat emphasis she thrust
the wailing bundle into Ressie's arms, and stumped down the
porch step.

"Nawsuh, honey! Not me! Hit say in de Good Book not to have
no truck wid no conjure 'oman. And dat little seb'm-sister of
yourn gwine be a plain-out, hard down conjure 'oman, sho as you
born! . . . Jes' keep her out in de corncrib; Dody won't take no
notice of her. Feed her on goat's milk. . . . Mm-mmm!" Aunt Fan
shook her head in wonder. "She sho is a funny color!"

It was a month after Mattie's funeral before Cap'm Jim came
down to the Old Place again with the boys and Miss Ruth. When
he heard, by neighborhood grapevine, that Dody's new baby was
being hidden out in the corncrib like an infant Moses, he stormed
down to the cabin with proper indignation.

He took one startled look at the baby, white as a slug that has
spent its life in darkness under a rock. Pink eyes blinked up at him
painfully. The little thing seemed to be thriving very well on
goat's milk, but the corncrib was draughty and full of rats. Cap'm
Jim attacked Dody with the good-natured tyranny of all Deep-
Southerners toward the darkies who trust and depend upon them.

"I'm ashamed of you, boy!"—Dody was over ten years older
than Dr. Saunders. "Making your own baby sleep out in a corncrib, just for some damn-fool notion that she's a hoodoo! And of
course she is your own baby. She's just an albino; that's why she's
so white."

Dody bobbed and scratched his head. "Yassuh, cap'm? Sho
nuff?"

"Yes. It's a lack of pigment in the skin . . . er. . . ." Dr. Saunders floundered, faced by the childlike bewilderment in the big Negro's face. "I mean, she's black, but her skin is white. She . . . Oh, the devil! You take that child into your cabin and treat her right, or I'll turn you out so quick it'll make your head swim!"

"Yassuh . . ." Dody grinned and bobbed again, turning his frayed straw hat around and around by the brim. "Yassuh, cap'm . . . You ain't got a quarter you don't need, is you? Seem like we's plumb out o' salt and stuff. Ain't got no nails, neither, to mend de chicken house. . . ."

Dr. Saunders grunted and handed him fifty cents. "Here. But if you spend it on bay rum and get drunk this weekend, I'll tan your hide!"

"Naw*suh!*" Dody beamed, and guffawed his admiration of the bossman's unerring shot. "I ain't gwine do dat, cap'm! Does you want me for anything, jes' ring de bell. I'll send Clarabelle on up to look after de boys."

Dody shambled off, grinning. Cap'm Jim let out a baffled sigh. He strode back toward the Place, well aware that Dody would be drunk on dime-store bay rum by nightfall, and that the big rusty plantation bell in the yard would clang in vain if he wanted any chores performed. But he had laid the law down about the new baby, and that order at least would be obeyed.

"A pure albino!" he told his wife later, at supper. "Poor little mite; it's amazing how healthy she is on that treatment! They won't even give her a name. They just call her Seven Sisters . . . and cross their fool fingers every time she looks at 'em! I'll have to say, myself, she is weird-looking with that paper-white hair and skin. Oh, well—they'll get used to her. . . ."

Cap'm Jim laughed, shrugged and helped himself to some more watermelon pickle.

Dody, with his fifty cents, rode mule-back to the nearest town five miles away. In a fatherly moment, while buying his bay rum at the five-and-ten, he bought a nickel's worth of peppermints for the young-uns. He bought salt, soda, and some nails.

Plodding back home up the highway, he passed Aunt Fan's cabin and hailed her with due solemnity.

"Us sho got a seb'm-sister, all right," he called over the sagging wire gate, after a moment of chitchat. "Cap'm Jim say she ain't no woods-colt. He say she black, but she got pigmies in de skin, what make her look so bright-colored. Do, my Savior! I bet she got de blue-gum! I sho ain't gwine let her chaw on my fingers like them other young-uns when she teethin'! I ain't fixin' to git pizened!"

"Praise de Lawd!" Aunt Fan answered noncommittally, rocking and fanning herself on the front stoop. "Reckon what-all she gwine be up to when she old enough to be noticin'? Whoo-ee! Make my blood run cold to study 'bout it!"

Dody shivered, clutching his store-purchases as though their prosaic touch could protect him from his own thoughts. If there was any way to get rid of the baby, without violence. . . . But Cap'm Jim had said his say, and there was nothing for him to do but raise her along with the others.

It was a fearful cross to bear. For, Seven Sisters began to show signs of "the Power" at an early age. She could touch warts and they would disappear; if not at once, at least within a few weeks. She would cry, and almost every time, a bullbat would fly out of the dusk, to go circling and screeching about the cabin's fieldstone chimney.

Then there was the time when she was three, playing quietly in the cabin's shade, her dead-white skin and hair in freakish contrast with those of her black brothers and sisters. The other pickaninnies were nearby—but not too near; keeping the eye on her demanded by Clarabelle without actually playing with her.

Willie T., five, was playing train with a row of bricks tied on a string. Booger and Gaynelle, twins of eight, were fishing for jackworms—poling a blade of grass down each hole, and jerking up the tiny dragonlike insects. Lula and Willene and Buzz, aged twelve, nine and thirteen, were engaged in a game of squat tag under the fig trees. They were not paying much attention to their queer-colored sister, though from time to time she glanced at them wistfully.

Willie T. it was who happened to look up and see the bird clumsily winging along overhead in the clear June sky. He pointed, not greatly interested.

"Look at dat ole shypoke!" Snatching up a stick, he aimed it at the flapping target, closed one eye and shouted: *"Bang! Bang! Babloom!"* in imitation of Cap'm Jim's rifle. The bird flew on.

The other children glanced up idly. Only the little albino, lonesome and longing for attention, feigned an interest in this byplay. Squinting eagerly up at the distant bird, she pointed the old chicken foot with which she was playing, and trebled in mimicry of her brother: *"Bang, bang! Boom!"*

And a weird, incredible thing happened.

The shypoke, flapping along, wavered suddenly, one wing drooping. With a lurching, fluttering motion it veered—then fell like a plummet, striking the ground not three yards from where the little girl sat.

Willie T. stared. The bird was dead. There was blood on its feathers.

In a stunned, silent, wide-eyed group, Mattie's other children backed away from their ghostly sister. She blinked at them, her pinkish eyes squinting painfully in the sunlight.

"*Bang-bang* . . . ?" Seven Sisters repeated in a hopeful under-
tone.

There was a shuffle of running feet. Her lower lip quivered
when she saw that she had been left alone.

She was always alone after that, partly because the other children shunned her, and partly because she could not see well
enough to run after them. She had developed a peculiar squint,
holding her tow-head to one side, slit-eyed, upper lip drawn back
to show her oddly pointed little teeth. For a "seven-sister" she
tripped over things and hurt herself twice as often as her brothers
and sisters who were not gifted with supernatural powers.

Cap'm Jim, on a flying visit to the plantation one Sunday, had
noticed the way the child kept always to the shadowy places.

"Weak eyes," he pronounced. "Typical of albinos. Have to get
her some special glasses. . . ." He sighed, mentally adding up his
vanishing bank account. "Oh, well—time enough when she starts
to school. Though, Lord help the little thing at recess!"

That preference for shadow was given another connotation by
dark-skinned observers.

"Dah! Ain't I done tole you?" Aunt Fan was triumphant. "See
jes' like a cat in de dark, but can't see hardly nothin' in de
daytime. Yessirree—she a plain-out, hard-down conjure 'oman,
and I knowed hit de first time I sot eyes on her!"

By this time, the lone screech-owl which had attracted Seven
Sister's birth had become seven screech-owls, hovering in a ring
around the cabin to demand Mattie's soul in return for the new
baby's "Power."

This "Power" mystified Seven Sisters, though she did not
doubt that she had it. Clarabelle and Dody had told her so, ever
since she could understand words. Now a thin, too-quiet child of
six, she accepted the fact as simply and sadly as one might accept
having been born with an interesting club-foot. But, because it

was the only way in which she could attract attention—half fear, half respect—the little albino drew on her imagination, and did not herself know where fact ended and fancy began.

The other children jeered at her but were frankly envious. The elders laughed and remarked that nobody but "ig'nant country niggers" believed in conjures any more.

Secretly they came to her by night, and hissed at her window, and proffered silver in return for her magic. Seven Sisters never saw any of the money, however, as the business was always transacted through Clarabelle or Dody.

Some of the things they wanted were incomprehensible to her at first. Mojoes—tiny bags of cloth that might contain anything at all, plus the one thing only she possessed: "the Power." In Atlanta, in Birmingham, and Memphis, especially in Harlem, a good one might sell for as much as ten dollars. These, according to whatever words the conjurer mumbled over them, were able to perform all sorts of miracles for the wearer—from restoring the affection of a bored mate to insuring luck in the numbers game.

Seven Sisters, with the precocity of all outcasts, caught the idea early. Like the little girls who started the witch-scare in Salem, she felt pains and saw apparitions for the bug-eyed approval of kin and neighbors. She made up words and mumbled them on every occasion, squinting weirdly and impressively. She hummed tuneless little chants, in the eerie rhythm of all darkies. She memorized the better-known household "conjures"; such as, burying three hairs from the end of a hound's tail under the front steps to keep him from straying. With a ready wit she invented new ones, then forgot them and supplied others on call.

True, most of these tricks had, at one time or another, been subtly suggested by Aunt Fan or Clarabelle as the proper procedure for a "seven-sister." But the little albino, pleased and excited by any substitute for affection, threw herself into the part—a pale wistful Shirley Temple in the role of Cybele.

She wanted to be admired, however. She did not want to be feared.

But even Clarabelle, who loved her in a skittish way one might grow to love a pet snake, gave her a wide berth after the incident of the stomachache.

It happened one sultry August day when Dody came stumbling into the cabin, drunker than usual and in a nasty mood.

"Whah dat low-down triflin' Seb'm-Sister?" he bellowed. "Whah she at? I gwine wear de hide off'n her back—takin' dat four-bit piece from Ole Man Wilson for a huntin' mojo. Hidin' it fum her po' ole pappy what feed her! Whah she at? . . . Young-un, you come out fum under dat table! I sees you!"

The other children, gnawing pork chop bones beside the fireplace—thanks to the sale of a "health mojo" purported to contain the infallible John the Conqueror root—stirred uneasily. In this mood Dody was apt to throw things at anyone within range. But it appeared that Seven Sisters, quaking under the table, was the main object of his wrath tonight.

"Come on out, you heah me?" Dody snarled, grabbing up a stick of lightwood from the hearth and advancing toward the culprit. "I'm gwine whup you good! Stealin' my four-bits. . . ."

"I . . . done lost it, pappy. . . ." Seven Sisters's childish treble was drowned out by his bellow of rage. "Don't whup me! I drapped it in de field. I couldn't see whereat I drapped it—I'll go git it. . . ."

"Now you's lyin' to me!" Dody roared, waving his club. "Come on out! I'll learn you. . . ."

The other pickaninnies, fascinated, stopped gnawing their chop bones for an instant to watch, their greasy black faces gleaming in the firelight. Dody jerked the table aside. Seven Sisters cringed. Then:

"Don't you hit me wid no stick!" the frightened child shrilled. "I'll put a hoodoo on you! I'll . . ."

Dody lunged, and fell over the table. His stick whistled dangerously close to the child's tow-head.

The next moment Dody was groaning with pain, doubled over, hugging his stomach. Sweat stood out on his black face. He stared at his weirdly white daughter: backed away, thick lips trembling. Seven Sisters made a dive through the open door and out into the friendly night.

Cap'm Jim happened to be at the Place that day; it was a Sunday. He rushed Dody to the nearest city in his car. Appendicitis, Cap'm Jim called it, to the man at the hospital. He and Miss Ruth had a good laugh over Dody's version of the attack.

But after that, Clarabelle stopped giving her little albino sister a playful spank when she was naughty. No one would touch her, even in fun.

"I done tole you!" Aunt Fan intoned. "Do, Moses! Puttin' a hoodoo on she own pappy! Dat ole Seb'm-Sister, she jes' born to trouble! She *bad!*"

For more than a week thereafter, Seven Sisters hid in the woods, creeping out only to sneak food from the kitchen. She was deeply frightened. So frightened that when Cap'm Jim came to bring Dody back from the hospital, she ran from him like a wild creature. If she had not tripped over a log and knocked the breath from her slight body, he would never have caught her.

Dr. Saunders helped her up and held her gently by the shoulders, marveling anew at her Negroid features and cotton-white hair and skin. Her single garment, a faded dress which had not been changed for eight days, hung half-off one shoulder, torn and filthy. She was trembling all over, squinting up at him with white-lashed pinkish eyes dilated by terror.

"Now, now, child," the tall bossman was saying, in a tone as gentle as the grip of his hands. "What have those fools been telling you? That it's your fault about Dody's appendix? Well, Heaven help us!" He threw back his head, laughing, but stopped when he saw how it frightened his small captive. "Why, don't be scared. Cap'm Jim won't hurt you. Look here—I've got a present for you! Don't let the other young-uns get hold of it, you hear? Just hide it and play with it all by yourself, because it's yours."

The little albino stopped trembling. Gingerly she took the proffered box and gaped at the treasure inside. A doll-baby a foot high! With real hair, red hair, and eyes that opened and shut. When she turned it over, it gave a thin cry: *"Mama!"* Seven Sisters giggled.

The Cap'm chuckled. "Oh, I don't reckon you want this old doll-baby," he made a pretense of taking it back, eyes twinkling. The child clutched at it. "You do? Well, then, what do you say?"

Seven Sisters ducked her head shyly. "I don' care," she whispered—polite rural South for "Thank you!"

Dr. Saunders chuckled again. "That's a good girl." He stood up; gave her a careless pat. Then he strode off toward the Place, frowning over his own problems—not the least of which was mother-in-law trouble.

He and Ruth and their two boys had been so happy in their touch-and-go way. Then his wife's mother, a forthright lady from Oklahoma, had descended upon them and decided to run their lives with a new efficiency. With her customary dispatch she had found a buyer for the old Saunders plantation, and was now raging at her slipshod son's reluctance to sell.

Even Cap'm Jim had to admit that the price was half again as much as the property was worth. Besides, his practice in Chattanooga had been dwindling of late. A mother-in-law could point out such matters so vividly . . . !

Seven Sisters blinked after his retreating back. Keeping to the shade of the pine coppice, she followed the tall white man a little way, the doll squeezed tightly against her soiled blue-gingham dress. Cap'm Jim waved at someone, who met him in the orchard —a pretty redheaded woman. They went on to the house together, arms about each other's waists. Seven Sisters watched them until they were out of sight.

Thereafter she listened attentively whenever Dody or Clary spoke of cap'm. She grew to love anyone that he loved, and to hate anyone that he hated, with a doglike loyalty. In her child's mind, Good became personified as Dr. Saunders, and Evil as the sheriff or Old Miz Beecher.

It was common knowledge about the mother-in-law trouble. Clarabelle, who cooked all year round for the Saunderses now, had passed along every word of the quarrel.

"Us'll git turnt out like white-trash if'n de cap'm sell de Place," Dody mourned. "Dat old Miz Beecher! Do, Lawd! Dat old 'oman mean as a cottonmouth! She don't care what happen to us niggers, nor nobody. Miss Ruth sho don't take after her none. I wisht she'd fall down de steps and bus' her brains out, so she wouldn't plague de cap'm no more! If'n he don' sell come Thursday, Thanksgivin', she gwine jes' make his life mis'able!"

Seven Sisters listened, huddled apart from her black kin in a shadowy corner of the cabin. Her little heart began to beat rapidly as a mad idea crept into her tow-head. Without a sound, she slipped out into the frosty night of mid-November.

There was a thing Aunt Fan had hinted to her one day—or

rather, to Clarabelle within her hearing, since no one ever spoke directly to a seven-sister in idle conversation. Something about a . . . a *graven image.* There was even, Aunt Fan said, a passage about it in the Good Book, warning all Christians to steer clear of the matter.

But Seven Sisters was not a Christian. She had never been baptized in the creek like the rest of Dody's brood. Nothing hindered the plan. And . . . it sounded remarkably simple.

". . . whatever you does to de image, you does to de one you names it!" Aunt Fan's solemn words came back to her clearly. "Jes' wrop somep'm around it what dey wears next to dey skin— don't make no never-mind what hit is. And dat's de conjure! Eh, Lawd, I seed a conjure man do dat when I was married up wid my first husband. And de 'oman he conjure drap daid as a doornail dat same winter. . . . And dey do say as how hit were a big black cat got in de room whah dey was settin' up wid de corp. Hit jump up on de bed and go to yowlin' like ole Satan hisself! Yessirree, dat's de Lawd's truth like I'm tellin' you!"

Seven Sisters, picking her way easily through the dark, slipped into the pine coppice. After a moment, heart pounding, she dug up something from under a pile of leaves. A faint sound issued from it, causing her to start violently—*"Mama!"*

Like a small white ghost, the child then ran through the peach orchard. The Place, dark now since Cap'm Jim had gone back to Chattanooga, loomed just ahead. Seven Sisters found what she was looking for, under the steps of the isolated kitchen—an old piece of silk nightgown that she had seen Miss Ruth's mother herself give Clarabelle as a polishing rag for the flat silver. The older girl had used it and flung it under the kitchen steps. Seven Sisters retrieved it now furtively, and padded swiftly back through the orchard.

Deep in the pine coppice, illumined only by the filtered light of a quarter moon, she sat down cross-legged. For a long time she stared at the lovely thing Cap'm Jim had given her, the only thing that had ever been truly her own. The hair was so soft, the glass eyes so friendly. But now the doll had taken on a new personality, a hated one. Seven Sisters glared at it, shivering a little.

Then, deftly, she tied the silk rag about its china neck, and stood up.

"Ole Miz Beecher—you's ole Miz Beecher!" she hissed with careful emphasis; then clarified, against all mistake, to whatever dark pointed ears might be listening: "Miss Ruth's mama. Cap'm Jim's wife's mama. Dat's who you is, doll; you heah me? Ole Miz Beecher . . . !"

With a fierce motion she banged the poppet hard against a tree trunk. The china head broke off and rolled at her bare feet.

"Mama!" wailed the headless body, accusingly.

Seven Sisters dropped it as though it were red-hot. She backed away, rubbing her hands on her dress like an infant Lady Macbeth, and shuddering in the Indian summer chill. Panting, shaken, she turned and ran back to the cabin.

But she paused in the half-open door.

Excited activity was going on inside. Aunt Fan was there, puffing with importance and fumbling for her box of snuff. Dody was shouting questions, wringing his big hands. Clarabelle, Ressie and the others were milling about like a flock of chickens, clucking and squawking in chorus.

". . . and de phome call say for you to clean up de fambly plot on de south hill," Aunt Fan made herself heard shrilly. "She gwine be buried fum de Place like Miss Addie. . . ."

"Oh, Lawsy! Ain't it awful?" This from Ressie.

"Sho is, honey," Aunt Fan agreed complacently. "I don't reckon the cap'm'll ever be de same, hit was so awful. I don't reckon he care what become of de Place, nor nothin', he so cut up about hit."

"Lawd he'p us!" Dody shouted for a fifth time. "When it happen? How come?"

"I done tole you," Aunt Fan repeated, relishing the drama of her words. "Truck run slap into 'em. She was plumb flang out'n de car. Cap'm want even scratched up. But it broke her pore neck. . . ."

The child in the doorway caught her breath sharply. The conjure had worked! So soon? A little knot of nausea gathered in her stomach, in memory of the china head rolling against her bare foot. Then an angry thought came.

"Aunt Fan—cap'm ain't gwine bury that old 'oman in de fambly plot, is he?" Seven Sisters piped above the chatter. "Not dat ole Miz Beecher . . . !"

The excited group barely glanced at her, impatient of the interruption.

"Miz Beecher?" Aunt Fan grunted. "Lawd, chile, hit ain't ole Miz Beecher what got killt. Hit was Miss Ruth. . . ." The aged Negress went on with her narrative, dwelling on the details with relish. "And de man tole Marse Joe Andrews over de phome. . . . Eh, Lawd; he say de cap'm jes' set dah by she bed and hold she hand. Don't cry nor nothin'. Jes' set dah and stare, like he daid, too. . . ."

Seven Sisters heard no more. A sound like falling timber roared in her ears. Through it, dimly, she thought she heard a screech-owl's quavering cry—eerie, mocking, malicious.

She turned and ran. Ran, blindly sobbing. Cap'm Jim's Miss Ruth! She had forgotten Miss Ruth's hair was red, exactly like the doll's. And . . . that soiled bit of nightgown might not have been ole Miz Beecher's at all, but Miss Ruth's. Cap'm Jim's Miss Ruth. . . .

Beyond the cornfield the black woods opened up to receive the small ghostly figure, running like an animal in pain; running nowhere, anywhere, into the chill autumn night.

Sawbriars tore dark scratches in her dead-white skin, but Seven Sisters did not feel them. She ran, careening into tree trunks and fighting through scuppernong vines, until the salt taste of blood came into her mouth. Twice she fell and lay in the damp leaves for a long time, her thin shoulders racked with sobs.

"Oh, cap'm! Cap'm Jim . . . I . . . I didn't go to do it!" she whimpered aloud once. "I didn't mean to! I didn'—hones' I didn'. . . ."

At that moment she heard the dogs baying.

Tense as a fox, she sat up and listened. Was it only Old Man Wilson, hunting with his pack along the north ridge? Or was it . . . the Law? A posse, with guns, following the deputy sheriff and his two flop-eared bloodhounds through the canebrake. Following a trail of small bare feet. *Her* feet. . . .

The little albino sprang up, her features contorted with panic. Harrowing yarns crowded her memory. Of the time Aunt Fan's preacher husband had hid in the canebrake for eight days, with the dogs baying closer and closer. And Aunt Fan's husband had only cut a man with his razor, while *she*. . . .

Just then she heard the screech-owl, right over her head.

Seven Sisters was running again, goaded now by the spurs of terror. But now the very woods seemed hostile. Gnarled branches snatched at her cottony hair and tore a jagged flap in her gingham dress. Old spider webs clung to her face. The dogs sounded nearer. Once more she tripped and fell, panting, but sprang up again with a scream as something slithered out from beneath her arm.

The screech-owl tittered again, from somewhere above her. It seemed to be trailing the ghostly little fugitive, so white against the ground.

Seven Sisters ran on, blindly, staggering with exhaustion. Once she cried out in her terror—oddly, the very name of the one she was running from:

"Cap'm . . . ! Cap'm Jim. . . ."

Of a sudden the ground dropped from beneath her feet. She pitched forward, and felt herself falling into space. Dark icy water rushed up out of nowhere to meet and engulf her. . . .

Mist rose from the cornfield in front of Dody's cabin. Dry leaves rattled. The gourds of the martin pole swung in the wind.

Somewhere a screech-owl quavered again, far away, in the direction of the creek—whose muddy waters had washed away the sins of many a baptized little darky.

THE DEVIL DOLL

BY BRYCE WALTON

Another of the many places where you'll find the practitioners of voodoo is New York City—and if you should happen to be as unfortunate as the Greenwich Village artist named Earl in this story, you might even discover that a voodoo devil doll is not always a wax or clay image, that in some cases it can come alive and take root and grow in your own flesh. Skeptical? So was Earl, until he realized that "you'll believe in anything, anywhere, even among the steel and concrete jungles of Manhattan—when it happens to you."

Like "Papa Benjamin," "The Devil Doll" was first published in Dime Mystery, *one of the leading "thrill" pulps; unlike the Woolrich story, however, it has been overlooked by fantasy/horror anthologists since that initial publication in 1947. Perhaps this is because its plot is somewhat reminiscent of Edward Lucas White's widely reprinted "Lukundoo" (but only somewhat); nevertheless, its eerie atmosphere, its surprises and abundant terrors invite comparisons to Woolrich and make its neglect insupportable. It is a pleasure to present it here.*

Bryce Walton was born in Missouri in 1918, headed West on a freight train after high school graduation, and held jobs as a placer miner, migrant fruit picker, sheepherder and sign painter before turning to the writing of short-shorts for newspaper syndicates. During World War II he was a combat correspondent for the Navy and, after being transferred to the Marine Corps, a staff correspondent for Leatherneck Magazine. *When the war ended he began to write extensively for the mystery/detective, science fiction and Western pulps; later, his work appeared in such magazines as* The Saturday Evening Post, Ellery Queen's Mystery Magazine *and* Alfred Hitchcock's Mystery Magazine *(which awarded his story "The Last Autopsy" first prize in its 1961 best story contest). He is also the author of seven novels, most of them juvenile adventure fiction, and has written and adapted TV scripts for* Captain Video *and* Alfred Hitchcock Presents. *He lives in Los Angeles, where he is at work on a new novel.*

JACK LONDON said it better than Earl could have said it. She was "fire in his blood and a thunder of trumpets." But no one could tell you of her laughter. It held undertones, suggestions of shadows and evil darkness.

Crita doesn't laugh any more, of course. Nor does Jean, though her laughter was never more than a thin cold smile. But Earl will always hear Crita's mocking laughter as long as he lives. And he will always remember the unspeakable little projection, with its soft, warm breath against his ear.

The small, piping voice. The thing's laughter and its tiny fingers, fine and delicate and wet, that ran over his face like mice in the dark. . . .

He had been drinking heavily. He had never been able to drink well. But he had needed courage to tell Crita that it was quits. The courage gained was not in proportion to the bourbon consumed. His suit was wet and cold against his thin, quick-moving body as he edged up the stairs.

It was in the Village, on Grove Street. And he climbed the narrow stair slowly. Sweat was cold on his thin face. His heart was pounding pain against his ribs.

Why should he fear to tell Crita? They'd made the arrangement long in advance—when one tired of the other, the affair would be gracefully dissolved, no regrets, no fuss.

But he had learned since then that Crita never surrendered anything. And she had claimed him. He had been a promising artist until a few months ago, when he had met Jean Morris. Something had happened to his artistic ambitions. He had quit painting because of Jean. He had begun to play. Jean had money, more money than she had ever bothered to count. She was pretty but nothing like Crita.

Crita had been a singer in a Village night spot, with promise of getting into the big time. But Earl had been selfish. Too selfish, but he couldn't help it. She had quit singing. He'd wanted her all to himself, you understand.

She loved him with a strange, almost terrifying possessiveness. To him, she was a violent, roaring flame. He lived in the flood of her fire. But Jean had taken him away—from his painting, from the Village, from Crita. Jean was a traveler, a trotter of grotesque dogs along Park Avenue. She was small, delicate, white.

He had to tell Crita now. Jean was impatient with his dual role.

He shivered. He blinked hot burning eyes. Crita had given up everything, everything, for him. She had cooked, washed, done a thousand and one small things to make his meaningless life easier. And he had to tell her that it was finished. He didn't want to. Money, the damned filthy compulsion. He hesitated outside the door. The narrow hall was confining, stuffy. He felt his breath suck in between tight lips. Then he opened the door.

The room was dark, the blinds drawn. A single candle burned in an onyx holder wound with red-eyed serpents, upon a small table. All the familiar things in the large, sky-lighted room were shadow-limned, distorted.

He saw her dark face framed by candlelight.

He backed away. Her eyes shone with a gleam of hateful understanding. Mingled with sudden horror in him was also relief, because now he wouldn't have to tell her. Crita knew about Jean. And she had already done something about it.

He didn't know that. There was much he didn't know.

Her skin was a deep bronze. He didn't know her origin, but her accent seemed subtly French. There was something primitive about her face, a beautiful savagery. Like an evil but beautiful jungle flower, hungry and unfolding.

Her lips were slightly parted, revealing strong teeth like white pearls. The deep brown of her eyes shone with that ineffable light of love that has frozen to hate and loathing.

Then he seemed to get the full implication of the props littering the shadowed room. They had always been there. But until now he had always considered them an affectation—"arty" stuff. He realized now that Crita's hobby of voodoo and black magic was more than a hobby. Maybe he had always known this, subconsciously. The voodoo drums on the walls. The "black magic" cult she belonged to.

Now the memory of these things came back. How strange she had seemed as she sometimes sat in the shadows, softly murmuring some alien chant, eyes closed, mouth lax, while her hands gently brought blood-throbbing rhythms from the drums.

She was familiar with Haiti. Maybe she came from Haiti. Haiti, dark island of voodoo, devil-devil. She made dolls, devil dolls, and also little packets which she called *ouangas*. Packets of carved bone, beads, potions.

That had been the thing about her songs at the clubs that made them different. Sultry, suggestive songs, half chanted, self-accompanied by the gentle, throbbing rhythm of a jungle drum.

"You're not going to leave me, Earl."

Her voice was low. The candle shuddered. Shadows swayed.

He moved toward her. He'd forgotten Jean for a moment. He had forgotten her delicate submissive slimness, the softness of her brown hair. Her wealth and her penthouse.

He stopped walking. The candlelight hurt his eyes. He was ill, very ill. He had been drinking much too much.

"How did you know about Jean and me?"

She laughed. Her eyes turned downward into the flame. He touched his wet lips. How had she known? A modern witch. Strange contrast. A beautiful woman, compact and full and rounded with a penchant for black magic—in the heart of New York.

She got up, the candlelight flickering over her green evening gown. It clung to the roundness of her bronzed figure. She came to him slowly. His arms reached out. He felt the warmth of her body reaching out to him. His hands cupped her shoulder blades and she didn't move, just watched mutely. She was firm and warm in his arms.

Her head went back and she shut her eyes. He kissed her. The candle flame flickered, and he felt her arms about his neck as the kiss became deep. Lilac perfume closed around him.

"You can't leave me, Earl. No matter how you try."

He shook his head. His hands dropped. The way she had said that. As though she *knew* he couldn't leave. He looked up at the ceiling to escape her eyes. It was a Gothic ceiling with heavy rafters in squared angles. Like a row of gibbets strung across the room. A creeping knot of terror grew tighter and tighter around his waist.

He pushed her away. She stumbled. He fell back as she crashed into the wall. The voodoo drum fell from its hook. A dull dead *boommmmm* floated across the shadows.

Her eyes blazed as she climbed slowly to her feet and came toward him again. His hands were rubber fish against his sides. He had to get out of there, get a drink. He couldn't see or talk to Crita any more. He tried to move, but he seemed rooted there by old passions, memories, fears.

He watched her hand move to his right shoulder, a kind of lethargic terror dulling him, freezing him there.

Her hand moved quickly. His coat slid down over his right shoulder. The sound ripped in his ear as her fingers clawed his shirt open, baring his shoulder.

Then she kissed his shoulder. Her lips burned. A river of white-hot flame exploded in his head. She dropped back, laughing. Laughing. Always the laughter.

He looked at his shoulder. Nausea caused by pain thickened in his throat. Red on his shoulder where her lips had been. He was swearing as he rubbed at the red marks. But it wasn't lipstick; it wouldn't come off. He scrubbed frantically. She kept on laughing.

He stumbled back to the door and opened it. A draft of cool air was a shock to his sweating skin.

"You'll try, but you can't leave me, Earl. I won't let you go."
He ran. Down the dark stairs fast. And into the night.

He remembered drinking heavily that night. Straight shots in
a dark booth where no one noticed him. But nothing could drown
the fear. . . .

The fear, nor the pain that was growing in his right shoulder.
He tried to ignore the pain later when he drove over to 61st Street
to see Jean and tell her that he had gotten rid of Crita. Jean knew
about Crita.

It wasn't that night that Jean died with his fingers around her
thin white throat, throttling off her cries, her million dollars. It
was later, maybe a week, maybe less. That isn't important to Earl.
But he couldn't forget Crita that night when he was with Jean.
The pain in his shoulder kept growing as they went walking in the
park, threw popcorn to the ducks, watched the lights from the
towers reflected on the water, watched other couples walking
along the dark paths.

He got rid of Jean, left her at home and ran away to his own
apartment. He ran frantically, sobbing. His shoulder was burning
agony. And—*something was alive there. Something moved.*

He tore off his coat and shirt. He looked in the mirror. His
face was a terrible image sculpted in wet, gray putty. His eyes
bulged. . . .

A figure danced on his shoulder. A little, living, chortling mari-
onette.

*She's here . . . with me . . . on my shoulder. Crita. In a green
dress. Only an inch high. But she's alive.*

She is growing out of my shoulder.

There were familiars. You believed in them, you feared them
in dark forbidden jungles and groveled in superstitious terror.

You'll believe in anything, anywhere, even among the steel and concrete jungles of Manhattan—*when it happens to you.*

"Go away!" he shrieked. He slapped at it. It slithered from the flat of his palm. "Get off me! Go away, damn you!"

The tiny swaying figure laughed.

Crita in miniature, growing out of his shoulder. A tiny, wispy body swaying to an invisible melody. And it leaned toward his ear. The laughter became high and shrill, then tiny, elfin.

He kept staring into the mirror. It was easier to see the thing there than to turn and see it directly, see it looking back at him from tiny pin-point eyes. Its little hands reaching for him, the elfin head tilted, and the shrill bleating laughter.

He reached up slowly with his left hand. But he couldn't grasp the devilish thing. He was afraid perhaps that he actually *could* touch it. And before his eyes, in the mirror, the ghastly miniature kept growing.

He stumbled about the apartment. It was hot, stuffy, damp. His clothes stuck to him. His right shoulder pained and twitched, and he felt its roots in his flesh.

He stumbled to the telephone and called Crita's apartment. He heard the phone ringing, over and over. But no answer. He dropped the receiver and groped his way to the bed, fell on it, shuddering.

From then on the thing on his shoulder talked to him. Talked and laughed.

"I'll not go way. I'll not go way. Not until you come back to Crita."

It was Crita's voice, only it was far away and tiny and silvery now. It mocked and laughed and swayed.

And through the hours, the laughter rose higher and more shrill in his ear. . . .

It was dark in the room. It was hot and sticky. Under his matted hair and through the stubble of beard, his eyes were depthless and terrified.

Suddenly, with a choking cry, he clutched at the thing on his shoulder. It squirmed in his grasp. He tore, wildly, gasping and gibbering. White-hot pain seared his arm, sizzled in his brain. He felt the warm lines of blood crawling down his chest as he slowly withdrew his hand.

The thing began to laugh again. He couldn't rid himself of it. Not that way. He staggered to the mirror. The thing was taller, more full-bodied now. It was four inches high. He knew he couldn't hurt it without hurting himself, and he couldn't stand pain.

He knew the thing laughing and growing from his shoulder was real. That Crita had sent it to him and was making it grow.

Voodoo. Witches in Manhattan. Black Mass on altars of chome and white walnut. He knew now. He believed now.

There was no sleep for Earl. There would never be sleep for him until he went back to Crita, back to her apartment in the Village, with the dusty paintings in the corner. . . .

Long nights, twisting and turning in a clammy shroud. The tiny laughter and the shrill voice mocking and beckoning as the Lorelei beckon.

He had called up Jean. He had tried to explain in a way she would believe. He formulated stories and none of them sounded credible. She kept calling him. He sat waiting for her calls while the thing in the green gown swayed from his shoulder. It was fat and sleek. Its voice was stronger now.

"Come back to Crita. Come back to Crita."

You can't leave me, Earl. The only way you can be free of me is to come back to me.

He phoned Crita's apartment again. He phoned many times. He couldn't remember now how many times. There was never any answer.

But Jean came to see him. She came unexpectedly, without phoning. The bell rang. He cried out, felt his muscles jerk with fear as he stumbled to the door, stood leaning against the wall.

The thing on his shoulder rubbed tiny fingers down his neck. He shivered.

"Let her in. It's Jean. Let her in."

He was muttering. Terror clawed and scrabbled in his heart. His lips felt wet and loose. The little voice whispered hoarsely, *"Let her in, Earl. Hurry. You'll never be able to come back to Crita until Jean's out of the way."*

His hand trembled as he managed to hook it around the knob of the door, and pull it open.

"Jean . . . don't. . . ."

She screamed in terror when she saw him.

"No, Jean. Don't. . . ."

"You've got to kill her, Earl—quick! You've got to stop that screaming!" the little voice whispered.

He slammed the door shut. His back was against it. He jumped. A sense of intense relief flowed through him, warmly, as her cries died between his hands. He kept his hands there, made them tighter and tighter.

"You . . . Jean, I was happy enough . . . things were nice . . . until you and your damned money . . . you . . . talking all the time about what we could do . . . where we could go . . . you laughed at my work. . . ."

He staggered back. He flattened against the wall. His breath was choked and heavy in his throat as he looked down at her. The little familiar on his shoulder twisted its head and looked at him. It laughed its shrill little laugh.

"Hurry, Earl. Come back to Crita. You haven't much time."

He taped the thing down. It shrieked and he tried to smother its cries, bind its lashing body. He put on a coat, then a topcoat. But he could still feel it squirming against him. He could hear its muffled cries as he drove blindly toward Crita's apartment in the Village. . . .

The hallway was still. A faint wind blew some white hall curtains gently. They floated faintly in the soggy darkness. A musty odor hung imprisoned by the flood of dim yellow light outside her door.

He listened. He couldn't hear anything from beyond the door. Only the muffled whispering of the thing on his shoulder, the familiar, the vicious little monster that had grown out of him.

He opened the door and edged into the room. It was very still and smothered in thick dusty shadows and hot breathless air. No songs now to ancient gods. No incantations to the monody of evil drums. There was an unfamiliar smell. Yet he should be able to recognize it—the unmistakable smell of death.

He lurched toward a window. Dead flies lay on the sill, dead flies and dust. He needed air. He cried out as he bumped into something, something that thudded hollowly against his face. Something that swayed back and forth now. There was a creaking sound overhead. The swaying form bumped him, slid around him, then twirled slowly around and around. . . .

Rafters strung across the darkened ceiling like gibbets. Crita! *Crita!* And a length of hemp squeaking on dry wood. Her body in its green gown hanging, stiff and cold and twisted.

He opened his mouth to scream, but nothing happened.

The miniature thing on his shoulder laughed.

We found him crouched in the dark corner of Crita Montez's apartment over a shattered pile of his dusty, abandoned paintings. He later admitted murdering Jean Morris. Crita had evidently committed suicide.

We found a doll in his hand. It was a very lifelike doll with a green dress. It was an amazing duplication of Crita Montez.

An odd case. There's a birthmark on his shoulder—a peculiar birthmark. It looks startlingly like the imprint of a woman's lips.

Police psychiatrist Dr. Joseph Wright says that as far as he can determine, Earl Gleason is sane.

KUNDU

BY MORRIS WEST

The true evocation of a primitive culture is not easy for most writers to capture on paper; the sights, sounds, smells—and, of course, insights—are not often fully realized and the treatment is generally superficial. Morris West, however, is not "most writers," and when he sets out to portray a primitive society, as he does in regard to the New Guinean aborigines in Kundu, *the results are both vivid and electrifying.*

Kundu, *which was West's second novel and first to be published in the United States (in 1956, as a paperback original by Dell First Editions), deals in large part with voodoo magic. The excerpts offered here describe the mating ceremony known as* kunande *and the powers of such sorcerers as* Kumo, *who are able to turn themselves into cassowary birds and run like the wind; they also offer a superior character study of a man named Max Lansing, one of the Australians who have migrated to the area. In sum, as the Dell edition's back cover blurb says, accurately if somewhat flamboyantly, "Here is a story of New Guinea's fetid villages and wind-*

cooled valleys, of barbaric natives and over-civilized whites—all finally made one in desire and fear by the timeless beat of the great kundu drums."

Although his first few novels achieved a certain success, it was the publication of The Devil's Advocate in 1959 that brought Morris West widespread critical acclaim as one of this generation's major writers. Such subsequent titles as The Shoes of the Fisherman, Tower of Babel, The Salamander and Harlequin enhanced that reputation and created a worldwide and ever-growing audience for his work. Born in Melbourne, Australia, in 1916, West now makes his home in Europe and is a fellow of the Royal Society of Literature and a member of the World Academy of Arts and Sciences.

Down in the village, they were making *kunande.*

There were perhaps a hundred of them, bucks and girls, squatting two by two around the little fires in the long, low hut. Behind them in the smoky shadows sat the drummers, crouching over the kundus, filling the fetid air with the deep insistent beat that changed from song to song, from verse to refrain, with never a pause and never a falter.

The couples around the fires leaned face to face and breast to breast, and sang low, murmurous, haunting songs that lapsed from time to time into a wordless passionate melody. And, as they sang, they rolled their faces and their breasts together, lip to lip, nipple to nipple, cheek to brown and painted cheek.

The small flames shone on their oiled bodies and glistened on the green armor of the beetles in their headdresses. Their plumes bobbed in the drifting smoke and their necklets of shell and beads made a small clattering like castanets as they turned and rolled to the rolling of the drums.

The air was full of the smell of sweat and oil and smoke and the pubic exhalation of bodies rising slowly to the pitch of passion. This was *kunande,* the public love-play of the unmarried, the courting time, the knowing time, when a man might tell from the responses of his singing partner whether she desired or disdained him. For this was the time of the women. The girl chose her partner for the *kunande,* left him when she chose, solicited him if she wished, or held herself cool and aloof in the formal cadence of the songs.

N'Daria was among them, but the man with her was not Kumo. Kumo would come in his own time and when he came she would leave her partner and go to him. For the present, she was content to sing and sway and warm herself with the contact of other flesh and let the drum beats take slow possession of her blood.

A woman moved slowly down the line of singers. She was not adorned like the others. Her breasts were heavy with milk, her waist swollen with childbearing. Now she would throw fresh twigs on the fire, now she would part one couple and rearrange the partners. Now she would pour water in the open mouth of a drummer, as he bent back his head without slackening his beat on the black kundu. This was the mistress of ceremonies, the duenna, ordering the courtship to the desires of her younger sisters, dreaming of her own days of *kunande* when she, too, wore the cane belt of the unmarried.

The drum beats rose to a wild climax, then dropped suddenly to a low humming. The singing stopped. The singers opened their eyes and sat rigid, expectant. Distant at first, then closer and closer and closer, they heard the running of the cassowary bird. They heard the great clawed feet pounding the earth—*chuff-chuff-chuff-chuff*—down the mountain path, through the darkness of the rain forest, on to the flat places of the taro gardens and into the village itself. Tomorrow they would go out and see the footprints in the black earth. But now they waited, tense and silent, as the beat came closer and closer, louder than the drums, then stopped abruptly outside the hut.

A moment later, Kumo the Sorcerer stood in the doorway.

He did not enter as the others had done, stooping under the low lintel. He was there, erect and challenging as if he had walked through the wall. He wore a gold wig, fringed with green beetle shards. His forehead was painted green and the upper part of his face was red with ocher. His nose ornament was enormous, his feathered casque was scarlet and blue and orange. His pubic skirt was of woven bark and his belt was covered with cowrie shells. His whole body shone with pig fat.

The boy who had been singing with N'Daria rose and moved back into the shadows. N'Daria sat waiting. Then Kumo gave a curt signal to the drummers and they swung into a wild loud beat as he moved down the hut and sat facing N'Daria. No word was spoken between them. They sang and moved their faces together as the others did, but N'Daria's body was on fire and the drums beat in her blood, pounding against her belly and her breasts and her closed eyelids.

Then, after a long time, slowly the drum beats died and the fires died with them. Quietly the couples dispersed, some to sleep, some to carry on the love-play in a girl's house, others to seek swift consummation in the shadows of the tangket trees.

Kumo and N'Daria left the hut with them and walked through

the darkness to the house of N'Daria's sister. Here there was food and drink and a small fire; and when they had eaten, two of the drummers came in with two more girls and they sat in pairs, backed against the bamboo walls to make the greater love-play, called in pidgin "carry-leg."

Kumo sat with his legs stretched out toward the center of the hut. N'Daria sat beside him, her body half turned to him, her thighs thrown over his left leg. His right leg locked over hers so that he held her firmly, and with his left arm around her shoulders, he drew her close up to his breast. Then the fondling began, a long, slow ritual of excitement, tentative at first, then more and more intimate and urgent. At first, they sang a little, snatches of the *kunande* songs; then they laughed, telling stories of other lovers and scandalous doings in the village and on the jungle paths. They made laughing flatteries of one another's bodies and their skill in the arts of love. Then, gradually, their voices dropped and their whispers became fiercer and more desirous.

"Does the white man touch you like this?"

"No, no." She lied and half believed the lie in the warmth of the moment.

"Is the white man as great a man as I am?" His fingers pressed painfully into her flesh.

"He is not a man. Beside you, he is a lizard."

"If he touches you, I will kill him."

"I would want you to kill him."

"I will make his blood boil and his bones turn to water. I will put ants in his brain and a snake in his belly."

"And I will watch and laugh, Kumo."

He caught her to him, suddenly. His nails scored into her body so that she gasped with the sudden pain.

"What does he teach you there in the little hut?"

She buried her face in his shoulder to hide the small smile of triumph. Kumo was a great sorcerer, the greatest in the valleys. Kumo could change himself into a cassowary bird and travel fast as the wind. But even Kumo did not know the secrets she learned in Sonderfeld's laboratory.

"Tell me. What does he teach you?"

She giggled and clung to him, her hands searching his body.

"What will you give me if I tell you?"

"I will give you the charm that makes children and the charm that destroys them. I will make you desired of all men. I will give you the power to strike any woman barren and make any man a giant to embrace you."

"I want none of these things."

His mouth was pressed to her ear. He whispered urgently, so that the others could not hear, "What do you want? Tell me and I will give it to you. Am I not the greatest sorcerer in the valleys? Does not the Red Spirit speak to me in the thunder and in the wind? Ask me and I will give. What do you want for the secrets of the white man's room?"

"Only that you should take me—now!"

His body shuddered with the flattery and the triumph of it.

"And you will tell me, when?"

"Tomorrow or the day after, when I can come without being seen. But not now—not now!"

Kumo laughed. His plumes tossed. His teeth shone. He swept the girl to her feet and half ran, half carried her out of the hut.

The consummation was a wild, brief frenzy that left her bruised and crumpled and only half content, alone in the tall and trodden kunai grass.

In the warmth of the rich mountain morning, Max Lansing walked home to his village. It lay in a deep saucer-shaped depression between Pere Louis's community and the Lahgi Valley. To reach it, he had to make a wide traverse westward of Sonderfeld's property and cross two steep saddles before he struck the path that led over the lip of the crater and downward into the taro plots and the banana groves and the dancing park. He would not reach it till the middle of the afternoon.

He had a water bottle hooked to his belt with a canvas knapsack filled with food from Gerda's kitchen and a bottle of Sonderfeld's best whisky. By midday he would have crossed the first saddle and he would rest and eat by the swift water that came singing down over the rocks from the high peaks. Then he would push on, with neither joy nor impatience, to the small bamboo hut on the outer edge of the village—his home for the years of his subsidized exile.

As he topped the rise that overlooked the plantation, he halted a moment and looked back. He saw the blaze of Gerda's garden, the nestling of the bungalow under its thatched roof, the long serried lines of the plantation trees. He saw the work boys moving about like leisurely ants and the white tall figure of Sonderfeld standing at the head of the first grove. He saw them all as a symbol of permanence and possession, a mockery of his own rootless, pointless existence.

Long, long ago he had been fired with zeal for knowledge—knowledge for its own sake, knowledge without thought of gain, profitless except in human dignity and spiritual enlargement. But the fire had burned out years since and he saw himself, not great among the solitary great ones, but a poor and tattered pedant, piling his dry facts like children's blocks, while the laughing, weeping, lusting, suffering world rolled heedless past his doorstep. Without faith in himself and in his work, he found himself without strength for dedication. He could no longer walk happily among the scholars and he had forgotten the speech of the marketplace. Even his love was a pedantry, dusty and dry beside the welling passion of Gerda.

When Sonderfeld had left the house, he had sat with her at breakfast on the verandah and he had tried to recapture the brief warmth of their night's embrace. But Gerda refused to match this mood. She had talked cheerfully enough about the dinner party, the guests, the plantation, the news from Goroka. But when he had urged her to discussion of their own relationship, she refused gently, but with finality.

"No, Max. All that can be put into words has been said between us. I am here, whenever you care to come. I will be with you as I have always been. But I will not talk—talk—talk! Better to kiss or make love, or simply walk among the flowers together. But why rake our hearts with words that mean nothing?"

To which, of course, there was no answer. Take it or leave it. He had not the courage to leave it and he lacked the wisdom to take it without question. He must itch and scratch and itch and scratch again until the warm and willing heart was scarred into a running sore.

He had risen abruptly from the table and gathered his things to leave. She had come to him then and kissed him with that maddening maternal gentleness.

"Don't be angry with me, Max. I am as I am. I cannot change. But before you go, let me tell you one thing."

"Yes?"

Let her tell him she loved him, and he would be happy again. Let her give him one small hope, and ambition would soar again, mountains high.

"Be careful, Max, I beg of you. Be careful!"

"Careful of what?"

Her hands made a helpless fluttering gesture.

"I don't know. I wish I did. But after what you said last night, my husband—"

"To hell with your husband!"

He caught her to him, crushing his mouth brutally on hers. Then he released her, picked up his knapsack and without a backward glance strode off, a lost and angry man, storming up the hillside.

When he came to the river he was sweating and exhausted. It was a long walk at the best of times, but for a lonely and unhappy fellow, it was twice as tedious. He plunged down to the water, and felt the humid air close round him like a curtain. A cloud of insects enveloped him. He beat at them irritably with his handkerchief and by the time he reached the sandy hollow near the ford, he was free of them.

He slipped off his knapsack, took a long pull at the water bottle and flung himself down at the edge of the clear singing water. He was too tired to eat, so he lay sprawled on his back, head pillowed on the knapsack, looking up into the dappled green of the jungle overhang, through a cloud of bright blue butterflies. He saw the flash of brilliant scarlet as a bird of paradise made his mating dance on the branch of an albizzia tree. A tiny tree kangaroo peered cautiously between two broad purple leaves. A lizard sunned himself on the rock beside him, and in the undergrowth he heard the scurrying of small animals, rooting for food.

The thought struck him that in his four-hour walk he had seen not a single human being. This was unusual, for the mountain paths were the highways of the tribes. Since the white man's law had abolished war and killing raids, there was a modest traffic between the villages in canes and bird of paradise feathers and gum and galip nuts and pigs and produce of the gardens.

This traffic had been increased of late by the movement of the tribes for the approaching pig festival. Yet today he had seen no one. Because he was tired, the thought nagged at him uneasily. He fumbled for a cigarette, lit it and watched the blue smoke spiral up toward the green canopy.

Then he heard it, distant but distinct—*chuff-chuff-chuff*—the unmistakable beat of a running cassowary. The sound was unusual enough to interest him. The cassowary bird was native to the high valleys, but the breed was being thinned out by killing and the survivors were retreating into the less populated mountains.

The footsteps came closer, thudding like the muffled beat of a train on steel rails. Lansing sat up. The bird was coming down the same path that he had followed. He wondered if it would break out on to the beach. He was not afraid, only interested. The big ungainly bird is easily frightened and will not attack a human being unless it is angered or cornered. The footsteps came closer and closer. Then they stopped.

He judged the bird was probably a dozen yards away, hidden by the dense screen of undergrowth. He could hear its rustling among the leaves and low branches. Then the rustling stopped, and after a moment Lansing lay back drowsily against the knapsack. He thought he would sleep a little, then eat before he continued his walk. He worked a hollow for his hip in the warm sand and turned comfortably on his side.

Suddenly, a yard from his face, he saw a small white snake, dappled with black spots. In the suspended moment of shock he saw the trail of its body in the white sand. It had come from the bush at his back, the deadliest reptile in the whole island. If it struck him, he would die, paralyzed and beyond help, within two hours. Cautiously, he moved his hand to get purchase on the sand, then, with a single movement, he thrust himself to his feet. In that same moment the snake moved, fast as a flicker of light to the spot where his head had lain. Its jaws opened and it struck at the stiff canvas of the knapsack. Before Lansing had time to snatch up a stick or stone it was gone again, a dappled death, slithering into the fallen leaves at the fringe of the bush.

Sick with terror, he stood looking down at the knapsack and the tiny dark stain of the ejected poison. Then he shivered, snatched up the bag and plunged across the ford, heedless of the water that swirled about his knees and the hidden stones that sent him half-sprawling into the icy current.

Gerda's parting words beat in his brain. "Be careful, Max. I beg of you, be careful."

Breathless, he scrambled up the steep bank and looked back at the small white beach. It was bare and empty of life. The jungle was like a painted backdrop, motionless in the heavy air.

Then he heard it again—*chuff-chuff-chuff*—the running feet of the cassowary, retreating into the stillness.

Suddenly he remembered the cassowary men. They were an old story in the valleys, an old fear among the tribes. They were sorcerers who, by common repute, had power to change themselves into cassowary birds and run faster than the wind. They were the Territory counterpart of the Carpathian werewolves and the jackal-men of Africa. The tribes believed in them implicitly and for proof pointed to the claw marks on the soft ground after a nocturnal visit from one of the sorcerers. Newcomers to the mountains scoffed at such rank superstition, but the old hands— traders, missionaries, senior men in the District services—were less skeptical. Each had his own stories to tell of phenomena apparently beyond physical explanation. But all had one thing in common: a healthy respect and a prickling fear of the dim border-lands of primitive mysticism.

At first Lansing had rejected the manifestations as pure charlatanry. But the more he studied, the less certain he became; and now, in the eerie solitude of the upland paths, he, too, was gripped by the cold, uncanny fear of the bird man.

It was late in the afternoon when he came to the village. The mountain shadows were lengthening and the first faint chill was creeping down the valley. He was hungry and tired and trembling as if with the onset of fever. He paid no heed to the curious stares of the villagers, but went straight to his hut, crammed a couple of suppressant tablets in his mouth, stripped himself naked and sponged himself with water from the canvas bucket.

When he was clean and dressed in fresh clothes, he poured himself a noggin of Sonderfeld's whisky and tossed it off at a gulp. He poured another, tempered it with water and stood in his doorway with the glass in his hand, looking out on the village.

The women were coming up from the taro gardens, naked except for the pubic belt, their thick bodies bowed under the weight of string baskets full of sweet potatoes which they carried suspended from their broad foreheads and supported on the small of their backs. In the far corner of the compound a young girl was feeding the pigs. They were blinded so that they could not run away and tethered to stakes of casuarina wood. They grunted and snuffled and squealed as she passed among them with fruit rinds and bananas and taro pulp.

The pigs and the gardens and the children, these were the charges of the women—and in that order. A woman would suckle a child at one breast and a piglet at the other. The men would make the gardens, laying them out, breaking the first soil, marking each patch with the small blunt mound of the phallic symbol crossed with the cut that represented the female principle. But it was the women who tilled them and dug the big ripe tubers that were the staple diet of the tribe.

As for the men, they sat as they sat now: one making a ceremonial wig of fiber and gum and flaring feathers and green beetle shards; another plaiting a cane socket for his obsidian axe; this one chipping a round stone for the head of his club; that, stringing the short cane bow which would bring down birds and possums and the furry cuscus whose tail made armlets for the bucks and the unmarried girls.

Looking at them there, bent over their small tasks, Lansing thought how like children they were—intent, mistrustful, jealous of their trivial possessions. The second thought came hard on the heels of the first. They were not children. They were adults, intelligent within the limits of their knowledge, bound by sanctions older than the Pentateuch, preoccupied with the problems of birth and death—and survival for the years between.

To the outsider their tasks were trivial, but in the small stringent world of the tribal unit, they were of major importance. Let a blight come on the taro patch, the whole village must move to new territory. If the pigs should be stricken with swine fever, they would have no protein in their diet—the ancient island of New Guinea is poor in all but the smallest animal life.

They went naked because there were no furs to give them warmth. They practiced abortion and birth control because there was a limit to the crops that could be raised in the narrow gardens and because the pigs were decimated at festival after festival by a meat-hungry people, bound, moreover, by the primal need to propitiate a hostile Pig God in whom lay the principle of fertility. They had no written language. They had never made a wheel. Their traditions were buried in ancient words and phrases that even the elders could not translate.

In their narrow uncertain world, love, as the white man knew it, did not exist. The girl who made the love-play in the *kunande* would be raped on her wedding night and her husband would scowl if she wore any but the simplest ornament. In certain villages a man chose his bride by firing an arrow into her thigh —an act of hostility and enslavement.

In this climate of fear, behind the closed frontiers of the razor-backs, superstition flourished like a rank growth and the old magical practices of the dawn people were the straws to which the simple clung for security and the clubs which the ambitious used to bludgeon them into submission.

As he sipped his whisky and watched the small but complex pattern unfold itself, Lansing was conscious of his own inadequacy. Two years now he had lived among these people. His notebooks were full of careful observations on every aspect of their life pattern, yet he was as far from understanding them as he had been on the day of his arrival. It was as if there were a curtain drawn between him and the arcana of their secret life and unless he could penetrate the curtain, his work would be without significance.

The missionaries did better. The old ones, like Père Louis, did best of all. They came unabashed to make commerce in souls and spirits. They had secrets of their own to trade. They offered protection against the sorcerers, an answer to the ambient mystery of creation.

But when you didn't believe in the soul, when you were committed by birth and training to the pragmatic materialism of the twentieth century, what then? You were shut out from the sanctuary, condemned to walk in the courts of the strangers, denied access to the mysteries and the sacrifice.

He tossed off the dregs of his whisky, rinsed the glass carefully and set it on the table. Then he walked out into the compound.

There was a girl in the village whom he had trained to look after

him, to wash his clothes and tidy his hut and prepare his food with
moderate cleanliness. He had not seen her since his arrival; he was
going to look for her.

First, he went to her father's hut. The girl was not there. The
old man was sitting outside the door sharpening a set of cane
arrows. When Lansing questioned him, he gave him a sidelong
look, shrugged indifferently and bent over his work. Accustomed
to the moodiness of the mountain folk, Lansing made no comment but walked over to a group of women bending over a fire
pit.

They giggled and simpered and exchanged smiles of secret
amusement, but they would tell him nothing. He was irritated,
but he dared not show it for fear of losing face. He hailed the
women coming up from the taro gardens. They shook their heads.
They had not set eyes on the girl. He tried the children, but they
drew away from him and ran to hide their faces behind the
buttocks of their mothers.

Then, suddenly, he became aware that the whole village was
watching him. They had not paused for a moment in their work,
but they were following his every movement, eyes slanting and
secret, their smiles a silent mockery. They were not hostile, they
were simply amused. They were watching a dancing doll, jerked
this way and that by forces beyond his control.

Anger rose in him, sour and acid from the pit of his belly. He
wanted to shout at them, curse them, strike them at least into
recognition of his presence. He knew he could not do it. The loss
of face would be final and irrecoverable.

He turned on his heel and with elaborate slowness walked back
to his hut. He closed the door and lit the lamp. His hands were
trembling and his palms were clammy with sweat. This concerted
mockery was new in his experience. Sullenness he had met and

had learned to ignore. Suspicion had been rasped and honed away
by the daily familiar intercourse. This was something different. It
was like . . . he fumbled for a tag to identify the strangeness
. . . like being sent to Coventry. But for what?

He knew enough of ritual and custom to make him careful of
their observance. He had crossed no one of the elders. He was
aloof from village scandal. There was no reason why they should
turn against him. Then, he thought of Sonderfeld and of Kumo
and of Gerda's cryptic warning; and he was suddenly afraid.

He thought of Père Louis and the dappled snake and the sound
of the unseen cassowary bird and his fear was a wild, screaming
terror. He was alone and naked and defenseless among the secret
people in the darkening valley.

Desperately he struggled for control. At all costs he must show
a brave face to the village mockery, must maintain the simple
order of his studious existence.

He broke out Gerda's package of food and tried to eat. The cold
food gagged him and he thrust it away. He lit the spirit lamp and
tried to work over his notes, but the letters danced confusedly
before his eyes and his trembling fingers could not control the
pencil.

Then, with the abrupt coming of darkness, the kundus began
their maddening climactic rhythm. He felt as though they were
throbbing inside his skull case, thudding and pounding till his
brain must burst into wild incurable madness.

Then he knew what he must do if he were to get through the
night. He set the whisky bottle and the water canteen on the table
in front of him, broke out a fresh pack of cigarettes, pushed the
lamp to a safe distance from his elbow and began carefully and
methodically to get himself drunk.

He drank slowly at first lest his empty stomach revolt and cheat him of relief. Then, as the liquor warmed and relaxed him, he poured larger tots and used less water, until finally he was drinking neat spirits and the level of the bottle was below the halfway mark.

Long before the drums were silent, long before the singers were dumb, Max Lansing was slumped across his table, with his head pillowed on his unfinished manuscript, one nerveless hand lying on an overturned bottle, the other dangling over a broken glass and a pool of liquor that soaked slowly into the earthen floor.

Then Kumo came in.

All through the solitary orgy he had been squatting outside the hut watching Lansing's slow collapse into insensibility. He was dressed in the ceremonial costume with the tossing plumes and the clattering ornaments of pearl shell. His long, crescent nose ornament gave him the look of a tusked animal. Tucked in his fur armband he carried a small closed tube of bamboo.

For a long moment he stood over the unconscious man, then with a sudden gesture he lifted Max's head by the hair and let it fall with a thump on the table. Lansing made no sound. His head lolled into equilibrium on one cheek and one ear. Kumo grunted with satisfaction, and took the bamboo tube in his hands.

First he rolled it rapidly between his fingers, then tapped it rapidly on the edge of the desk, making a dry, drumming sound. Finally, he held it a long time against the hot glass of the lamp, so that the warmth soaked through the pithy wood and into the hollow center.

Now he was ready.

Carefully he took up his position between the edge of the table and the open door of the hut. Then he bent over Lansing, holding the butt of the tube in one hand and its cap in the other, the cap end pointing downwards, six inches from Lansing's face. With a sharp movement, he pulled off the cap and stepped backwards. There was a soft *plop* and a small dappled snake fell onto the desk.

Maddened by the noise and the movement and the heat, the snake struck and struck again at Lansing's cheek. Then it slithered off the table and disappeared in the shadows of the hut.

Anesthetized by the liquor, Lansing felt no pain and made no movement. Kumo stood a moment looking down at his victim and at the twin punctures just below his cheekbone. Then, silently as the snake, he, too, went out into the darkness and soon, over the beat of the drums, the villagers heard the thudding feet of the cassowary bird.

PART III

THE "ULTIMATE" VOODOO

TÏE CANDIDATE

BY HENRY SLESAR

The plot of this "ultimate" voodoo story is doubly intriguing: not only is it a brilliant and unique fiction idea, it may also be "an idea whose time has come" for practical application. There are a lot of people in this world who have harmed others—dozens or hundreds or thousands of others—and who would make the good Earth a happier place by departing it. Just think of the politicians alone who fall into that category. . . .

Could it work, this unique idea, this "ultimate" voodoo? Could an organization such as the Society for United Action be formed and achieve the results postulated herein? Perhaps. After all, we know that almost anything is possible these days. Almost anything at all.

One thing is certain: no one would want to be in Burton Grunzer's shoes.

Since he began writing in 1956, while in his late twenties, Henry Slesar has accumulated a list of credits that any ten average authors would be hard-pressed to equal in a lifetime: some five hundred and fifty short stories in periodicals ranging from Ellery Queen's Mystery Magazine *to* Playboy; *two collections; five novels, the first of which,* The Gray Flannel Shroud, *received the Mystery Writers of America Edgar Award as Best First Mystery of 1959; twenty radio plays for* CBS Radio Mystery Theatre; *well over a hundred teleplays for such shows as* Alfred Hitchcock Presents *(which alone produced sixty of his scripts),* Run for Your Life, Batman, *and* The Man from U.N.C.L.E.; *and, last but by no means least, all the scripts for the much-acclaimed daytime TV serial* The Edge of Night, *which won the National Academy of Television Arts and Sciences Emmy Aware in 1973. (At the same time, for two years, he was head writer for another daytime serial,* Somerset.) *TV* Guide *once called him "the writer with the largest audience in America." Little wonder. At present he lives in New York City, not all that far from his Brooklyn birthplace.*

A man's worth can be judged by the calibre of his enemies. Burton Grunzer, encountering the phrase in a pocket-sized biography he had purchased at a newsstand, put the book in his lap and stared reflectively from the murky window of the commuter train. Darkness silvered the glass and gave him nothing to look at but his own image, but it seemed appropriate to his line of thought. How many people were enemies of that face, of the eyes narrowed by a myopic squint denied by vanity the correction of spectacles, of the nose he secretly called patrician, of the mouth that was soft in relaxation and hard when animated by speech or smiles or frowns? How many enemies? Grunzer mused. A few he could name, others he could guess. But it was their calibre that was important. Men like Whitman Hayes, for instance; there was a 24-carat opponent for you. Grunzer smiled, darting a sidelong glance at the seat-sharer beside him, not wanting to be caught indulging in a secret thought. Grunzer was thirty-four; Hayes was twice as old, his white hairs synonymous with experience, an enemy to be proud of. Hayes knew the food business, all right, knew it from every angle: he'd been a wagon jobber for six years, a broker for ten, a food company executive for twenty before the old man had brought him into the organization to sit on his right hand. Pinning Hayes to the mat wasn't easy, and that made Grunzer's small but increasing triumphs all the sweeter. He congratulated himself. He had twisted Hayes's advantages into drawbacks, had made his long years seem tantamount to senility and outlived usefulness; in meetings, he had concentrated his questions on the new supermarket and suburbia phenomena to demonstrate to the old man that times had changed, that the past was dead, that new merchandising tactics were needed, and that only a younger man could supply them. . . .

Suddenly, he was depressed. His enjoyment of remembered victories seemed tasteless. Yes, he'd won a minor battle or two in the company conference room; he'd made Hayes's ruddy face go crimson, and seen the old man's parchment skin wrinkle in a sly grin. But what had been accomplished? Hayes seemed more self-assured than ever, and the old man more dependent upon his advice. . . .

When he arrived home, later than usual, his wife Jean didn't ask questions. After eight years of a marriage in which, childless, she knew her husband almost too well, she wisely offered nothing more than a quiet greeting, a hot meal, and the day's mail.

Grunzer flipped through the bills and circulars, and found an unmarked letter. He slipped it into his hip pocket, reserving it for private perusal, and finished the meal in silence.

After dinner, Jean suggested a movie and he agreed; he had a passion for violent action movies. But first, he locked himself in the bathroom and opened the letter. Its heading was cryptic: *Society for United Action.* The return address was a post office box. It read:

Dear Mr. Grunzer:

Your name has been suggested to us by a mutual acquaintance. Our organization has an unusual mission which cannot be described in this letter, but which you may find of exceeding interest. We would be gratified by a private discussion at your earliest convenience. If I do not hear from you to the contrary in the next few days, I will take the liberty of calling you at your office.

It was signed, *Carl Tucker, Secretary.* A thin line at the bottom of the page read: *A Nonprofit Organization.*

His first reaction was a defensive one; he suspected an oblique attack on his pocketbook. His second was curiosity: he went to the bedroom and located the telephone directory, but found no organization listed by the letterhead name. *Okay, Mr. Tucker,* he thought wryly, *I'll bite.*

When no call came in the next three days, his curiosity was increased. But when Friday arrived, he forgot the letter's promise in the crush of office affairs. The old man called a meeting with the bakery products division. Grunzer sat opposite Whitman Hayes at the conference table, poised to pounce on fallacies in his statements. He almost had him once, but Eckhardt, the bakery products manager, spoke up in defense of Hayes's views. Eckhardt had only been with the company a year, but he had evidently chosen sides already. Grunzer glared at him, and reserved a place for Eckhardt in the hate chamber of his mind.

At three o'clock, Carl Tucker called.

"Mr. Grunzer?" The voice was friendly, even cheery. "I haven't heard from you, so I assume you don't mind my calling today. Is there a chance we can get together sometime?"

"Well, if you could give me some idea, Mr. Tucker—"

The chuckle was resonant. "We're not a charity organization, Mr. Grunzer, in case you got that notion. Nor do we sell anything. We're more or less a voluntary service group: our membership is over a thousand at present."

"To tell you the truth," Grunzer frowned, "I never heard of you."

"No, you haven't, and that's one of the assets. I think you'll understand when I tell you about us. I can be over at your office in fifteen minutes, unless you want to make it another day."

Grunzer glanced at his calendar. "Okay, Mr. Tucker. Best time for me is right now."

"Fine! I'll be right over."

Tucker was prompt. When he walked into the office, Grunzer's eyes went dismayed at the officious briefcase in the man's right hand. But he felt better when Tucker, a florid man in his early sixties with small, pleasant features, began talking.

"Nice of you to take the time, Mr. Grunzer. And believe me, I'm not here to sell you insurance or razor blades. Couldn't if I tried; I'm a semi-retired broker. However, the subject I want to discuss is rather—intimate, so I'll have to ask you to bear with me on a certain point. May I close the door?"

"Sure," Grunzer said, mystified.

Tucker closed it, hitched his chair closer and said:

"The point is this. What I have to say must remain in the strictest confidence. If you betray that confidence, if you publicize our society in any way, the consequences could be most unpleasant. Is that agreeable?"

Grunzer, frowning, nodded.

"Fine!" The visitor snapped open the briefcase and produced a stapled manuscript. "Now, the society has prepared this little spiel about our basic philosophy, but I'm not going to bore you with it. I'm going to go straight to the heart of our argument. You may not agree with our first principle at all, and I'd like to know that now."

"How do you mean, first principle?"

"Well . . ." Tucker flushed slightly. "Put in the crudest form, Mr. Grunzer, the Society for United Action believes that—*some* people are just not fit to live." He looked up quickly, as if anxious to gauge the immediate reaction. "There, I've said it," he laughed, somewhat in relief. "Some of our members don't believe in my direct approach; they feel the argument has to be broached more discreetly. But frankly, I've gotten excellent results in this rather crude manner. How do you feel about what I've said, Mr. Grunzer?"

"I don't know. Guess I never thought about it much."

"Were you in the war, Mr. Grunzer?"

"Yes. Navy." Grunzer rubbed his jaw. "I suppose I didn't think the Japs were fit to live, back then. I guess maybe there are other cases. I mean, you take capital punishment, I believe in that. Murderers, rape-artists, perverts, hell, I certainly don't think *they're* fit to live."

"Ah," Tucker said. "So you really accept our first principle. It's a question of category, isn't it?"

"I guess you could say that."

"Good. So now I'll try another blunt question. Have you—personally—ever wished someone dead? Oh, I don't mean those casual, fleeting wishes everybody has. I mean a real, deep-down, uncomplicated wish for the death of someone *you* thought was unfit to live. Have you?"

"Sure," Grunzer said frankly. "I guess I have."

"There are times, in your opinion, when the removal of someone from this earth would be beneficial?"

Grunzer smiled. "Hey, what is this? You from Murder, Incorporated or something?"

Tucker grinned back. "Hardly, Mr. Grunzer, hardly. There is absolutely no criminal aspect to our aims or our methods. I'll admit we're a 'secret' society, but we're no Black Hand. You'd be amazed at the quality of our membership; it even includes members of the legal profession. But suppose I tell you how the society came into being?

"It began with two men; I can't reveal their names just now. The year was 1949, and one of these men was a lawyer attached to the district attorney's office. The other man was a state psychiatrist. Both of them were involved in a rather sensational trial, concerning a man accused of a hideous crime against two small boys. In their opinion, the man was unquestionably guilty, but an unusually persuasive defense counsel, and a highly suggestible jury, gave him his freedom. When the shocking verdict was announced, these two, who were personal friends as well as colleagues, were thunderstruck and furious. They felt a great wrong had been committed, and they were helpless to right it. . . .

"But I should explain something about this psychiatrist. For some years, he had made studies in a field which might be called anthropological psychiatry. One of these researches related to the voodoo practice of certain groups, the Haitian in particular. You've probably heard a great deal about voodoo, or Obeah as they call it in Jamaica, but I won't dwell on the subject lest you think we hold tribal rites and stick pins in dolls. . . . But the chief feature of his study was the uncanny *success* of certain strange practices. Naturally, as a scientist, he rejected the supernatural explanation and sought the rational one. And of course, there was only one answer. When the *vodun* priest decreed the punishment or death of a malefactor, it was the malefactor's own convictions concerning the efficacy of the death wish, his own faith in the voodoo power, that eventually made the wish come true. Sometimes, the process was organic—his body reacted psychosomatically to the voodoo curse, and he would sicken and die. Sometimes, he would die by 'accident'—an accident prompted by the secret belief that once cursed, he *must* die. Eerie, isn't it?"

"No doubt," Grunzer said, dry-lipped.

"Anyway, our friend, the psychiatrist, began wondering aloud if *any* of us have advanced so far along the civilized path that we couldn't be subject to this same sort of 'suggested' punishment. He proposed that they experiment on this choice subject, just to see.

"How they did it was simple," he said. "They went to see this man, and they announced their intentions. They told him they were going to *wish him dead*. They explained how and why the wish would become reality, and while he laughed at their proposal, they could see the look of superstitious fear cross his face. They promised him that regularly, every day, they would be wishing for his death, until he could no longer stop the mystic juggernaut that would make the wish come true."

Grunzer shivered suddenly, and clenched his fist. "That's pretty silly," he said softly.

"The man died of a heart attack two months later."

"Of course. I knew you'd say that. But there's such a thing as coincidence."

"Naturally. And our friends, while intrigued, weren't satisfied. *So they tried it again.*"

"Again?"

"Yes, again. I won't recount who the victim was, but I will tell you that this time they enlisted the aid of four associates. This little band of pioneers was the nucleus of the society I represent today."

Grunzer shook his head. "And you mean to tell me there's a *thousand* now?"

"Yes, a thousand and more, all over the country. A society whose one function is to *wish people dead.* At first, membership was purely voluntary, but now we have a system. Each new member of the Society for United Action joins on the basis of submitting one potential victim. Naturally, the society investigates to determine whether the victim is deserving of his fate. If the case is a good one, the *entire* membership then sets about to *wish him dead.* Once the task has been accomplished, naturally, the new member must take part in all future concerted action. That and a small yearly fee, is the price of membership."

Carl Tucker grinned.

"And in case you think I'm not serious, Mr. Grunzer—" He dipped into the briefcase again, this time producing a blue-bound volume of telephone directory thickness. "Here are the facts. To date, two hundred and twenty-nine victims were named by our selection committee. Of those, *one hundred and four* are no longer alive. Coincidence, Mr. Grunzer?

"As for the remaining one hundred and twenty-five—perhaps that indicates that our method is not infallible. We're the first to

admit that. But new techniques are being developed all the time.
I assure you, Mr. Grunzer, *we will get them all.*"

He flipped through the blue-bound book.

"Our members are listed in this book, Mr. Grunzer. I'm going
to give you the option to call one, ten or a hundred of them. Call
them and see if I'm not telling the truth."

He flipped the manuscript toward Grunzer's desk. It landed on
the blotter with a thud. Grunzer picked it up.

"Well?" Tucker said. "Want to call them?"

"No." He licked his lips. "I'm willing to take your word for it,
Mr. Tucker. It's incredible, but I can see how it works. Just
knowing that a thousand people are wishing you dead is enough
to shake hell out of you." His eyes narrowed. "But there's one
question. You talked about a 'small' fee—"

"It's fifty dollars, Mr. Grunzer."

"Fifty, huh? Fifty times a thousand, that's pretty good money,
isn't it?"

"I assure you, the organization is not motivated by profit. Not
the kind you mean. The dues merely cover expenses, committee
work, research and the like. Surely you can understand that?"

"I guess so," he grunted.

"Then you find it interesting?"

Grunzer swiveled his chair about to face the window.

God! he thought.

God! if it *really* worked!

But how could it? If wishes became deeds, he would have
slaughtered dozens in his lifetime. Yet, that was different. His
wishes were always secret things, hidden where no man could
know them. But this method was different, more practical, more
terrifying. Yes, he could see how it might work. He could visualize
a thousand minds burning with the single wish of death, see the

victim sneering in disbelief at first, and then slowly, gradually, surely succumbing to the tightening, constricting chain of fear that it *might* work, that so many deadly thoughts could indeed emit a mystical, malevolent ray that destroyed life.

Suddenly, ghostlike, he saw the ruddy face of Whitman Hayes before him.

He wheeled about and said:

"But the victim has to *know* all this, of course? He has to know the society exists, and has succeeded, and is wishing for *his* death? That's essential, isn't it?"

"Absolutely essential," Tucker said, replacing the manuscripts in his briefcase. "You've touched on the vital point, Mr. Grunzer. The victim must be informed, and that, precisely, is what I have done." He looked at his watch. "Your death wish began at noon today. The society has begun to work. I'm very sorry."

At the doorway, he turned and lifted both hat and briefcase in one departing salute.

"Goodbye, Mr. Grunzer," he said.

BIBLIOGRAPHY

NONFICTION:

Asbury, Herbert. *The French Quarter.* New York: Alfred A. Knopf, 1936. Chapter entitled "Voodoo."

Bach, Marcus. *Strange Altars.* New York: Bobbs-Merrill, 1952.

Cave, Hugh B. *Haiti: Highroad to Adventure.* New York: Henry Holt, 1952.

Deren, Maya. *Divine Horsemen: Voodoo Gods of Haiti.* New York: Delta Books, 1972.

Douglas, Drake. *Horror!* New York: Macmillan, 1966. Chapter entitled "The Walking Dead," which deals with voodoo and zombies in film and literature.

Dunham, Katherine. *Island Possessed.* New York: Doubleday, 1969.

Gonzalez-Wippler, Migene. *Santería: African Magic in Latin America.* New York: Julian Press, 1973.

Haskins, James. *Voodoo and Hoodoo.* New York: Stein & Day, 1978.

Herskovits, Melville J. *Life in a Haitian Valley.* New York: Alfred A. Knopf, 1937.

Hill, Douglas and Williams, Pat. *The Supernatural.* London: Aldus Books, Ltd., 1965. Chapter entitled "Land of Voodoo."

Hurston, Zora Neale. *Mules and Men.* Philadelphia: J.B. Lippincott, 1935.

Huxley, Francis. *The Invisibles.* New York: McGraw-Hill, 1969.

Kerboull, Jean. *Voodoo and Magic Practices.* London: Barrie & Jenkins, Ltd., 1978.

Kristos, Kyle. *Voodoo.* Philadelphia: J.B. Lippincott, 1976.

Langguth, A.J. *Macumba: White and Black Magic in Brazil.* New York: Harper, 1975.

Loederer, Richard A. *Voodoo Fire in Haiti.* New York: Doubleday Doran, 1935.

Martin, Kevin. *The Complete Book of Voodoo.* New York: G.P. Putnam's Sons, 1972.

Metraux, Alfred. *Voodoo in Haiti.* New York: Schocken Books, 1959.

Rigaud, Milo. *Secrets of Voodoo.* New York: Arco Books, 1970.

St. Clair, David. *Drum & Candle.* New York: Crown, 1971.

St. John, Spencer. *Hayti; or the Black Republic.* London: Smith, Elder & Company, 1884.

Seabrook, W.B. *The Magic Island.* New York: Harcourt Brace, 1929.

Tallant, Robert. *Voodoo in New Orleans.* New York: Macmillan, 1946.

Williams, Sheldon. *Voodoo and the Art of Haiti.* London: Morland Lee, Ltd., 1969.

FICTION:

Avallone, Michael. *The Voodoo Murders.* New York: Gold Medal, 1957.

Barrett, Monte. *Murder at Belle Camille.* New York: Bobbs-Merrill, 1943.

Bourne, Peter. *Drums of Destiny.* New York: G.P. Putnam's Sons, 1947.

Brandon, Michael. *Nonce.* New York: Coward-McCann, 1944.

Cave, Hugh B. *The Cross on the Drum.* New York: Doubleday, 1959.

———. *Legion of the Dead.* New York: Avon, 1979.

Chesnutt, Charles G. *The Conjure Woman.* Boston: Houghton-Mifflin, 1899. Collection of folkloric short stories.

Esteven, John. *Voodoo.* New York: Doubleday Crime Club, 1930.

Foran, W. Robert. *Drums of Sacrifice.* London: Hutchinson, 1934.

Gibson, Walter B. *Voodoo Death.* New York: Tempo Books, 1969.

Janson, Hank. *Voodoo Violence.* London: Roberts, 1964.

Lecale, Errol. *Zombie.* London: New English Library, 1975.

Meik, Vivian. *Devils' Drums.* London: Philip Allan, 1933. Collection of short stories.

Perkins, Kenneth. *Voodoo'd.* New York: Harper & Brothers, 1931.

Rohmer, Sax. *The Island of Fu Manchu.* New York: Doubleday Crime Club, 1941.

Tallant, Robert. *Voodoo Queen.* New York: G.P. Putnam's Sons, 1956.

Thoby-Marcelin, Philippe and Marcelin, Pierre. *Canapé Vert.* New York: Rinehart, 1944.

————. *The Beast of the Haitian Hills.* New York: Rinehart, 1946.

————. *The Pencil of God.* Boston: Houghton-Mifflin, 1951.

West, Morris. *Kundu.* New York: Dell Books, 1956.

Whitehead, Henry S. *Jumbee and Other Uncanny Tales.* Sauk City, Wisconsin: Arkham House, 1944. Collection of short stories.

————. *West India Lights.* Sauk City, Wisconsin: Arkham House, 1946. Collection of short stories.

PLAY:

St. Clair, Robert. *The Zombie.* Evanston, Illinois: Northwestern Press, 1941. Three acts.

FILMS:

Devil's Own, The (British, 1966). Joan Fontaine, Kay Walsh.

Disembodied, The (1957). Paul Burke, Allison Hayes.

Ghost Breakers, The (1940). Bob Hope, Paulette Goddard, Willie Best.

I Walked with a Zombie (1943). Frances Dee, Tom Conway, James Ellison. Written by Curt Siodmak and produced by Val Lewton; directed by Jacques Tourneur.

King of the Zombies (1941). John Archer, Henry Victor, Mantan Moreland.

Revenge of the Zombies (1943). John Carradine, Gale Storm, Mantan Moreland.

Revolt of the Zombies (1936). Dean Jagger, Dorothy Stone.

Voodoo Island (1957). Boris Karloff, Beverly Tyler, Murvyn Vye.

Voodoo Man, The (1944). Bela Lugosi, John Carradine.

Voodoo Tiger (1952). Johnny Weismuller, Jean Byron.

Voodoo Woman (1957). Marla English, Tom Conway.

White Zombie (1932). Bela Lugosi, Madge Bellamy, Robert Frazer.

Zombies of Mora Tau (1957). Gregg Palmer, Allison Hayes. (Also released as *The Dead That Walk.*)

Zombies on Broadway (1944). Bela Lugosi, Wally Brown, Alan Carney.